SILVER SKULLS:
PORTENTS

WARHAMMER 40,000 ®

SILVER SKULLS: PORTENTS

S P Cawkwell

BLACK LIBRARY

For Christian, who knows why, the always-dependable Lee
and Alec for patiently dealing with my panicking
and especially for Qui Gon Jim, for all the 'five minute' conversations.

A BLACK LIBRARY PUBLICATION

First published as an eBook in 2014.
This edition published in 2015 by
Black Library
Games Workshop Ltd
Willow Road
Nottingham NG7 2WS UK

10 9 8 7 6 5 4 3 2 1

Produced by the Games Workshop Design Studio

See Black Library on the internet at

blacklibrary.com

Find out more about Games Workshop
and the world of Warhammer 40,000 at

games-workshop.com

Printed and bound by CPI Group (UK) Ltd, Croydon, CR0 4YY

It is the 41st millennium. For more than a hundred centuries the Emperor has sat immobile on the Golden Throne of Earth. He is the master of mankind by the will of the gods, and master of a million worlds by the might of his inexhaustible armies. He is a rotting carcass writhing invisibly with power from the Dark Age of Technology. He is the Carrion Lord of the Imperium for whom a thousand souls are sacrificed every day, so that he may never truly die.

Yet even in his deathless state, the Emperor continues his eternal vigilance. Mighty battlefleets cross the daemon-infested miasma of the warp, the only route between distant stars, their way lit by the Astronomican, the psychic manifestation of the Emperor's will. Vast armies give battle in His name on uncounted worlds. Greatest amongst his soldiers are the Adeptus Astartes, the Space Marines, bio-engineered super-warriors. Their comrades in arms are legion: the Astra Militarium and countless planetary defence forces, the ever-vigilant Inquisition and the tech-priests of the Adeptus Mechanicus to name only a few. But for all their multitudes, they are barely enough to hold off the ever-present threat from aliens, heretics, mutants – and worse.

To be a man in such times is to be one amongst untold billions. It is to live in the cruellest and most bloody regime imaginable. These are the tales of those times. Forget the power of technology and science, for so much has been forgotten, never to be re-learned. Forget the promise of progress and understanding, for in the grim dark future there is only war. There is no peace amongst the stars, only an eternity of carnage and slaughter, and the laughter of thirsting gods.

ONE

BLOOD OF KINGS

Only five remained.

They perched high on the ragged lip of an ancient impact crater, their eyes turned to the dust-clogged complex squatting far below. The blocky buildings, the sagging remains of a long-forgotten explorator expedition, had definitely seen better years. Several outhouses surrounded a larger central edifice bristling with rusting masts and stained comms-dishes. The lamps sweeping lazily around the perimeter of the complex were much newer additions. *Those* were the work of the enemy.

Of the ten who had initially deployed on the mission, not enough were left to reasonably allow a direct assault on the objective. Despite this, they remained motivated, had adapted accordingly and refused to acknowledge the possibility of defeat. With each successive loss, the dynamic within the squad had altered, the burden of leadership falling naturally and without any preamble from one pair of broad shoulders to the next.

Over the years they had spent in one another's company, they had developed solid bonds of brotherhood. But now, those bonds were being strained to the limit. Finding themselves tested as never before, each remaining warrior was identifying hitherto unnoticed chinks in their individual personal armours of arrogance. Doubts were beginning to creep in and were dutifully cleansed by a muttered litany, or a few words of support from a comrade. After all, four of the remaining warriors knew each other intimately, their shared experience binding them together. They were closer than brothers born.

And then...

Then there was the fifth, the last member of the team, who had been introduced to the group only two days before. Despite the closeness of their age, the fifth had undergone the majority of his training at the hands of very different masters. His was a talent that was formidable in the extreme and worthy of very great respect. Nicodemus was a psyker and all those of his creed were revered within the Chapter, particularly those who became squad and company advisers.

But Nicodemus was no Prognosticator. This young warrior could not divine the skeins of fate and never had been able to. But from the beginning of this mission, he had demonstrated courage and initiative that shone above his peers. He had declined leadership at the start but now it had fallen to him whether he desired it or not.

Not gifted with the holy blessing of foresight, this young warrior was well on the path to becoming a Prognosticar, one of the battle elite of the Silver Skulls Chapter of the Adeptus Astartes. But for now he was still a novitiate, his training incomplete. He had spent many years learning and studying alongside the Chapter's finest minds. He had then gone on to spend the requisite time on the funereal moon of Pax Argentius under the tutelage of the sombre Chaplains. There, he had been instilled with a furious zeal and passion for battle that had served him well during these last two days.

Forty-eight hours previously, Nicodemus had exited the drop-ship onto this desolate world and taken his place within a squad of ten warriors. He had obeyed all commands without question and had demonstrated great strength of character and tenacity. Now it seemed that it had become his duty to lead.

If this new responsibility fazed or unnerved him at all, it did not show in the strength of his voice as he issued orders to the others. The five Silver Skulls were in cover, a deep crater that had been formed by a long-ago orbital bombardment. The air was thick with the ash and dirt of the years; their passage across the plains of this planet had stirred up debris that had been left undisturbed for an age, and a perpetual dust-haze obscured their vision. A kilometre to their west was a crumbling ruin that had once been a military installation but was now home to their enemy. It had taken them hours of cautious approach to get this far and they had made many errors of judgement on the way, lost brothers before their time.

Nicodemus studied the remaining warriors. In a short space of time, he had learned much about them. He was acutely aware of their strengths, their weaknesses, what made them react well and what caused them to falter. He had observed every one of them in battle and they had executed their duties with admirable ferocity, if not success. He was certainly proud to be one of their number, but pride was no longer enough to ensure their victory – even if only partial – in this mission.

The velvet half-light of the planet's dusk had given way to night-time and bright stars studded the dark backdrop of the world's blackened skies. There was a waxing moon on the quarter phase hanging low in the sky, and turgid clouds were rolling in from the south. Within a few short moments they had muted much of the pale, argent light and only a ghostly silver outline glimmered behind their ominous presence.

Sweeping lumes blazed from the installation and the low, distant hum of a promethium-powered generator could be felt as much as heard on the still air. Nicodemus gave a slightly crooked smile as he thought swiftly.

'Caution is the byword now, my brothers. We can proceed no further without a full understanding of what it is that we face,' he said. Glittering, emotionless eyes glanced from one battle-brother to the other. 'We have presumed too much throughout this mission and it has cost us greatly. Teris, take Achak and skirt the east edge of the crater, and provide covering fire. Motega, Nahuel and I will circle west and use the rocks there to cover our approach.' He considered his own words briefly, before nodding. 'We will attempt to infil-trate the facility via the outbuildings. But first, let's make it a little tougher for them.' He raked his fingers through his cap of short dark hair and closed his eyes briefly. He reached out with his psychic senses with fluid ease.

Immediately, the bitter taste of promethium flooded his mouth as he located what he sought. Piece by piece, the generator took shape in his thoughts. With the minimum of effort, he was able to reconstruct it cog by cog within his mind. When his powers had first been assessed, before he had been sent to the Prognosticatum, they had mistaken a psychic ability to manipulate machinery for the early signs of a gifted Techmarine. However, as time had gone by, it became apparent that he would have made a terrible servant of the Omnissiah. Nicodemus had a capacity for destroying machines and mechanisms by thought alone. With some effort, he could disable mechanical systems and had a natural gift for disrupting the delicate balance of the machine-spirits in a firearm.

Such a gift had won him respect from his peers, but those who *did* serve the Omnissiah had not been so easy to impress. His ability – just one of many – was anathema to them. The brothers of the Mechanicus were not here to be unnerved by him, however, and so he made his choice easily. When specifically targeted, his power had the potential to disarm an unsuspecting warrior or could be used as an exceptionally effective distraction, though the effort of will was swiftly taxing.

He let his mind drift through the heart of the machine until he found the right combination of thoughts. He urged his investigative mind forward gently, whilst his hand reached out and closed around something unseen. Then he tugged backwards rapidly. The low, distant hum became a discordant whine for an instant and then the generator coughed into silence.

Across the compound beyond the crater, lights guttered and died. Nicodemus's eyes opened again and he nodded in satisfaction as he gestured to his companions to take up their positions. He unclamped his bolt pistol from his thigh and checked that it was primed and ready. Ammunition was not unlimited and a lot had been spent already. Too much.

'Assess the threat,' he ordered across the squad vox. 'Take

11

whatever action is necessary to eliminate opposition, but make every shot count, brothers. This must be a precision strike – we cannot afford to waste a single round.'

His eyes met those of Teris. Though no words passed between them, the hot-headed Teris would know exactly where that particular order was directed. Quick on the offensive but slow to plan, Teris was charismatic and Nicodemus had been surprised that he had not assumed command of the squad. He would learn in time that Teris may have been a natural leader, but he was also imbued with great humility.

'Aye,' came the murmured replies. Nicodemus nodded brusquely and gave the order with a confidence in his tone that he certainly did not feel.

'Then we are ready. Deploy.'

The enemy had not been in place long enough to install secondary power and as the Silver Skulls approached from two separate directions, the area remained dark. Occasional slivers of light cut through the gloom as the enemy forces employed their weapon lights or torches. The bright circles emanating from these sources danced on the ground and low voices could just be heard on the edge of awareness.

'Nicodemus. We count eight on this side of the compound.' Teris's voice crackled softly across the vox and Nicodemus nodded, even though he knew his companion could not see the gesture.

'I have counted at least twelve here. They are armed every bit as lethally as we are.'

'How many of their weapons could you jam at one time?' Motega spoke from Nicodemus's right side. The psyker frowned.

'One, maybe two, but it would be a struggle,' he said. 'Not enough to even the odds in our favour. No, we are going to have to approach with caution. Teris, is there any sign of the primary objective?'

'Negative.'

Nicodemus cursed softly and considered the situation. The primary objective of their mission had been to recover a stolen artefact – a valuable relic of the Chapter. Intelligence reports that had been fed to them had brought them to this distant world. They had not expected such a considerable enemy force, and each one of the squad harboured the same thought. With such a disproportionate number of foes ranged against them, the chances of success were slim.

'Nicodemus?' Teris's voice crackled through again. 'What are your orders, brother?'

With that single question, the young psyker discovered the true weight of command. The fact that the remaining squad were relying on him, looking to him for guidance and expecting him to lead them to victory, suddenly landed on his shoulders. He learned, several seconds later, that self-doubt had no place in his mind.

The first sounds of gunfire echoed across the crumbling compound and Nicodemus started. He reached for his bolt pistol and gestured to his companions to move into cover.

'Teris, report!' Nicodemus snapped into the vox, but there was no reply. The young psyker swore loudly and joined Motega and Nahuel behind the remains of a column.

'We have to presume the other team has been compromised,' he said. 'There is no word from them on the vox and the sounds of that firefight do not bode well.' Beyond the edges of the compound, they could hear the battle taking place. Several voices were calling out, orders being shouted from one of the enemy soldiers to another. Nicodemus nodded, coming to a decision.

'We use their distraction to our advantage,' he said. 'This is our opportunity. We have to strike hard and we must strike fast. Retrieve the relic and withdraw as swiftly as we can. We cannot afford to get pinned down or to confront our enemy directly.' He indicated with his pistol. 'Make for the entrance and do not stop. Not for anything.'

It was darker within the building. Only the faintest slivers of light from the beclouded moon filtered through the shattered skylights to afford any sort of illumination, but it was enough for Nicodemus's enhanced senses. He inched along the interior wall with extreme caution until he found himself at a corner. He could hear low voices ahead and checked the magazine in his pistol. This would have to be swift and decisive.

Despite the fact that he felt calm, he cursed the sound of his breathing. To his ears, it seemed loud and ragged even though he knew it could not be. He took a single deep, calming breath and listened to the voices again. Three... no, four distinct voices ahead of him. He could deal with that threat in short order, but undoubtedly pistol fire would attract attention. There was no way he could slip unnoticed past them. A smoke bomb would distract them, but not for long enough. And despite the confidence he had projected to his brothers, he did not truly know if the relic was even in this building any longer. Or indeed if it had ever been here at all.

Nicodemus closed his eyes and drew on the core of inner strength that he had cultivated during his time learning from the Chapter's finest psykers. He reached down deep within himself and allowed a sense of complete calm to settle over his emotions.

'I am a son of Varsavia,' he whispered under his breath. 'I will prevail.'

'No.' The voice, when it came, was right behind him. 'No, you will not.'

Before Nicodemus could turn, his enemy had squeezed on his pistol's trigger. The projectile sliced across the room and was deflected by an immediate reaction from Nicodemus. The near-instant, reflexive kinetic barrier that he had learned early on in his psychic training spared him and the shot went spinning off into the wall. He levelled his own weapon at his assailant and prepared to return fire. With a glaring flash of white light, the huge figure looming before him detonated a blind grenade.

Momentarily disoriented, Nicodemus staggered backwards into the wall behind him and fired wildly. Another *crack* sounded from the weapon that had been pointed at him. He felt the impact of projectiles against his chest and put his hand to the spot. In his blurred, clearing eyesight he could see that it came away stained with red.

'No,' he said, fury rising in the pit of his stomach. 'No. I will not die like this.'

He hurled a thought towards the gun in his enemy's hands and was rewarded, however briefly, with the resulting click of a weapon jam. He took full advantage of the moment and snapped several shots at where he believed his assailant stood, yet nothing but the shatter of old plascrete answered his assault. His attacker was no longer where he had been.

An arm clamped around his neck and pulled hard, slowly crushing his windpipe. He struggled desperately, but there was no way he was going to get free from the iron grip that had him.

'By rights, you should have died outside the compound, novitiate,' said the huge warrior behind him. 'This mission was a failure from the moment you hesitated.' He released the boy and let him drop to the floor. Nicodemus gasped for air and swallowed back a retort.

'This is Sergeant Makya,' said the Space Marine across the vox. 'Training scenario ends. Mission failure. Assemble for debrief.' Makya cast a glance down at the prone psyker. 'On your feet, boy. You have to deal with the consequences of your poor decisions.'

'Yes, sergeant,' said Nicodemus, slowly getting to his feet. Disappointment was writ large in his face and he could not meet the sergeant's eye. The mission had failed and it was because of his inability to lead. Because of him, ten young men would face further testing and scrutiny to assess their suitability to go forward to the transcendence – to be given the ultimate honour of undergoing the last rites of ascension.

The guilt of that knowledge was not a pleasant reward for nearly three full days of fighting and infiltration.

'You are warriors born,' said Makya as he glanced from one young man to another. The youths who had been shipped to this distant training world for their final observation mission variously sat or stood around the interior of the compound. Whenever they had been tagged and 'killed' during the various stages of the three-day mission, they had joined Makya in making up the numbers of the enemy. Little was simulated; weapons held low-velocity solid rounds that could cripple but rarely kill, and the youths were encouraged to forge their own bonds of brotherhood and to act on their initiative rather than remain within set parameters.

Makya continued to study each of the boys. They were a variety of sizes and colourings, but were all around sixteen years of age. This tactical assessment was the final one before they were accepted – or otherwise – for the rites of ascension. Those who were passed through by Makya would return to Apothecary Malus on Varsavia and genetic implantation would commence.

Some distance behind him stood Prognosticar Linos. Normally only Makya would oversee a training session of this level, but with Nicodemus included in the squad, it was essential that an experienced psyker be present. No matter the self-control or the tenacity of the young warrior, there was always a danger in allowing an untried psyker to unleash his power. Linos had been there to step in should Nicodemus have lost control. But he had not. That, at least, was something the young psyker could take pride in.

'You have all demonstrated your skills over the course of this mission,' Makya said. His voice was dry and expressionless and if any of the boys hoped to glean any sort of clue as to their collective fate, he gave them none. 'You have been observed and you have been judged.'

Nicodemus remained stock-still, his eyes locked on a particularly interesting rock on the ground at his feet. He chewed at his lower lip anxiously. The entire group would be judged poorly because of his failure at the mission's end. He would be sent back to Varsavia in shame. If he was lucky, they would allow him another trial. But of the group, he was among the oldest. Too much longer and he would not be suitable for any further genetic work. He would end

17

up as a Chapter-serf, the Silver Skulls equivalent of being sent home in shame.

'We return to Varsavia tomorrow,' Makya said in the lengthy silence. None of the novitiates had spoken a single word. Most of them were looking weary and Nicodemus was acutely aware of the gnawing ache of hunger in his own belly. What it must be, to be one of the Emperor's Angels and be freed completely from the need for sustenance and rest.

'I will speak to each of you in turn before we arrive and advise of what awaits you. Some of you will proceed to Apothecary Malus with immediate effect. Others… will not.'

Was it his imagination, or did Makya catch his eye when he said that? Nicodemus sighed inwardly and held his head up high. Whatever happened, whether he became a warrior with the blood of kings flowing through his veins or whether he became a humble Chapter-serf, he would accept his fate with pragmatism and the loyalty that he had always demonstrated. The gnawing doubt ate away at him.

'Nicodemus,' said Makya. 'You will be first.'

'Yes, my lord,' replied the youth in a voice that shook despite his best efforts. In scant minutes, his fate would be set in stone. Feeling once again that peculiar mix of shame at his failure but pride at his efforts, he stepped forward and bowed his head. He made the sign of the aquila across his chest and without casting a glance back at his fellows, followed Makya inside the run-down building where barely hours before he had laid the grounds for his future.

+++

Security Level Maxima Pheta.
Breach of this code is considered
an act of traitoris extremis.
Any non-authorised individual attempting to view
these documents will be dealt with severely.

+++

Transmission Begins

+++

Thought for the day: It is not in my mind to ask
questions that cannot be answered. That is the
soul standing upon the crossroad of vacillation.
You search for wisdom, but achieve only a stasis
of will.

Subject: Mission Alpha Forty-Seven

Varsavia Quintus (Varsavia) is the fifth planet in a
system of seven. It is an ice world orbited by five
moons set in the galactic north of the Segmentum
Obscurus. For what is tantamount to a death world,
there is a considerable array of indigenous life,
much of it hostile in the extreme. This is a
marvel, given the natural disaster that saw most
of the planet locked in permafrost and an erratic
orbit between the binary stars. What is even more
unexpected is that humanity survives here.

Varsavia is the only inhabited planet in the system
and has three volcanoes, each one known to be
active. A check of records suggests that there have
been no logged eruptions for several hundred Terran
standard years. There are three continental land
masses, but only one sustains human life and it is
split approximately in half by a landlocked sea.
The southern lands are inhabited almost exclusively
by the tribal people who are descended from the
planet's original settlers. It remains a mystery as
to how they endured the series of volcanic eruptions
and subsequent disruption of the planet's weather
system. Nonetheless, these tribes thrive.

They are considered primitive in nature and the
creed of the God-Emperor has been slowly introduced
to them, one tribe at a time. Most have embraced
these teachings and whilst they have eschewed the
opportunity of moving to the civilised north,

nonetheless show their fealty. A number of Adeptus Astartes are drawn from these peoples and they make tenacious warriors.

A few isolated tribes have remained resistant to our missionary efforts, but in due course this will be addressed. They are made up of hardy stock that will provide an excellent recruiting ground for the Adeptus Astartes, and may yet provide a founding for a regiment of Astra Militarum.

The fortress-monastery of the Silver Skulls Chapter is situated in the far north of the continent, built into the side of the largest mountain in a range. Silver veins run through the rocks here and it is believed this is why the Silver Skulls selected Varsavia as their new home world when the unfortunate events of Lyria (see Appendix IV) pushed them from their original home.

As for the Silver Skulls Chapter, they are presently led by Lord Commander Argentius, the twenty-seventh incumbent to hold the title. The present Argentius is believed to have formerly been Captain Artreus, commander of the Sixth Company, whose battle record was outstanding. This has yet to be verified, something that will be done when the investigative team arrive on the planet.

They acquit themselves with honour on the field of battle and are in possession of a considerable fleet that has proved its worth on more than one occasion.

The Silver Skulls have taken responsibility for patrolling a number of neighbouring star systems and shipping lanes, including the treacherous Gildar Rift.

As warriors, they are known to have close alliances with a number of other Chapters. Conversations with warriors of these allied Chapters have affirmed the understanding that the Silver Skulls are brutal on the field of battle, perfect examples of the Emperor's maxim that 'they shall know no fear'.

Yet for all the positive information that has been gathered on the Silver Skulls, one thing continues to cause concern. Perhaps in part because of their tribal nature, they hold fast to potentially deviant superstition. Their Librarium is not arranged according to the Codex Astartes. Instead, they utilise a body known as the Prognosticatum.

This body consists of Prognosticators, Prognosticars and the handful of Chaplains who serve the Chapter. At its head sits the Chapter Master's equerry and chief adviser, Vashiro (another affected title). The Vashiro and Prognosticators are set apart from the others due to their apparent ability to read the threads of fate and predict outcomes of future events. The entire Silver Skulls Chapter has been known to refuse to take the field of battle when a Prognosticator has said that the omens were poor.

Moreover, and more worryingly, there is evidence that they claim these visions are delivered to

22

them by the voice of the most glorious God-Emperor of Mankind. This, in conjunction with the highly unsatisfactory recent gene-seed tithe, is primarily the reason that my operatives and I have been called in to investigate. It is most fortuitous that a situation outside of this investigation has arisen that provides me with the perfect reason to travel to Varsavia.

Rest assured, my lord, that the primary objective of this mission will not be forgotten. You have my word and that is — as it always has been — my bond.

Ave Imperator!

Inquisitor L. Callis
Ordo Hereticus

+++

Transmission Ends

+++

TWO

HOMECOMING

One Year Later
The Fortress-Monastery, Varsavia

The feral backwater world of Varsavia stood testament to
the sheer determination of mankind. Despite its harsh environs, regardless of the countless predators who roamed the
tundra and the mountainsides, the human race had still
somehow managed to prevail. Tribes existed wherever they
could eke out a living and survival was bred into them from
the moment of their birth.

There were only three major land masses on the planet,
although countless islands and archipelagos were dotted around oceans that were partially frozen for much of
the Varsavian year. Occasionally, temperatures would rise
enough to allow a slow melt to begin, but the thaws never
lasted. The harsh, often cruel landscape was only the first
of the challenges that faced the warlike tribes scattered

amongst the ice-locked hills and valleys. The animals that prowled and hunted were savage and as desperate to survive as the people, and the battle for supremacy was as much a part of Varsavia as the silver giants who had arrived here and claimed it as their home world.

From the observatorium aboard the strike cruiser *Silver Arrow*, Gileas Ur'ten stared down impassively at the slowly turning blue-white planet that was his birthplace. Feeble binary stars possessed of barely any strength did little to bring sunlight to a world that was wreathed in perpetual twilight for the better part of the solar year. The surface was blanketed in ice and snow that gave the landscape a uniform colouring of ghostly white.

Yet once every two Varsavian years, when the world's erratic orbit passed directly between the two stars, an explosion of life would burst forth. The ice never melted fully, but the rivers flowed sluggishly. Unbound from their cold prison, the waters were the spawning ground and lifeblood for the tenacious wildlife that teemed across the surface of the planet and lived within the oceans. This cycle was a true miracle. It was a harsh world, of that there was no doubt.

It was harsh, but it was also the world that had become the foundation of his Chapter. The world they had selected following the destruction of Lyria so many thousands of years before.

Varsavia was *home*.

Sergeant Gileas Ur'ten had not initially been keen to return to Varsavia. Recall by the Chapter Master left little room for discussion on the matter, however, and during the journey, which had taken several weeks, he had been able to reflect on the order.

When he had considered it, he had been surprised to realise that it had been decades since he had visited the fortress-monastery. The closer the planet came, the more he found himself looking forward to returning. Just the thought of speaking the litanies in its beautiful chapel filled his heart with pleasure.

Three days ago, the Silver Skulls had translated from the warp and begun their orbital approach to Varsavia. Even for a returning fleet ship, there were protocols and formalities that had to be endured. *Endlessly.* After his initial resentment at the recall to the fortress-monastery, the need to set foot in the place of his rebirth had become all-consuming. Thus, he was in an uncharacteristically good mood as the Thunderhawk bore him and several of his company down through the icy mists on the final leg of the journey.

His company. That was what they were, really. He had taken temporary command following Captain Meyoran's death. Bast, the Eighth's Prognosticator, had informed him that it was by general consensus.

'Nobody is as well suited to the role as you, sergeant,' he had said. Gileas had accepted the honour of acting captaincy in his usual stoic way. The ultimate choice would rest with Vashiro, and he would gladly adhere to any decision that was made. Gileas Ur'ten was not a man to challenge fate... although some might have suggested that his personal history belied that contention.

'It feels good to be coming home,' he murmured. He was addressing his squad, but after a few grunted replies – most of which were similarly in the affirmative – a deep, low rumble sounded in his ear. It hissed and crackled with static, and seemed distant. Gileas adjusted the reception and what he heard brought a smile to his face.

'If you were stationed here for your year's duty, Ur'ten, you would not be so eager to return. The place is a wasteland. Nothing but snow and ice in all directions.'

Another of those pauses and then the voice crackled through the vox once again.

'Although in fairness, I may have seen some sleet once.'

The words were dour and dry, without any hint of sarcasm. This was a voice that belonged to a warrior who saw the very worst in any given situation. His pessimism had long served him well; he had risen swiftly to the position he now held. This was a voice that belonged to a psyker whose powers of precognition would be hard pushed to ever see a positive outcome for the Silver Skulls. Fortunate then that his destructive talents had taken him down the other path open to the psychic brethren of Varsavia.

The voice belonged to a man Gileas had fought alongside on more than one battlefield and whom he considered his friend. Renowned for his tenacious ferocity, the speaker was revered by all. His ability to take skulls was unparalleled and none had ever come close to his record of one hundred and sixty trophies from a single battle. His was the benchmark by which the other Silver Skulls judged their own victories. His very legend was the measure by which they gauged *themselves*.

'Phrixus,' Gileas said warmly. 'It is good to hear your voice. It has been too long since we last met in these hallowed halls, my brother.'

'I do not like what I hear in your tone, *Hathirii*. Mark my words, boy, I guarantee that this infernal cheer will soon desert you. I suspect your pleasure will not last beyond a few hours, particularly when you are lying flat on your back in the training cages.'

The rest of the Space Marines aboard the Thunderhawk were enjoying the exchange. Reuben in particular wore a grin that threatened to split his face apart. Gileas chuckled at Phrixus's words.

'And who exactly is going to put me there, Phrixus? You?'

'I have done so on every occasion so far,' came the pragmatic reply. 'You do not wish to test me again, do you, sergeant?'

'Always, Phrixus. You remember that is my primary role, surely?'

Another one of those long pauses. The First Prognosticar weighed his words like they were ammunition, distributing them in carefully measured parcels for maximum effect. When his voice came again, there was a remarkable and unexpectedly warm undertone to it.

'It is good to hear your voice too, Sergeant Ur'ten. I have missed your fire.'

'Aren't you going to welcome me home?'

'No.'

The vox went dead and the grin on Gileas's face became a warm smile. He leaned back in his seat and closed his eyes, listening to the rumble and roar of the Thunderhawk's engines as it completed its descent to the landing grounds. How could he ever have felt reluctance at the idea of returning home? Varsavia was the place of his birth and of his rebirth.

'I am home,' he said.

'Preliminary tests suggest that he has seen nine winters,' said the medicae officer. She was a slight woman with hair the colour of burnished bronze and a prematurely lined and tired face. 'He is slightly malnourished and his body appears to be home

29

to several species of lice, but apart from that…' She shook her head. *'He is alive. That should probably tell you all you need to know about him.'*

The child of whom she spoke was sleeping peacefully. He had been given a hard cot to lie on, but had snatched the blanket and retreated to a corner. He had curled up in a ball like one of the big felines who roamed the halls of the fortress-monastery and had gone to sleep there. One of the cats, barely more than a cub but still as high as a Space Marine's knee, had curled around his sleeping form protectively.

Janira handed the data-slate containing the boy's medical information to the massive figure standing opposite her. As the current incumbent Master of the Watch, Andreas Kulle had been informed of the child's arrival and was simply following up the report. The story he had been told had intrigued him and he had paid the young guest a personal visit. Apparently, the boy had clambered up the east face of the mountainside and emerged, bloodied and triumphant, in the fortress-monastery courtyard where he had promptly engaged in creating havoc.

'So is it true that he marched right up to the entrance and demanded to be allowed in?' There was a note of amused warmth in Kulle's voice. He had been told stories before of determined individuals making their way up the Argent Pass to the mountaintop, but never a child.

'True as I am standing here, my lord. At least, it was what he appeared to want. He speaks solely in his tribe's dialect. I understand about one word in six.'

Kulle grunted and glanced over at the sleeping boy. He was dark-haired and his skin was already weathered by a life spent outdoors. Asleep, he bore all the innocence of youth. Kulle was intrigued.

'And he gives no indication of his origin?'

'The brand at the base of his neck is that of the Hathirii tribe, but our records suggest that tribe has always been settled in the far south. He is a child. He could not have travelled all that way alone. Perhaps a nomadic sect of the Hathirii who strayed further north? I will speak with him more in the morning. Or at least try to.'

'I would speak with him also.'

Janira chewed her lip, choosing her next words carefully. 'We should give him a day or two to recover his senses. I mean no disrespect, my lord, but you are more than a little intimidating, even for human adults. I cannot imagine how you must seem to a child who has never experienced the Adeptus Astartes. We should address one issue at a time. He needs rest and sustenance first.'

'And sanitisation might not go amiss,' came the wry response. 'Very well, Mistress Janira. I leave the boy to your care.'

Gileas had no recollection of his arrival at the fortress-monastery so many years before. Years of war and intensive hypno-doctrination had wiped nearly all his early memories from him. Yet as he stepped down the ramp of the Thunderhawk and gazed up with deep pride and honour at the gateway looming before him, it was as though he had never left. Old feelings stirred from the depths of memory and threatened to surface. When Reuben spoke, Gileas was glad. He had sensed that some of his memories were unwelcome ones.

The Thunderhawk had set down on the east side of the mountain face; a natural cleft in the rock that had been hollowed out further and widened for use as a landing pad. Capable of housing as many as three gunships at a time, it was generally used for the relay of materials between the fortress-monastery and the larger space port maintained at the tip of the northern peninsula.

'It has been too long,' murmured Reuben as his friend moved to stand behind him. 'Feels good to be home.'

'Aye, brother, I am with you there.'

The vast archway that led into the fortress-monastery here was by no means as beautiful or ornate as the one that was worked into the stone over the main entrance, but still this one was carved and shaped with consummate skill until it was impossible to tell where nature left off and the intervention of man began. Set in a recess in the side of the peak, it was adorned with stonework skulls that rose from either side to meet the Imperial aquila standing proudly in the centre.

As they passed beneath the archway, they stepped into the lee of the wind and the young men who walked with them received a brief reprieve from the biting air that had greeted them on stepping from the ship. In this courtyard, servitors and Chapter-serfs busied themselves with the day-to-day tasks that kept them occupied. At the top level of the fortress-monastery, in a vast, armourglass-domed courtyard, was an entire human settlement. It was here that the majority of Chapter-serfs lived, some marrying and dying here without ever seeing life beyond the mountain. Lives spent in loyal and faithful service to the Silver Skulls. It was said, although nobody had ever tested the claim, that the Lord Commander knew every thrall by name.

'I will take the recruits to Attellus,' said Reuben, referring to the knot of youngsters they had recovered from their last mission. Gileas put a hand out to catch his brother's arm.

'No,' he said. 'That is my responsibility. You take the rest of the company down to the dormitory levels and disperse them for maintenance. I will establish how long our stay is likely to be and let you know as soon as I can.'

'Aye, captain.' Reuben's eyes glinted mischievously as Gileas frowned at the honorific. 'You really should start getting used to that, you know.'

'Perhaps. Now get going.'

The two warriors clasped one another's forearms and moved off in separate directions. Gileas headed towards the boys who had been recovered from the dark eldar during the skirmishes on Cartan V. Throughout the journey back to Varsavia, they had spent a lot of time being instructed in what to expect on their arrival. Now that they were actually here, however, it was far more than they could have anticipated. Several of them stared up at the archway with obvious awe on their faces. At Gileas's approach, most of the children stood to clumsy attention. One or two did not, fascinated by their surroundings. When the Space Marine spoke, they jumped visibly and fell into loose formation.

'Listen to my words carefully. Every last one of you is honoured beyond all others,' said Gileas, letting his dark blue eyes sweep across the gathered youngsters. 'You stand here at the gateway to your future. Thousands of warriors and heroes have crossed the threshold of the Varsavian fortress-monastery, and you must consider yourselves deeply honoured to be granted that privilege.'

He had chosen his words well. Many pairs of eyes shone brightly with great optimism. 'Some of you will ascend to the ranks of the Emperor's chosen. Some of you will not. But whatever becomes of you, you will be reborn in one form or another. Everything that happens here in the heart of Varsavia is for the good of the Emperor.' The boys were staring up at him in fascination. Gileas felt the faintest sense of discomfort. The sooner he delivered these youths into the hands of Attellus, the better. He had never felt comfortable around children.

'I will take you now into the lower levels,' he continued, pushing the thoughts from his mind. 'There you will be assigned dormitories and shown where you will be training and studying. You may find your way around by yourselves, but I warn you in advance – do not stray beyond your designated areas. A certain tolerance will be shown, but if you do not learn quickly, then you will go no further with your training.'

He had done exactly that as a child: gone exploring where he had specifically been told not to venture. It was one of the few memories of his younger years that remained as clear as a bell. Hand in hand with that was the memory of the shame he had felt when he had been brought before his mentor and forced to explain his actions. Kulle's disappointment in him had been a harder lesson than any of the physical punishments that were frequently meted out.

'The Silver Skulls are an ancient Chapter,' he continued, acutely conscious of them all watching him intently. Evidently, something more was expected of him. 'Our ways are considered archaic by some. But the very fact that we remain, millennia past the time of our founding, speaks for itself. You now leave behind all that you were and become all that you can be. Do not fear what awaits you, for you are chosen. Remember the feeling of pride this gives you. Hold on to it and nurture it, for you will find that it serves you well during the trials to come. Now fall into line and follow me.'

He could tell by the look in their eyes that his words had reached them. He turned away from them to lead them into the halls, but also to hide his smile.

THREE

DENIAL

Scout Captain Attellus was a grizzled knot of sinewy muscle and intense surliness. He had been that way for as long as Gileas could remember and it was more than likely that he would remain that way until the day he died.

Unlike most of the Silver Skulls captains, he had not elected to have graceful tribal whorls or beautiful designs tattooed on his face. He didn't even have something as fearsome as the skull that First Captain Kerelan had adopted. Instead, his face was quite simply a mask of red and black marks. Single strokes, crossed at regular intervals to make adding them up a quick process, the black marks were a tally of personal kills. Each red mark was for a brother he had stood beside and lost.

There were far more black strokes than there were red.

He was on the training levels, wearing a simple tunic and combat fatigues, putting a group of young Scouts through their paces. He stood to one side, his arms folded over his massive chest, watching each one closely and with an instructor's ease. Occasionally he would bark out a command or admonishment and Gileas kept his peace for a while. He had learned many years ago that Attellus spoke when Attellus was ready.

'Well, now,' the Scout captain said, shifting his grey eyes to Gileas. 'The wandering savage returns, eh?'

'Captain,' replied Gileas formally. 'The Lord Commander has ordered me back to Varsavia and I have brought you a new batch of recruits.'

'So I hear,' sniffed Attellus. He turned to his charges and beckoned one young man. The youth jogged over obediently. 'Nicodemus, you have command until I return. Do not get too used to it.'

'Yes, captain.' The boy inclined his head graciously. He cast a single, curious glance at the sergeant and turned to the drilling young warriors. Attellus watched him go, his arms still folded across his chest.

'Some are easier to train than others,' he mused. 'That one will be good as soon as he learns to curb his arrogance. If he can do that, he's likely to be able to give Phrixus a run for his money.' Attellus waved a hand that took in the assemblage. 'This group completed their rites only a few weeks ago. We lost three in the process, unfortunately. It could have been worse.' He watched Nicodemus again for a few moments before turning the full force of his attention onto Gileas.

The Scout captain looked over the younger warrior with the expertise of a man who knew his craft well, noting at a single glance the new scars that marred his flesh and the change in Gileas's stance and demeanour. There was acquired experience in the Space Marine's eyes that had been missing the last time the two had met. Attellus scowled and sniffed indifferently.

'I see you have not got any prettier to look at, Ur'ten.'

'And you are still as sour as a kumari fruit.'

The ritual trading of insults completed, Attellus's face broke out in a grin and he unfolded his arms to clasp Gileas's shoulders. 'By the Emperor, it is good to see you again, boy. When I heard about Meyoran…' Gileas cast his eyes down briefly at the mention of his former commander. 'I feared the worst for the Eighth.'

'Bast saw us through.' The company's Prognosticator had been invaluable during the transitory period following the captain's death. It had been Bast who had guided Gileas during his time as acting captain and it would be Bast who would be making his report to Vashiro even now. 'It has not been easy.'

'I should hope not,' retorted Attellus. 'Hardship was ever the mother of tenacity. A harsh trial for you and your warriors, but a necessary one nonetheless.' He reached up and scratched thoughtfully at his salt-and-pepper beard, and began to walk. He indicated that Gileas should follow. They were of a height, but where Gileas was a solid slab of muscle, Attellus's strength seemed somehow wiry. The two warriors walked in companionable silence for a while around the training halls. Around them, Scouts and fully fledged battle-brothers trained together.

The Silver Skulls had always encouraged the training of Tenth Company alongside the more experienced warriors of other companies. Contests of strength and ability were regularly staged in the training cages and in the small fighting arenas that were dotted around. The Silver Skulls were invariably born into warrior tribes and even once ascended, they retained much of that tribal spirit. Competitiveness was openly encouraged, sometimes to extremes. The commanders of the Chapter had always believed it fostered an eagerness to excel.

'You have my deepest condolences on the loss of Meyoran, lad,' said Attellus in time. 'I know that he looked on you with great favour.'

'Aye,' replied Gileas. 'He was a great warrior, a good captain. And he was my friend. I have lost too many mentors over the years, present company excluded. And the Emperor knows I have tried my hardest to get rid of you.'

'I was never your mentor,' retorted Attellus. 'I was just the man who told you what to do. If I was lucky, you listened. You were always one step ahead of your training, Ur'ten. There were times I believed you would not accept the fact that you would never know it all. Kulle knocked that out of you in the end.'

'True enough.' Gileas gave Attellus a sheepish grin. He had been a belligerent child and a temperamental adolescent, and many of those qualities had been brought with him through to genhanced adulthood. They had been encouraged in him, although this was something he had only realised in hindsight. Andreas Kulle, a seasoned warrior and a man Gileas had come to love like a father, had been a steadying influence.

'Enough of the reminiscing, pleasurable as it may be. I have seen more battle-brothers come and go over the years than I care to recall right now. It does not do to linger. Will you be undertaking a pilgrimage to Pax Argentius whilst you are here?'

'If the chance presents itself, most certainly,' confirmed Gileas. 'Whilst we have been unable to return the captain's body, I am keen to take tales of his greatness to the Halls of Remembrance.'

'Then for the sake of his memory, I hope you get the opportunity. Now enough of the melancholy. Tell me of the new blood.'

Grateful for Attellus's skilful change of topic, Gileas presented his report efficiently. He detailed the circumstances under which he had collected the youths who even now were undergoing medical assessments in the apothecarion. He listed those who had demonstrated leadership potential and those he believed might be more difficult to control. Attellus nodded without speaking, mentally absorbing every word.

'On the subject of leadership potential, I have a favour to ask of you.' Attellus moved smoothly and without hesitation on to a new topic.

'Of course, captain.'

'The boy, Nicodemus.' Gileas turned to follow Attellus's gaze. The young man was leading his fellow Scouts in a training exercise. On first glance, the boy was evidently strong and confident in his abilities and the others heeded his every command without question. Gileas studied the youth carefully, recognising something of the southern Varsavian in his colouring and stance. He sported dark brown hair which showed evidence of having been shaved during the gene-enhancement processes, but it was growing back. He fought bare-chested and his skin was wind-tanned and smooth.

'What of him?'

'Perhaps you would be prepared to train with him a little whilst you are here? The boy is as savage and untamed as you were at his age.' Attellus gave a slight smirk. 'As a future

Prognosticar, he will prove his worth a thousand times over. I am told that he exhibits much potential, although he's pretty much raw talent right now. But he relies on his psychic abilities too much. He needs careful handling and schooling in the finer arts of battle. He acts first and considers his options later. In that, I feel he could benefit from your experience. I would say your experience and wisdom, but I remain to be convinced that you have yet attained any of the latter yourself.'

'I would gladly do that, captain.'

Gileas watched the boy train for a few moments. His movements were lithe and graceful, but there was a core of strength in his attack that was impressive to watch. Once he was deployed on a mission, he would excel. He had confidence, but Gileas knew from cold experience that confidence was not enough.

'You might even enjoy it. And maybe you will learn a new trick or two in the process.'

Their pleasant exchange was interrupted by the arrival of a Chapter-serf who came into the training halls and headed straight for the pair.

'Sergeant Ur'ten? The Lord Commander has requested your presence as soon as possible, my lord.' The man bowed deeply and respectfully.

Attellus clapped Gileas on the back in an unexpected gesture of warm camaraderie. It was not unwelcome.

'Go and excel, boy,' he said. 'Prove your worth. I have every faith that by the end of this day, you will be planning your first captain's tattoo. And well deserved it will be, too.'

'I would not dare to presume,' responded Gileas cautiously. 'I will see you again, captain.'

'Call me Attellus off the battlefield, boy.'

Gileas smiled, his sharpened incisors flashing briefly. It was a startling thing, this sudden acceptance as a peer despite no captain's laurels on his armour.

As Gileas followed the Chapter-serf from the training halls, he tried hard to dismiss the thought that Attellus's confidence in his impending promotion was poorly placed.

Even in the years after the child had ascended to join the ranks of the Chapter, Andreas Kulle had never really understood why it was that he had screened the boy for suitability. Perhaps it was just the evidence of his tenacity. Whatever it was, three days after he had arrived, Kulle sat opposite the child, who kept his sullen, dark-eyed gaze defiantly on the giant who had come to talk with him.

He had not been able to communicate with anybody in the medicae centre other than through gestures and expressions. It had come as something of an obvious relief to the boy when Kulle had cycled through a number of tribal dialects, finally finding one which they both spoke. Due to the necessity of recruiting tribesmen to their ranks, all of the Silver Skulls had multilingual communications programmed into their hypno-doctrination process.

Once contact was established, the boy began to talk at an astonishing speed until Kulle had finally barked at him to be silent. His eyes widened in shock and he fell quiet.

'Good. Now, then. Let us start from the beginning, boy. What is your name?'

The boy hesitated for a second and then he shook his head. 'I haven't reached my naming day yet,' he replied. 'I was supposed to get my name at the next turn of the moon. Right now, I am ur'ten.'

Kulle scratched at his chin thoughtfully. The word translated roughly as 'orphan'. The tribal language that they were both speaking was an ancient one, but there was something musical in its cadence and the elegance of its sound. It made the child seem far older than his years, something which was reflected in his eyes. The boy had seen a lot and had evidently suffered greatly but he had never given up.

'Ur'ten? Can you tell me what happened to your family?' Kulle asked the question cautiously, sensing that he knew the answer.

A look came into the child's face that Kulle recognised immediately as grief. He chose not to interrupt and let the boy deal with his emotions as he saw fit. Two slightly grubby little fists ground into a pair of tired eyes, physically fighting back tears. 'They're dead. My mother, father and my three sisters. All dead.'

'How long ago?' The child counted on his fingers, then held up both hands with all the fingers stretched out. He stared at Kulle crossly and the Space Marine read his silent question easily.

'Ten,' Kulle said gently.

'Ten rises of the moon,' the child replied. 'We were travelling north. My father… he was bringing me here. He said that it was the Shiro's vision that I was to come to the mountains in the north.'

Shiro. The seer. The root word that had given Vashiro, he who sees, his title. Kulle had heard such stories before. Without exception, all of the 'seers' who had been brought to the attention of the Silver Skulls were not psykers, but simply men and women of great intuition and with an understanding of the human condition that was unsurpassed. The rest of their art was accomplished with the aid of various herbal preparations, sometimes smoked and sometimes drunk, powerful enough that they could induce visions in anyone.

'Why was it that your Shiro said this thing?'

'He had a vision. He told my father of the silver giants in the north. *That I should be brought here. We all came together.'* The boy fell silent again, obviously struggling to contain his grief. Although his years of service had largely stolen him of the ability to feel sympathy, Kulle nonetheless felt a stirring of emotion. He likened it to respect for the boy. He had lost his whole family and had still struggled to the end of his journey.

'What happened on the journey?' He waited for the child to get his churning emotions under control. Dark blue eyes lifted, barely visible beneath the tangle of dark curls that fell into them, and the grief was replaced with utter hatred.

'Xiz.'

The rogue, cannibalistic tribe who roamed Varsavia's southern wastes and even strayed north. Known for attacking travellers, they were fearsome fighters. Not one had ever been selected for recruitment. Not one possessed sanity enough to earn the attention of the Adeptus Astartes. They were animals with a penchant for human flesh. Of late, they had become increasingly active and the Silver Skulls had debated moving to deal with them once and for all.

But Vashiro had communed with the Emperor, who in turn had said that to extinguish the threat of the Xiz would be to interfere with the path of the future. The cannibals were to be left to roam free. In time, their prominence would wane and equilibrium would be restored.

'How did you escape them?'

'My father… dug down. Hid me beneath the snow. I didn't come out until I couldn't hear them any more. I was alone.' The moment of intense hatred bled from the boy's eyes and a resigned weariness that seemed too old for him seeped in. *'I came here. I had nothing else. Nowhere else to go.'*

'Yes.' Kulle offered a brief smile. *'You came here.'* He examined the data-slate before him, finally looking up at the ragged

child seated opposite. 'Tell me, boy. You travelled here alone and made your way up the side of a dangerous mountain. You are surrounded by things and individuals of which you have no true comprehension. Are you not afraid? Or do you consider yourself courageous? Above such fears?'

The dark-eyed gaze was steady and the confidence wavered only slightly. He shrugged one shoulder again.

'Of course I'm afraid,' he replied. 'But my father told me that courage wasn't just a case of not being afraid. He told me that courage is about being afraid but still doing what it is that you must do. Regardless of that fear.'

With those words, the boy's future was sealed. 'He was a wise man indeed,' said Kulle, nodding slowly as he made a check on the data-slate. He set the object down and leaned forward, setting his elbows on his knees. His fingers knotted together and he rested his chin on them. 'What was his name?'

'Gileas. He was a warrior. First warrior of our tribe. But he couldn't defend us against the Xiz. They were... they were too many.' The challenging look in the child's eyes dared Kulle to call his father a failed warrior. Instead, Andreas Kulle noted something down on the data-slate and reached over a huge hand to clasp the boy's shoulder.

'Then in memory of your father, whose wise words brought you to us... and to honour the traditions of your tribe, I give you a name by which you will be known from this point on. Your name, boy, will be Gileas.'

And so it was done.

He had never been in the Chapter Master's personal chambers before and Gileas felt distinctly overwhelmed by the fact that he had been invited there now. He had stood in the presence of Argentius only a handful of times, and never previously before this particular incumbent. He knew the warrior who bore the rank well, however. They had even fought together on the field of battle.

It was hard not to let the approval flicker onto his face. The Chapter Master's quarters were not lavishly furnished, but they were comfortable in a spartan way. The slate-topped table that dominated the room was covered with ledgers and tomes of deepest midnight blue embossed with silver runes. The walls bore no decoration and one side of the huge room opened out onto the training courtyard. From here, the Chapter Master could oversee his battle-brothers undergoing rigorous training below him.

A thick rug made from the hide of a Varsavian native beast graced the floor and it was on this that Gileas stood before a man he had once stood alongside. He looked across the table at Argentius. In so many ways, they were physically opposite. Although his hair was presently shorn to the scalp, Gileas knew that the Lord Commander was blond and his eyes were a light blue, where Gileas was dark of both eye and hair. Argentius had the pale cast of those born in the northern cities. Gileas's swarthy skin bore the deep olive tones of a southern-born. Argentius carried himself with the easy assurance that when he spoke, people would listen to him and that was indeed the case.

Blessed with natural charisma that had seen him rise rapidly through the ranks to where he was now, Argentius – in the days before he had assumed that title – had been well respected and well liked. Space Marines and Imperial forces alike found themselves drawn to his easy manner and quietly commanding presence. It felt as though Argentius never ordered those under his leadership. It felt as though he simply guided and shaped them.

Gileas wondered wildly if the Lord Commander even remembered him and immediately berated himself for such a foolish thought. The question was answered with Argentius's opening words.

'Sergeant, please stand at ease. You look so tense that if you moved even a muscle in your face you would fracture. I appreciate the sentiment, but please, brother. Do not stand on ceremony. Not with me.' His smile was warm and friendly. 'We have shared enough of our time in service to the God-Emperor as brothers-in-arms not to let a small thing like my promotion to this lofty position come between us now, surely?'

Gileas had not even realised how straight he had been standing. There was an amused look in Argentius's eyes and the younger warrior relaxed, but only slightly. Realising that he was not going to put Gileas at ease at all, Argentius shook his head with a wry smile on his face before he moved onto business.

'Thank you for responding to my message with such alacrity, Sergeant Ur'ten. It is often many weeks before a recall to Varsavia reaches a ship of the fleet. You were engaged with the eldar for longer than anticipated.'

'Yes, sir. In the wake of the captain's... in the wake of Captain Meyoran's disappearance, we sought out and destroyed as many of the eldar in that system as we could find. We have reason to believe that they will not be back for a good long while.'

'Something which gives cause for satisfaction, no doubt?' Argentius turned away from Gileas and strode across the floor to the balcony overlooking the inner training halls.

'I am not sure I follow your meaning, sir.'

'Revenge, Gileas, is a dish best served cold – or so they say.

46

You could have fallen back from the assault on the eldar. Gathered together more of a battle force. Yet you did not. Was this on Bast's advice?'

'Yes, my lord. And if I speak truth, on my instincts as well. It just so happened that our thoughts ran parallel on the matter.'

'As it should be. I would not like to think that you did not listen to the words of your Prognosticator. Where would our Chapter be if we were to forsake our most holy tradition?' There was a faintly bitter tone in the Chapter Master's voice, hinting at undercurrents of tension which Gileas did not dare to question. Argentius turned from the balcony and moved back into his chamber.

'I have already seen the manifest from the *Silver Arrow*. You have brought back a goodly number of recruits. Excellent work... again. But you also return to me missing something vital.'

'Aye, sir. Captain Meyoran's body was lost during the engagement with the eldar. He was torn apart by one of the xenos' devices. Not even armour scraps remained. I intend to take a personal pilgrimage to Pax Argentius and speak the Catechism of Remembrance for him as soon as I am able to do so.'

'You have handled the events of these past weeks well, my brother,' said the Chapter Master, his voice dropping to something softer and entirely more informal. 'It cannot have been easy on you, being forced to take command of the Eighth Company.'

'I relished the challenge, sir.'

'Of course you did, Gileas – I expected nothing less of you. And you will receive commendation for that in due course, I assure you.' Argentius looked up as another figure came in through the doorway. 'Vashiro. Thank you for coming.'

Gileas took to his knee immediately. Every battle-brother within the Silver Skulls revered their Head Prognosticator with fierce loyalty and a deep, abiding respect. As the old psyker moved past Gileas, he laid a hand on the sergeant's head.

'Deference noted, boy,' he said. 'Please stand up.'

'My lord,' said Gileas as he got to his feet, his voice choked with awe. To be standing in such august company as the two senior commanders of the Chapter was something that not many achieved. He dared a glance at the Head Prognosticator. The man's face was lost behind a plethora of tattoos, faded and indecipherable with the ages. He had held his position for as long as Gileas could remember and yet he had not changed much.

Clad in soft flowing robes of steel grey, his stature was as great as the two warriors who stood with him. He was every bit as broad across the shoulders, every inch an Adeptus Astartes. But he was first and foremost a Prognosticator. He still took the battlefield when duty called him to attend, and fought alongside the Prognosticators. Gileas had not seen him in battle, but the tales were legion. A warrior who moved as silently as a wraith across a field of war, reaping skulls for the Chapter in the tens of thousands.

'Gileas Ur'ten, you have been a difficult man to deal with,' said Vashiro. A faint smile on his lips removed any stern undertone that might have been implied. 'I have spent many long hours in communion with the Emperor regarding your future.'

He stepped closer to Gileas and stared into the sergeant's

dark blue eyes thoughtfully. 'I mean these words not as an insult, Gileas, but hear me out. I always did feel that you were a complicated boy. Age and experience, it seems, have not robbed you of that honour.' Vashiro's eyes narrowed and his next words came out as a snap. 'Guard your thoughts with more care. A child could read them.'

Startled by the sudden reprimand, Gileas realised that he could feel the faint sense of tingling that always accompanied the action of psychic powers. Argentius watched the exchange but did not speak. He had decreed that since Vashiro had made the decision, he would be the one to give Gileas the news.

'You have done sterling work leading the Eighth Company in the wake of a tragic loss,' he said. 'The Chapter Master and many others here have spoken highly in your favour. Even Kerelan has been involved in the discussions.'

'The Talriktug are presently in residence here,' interjected Argentius. Gileas moved his gaze with some difficulty from the psyker to glance at the Chapter Master. Vashiro's lips twitched slightly as he plucked the surface thought that flashed through Gileas's mind on hearing this news. The Talriktug. First Company champions every one, with First Captain Kerelan at their head. It would be quite the honour to spend time learning from them and this lifted Gileas's spirits briefly.

'So there have been a great number who have spoken up in favour of you taking permanent command of the Eighth Company. Your battle record speaks for itself. You are loyal and you are honourable.' Vashiro's heavily inked face twisted into a frown. 'But you are still hot-headed and impetuous. Your rage is like a wild thing that is chained and kept in check. It is always there, straining at its bonds, a danger to yourself and your brothers. This is not the way of the Silver Skulls. This you must learn, Gileas.'

Argentius was watching the warrior carefully, gauging his reaction to these words. Vashiro nodded slowly, once more taking the thoughts from Gileas's mind as though he had written them down.

'You are correct, of course. The captaincy of the Eighth will not be yours at this time.'

If Gileas was surprised or disappointed, he did not let it show. Instead, he nodded in understanding.

'If I may ask,' he said, his voice steady and calm, 'to whom will I be reporting?'

'Sergeant Kyaerus has received a message to return to Varsavia,' replied Argentius. 'Seventh Company have been deployed to support others in a conflict in the Herios system. He will be given the position with immediate effect on his arrival. But I have a special, personal favour to ask of you.'

'My lord?' There seemed to be a lot of personal favour requests of him today and Gileas was startled for a second time.

'It has been a long time... a very long time since warriors of Eighth Company took their place as defenders of the fortress-monastery. I would consider it a great honour were you to retain a number of your battle-brothers for a term and fulfil that duty.'

Gileas barely stopped the derisive snort that threatened to explode out of him. Fortress guardianship was called an honour, something that the Chapter Master 'requested' of a company from time to time. 'Honour' was not the word that the lower ranks used to describe it. A term usually lasted a full Varsavian year, during which they did not go off-world unless terms of engagement dictated otherwise.

He had not spent any prolonged period of time on Varsavia in over eighty years.

Strange, he thought, how he had yearned to return to its chill embrace only that morning. Now it seemed that he would be there longer than he thought.

'There will be many opportunities for your men to train alongside the Talriktug,' offered Argentius, but he could tell from the look in Gileas's eyes that even the thought of training alongside the Chapter's First Company elite was a poor substitution for being returned to active duty. 'And I am sure that Attellus would appreciate your insight in dealing with the novitiates.'

'As my lord commands, so I will obey.'

'It is the Emperor's will, Gileas.' Vashiro sounded surprisingly apologetic. 'It is the way things must be.'

'Of course, my lord.' Gileas gave Vashiro a careful look. 'I would never question the Emperor's will. I would hope that you know that of me at the very least.'

'It is the way things must be, that much is true. But I feel that this is only for now,' added Argentius. 'Your time will come, brother. Of that, I am sure.'

'Yes, sir.'

The rest of the conversation was taken up with logistical detail and Gileas was more than happy to sink his teeth into talk of training schedules and duty rosters for the time he would spend on the Chapter's home world. But the disappointment was there. It was plain in his posture, the set of his shoulders and the occasional distracted look on his face.

They saw his disappointment, but they could offer no words to alleviate it.

It was, after all, the Emperor's will.

My Lord

I trust that this message finds you well and that your burden is not too great at this time. I am sending this astropathic communication to you in order that you may be assured that your task has been taken in hand.

My recent trip to the gene vaults of Terra was less than conclusive, although I have had long discussions with representatives of the Adeptus Biologicus regarding the matter. A full enquiry has been promised and the results should be available in due course. Fortunately, expedience is not the watchword in this matter, particularly when we need to gather as many accurate facts as we can.

At the moment, my time is being taken up with matters in the Ultima Segmentum, but I have tentatively scheduled time to visit our mutual friends within a Terran year. In the meantime, I am working to obtain as much conclusive documentation as possible on their history, their planet's history and specific individuals who may be of interest to us in times ahead.

I must stress that preliminary checks have revealed much that is good about our subjects. Those who have worked and fought alongside them have little disparaging to report, although the thread of superstition continues to run through everything I have gathered so far. I will consolidate what I have and transmit this to you accordingly.

* * *

You can be assured that I am continuing to extend enquiries into this matter. If and when time allows, we will arrange for a more formal information-gathering process to commence.

My discretion and my loyalty are guaranteed.

I will contact you again soon.

Ave Imperator!

Inquisitor L. Callis
Ordo Hereticus

+++

Transmission Ends

+++

FOUR

THE EMPEROR'S WILL

It was not going to be easy returning to his squad in the wake of the news, but Gileas was eventually dismissed from the Chapter Master's presence and it was to them that he immediately returned. He found Reuben first, holed up in the armoury. His oldest friend had stripped back his armour completely and had started work on maintenance. Dents were being carefully hammered out and Reuben handled every piece of the steel-grey plate with loving care and attention and complete concentration.

Let other Chapters leave the cleansing and repair of sacred battle armour to their serfs. The Silver Skulls, deeply superstitious, considered that bad luck and more than a little insulting to the machine-spirits. Chapter-serfs had their place in the process, of course: they were tasked with the job of maintaining armour that was not in use. Once the warriors had painstakingly hammered out every dent and lovingly polished every last inch of ceramite plate, the serfs would maintain regular tests and checks to ensure its battle-readiness.

Around the armoury, other brothers from Eighth Company were similarly working on their battleplate. Some would be elsewhere, maintaining weapons or jump packs. Others were probably already in the training cages and Gileas didn't doubt for a second that most – if not all – had already been to the chapel. He had yet to attend to that part of his duty. Most of them acknowledged the sergeant's presence as he strode in.

Reuben on the other hand did not even look up and Gileas felt a moment's relief. If Reuben didn't acknowledge him, it would give him a little time to marshal his thoughts before the inevitable questions began. He walked past his battle-brother and headed for the armouring servitors. He gave them a few curt orders and stood still whilst they complied with his request. Four of them attended him immediately, removing the rivets that held his armour in place.

Due to their ongoing engagements and the need to appear in full battleplate in front of his Chapter Master, Gileas had not been properly freed from its confines for any length of time in many weeks. At most, he had been relieved of the bracers and the pauldrons, but readiness had been an absolute requirement. As the first of the heavy ceramite plates was removed from his body, he felt curiously light.

The armour was stripped away from him carefully, piece by piece, and mounted on a rack that stood to the side. Some other Chapters, so Gileas had heard, employed artificers to maintain their wargear. That was fine for weapons and jump packs, but to a Silver Skulls warrior, his armour was personal. Each set of wargear was a hereditary thing and to show it anything less than the utmost reverence would be disrespectful.

Finally, clad in nothing but the black bodyglove that he wore between his skin and his armour, the sergeant stretched out his shoulders. A Chapter-serf hurried up and provided a simple grey surplice that Gileas slid on over his head. It was made from a rough-edged fabric that would have itched terribly if not for the bodyglove. He was relieved at the reprieve from his armour.

He took his place on a bench opposite Reuben and took up one of his leg guards. He turned it over in his hands, inspecting it for minute dents or scratches that might weaken its structural integrity, or tiny nicks in the ceramite that might mar its perfection.

'So, then?'

Reuben asked the question without looking up. He held part of his breastplate in his hands and the soft cloth that he had been using to wipe its surface in meticulous circular motions had stilled.

'So, then.' Gileas's reply was carefully spoken in a completely neutral tone. 'It looks as though you will not be getting rid of me as your squad commander any time soon.'

'I see.'

Gileas knew Reuben well enough to recognise the early signs of his battle-brother's anger. He shook his head as he peered carefully at the leg guard. 'This is going to need some serious repainting.' Similarly, he knew Reuben well enough to know how to handle that particular mood swing.

'If not you, then who?'

'Kyaerus.'

'Kyaerus? Of Seventh Company? He is little more than a

boy!' Reuben's outrage was tempered by the unintentional humour implicit in his words. Gileas gave a small chuckle.

'*Captain* Kyaerus is at least half a century older than you or I, Reuben.'

Reuben snorted and set aside his armour. He lifted his head to glare at Gileas. 'Did they give any sort of reason for this insult?'

'Watch your tone, Reuben. The decree comes directly from Vashiro and I would not seek to question his wisdom in such matters.'

'From Vashiro?' Reuben's irritation did not give way under the revelation of this news.

'It is the Emperor's will.' Gileas finally looked up and met Reuben's angry stare. His eyes were clear and calm and their gazes remained locked for a while. Reuben looked away first, but not before Gileas had seen the bitterness in his brother's thoughts.

'Kyaerus though.' Reuben laughed without humour. 'I have fought alongside him many times. He is–'

'Mind your words, Reuben. I may not be captain, but I am still your sergeant and your commander.'

Reuben smirked a little, but the expression faded when he realised that Gileas was serious.

'I was going to say he is a fine warrior. But he is not you, Gileas. His heart does not beat with the Eighth.'

'It is a curse of my birth, Reuben. You knew that yourself long before I assumed temporary command. No southern-born who has ascended to the Silver Skulls has gone beyond the rank of sergeant. There have been no signs, no auspices to suggest that I am in any way different.' One huge shoulder shrugged easily. 'It is the way it must be.'

'Every warrior in our company assumed that the honour

of command would be yours. This will not sit well with them.'

'They are sons of Varsavia all,' Gileas retorted, setting down his leg guard and taking up a gauntlet. 'Vashiro has spoken. I have accepted it. You should do likewise.'

'Have you, Gileas? Really?'

The two Space Marines stared at each other for a long while. They had been friends for the better part of a century and had fought side by side during virtually every campaign in that time. They knew each other well. Gileas's expression shifted into a slightly sardonic, self-mocking smile.

'The Chapter Master has given me other orders, but now is not the time to discuss those. Now is the time to prepare for our duties. That means enough of this idle banter and getting back to your rites of maintenance, brother.'

'Is that an order?' There was a challenge there and Gileas ignored it, falling into thoughtful silence. Reuben shook his head and returned his attention to his own armour.

Perhaps it was simply being back amongst the familiar surroundings of the fortress-monastery or perhaps it was something entirely different, but Gileas chose to make the most of the opportunity to indulge his body in the luxury of truesleep. Lying down and closing his eyes, allowing sleep to come naturally, was something that was rarely practised during a deployment and it took Gileas a while to relax into a state where he could embrace it.

He woke some hours later, his twin hearts pounding and his hand reaching for a weapon at his side that was not there. He sat up, swinging his legs round and off the narrow bed that stood against one side of the small room that was his own by dint of his rank, lowly as it might be in the great scheme of things. His squad shared quarters a few rooms down from him and he realised how much he missed their easy banter and camaraderie.

Rubbing the heels of his hands against his eyes, he breathed deeply and allowed the dream to fade. His body was singing with the adrenaline rush that had occurred automatically when his mind had believed he was under attack, and he slowly allowed the effects of the moment to lessen. His breathing slowed and calmness returned. He had not expected so vivid a dream after so long without rest.

In the corner of his room, a lume-globe that he had not extinguished still burned, giving off a gentle glow that cast flickering shadows on the stone walls. Its light caught on the polished blade of Eclipse, the relic chainsword that he had been given by a dying captain several years before. The weapon was his pride and joy and he was well aware that there were many in the Chapter who did not feel a lowly sergeant – and a Hathirii at that – should be entrusted with such a relic. But a bequeathed weapon entrusted to another at the moment of death was not something that would ever be disputed.

He had always maintained Eclipse with the sense of honour and duty that owning such a cherished weapon brought and it gleamed as brightly as the day it had been gifted to a long-dead Lord Commander of the Chapter, hundreds of years before. His eyes rested on it for a long while as he processed the memories stirred by its proximity. Most were glorious recollections: fleeting and fading recalls of battles won. Countless numbers of enemy forces and traitors ended with a bite from its dreadful teeth. Such memories went a long way to calming his troubled thoughts.

Within the confines of both the cell and the fortress-monastery at large, there was no way of telling day from night. On the serf levels, lume-strips were used to simulate the passage of the hours, but lower down in the domain of the Adeptus Astartes, such methods were unnecessary.

Rising from his bed, Gileas reached for the light tan combat fatigues that he preferred when out of his armour and drew a tabard across his head, belting it at the waist. The emblem of the Chapter was rendered on it, worked in silvery thread that glinted in the weak, fading light of the globe. Moving over to the other side of the room, he reached up and took Eclipse down from the wall. Once it was in his hands, he felt entirely more comfortable. Its familiar weight and balance was something he had always welcomed and despite the fact that he had no call to go armed in this sanctuary, he still felt better having it with him.

He slid the weapon into the scabbard that hung from his belt. He usually preferred to wear the blade strapped across his back when he was fully armoured, but this was more comfortable. With a little reluctance, he abandoned the idea of sleep and headed towards the training cages. At least if he was there his mind would be occupied.

Servitors bustled through the hallways of the fortress-monastery, emotionless automatons who chattered endlessly as they carried out the various tasks for which they had been programmed. Gileas passed them by without a second glance, but he did make a point of acknowledging any of the thralls he encountered on his way down. There were barely any of them this deep into the fortress-monastery; the space that the Space Marines occupied was considered sacred and even novitiates were forbidden without receiving permission.

The training levels were never silent and as he entered through a vast archway adorned with exquisitely carved skulls, familiar noises washed over him. It was a complex layer of sound. Grunts of effort and occasional pain, words of encouragement, and overlying it all the metallic clash of blades meeting. He took a moment to look around and noted several of his own company were already down here as well. No doubt they had experienced similar difficulties adjusting to this sudden downtime. Relaxation was not a natural state of mind for a Space Marine.

They all greeted him warmly. He may not have been their captain, but as Reuben had said earlier in his moment of temper, the sergeant was deeply respected by the Eighth Company. They had all shared experiences, shared grief at the loss of Meyoran to the eldar, and the bonds of brotherhood that had formed could not be easily broken.

'I admit that I am surprised it has taken you this long to find your way down here, Gil.' Reuben stood with his arms folded across his barrel chest, a sly smirk on his face. Like Gileas, he was wearing fatigues and a tabard. A few healing marks on his bare arms told that he had already been in training. 'The rest of us have been here for hours already.'

'Of course you have,' countered Gileas with a flash of a grin. When he smiled, the tips of his razor-sharp incisors glinted in the noticeably brighter light of the training floor. Reuben's own chainsword rested casually across his shoulder and a trail of sweat on his neck suggested that he had been working hard. 'And I imagine you have an elaborate excuse to avoid sparring with me again?'

'Now you mention it...' The two warriors laughed warmly. Their banter was old and recalled the many times they had fought opposite one another in the cages. In unarmed combat and with the chainsword, Gileas rarely lost a bout. It was not unheard of, but he was a challenging opponent.

'There is one reason you may not want to spar with me,' said Reuben after the laughter dissipated. 'The Talriktug are here. Always target the biggest game – isn't that the Hathirii way?'

The smile slid from Gileas's face and a strange expression came into his eyes. 'They are? All of them?'

'Djul is here, along with Vrakos and First Captain Kerelan.' There was undisputed reverence in Reuben's voice as he spoke the First Captain's name, and with good reason. The fearsome leader of the Chapter's most elite squad of Terminators had a reputation that all strove towards matching.

In all his years, Gileas had never engaged in lengthy conversation with Kerelan. Vrakos he knew well of old; the veteran had been a former sergeant of his. And as for Brother Djul... there was a complicated twist to that particular relationship.

'I should pay my respects,' said Gileas, looking over Reuben's shoulder at the distant end of the training hall where a small group had gathered.

'I thought you might feel that way. So shall I consider our bout postponed?'

'Think yourself lucky that you are not picking yourself up from the floor already, brother.' Gileas nodded a farewell before striding down the length of the training hall. All about him, Silver Skulls warriors of all ages and ranks were fighting, sometimes as opponents, sometimes alone, occasionally as groups against the many and varied machines that could be programmed to provide differing levels of resistance.

At the far end of the hall, three warriors were engaged in

conversation. All wore training tunics and all looked up as Gileas approached them. One, a shaven-headed warrior with an intricate facial tattoo that covered every inch of his skin, tipped his head onto one side. As he smiled, the representation of a skull that had been worked into his face contorted horribly in a parody of a skinless creature's death scream.

'Sergeant Ur'ten. I wondered how long it would be before we saw you.'

'First captain.' Gileas inclined his head in deep respect. 'It is an honour.'

'My condolences on the loss of Meyoran. He was a fine warrior and an honoured friend.'

'His memory will live on in the Halls of Remembrance. You have been there, I take it, sergeant?'

Djul's interjection came as no surprise. Pious to the extreme, the sour-faced veteran sergeant was a daemon on the battlefield and the most zealous preacher off it. His face was free of tattoos, but the intricate and tiny script marking his arms and what was visible of his shoulders beneath his tabard told tales of his deeds. His eyes, hard green emeralds, bored into the sergeant as though seeking a reason to declare blasphemy.

Gileas hesitated only briefly before responding. There was an undertone of scorn in Djul's voice that he was used to from others. Once, he might have lost his patience with the prejudiced attitude of those who sneered upon the accident of his birth. He knew well what Veteran Sergeant Djul thought of him, but Gileas Ur'ten had not survived this long without learning the hard way. His reply when it came was unfailingly polite and courteously respectful.

'I have not. Not yet. I intend to go within the week. There has been much to do and I have only been back on Varsavia these past few hours.'

Djul said nothing, but a sneer lifted the corner of his lip. He shifted the bulk of his body slightly so that he was no longer looking directly at Gileas, an obvious and very clearly intended insult to the sergeant. 'You do your captain's memory great dishonour by waiting, Ur'ten. Of course, I expect nothing less of a savage.'

'Djul.' Kerelan said nothing beyond his battle-brother's name, but the threat implicit in the single syllable was all too clear. Djul's eyes flashed contempt and without another word, he strode off. Kerelan watched him go and folded his arms across his chest.

'You will forgive him, of course,' said the first captain mildly. 'Brother Djul has an arsenal of difficulties when it comes to acceptance. He felt Meyoran's loss as keenly as any and has been concerned for the future of the Eighth Company.' The skull tattoo on Kerelan's face glinted silver in the light as his eyes studied Gileas carefully. The sergeant could feel Kerelan taking the full measure of him in that look. All the strength and every weakness he possessed was being registered and weighed in the cool gaze.

'Would you care for a bout in the cages?' Gileas's look was so startled that the first captain roared with laughter. 'You look as though I have asked you to enter a nest of tyranids alone, brother. I have heard many good things about you, Gileas, and I would see your quality for myself.'

'I would be honoured, first captain.' Gileas bowed his head again. Kerelan grinned at him, the skull contorting horribly once again.

'You say that now,' he said. 'Let us see what you say in a few moments.'

Gileas chose fists to battle against the first captain. On the battlefield, Kerelan fought with an exquisitely forged relic sword that was the height of a normal man. Gileas's usual style, adapted to the short range and quick-flurry blows of a chainsword, would have led to a very scrappy demonstration indeed. Like most young aspiring officers, Gileas felt a burning need to somehow prove himself in the eyes of his superiors and fighting with their hands would put the two on an ostensibly equal footing.

The Silver Skulls took their unarmed combat training very seriously. Not only was it good for improving agility, it frequently became a necessity in the type of warfare the Chapter favoured. 'Up close and personal' was how Gileas had once heard it described, and he had witnessed many battle-brothers who had been divested of weapons or ammunition simply throw themselves into the fray with their fists flying. Such was the strength of the Adeptus Astartes that with the correct training their fists could prove to be every bit as lethal as the weapons with which they fought.

The Chapter had a reputation as fearsome opponents, and it was not without reason.

The two warriors had already circled one another, each taking in the other's build and obvious strengths. They had both discarded their tunics and fought bare-chested. Kerelan's body was a mass of tattoos, mostly the tribal whorls of his people. Where there were gaps between these, inscriptions and litanies were worked in decorative script. Ugly, disfiguring scars crept across the surface of his skin, marring the once-perfect body art.

Gileas's body bore its own share of scars too, although, being junior by far, he had not yet accumulated such a wealth of honour to decorate his skin. The fading white, jagged edges of a scar that ran from his neck down across the solid mass of his fused ribcage and down to his abdomen stood out starkly in contrast to his olive-dark skin. He wore that scar more proudly than any honour marking.

It was inevitable that a martial display of this kind would draw something of a crowd, but Gileas did not notice immediately the fact that most of those present in the training halls had edged closer to watch the two fighting.

Kerelan and Gileas came together with an audible impact and blows began flurrying with alacrity, each attempting to find the way past the other's defences. Gileas drew his head back to avoid a punch aimed precisely for his jaw. He bent his huge body backwards and twisted so that he was in a position to bring up a kick towards Kerelan's torso. His booted foot was grabbed by the first captain and wrenched aside. He lost his balance for a moment before righting himself.

As he always did, Gileas soon became lost in the untold ecstasy of battle. When Eclipse was in his hand, he always considered it less of a separate weapon and more of an extension of his own body. He controlled it; he guided it to where it needed to be. But with or without its snarling power in his grip, he was a formidable warrior. Kerelan commented as much as they fought.

'Andreas Kulle trained you well. He picked up a lot of unconventional tactics in the years he served with the Deathwatch, so they say.'

They were words that annoyed Gileas. Kulle had indeed been less orthodox than many other Silver Skulls in his manner of executing warfare and Gileas had taken a number of cues from his mentor. Something of the irritation he felt must have flashed in his eyes.

'Do not fall prey to that southern temper of yours, sergeant,' Kerelan said and brought his leg round in a sudden movement. He hooked Gileas behind the knees and the younger warrior crashed onto his back. Kerelan was immediately ready with another blow, but Gileas rolled clear.

'My temper is in check, first captain.'

'No,' said Kerelan, taking a step back and eyeing his opponent warily as Gileas got to his feet. 'No, it is not. It is there for any to take advantage of. Lose your focus in a battle situation and you lose the advantage. A rush of anger may lend you strength and determination, but it also breaks your concentration. And when that happens...'

When he moved, he did so with such nimble speed that Gileas did not stand a chance. The relentless first captain barrelled into him with all the power he could muster and the pair of them went flying. Gileas crashed against the side of the training cage, which shook under the sudden impact but held firm. Kerelan was back on his feet with cat-like agility and stood with his foot planted on Gileas's chest.

'Enough yet, Ur'ten?' The gruesome skull leered down at him and in that instant it became readily apparent why it was that Kerelan was so feared on the battlefield.

'I am not the kind of man who gives up, first captain, but in this instance I feel you have made a very valid point.' Kerelan laughed at the younger warrior's words and stepped back. He offered out a hand to help the sergeant up and Gileas clasped it, standing once again with the minimum of effort.

'You fight well, Gileas. Of course, there is always room

for improvement. You must strive to be the best you can be in everything that you do.'

'I always have, sir.'

Kerelan's eyes narrowed. He dropped his voice down so that Gileas alone could hear him. The gathering of battle-brothers was beginning to dissipate now that the demonstration was over but it was evident that Kerelan still wanted to keep his words for Gileas's ears only.

'Do not pay heed to Djul's barbs. He will test your patience to its limits because he feels that it is his duty to do so.'

'I do not understand, sir.'

'No, Gileas, you do not. For that, you should be grateful for your youth. Your generation has been entirely more tolerant of the cultural differences that exist between the people of Varsavia and those of other recruiting worlds. Djul is a Varsavian to the core.'

'As am I,' countered Gileas. He knew precisely where the first captain was heading with this conversation but he felt obliged to see it through to its natural conclusion. Something like annoyance kindled in him, but he pushed it down.

'True enough. But you are from what those of Djul's upbringing would call the "savage south". He was born to the privilege of the northern cities and received education and schooling before he was even handed over to the Silver Skulls. A certain prejudice is so deeply ingrained in those of his ilk that it is difficult to remove. He considers you little more than a tamed animal – an animal with the potential to turn on its masters at any time.'

'He questions my loyalty?' Gileas's brow feathered together in obvious distaste and Kerelan shook his head.

'No, brother. That is perhaps the one and only thing that

71

he does not question. He is against your suitability to command based purely on historical accounts of others from the south of this world. You know of what I speak, of course.'

Gileas did. Battle-brothers initiated into the ranks of the Silver Skulls from the tribes scattered across the vast southern continent of the Chapter's home world were almost invariably fiery souls who burned brightly and died swiftly. There were exceptions to the rule, of course – there had been tribal-raised Prognosticators and even a Chaplain – but the reputation of southerners as savage warriors was not unfounded.

'I have done nothing but serve my Chapter, my Chapter Master and the Emperor from the day I swore fealty to the Silver Skulls,' said Gileas, his tone less neutral than it had been before. He had been away from Varsavia for many years but it seemed that the ancient prejudices that caused friction within the Chapter had not diminished. 'Every one of my men…' He paused, correcting his own words. 'Every brother in Eighth Company followed my orders without question. We took losses, but they were minimal. I have the ability to lead. Brother Djul should be made aware that it was the Emperor's word which stayed my progression through the ranks, not any accident of my birth.'

'He is aware of this, Gileas. But Djul is… complicated. I merely ask that you do not rise to any slights he may put before you. You will not come out of such an altercation well.'

'I hear your words, first captain,' said Gileas. 'I hear them, but they sit poorly with me. I had thought our Chapter beyond such conflict.'

'Whatever you may think, heed my advice, sergeant.' Kerelan studied Gileas's face without expression in his eyes.

'You will do yourself no favours if you fall to infighting. I will speak with Djul separately on the matter. Our Chapter is going through complicated times. We do not need to perpetuate them from within.'

'I swear to you that I will hold my tongue and keep a tight rein on my temper,' said Gileas after a time.

'Good,' said Kerelan. 'Then get back to your training. A pleasure sparring with you, boy. Perhaps we can do so again whilst you are here?'

'I would consider it an honour to train alongside the Talriktug, sir.'

'Yes,' said Kerelan conversationally. 'I suppose it would be.'

The funereal moon of Pax Argentius orbited Varsavia and was considered one of the Chapter's most sacred places. Elaborate white marble tombs and vast mausoleums sprawled across its airless grey surface. There were also many halls and places of sanctuary, heavy with icons dedicated to the Imperial creed, for those who preached the Emperor's word but were not gifted psychically were trained here under the banner of the Chaplains. The sheer majesty of Pax Argentius was enough to silence even the most loquacious of tongues, but in this sombre labyrinth, the warriors of the Silver Skulls could find words of inspiration to calm the soul.

As the shuttle circled to prepare for a landing, Gileas stared out of the window across the vast rows of headstones. Down there were the remains of battle-brothers he had fought alongside, and hundreds of others he had not. All had died in service to the Emperor. It was traditional to cremate the bodies of the fallen and place a tombstone in remembrance, although those who had performed above and beyond the call of duty were laid to rest within one of the ancient mausoleums.

'This is the first time I have seen this and truly understood what it means.'

The voice belonged to Nicodemus, who sat opposite Gileas. At Attellus's request, the sergeant had agreed to bring the youth with him. Thus far the boy had been mostly silent, but it was a respectful silence rather than the awe of travelling alongside an accomplished warrior. Gileas appreciated the thoughtfulness of the gesture; he had spent much of the journey here in silence himself, his mind caught up in memories of brothers and mentors long gone.

He looked up now and considered Nicodemus. If ever there had been a youth who reminded him of what he had once been – both physically and psychologically – it was this one. He had not been surprised to discover that Nicodemus was also a southern-born warrior. It had created an instant bond between the seasoned sergeant and the untried boy. Gileas liked the youth; there was something of Andreas Kulle in his manner and choice of words, and that ensured an immediate friendship between them.

'And what do you make of it?'

'It is...' Nicodemus shook his head and stared out of the viewport. 'It is overwhelming. So many graves. So many lost battle-brothers. It is curious, sir. I spent time with the Chaplains on this world for a number of months, but never really paid full attention to my surroundings. I was too lost in my studies.' The boy's face was pressed up against the plex-glass viewport. Gileas chuckled quietly.

'The Silver Skulls are proud warriors of the Second Founding, Nicodemus. Over the thousands of years we have served the Golden Throne, we have lost many. There have been times when engagements have stolen away great numbers of our brotherhood. But always...' Gileas also stared out at the grey, colourless world with its similarly colourless tombstones. 'Always, we rebuild. We are Silver Skulls. We will prevail. Never forget that.'

Even as he spoke the words, Gileas felt a brief ache of grief in the depths of his soul. Not just for the recent loss of his captain, but for all those he had lost. He yearned now to stand in the Halls of Remembrance and to speak the words that would commit the memory of Keile Meyoran to the ancestors.

FIVE

ABSOLUTION

'I know why you are here, brother. Release the burden you carry and your soul will be better prepared for what comes next in your service to the Golden Throne.'

Gileas knelt before the statue of the God-Emperor that stood in pride of place at the front of the vast Halls of Remembrance. He had been there for several hours, reciting litanies and prayers. The sergeant had fervently given thanks to the God-Emperor for His wisdom and benevolence, and he had pledged oaths of vengeance for his captain's death over and over.

The cavernous hall was a creation of breathtaking and exquisite beauty. The chapels on board the strike cruisers and battle-barges in which the sergeant had travelled during his many years of service had always been places of great humility and awe. But they were as nothing compared to the majesty of Pax Argentius, the spiritual home of the Chapter.

Within its sepulchral walls Chapter Masters were invested,

and when they reached the end of their lives, their remains were interred in the catacombs that wound beneath it. A warrior could walk into this holy space with a heavy heart or troubled soul and leave with a clear conscience… as long as he paid the dues he owed to the Emperor.

The Halls of Remembrance were a clear analogy for birth and death. This was a place where events transpired to shape a living, breathing Chapter. Its very existence was a testament to the pious nature of the Silver Skulls and, at the same time, it was an unholy shrine to what some considered their most barbaric practice.

Silvered skulls, trophies from countless engagements across a thousand star systems, were mounted on plinths or displayed in artfully designed recesses in the walls. Every race ever encountered by the Silver Skulls was on display here for all to see. A clear statement of martial capability, they were at once gruesome, freakish things and beautifully rendered works of art.

The vast stained-glass window that stood behind the statue of the God-Emperor was plain in design: an intricately crafted representation of the Chapter's insignia. Shafts of pale light that trickled in from Varsavia's binary stars fell on the marbled floor within, their colours dappled and magnificent.

Nicodemus stood some way behind the sergeant, his eyes lowered. The aching, stark beauty of the chapel stirred emotions in him that he had never previously experienced with the heightened sensations of one raised to the ranks. He had begun to become accustomed to his enhanced senses; the shifting colours on the floor were vibrant and alive in a way they hadn't been when he had been fully mortal. Even the scent of the place was filled with curiosity. He could detect the trace scents of the other two Space Marines nearby: the one with a definite air of promethium lingering from his chosen weapon, and the other garbed in a dry, dusty scent that spoke of his time amongst the dead.

They both bore the clean ice aroma of Varsavia and yet there were subtle differences that meant Nicodemus could have distinguished between them in the dark even if his eyes failed him. He marvelled quietly at the wonders that had been wrought upon his body.

Gileas raised his bowed head and met the eyes of one he knew well but had spent precious little time with in recent years. Sensations of guilt flooded through his system. Chaplain Akando laid a hand gently on the sergeant's dark hair.

'You should be at peace, Gileas. Keile's death was no more your fault than that of any of the Eighth. To bear the weight of that will serve you poorly, my brother. And what serves you poorly affects your judgement. You can ill afford such a luxury at this time.'

'It is difficult to let it go, my lord.' Chaplains such as Akando were rare within the Chapter. Not psychically gifted, the Silver Skulls nonetheless revered them every bit as much as the powerful psykers of the Prognosticatum. 'Captain Meyoran trusted in me as his second-in-command and I was unable to stop the events that took him from us.'

'He died as he would have wanted, bringing death to the enemies of mankind. His life was given in the service of the Emperor. You know yourself that such an end is the best that any of us wish for.' Akando's words were wise and spoken softly to a warrior who struggled to conceal his emotions: the sergeant's guilt was written across his face. The Chaplain tipped his head to one side. 'What is it that you seek in this place, Gileas?'

'I am unsure, my lord.' Gileas's brow furrowed. 'Forgiveness of some sort, perhaps. Peace of mind. Absolution.'

'Then think on this. Meyoran was right to have chosen you for that duty,' Akando reassured. 'You are stoic of spirit and strong of will. The Emperor elevated you above mortal men and you were granted a second life as one of His Angels of Wrath. You serve the Chapter and the Imperium with all your heart and soul. I have heard you recite the Catechism of Hate over and again. Sometimes, Gileas, you even get it right.'

The Chaplain's expression did not change. 'You did what you had to do. Nothing more, nothing less. I have told you to be at peace. Now heed those words, for there is nothing to forgive, brother.'

A flicker of a smile played around Gileas's lips and he rested back on his heels. Akando stood towering over him, wearing a tabard not dissimilar to that which Gileas wore. In deference to his role and function within the Chapter, however, Akando's tabard was black. The Chaplain, like Eighth Company, had recently been recalled to Varsavia and was serving his own term of duty. Only for Akando, that duty would be spent almost entirely on Pax Argentius, amongst the dead and the remembered.

'It is difficult,' Gileas said eventually. 'To be here amongst the fallen and have nothing of Captain Meyoran's body to lay to rest. I feel as though he deserves more than just my words.' The sergeant glanced over his shoulder to where Nicodemus was seated in a meditative pose. The boy's reverence for the Halls of Remembrance, a place forbidden to novitiates, had been pleasing. 'But I have chosen to make the offering in his stead.'

Akando nodded again. 'Get to your feet, Gileas. Between

the sons of Varsavia there should be nothing but equality. I cannot speak to you as my equal whilst you are down there.'

Gileas got to his feet and he and Akando briefly gripped one another's forearms. The greeting was very much brother to brother. The two were of an age, with Akando Gileas's slight senior, and they had faced many enemies together before. There were obvious genetic similarities between them, but they were comparatively few. Akando was a warrior recruited from a different planet, not even having been born on the Silver Skulls home world. His hair was closely shaved to his head but Gileas knew that were he to let it grow, it would be the same coppery shade shared by Tikaye, one of his own squad.

'To make the offering for one who has fallen beyond reclamation is an act of selflessness, Gileas Ur'ten. The Emperor looks with great favour on those who perform such a gesture. But it is not a necessity.'

'It is for me. It is the least I can do. He is worth more than just a name on a tombstone. And ultimately, we are all brothers. The same blood flows through our veins. What good is that bond if we do not value it?'

'Fine words. Very well then, it shall be as you wish, brother.' Akando gripped Gileas's forearm and then turned to the altar before the Emperor's likeness. He gathered up two pieces of stone mined from Argent Mons, where the fortress-monastery was nestled. Tiny veins of silver ore ran through the dark grey stone.

'Nicodemus.'

Gileas spoke softly to the young Scout-in-training, whose eyes opened obediently. He gazed quizzically at the sergeant and Chaplain.

'Sir?'

'Come here, boy. I wish for you to bear witness to this act of remembrance.'

'As you command.' Nicodemus unfolded his limbs and moved across to join the others. At the earliest stage of his new growth, the young warrior still had a few months of filling out to go through and he felt self-consciously undersized next to Gileas and Akando. But if it made him uncomfortable, he did not let it show.

'What is the tradition, Nicodemus?' Akando asked the youth directly, and received a textbook answer.

'The blood of the fallen becomes one with the stone. It is a symbolic harmonising of spirit, and the stone tethers the spirit. In accordance with our practices, the body of the fallen is reduced to ash and scattered to the winds of our home world. In this way, none will claim our skulls as we claim those of our hated enemies. One stone is placed within the grave, the other released into the void.'

'The light of the Emperor will guide the spirit of the fallen to His side,' completed Gileas. 'In this way, the spirits of the dead find their rightful place in the world beyond comprehension. But the fallen cannot always be retrieved.' Gileas looked at Akando, that same grief in his expression. 'I cannot let the captain's spirit wander without purpose through the ages.'

'Then make the offering, brother.' Akando stepped back to allow the sergeant to move forward.

Gileas nodded and drew his combat knife from its sheath in the belt at his waist. The blade was wickedly edged, and he laid it on the altar. He looked up at the effigy of the Emperor and reached up to lay a hand on its cold surface.

'Ultimate Father of us all. Great Primogenitor. I am but one of Your loyal servants, barely worthy of Your attention.

But hear my prayer now.' He closed his eyes briefly and drew in a deep, cleansing breath. 'I beg that You take the spirit of Keile Meyoran, Captain of the Silver Skulls Chapter, to Your side. And with this offering, I swear to bind myself to the oath of moment. Every eldar who crosses my path will bleed in his name. On the bones of our ancient home world and on the blood that courses through my veins, I so swear.'

He took up the knife and drew it swiftly across his palm. Moving quickly, before the Larraman cells in his blood could begin clotting and healing, he took up first one rock and then the other. The bright, highly oxygenated blood stained the dull grey stone instantly.

'Well spoken, brother.' Akando's voice was approving. 'With this gesture, you give Keile's spirit a chance to find its way in the void. He would have been proud of you.'

Gileas wiped the knife clean on his tunic and slid it back into its sheath. 'Perhaps,' he said. 'But I will never know. Not now.'

He touched his uninjured hand to the statue of the Emperor one last time before turning and walking from the Halls of Remembrance. Nicodemus, who had watched the entire situation with eager interest and great solemnity, glanced up at the statue, then trailed after Gileas, his mind filled with questions that he dared not ask.

The change of the seasons on Varsavia was barely worth noting. Winter and spring were identical, with only a brief spate of warmth to lift the ambient temperatures above freezing. Summer, when it eventually arrived, lasted only a few weeks before the ice returned and fresh snow came.

For four months, Gileas had served what he still saw as a term of penitence. He yearned to return to active duty, but kept his peace. He threw his exasperated energies into bettering his own combat skills and barely a day passed when he could not be found in the training areas, sometimes with the others of Eighth Company, more frequently alone. When he was not there, he could be found in the heart of the Great Library, absorbed in the Chapter's sagas, or seeking solace in the chapel. He was every inch the diligent warrior and at Kerelan's request had kept himself as much out of Djul's way as possible.

The veteran sergeant had acted in exactly the way Kerelan had predicted he would. Whenever he and Gileas crossed paths, the older sergeant found some reason to criticise his younger battle-brother. The way he walked. The manner in which he fought. Always small, insignificant things. Gileas, to his great credit, ignored Djul's carefully barbed comments with surprising restraint. But Reuben, his closest friend and most trusted confidant, recognised the growing danger.

'You should speak to him.'

They were sparring together with practice blades when he finally made the suggestion. Gileas lowered his weapon and studied Reuben with a calculating stare.

'What are you talking about?'

'Djul,' replied Reuben, stepping back and lowering his own blade. 'You should deal with this problem now. Before it gets out of hand.'

'I am dealing with it. I am ignoring him.'

'That is not what I mean, Gil. You know what I am saying. Every time he speaks to you, your temper frays one more strand. It is giving him exactly what he wants.' Reuben altered his stance and set his feet firmly on the ground ready to begin the next bout. 'I know you, you will snap eventually. You should just get it out of the way. Address this resentment he harbours. You are both excellent warriors. You are battle-brothers, for the love of the Emperor. There is no logic in this hate he holds for you. You can reason this out.'

'Reuben, he does not hate me.' Gileas grinned, but there was no humour in it. 'It is not personal. Have you not understood that yet? Djul hates what it is that I represent. *What* I am, not *who*. Now enough of your endless sermonising.'

The two warriors resumed their training. Well-matched as they were, Gileas had always been more wily than Reuben and had disarmed him within a few short minutes.

'Your technique is poor.'

As though talking about him had somehow brought him to their side, Brother Djul stood just beside them on the training floor, watching the bout with an affected air of bored disinterest. Gileas was roused to respond.

'My technique is fine. I took his weapon, did I not?'

'Your technique is poor,' Brother Djul shrugged. 'You fight with all the grace of an ork. There is no finesse to what you do and frankly, it is ugly to watch. This is merely an observation, sergeant.'

'Gil.' Reuben caught his sergeant's arm as Gileas turned to stare at the veteran. The words left Gileas's mouth before his brain intervened to temper them.

'I learned very early on that finesse is often a luxury best left to those who are idle enough to practise it.'

For the first time since he had returned to Varsavia, Gileas saw his poorly chosen words genuinely shock Djul. 'You would accuse me of idleness, Hathirii?' He put an accent on the final word, the name of Gileas's hereditary tribe. This very deliberate choice spoke volumes about his opinion of them.

'Not at all.' Something dangerous flashed in Gileas's eyes. 'It is merely an observation, sir.'

They held one another's gaze for an achingly long time. Eventually, Djul nodded.

'Very well then. I see how it must be, Ur'ten. Brother Reuben – give me your blade and step out of the arena. I believe our training together is long overdue, Gileas. I will prove to you that there are ways to fight that do not rely on strength alone.'

'You do me great honour, sir.' Gileas raised his practice blade in courteous salute. 'I look forward to seeing what you have to teach me.' His words were genuine and heartfelt; it *was* an honour to fight against one of the Chapter veterans. Perhaps it was the honesty in his tone that caused a ripple of annoyance to twist Djul's perpetually sour face into a full scowl.

'Your veneer of good grace and manners do not hide what you are, boy.' Djul considered his opponent carefully. 'A former captain of mine once said that you could clad a savage in armour and give him a weapon, but he will still be a savage. He will just be slightly more dangerous.'

'I request that you cease describing me in this way, brother.' Gileas lowered the practice sword very slowly, his gaze steady. 'The persistent implication that I am little more than an animal is becoming wearisome. I could retort with an observation on the childish nature of your wordplay, but I do not.'

'You *are* a savage, Ur'ten. That is not your fault.'

'Perhaps,' said Gileas and he grinned, baring his teeth. 'Let us see how much of a savage I am.' He raised his blade once again and Djul did likewise. The two warriors came together immediately with a clash, their blades meeting and locking. They stared into one another's eyes.

'Your strength is commendable,' commented Djul, the closest he was likely to come to a compliment. 'But you lean too far forward. It will throw you off balance.' To demonstrate his point, he drove his blade upwards, forcing Gileas to step back to avoid stumbling. Without hesitating, Djul swung his sword towards the sergeant's torso. Gileas adopted a defensive stance and barely managed to block the attack.

Djul took advantage of the clumsy defence and pressed his assault more firmly. Before Gileas could renew his efforts to parry the blade, Djul had pulled free, spun gracefully around and brought the blade in with a heavy blow against Gileas's hip bone. He moved to the side as the sergeant swivelled to strike back and brought the sword round again. This stroke connected with Gileas's upper arm, and the sound of the blade on flesh was one that caused several of the gathering spectators to nod with approval. The blow had been a fine one. Whilst the practice weapons did not carry an edge, they were heavy and more than capable of causing injury if the trainees did not take care.

'You are losing control of the fight already,' Djul said and the sneer in his voice was unmistakable. 'Put some effort into your defence, brother. You cannot rely on an ability to attack indefinitely. Sooner or later...' Djul dodged an incoming low sweep from Gileas easily, practically dancing out of the way and moving behind the sergeant. He brought his blade down heavily between Gileas's shoulder blades, sending the younger warrior sprawling. 'Sooner or later, you will learn that the best attack is a good defence. Assuming that primitive mind of yours absorbs anything of worth.'

Countless years of training meant that Gileas was back on his feet in seconds. He had still not spoken a word. But his eyes now blazed with a fury that he had spent many years trying to contain. It had been a long, long time since he had allowed his fiery temper to surge to take control of his good sense, but there was a limit and Djul had just pushed him over it.

'I see from your expression that you are desperate to prove me right.' The veteran sergeant's jibes were filled with contempt. 'Bring all that you believe you can throw at me, boy. You do not stand a chance. How can you hope to master an enemy if you cannot master yourself? That you have risen to the rank of sergeant remains a mystery to me.'

Gileas was acutely aware of the number of fellow Silver Skulls watching them fight and he felt a keen shame at the fact that Djul was doing everything in his power to humiliate him. He should not rise to the baiting. He had promised Kerelan that he would not. But the sneer on Djul's face, the disdain he could hear in the other warrior's tone… all of it combined to ignite the smouldering core of rage that he had kept under tight control.

It blazed forth in a sudden surge of strength. He flung himself at Djul, the practice blade a living thing in his hand. It sang as it cut through the air, connecting with his opponent's outer thigh with a slap. Djul returned the blow in kind, taking advantage of Gileas's fury to cut through his minimal defences. The practice sword hit Gileas in the jaw. There was a resounding *crack* as the bone dislocated, followed barely seconds later by another as Gileas forced it back the other way. Before he could even turn his attention back to the duel, Djul had turned the blade round and smashed the hilt directly into Gileas's face with not-inconsiderable force.

'We should stop this,' murmured Tikaye. He had joined Reuben in watching the demonstration. 'It has gone beyond a lesson, brother. There is nothing being taught here. Djul will kill him given the chance.'

Reuben nodded and took a step forward. Blood streamed from Gileas's temple, thickening even as he watched. It would take a sight more than a thump to the skull to bring down his sergeant. He had watched Gileas remain fighting under far more of an onslaught than a single warrior. But Gileas was not fighting back. Reuben willed him to retaliate, but his friend would not give Djul the satisfaction.

Damn you, Gileas. Reuben clenched his hands briefly into fists. Of all the times to find your pride, you could not have chosen more poorly.

He did not have a chance to bring the conflict to a halt. A voice sounded across the training floor, amplified with ethereal power that gave it unnatural volume and timbre.

'Enough!'

Several heads swivelled to watch the newcomer approach. A ripple of recognition rose in a whisper as a dark-haired, battle-scarred warrior strode towards the battling pair.

'Djul, Gileas, cease this foolishness. I believe your audience has seen enough of this display. Leave the arena immediately.'

Blood crusting on his cheekbones from Djul's vicious attack, Gileas lowered his head in respect. Djul did likewise, letting his practice blade drop to the floor with a disdainful clatter. He stared at the other warrior.

'First Prognosticar Phrixus. It is not like you to spend time in training with us. We are honoured by your presence.'

'Yes, you are,' retorted the psyker. The scars on his face were unsightly, marring the skin and giving him a fierce demeanour. He ran a forefinger across the longest, which ran from his forehead to his chin in a nearly perfect diagonal line. 'But I believe you are encroaching on time our brother here promised me.' Phrixus smirked over at Gileas. 'It seems that you are learning a hard lesson at the hands of Djul here, lad.'

Gileas shrugged one shoulder. 'I have much to learn. I am deeply grateful to Brother Djul for showing me methods to improve my technique.' His words were filled with carefully pitched diplomacy and more than a hint of sarcasm, which did not go unnoticed by the veteran sergeant. Djul scowled at the younger warrior.

'As well you should be,' said Phrixus approvingly. 'And much as I hate to disturb this lesson, First Captain Kerelan requests you attend him immediately, Djul.'

'Of course, brother.' Djul did not wait for anything further, but turned on his heel and walked away without as much as a farewell. Gileas raised a hand to his mouth and wiped off some of the blood that still drizzled there.

'And you, Sergeant Ur'ten?' Phrixus turned a piercing stare onto the battered warrior. 'Lesson learned?'

'I learned something,' replied Gileas with a grim smile. 'I am not sure whether it was the lesson Djul intended to impart, however.'

Phrixus glanced around at the gathered battle-brothers. 'This is over,' he said. 'Attend to your training.'

The crowd dispersed instantly. Phrixus was not known for his patience. In a few short seconds, only the First Prognosticar and Gileas remained.

'You let him bait you, Gileas.' Phrixus shook his head. 'That disappoints me.'

'I had little choice, sir. And if I am truthful, I had thought that he genuinely meant to instruct me on my fighting technique. Before it turned unpleasant.'

'There is always a choice. Kerelan warned you about Djul and his prejudices. We are working to address it, but it seems that your presence here does not please him. Fortunately, he is leaving Varsavia for a short while on a mission. In the time he is gone, I propose you work on those skills with others. Then, when the inevitable happens and he challenges you again...' Phrixus's smile was grim.

'I am sorry if you are disappointed in me, sir.'

'I am not really disappointed in you, Gileas.' Phrixus sighed. 'I am disappointed in the situation. You understand of course that Djul's hatred is not truly directed at you but comes from lifetime of distrust?'

'Perfectly, Brother-Prognosticar. It *feels* personal, but I know that it is not.'

'Good. Now do you feel you have had enough training for one day or is it time for that bout you promised me months ago?' Phrixus leaned down and picked up the weapon that the veteran sergeant had left behind.

Gileas reached up and tested his jaw. It was comfortably back in place and whilst it might ache for a short time, his enhanced biology would soon numb that pain. He considered Phrixus for a moment or two. He knew categorically that the psyker outclassed him in every way; that he would be likely to face another gruelling challenge and another solid beating...

'Ready when you are,' he said, adjusting his grip on his practice blade.

SIX

PROVING GROUND

For days following the humiliating lesson that Djul had delivered, Gileas was forced to deal with the repercussions. Reuben's response to the situation had been less than favourable and he had engaged in conversation that bordered on argumentative with his battle-brother.

'It was an insult plain and simple, Gileas. You cannot possibly let this go unanswered!' Reuben was pacing the length of Gileas's arming chamber. The sergeant sat with his armour, meticulously working on it and occasionally looking up at the other Silver Skull.

'Djul has ever been my adversary, Reuben. I am not going to change his mind with words and argument. All I can hope for is that my actions speak for themselves in time. Kerelan advised me to avoid him as much as I could.'

'It seems cowardly to me.'

'Are you accusing me of cowardice?' Gileas set down the

greave that he was repainting and got to his feet. Reuben shook his head in irritation.

'You know I am not doing that. Cowardly was a poor choice of word, brother. Forgive me. But there is a difference between not rising to Djul's bait and actively avoiding engaging him in the level of combat I know you are capable of.' Gileas folded his arms across his chest and shook his head.

'Djul wanted me to fight back,' he said. 'I gave him a textbook performance. I was not going to do anything that might strengthen his arguments. He may have passed through an assault company many years ago, but some tactics have since changed and it would seem that he does not approve of them. If he has it in mind to discredit me anyway, what purpose would I have served by using some of Captain Kulle's methods?'

'You make a valid point,' conceded Reuben grudgingly. 'It just angers me that the situation even exists.'

Things had been alleviated due to Djul and the rest of the Talriktug being dispatched off-world. The tension that ran between the hulking champion and Gileas's squad had been something that the sergeant had realised would need to be addressed. But for now at least, Djul's absence lifted some of the concerns from his shoulders and he was able to relax into his duties at the fortress-monastery more easily.

'Old prejudices run deep, brother,' Gileas reflected, sitting back down to return to his work. 'Djul has served the Chapter for more than two centuries and remembers a very different Varsavia to the one that now exists. A Varsavia that I am keen to get out into.'

'You took Attellus up on his offer, then?'

Gileas grinned. 'The opportunity to hunt for game out

on the ice fields? Did you ever really believe that I would refuse such an invitation? It has been a long time since I had the pleasure of doing that.'

The tension flowed out of Reuben's stance. The Scout captain had approached Gileas and his squad and secured their agreement to work with the young Scouts. It had been fruitful and occasionally entertaining work and every one of the Assault Marines had found their own reward in spending time with the Chapter's next generation of warriors.

They were halfway through their year's duty now and from his original disdain for the work, Gileas had shifted to gratitude. Time spent in the fortress-monastery had given him pause for thought and an opportunity to reflect on his service to the Golden Throne. He was able to address his own issues and engage in conversation with others who could better guide him. Now Attellus had asked him if he would accompany a group of five Scouts on a traditional rite of passage.

The Hunt was a trial that all the Silver Skulls took part in at some point during their early training. Varsavia's vast ice fields were teeming with tenacious life that clung to existence in the harshest of environments. Much of that wildlife was vicious and highly prized. On a leather thong around his neck, Gileas wore the only thing he had kept from his life before he had been taken in by the Silver Skulls: the tooth of one of the great predators of the *Tsai Chator*, the territory more commonly known as the Ice Wastes, polished to a fine finish.

His father had long ago hunted the big feline beast and had given one of the massive animal's teeth to the wide-eyed boy as a trophy. He had promised his son that one day he too would prowl the wastes and become a man. That truth had come to pass in time, but he had not battled the beasts at his father's side. Instead, he had fought off the predator and countless others like it with the aid of other young men he came to know as his battle-brothers.

Gileas stood at the entrance to the fortress-monastery, staring out over the trackless, mountainous landscape. Gathering clouds in the south-west suggested a storm was imminent and from what he could make out, it looked as though it would soon break. The temperature had increased marginally over the past few days and Varsavia would soon enter its chill equivalent of a spring.

It was strange, the sergeant thought, how much he had got used to variable weather patterns. It had been easy to forget that his home world was largely covered in permafrost that never went away. In the far south, beyond the land-locked ocean that divided the main continental landmass, there were sheltered valleys that harboured a little warmth: areas where the snow was largely absent and hardy tundra vegetation thrived. He had grown up in such an area, although when his father had made the decision to take his son to the legendary 'silver giants' in the north, he had left all that behind.

What little melt came to this part of the planet showed in the swell of the river that snaked across the landscape. With the turn of the season, the surface ice had broken up a little and was carried along in the sluggish flow of the water as it strove to break itself from its winter prison and head to the ocean. Where the river went, it brought a renewal of hope to the creatures that had been deprived of its life-giving properties through the cruel winter months.

While Varsavia was perfectly nestled between the twin suns, life had a chance. And with that surge of vigour for the planet's hardy wildlife came grand opportunities for hunting. Many of the predators who roamed the ice were no match for a party of young Silver Skulls warriors desperate to prove their worth. Gileas remembered well his own first hunt with his new-found strength and abilities. The opportunity to lead the Scouts out was a great honour.

There would be five of them under his supervision, young Nicodemus included. Gileas had spent much time in combat training with the psyker and found in him the sort of kindred spirit he had never thought to find. The similarities in their upbringings gave them instant common ground. As for the future Prognosticar, he found Gileas's blunt honesty remarkably refreshing.

No supervising psyker would be coming on the trip. The young warrior's psychic hood had been adjusted to ensure he could not exert the full force of his power. If he pushed it beyond a certain level, enough suppression drugs would be injected into his system to render him unconscious, neutralising the threat.

A distant rumble brought Gileas's attention back to the approaching thunderheads and his brow furrowed. The weather was most definitely not shaping up to be conducive to an easy hunt, which for him, a seasoned warrior, presented little problem. But the five boys who he would be taking out had not been in possession of their implants for long. They were still learning.

For a moment, Gileas doubted his suitability to lead the Scouts. It felt like so long since he had been a newcomer to the ranks of the Silver Skulls that he could barely recall any memory of what it had been like before. A flood of sympathy for lesser man flowed through his body. How glorious it was to be chosen, to be set apart from the rest of humanity through the gift of a genetic legacy bestowed upon the grateful and faithful few. What an honour to serve the Golden Throne through the strength and power of body and mind.

Any feelings of doubt that he had harboured drained away as he swept his gaze once more across the snowy landscape. He had been given a duty to discharge and he would prosecute it to the best of his ability. When they returned from the month-long hunting trip, the boys would be well on the way to becoming warriors.

The sergeant's lips lifted into a crooked grin and he turned away to head back inside. There were preparations to be made.

'But I thought…'

'At this point in your service, it is not your place to think, Nicodemus. It is your place to learn to respect the chain of command. And on this expedition, that chain of command begins with *me*. Now hold your tongue and listen.'

The young psyker fell silent, a dark look of mutiny on his face. Gileas studied him briefly, fighting back amusement at the Scout's expression. *A wilful soul who would take careful handling* – that was how Attellus had described him. The other Scouts were all compliant and obedient to the point of frustration. Gileas knew that over time their personalities would emerge, but for now at least, they were perfect specimens of their kind. They were fledgling Adeptus Astartes through and through.

'You are each allowed to select one weapon to take on the hunt. I recommend that you choose whichever suits your talents. It is not a time to experiment with new skills. Marksmen choose your rifles, duellists to your blades. Both will be required against the creatures we will face.'

'I relish the challenge of the knife,' said Achak, stepping forward. Gileas gave him a critical look and a smile slid onto his face.

'Of course you do,' he replied. 'And your attitude is commendable. However, do not act in haste. There is wisdom in the use of the rifle against many of the beasts that prowl the wastes. Far better that they remain out of reach where a well-placed shot will spare you the rending jaws of a *wessen-luk*. I have seen men lose limbs and even their lives at the teeth of the predators we will find during this hunt. Yes – even full-fledged battle-brothers.' He pre-empted Nicodemus's question before the psyker could speak.

It was no exaggeration and the words had the desired effect. The five Scouts immediately drew together in a huddle to discuss the matter, although Gileas could not help but notice that Nicodemus remained slightly apart. When they broke, only two of the five selected melee weapons.

'You chose well,' Gileas said approvingly. 'And you, Nicodemus?' He looked down at the bolter in the youth's hand. 'Is this most suited to your particular... talents?'

'Not necessarily, sir,' replied the psyker. 'But I have learned the art of improvisation since my training began. I have yet to truly find what works best for me.' He patted the bolter that he cradled. 'This will serve well enough for now. And besides, we are going out on the Hunt. The prey we stalk is unlikely to have the kind of equipment that will feel the benefit of my particular talents.'

Gileas grunted and took up his own trusted chainsword. It had been his weapon of choice even before he had been placed in the assault company and he suspected it would be his preferred means of delivering death for as long as the Emperor's grace kept him alive. 'Bolters are well and good,' he said to Nicodemus conversationally, 'but when you fight face to face with your enemy, whatever he, she or it may be, you touch the glory of the moment. That fatal second when they finally see the Emperor's light and come to know the error of their ways.' He gave a sharp-toothed grin. 'Then I obligingly extinguish that flawed existence. This weapon's name is Eclipse for a reason, brother.'

None of the warriors wore power armour, but were clad in lightweight carapace suits that were painted a universal shade of charcoal grey. The Silver Skulls Chapter sigil was worked in painstaking detail on the pauldron of each suit. Even Gileas, who had long ago been gifted his black carapace, had not donned his sacred battleplate. The purpose of this trip was complex. It was far more than just a simple rite of passage; it was an opportunity to give the youths a chance to learn how to work with their new implants. The year's worth of hypno-doctrination that explained what would happen to them during ascension was as nothing to heading out and learning the sheer reality of what they had become. During the Hunt, the training games stopped and the new life of a Silver Skulls battle-brother began.

'Meet at the Thunderhawk in ten minutes,' Gileas ordered. 'No later. Check that your weapons are in perfect order and for your own safety be sure to test that your vox-links are functioning correctly. Never mind boasts of your proficiency with the chainsword or your unerring aim with a sniper rifle. Attend to your rites of maintenance. Checking the simple things thoroughly could well prove to be what saves your life.'

One or two faces looked slightly embarrassed at Gileas's words and he adjusted his tone slightly. They were boys. They were eager to prove themselves as men and he needed to start treating them as such. His eyes ranged down the line and his expression grew serious.

'Never think of this venture as just a hunt. This will be the chance you need to prove yourselves worthy of the blessing you have received. Warriors are prepared through training and study, but their true strength is tempered in the forge of battle. In years to come, you will remember the day you stepped out onto the Tsai Chator and you will recall with vivid clarity the moment you became battle-brothers.'

He moved from one to the other, laying a hand on each shoulder, and then he spoke the ritual words. 'Let us go forth and hunt well, my brothers. May our prey fall swiftly to our blades and bolters and may the tale become the stuff of legend.' He bowed at the waist, a very obvious sign of deference that lit up the eyes of the eager boys.

'Yes, sergeant!' The young warriors made the sign of the aquila smartly and wheeled around to head away from the armoury. The sergeant watched them go and shook his head. Had he *ever* been that young and enthusiastic? If he had been, it was a struggle to recall it. How bitter time was making him.

How bitter and cynical.

In every direction for as far as the eye could see there were layers upon layers of ice and snow. Here and there, black specks showed through where jagged rocks crested the frozen surface, and some way below them, they could make out the very top of the white forest canopy. Several of the tallest trees grew to a phenomenal height and they towered above the ground like spindly sentinels. Their branches were thick and heavy with snow, and from time to time the soft sound of the build-up could be heard as it rustled down to the ground. The Tsai Chator ice field was a deadly place for those who travelled unprepared. But for the warriors of the Silver Skulls it was a perfect proving ground and fine hunting area.

Having deposited its passengers, the grey Thunderhawk fired its thrusters and rose into the air. A voice crackled through the vox.

'We will see you at the end of the mission, Sergeant Ur'ten. Good hunting.' With a throaty roar of its engines, the gunship turned and accelerated away to the north, back to the fortress-monastery. Gileas and the Scouts were left alone with rudimentary supplies and medicae packs.

'So then, Squad Ur'ten, this is where it begins.' Gileas spoke with obvious pride, his breath ghosting in a fine mist before his face. 'This is where you come into your birth-right... or die.' The ambient temperature was well below freezing but thanks to their genhanced physiology, none of them felt the cold. It would be a necessity to perform regular and close maintenance on their weapons, however, as the danger of mechanical parts freezing was very real.

Nicodemus stood towards the back of the assembled group, his face raised to the frigid air. He inhaled deeply, feeling the stark bite of its chill hit the back of his throat. Barely months before it would have been the kind of cold that hurt to breathe and froze the lungs from within. The human tribes inhabiting the south had adapted enough to travel and hunt only when temperatures allowed. Now that he was an Adeptus Astartes the thin, bone-chilling air merely afforded slight discomfort. He drew another breath and let it go slowly. His eyes ranged over the snow fields and he could physically sense his optical implants adjusting to the light levels.

The newly ascended warriors had not been out this far into the mountains since they had undergone their penultimate implant and Nicodemus was briefly fascinated by the way he could instantly filter out the increased ultraviolet wavelengths so that they caused no damage to his retinas.

It felt good to be deployed with the other Scouts again. Much of their training was separated, but the Chapter held firm to their strong belief in the presence of a psyker on all deployments and so young Prognosticators and would-be Prognosticars like Nicodemus were inserted into Scout squads wherever possible.

The sergeant had consulted with Bast, Eighth Company's serving Prognosticator, prior to deploying on the Hunt and had reported back that the portents for the Hunt had been good. He had delivered these words with no change in his expression, but it had not been hard for Nicodemus to gauge that it was also the truth. Sergeant Ur'ten was every bit as enthusiastic about this expedition as the Scouts themselves were.

'For several kilometres, you will encounter no animal life,' Gileas said. 'At this altitude, no plants survive above the ice and so the grazers seek out lower ground. We may see a few of the hardier predators intent on capturing birds of prey, but it is unlikely for what reason, Honon?'

He rounded and landed the question on the Scout without warning and the youth blinked in surprise. Glancing up at the sky and sniffing deeply, he offered his reply.

'A storm is coming,' he said. 'From the south-west. This face of the mountain range is exposed to it.'

'Quite right,' approved Gileas with a curt nod. 'What does that also mean, Motega?'

'That we should prepare ourselves against the worst of the

weather, sir. On finding out where we were going, I took the liberty of studying some of the topographical data of this area. A cave network that we can enter to the north extends approximately twenty kilometres in every direction. We could perhaps start...'

Gileas flashed a brief smile. 'The storms are brutal, brother and it is good to know where shelter can be found. Excellent work on familiarising yourself with the lie of the land before we even arrived. A good display of forethought.' The words came easily and he became silent again. He was here to observe, not to praise. He should let the neophytes do the majority of the legwork and only intercede when it was absolutely necessary. To compensate, he added a caveat.

'A good idea,' he said to Motega. 'And you can bet your life that a whole host of other creatures caught in the storm will be contemplating finding shelter.'

'Yes, sergeant.' The look of smug elation on Motega's face slid right off again.

'We should head to cover regardless,' offered Nicodemus. 'Incoming winds will challenge our vision and ability to gauge distance accurately.'

'Right. This is the first thing you learn about becoming a battle-brother. Our gifts from the Emperor are marvellous things, each and every one of them. But they are not infallible. You will all have noted how your eyes have adjusted to the poor light levels. Once the blizzards hit and all you can see is white, you will have to adapt to using your other senses... particularly you, Nicodemus. It will happen naturally, but it *will* disorient you.'

Tapping thoughtfully at the auspex that he held in one hand, Gaelyn looked up to the threatening skies. 'Typically, these winds are strong enough to scour the mountains clean and hurl boulders around. As the sergeant said, visibility will suffer and if we are not careful, we could be seriously compromised.'

'We could take shelter in the caves Brother Motega mentioned. At least until the worst of it has passed?' Honon supplied the suggestion and a lively conversation ensued about other methods of taking shelter from the storm. Everything from continuing with the Hunt to digging ice holes was discussed and they ultimately decided that finding their way to the caves was the simplest and most effective option.

Finally, the psyker nodded. 'Brother Gaelyn and I will take point,' he said. 'We will head towards the cave system.'

Gileas said nothing and let the Scouts fall into formation. He brought up the rear, carefully keeping one eye on the gathering gloom in the skies above Varsavia.

The blizzard hit less than thirty minutes later and did not ease for hours. A slight increase in the wind turned into a fierce gale that lifted the snow and flung it gleefully back into the air. Hard shards of ice were ripped up by the storm and lashed ceaselessly at the six giant figures labouring their way through the natural barrage.

It slowed their progress, but they finally reached the cave system. The blizzard had all but buried the entrance with banked snow and they spent some time struggling against the high winds until they cleared a way through. The passages were low-ceilinged and exceptionally uncomfortable, particularly when filled with Space Marines, but they offered sufficient shelter. It provided an opportunity to train them to lull into semi-sleep, resting parts of their brains whilst their catalepsean nodes allowed them to remain alert.

The worst of the blizzard blew out towards mid-afternoon

the following day and they dug their way back out of the freshly covered cave entrance. By softly discussed consensus they turned into the wind and forced themselves to struggle against the elements. Finally, the howling winds began to diminish. Snow continued to fall, stifling visibility down to just a few metres.

Gaelyn had instinctively kept tightly to the curve of the mountain face as a guide to their direction and for now at least, they had some shelter in the lee of the crag. But the storm did not seem inclined to release them from its clutches completely.

At the back of the group, Gileas had taken his attention off the neophytes and had employed other senses. The scent and taste of the air that was carried to him with the winds bore the flavour of death, suggesting that something had been killed nearby. It was still reasonably fresh, too. His mind recalled the Varsavian bestiary and he assimilated the data instantly. Within a few heartbeats he had narrowed the possible predator threat in the immediate area to a handful. Most likely were the big cats that prowled the wastes in their camouflage of white fur. But there were other things dwelling on Varsavia for which no comparison could be drawn.

Such things rarely came this far up into the peaks, although there were documented and proven sightings. Gileas felt confident that the felines were more likely to be their first prey. He sniffed the air again and... yes. There it was. So faint he might be wrong, but he could just detect the hint of animal life some way to the west.

He could make out the shapes of his charges through the thick snows. Already he had distinguished one from the other by the slope of their shoulders, the way they carried themselves and the weapons they had chosen. Nicodemus stood out, of course: his psychic hood rippled with ever-present energy. Over the months since his ascension, the boy had begun to get a lock on his powers and abilities, but there was still room for improvement. There was a lot of nascent power there, so his assessments read. But a lot of power was not always a good thing. There was a long way to go before Nicodemus could fully harness his potential.

'We should bear west,' said Motega, his voice rising to be heard above the incessant roar of the blizzard.

'For what reason?'

Motega hesitated. 'I am certain that there is something in that direction,' he said. 'I can... There is a strange scent on the wind. I do not recognise it.' The moment the words left his lips, the other Scouts raised their heads and tried to filter out such a thing from the air.

'This storm should pass us by soon,' Nicodemus stated confidently. 'Keep moving on for now... but slow the pace down and keep your senses sharp. We will do as Motega says and turn west.'

'A good choice.' The sergeant nodded his approval. 'Just one thing to add. Stop putting so much faith in the rock-face. If we maintain this heading, we will drop into a crevasse. I have little desire to report back that the reason for your death was that you fell off the mountain in poor visibility.'

The edge of lightness in his tone invited a slightly uncertain ripple of laughter from all of the boys and Gileas saw several stiffly held shoulders relax. This was good. He would be lying if he said that he could clearly recall the complicated transitions he had made in his life: from a wild, half-feral boy to a gangly untamed youth, to an eager acolyte and finally to the day he had been introduced to his first suit of sacred power armour. But he could recall enough. The boys – he could not stop thinking of them as such – were going through a strange time. They were born again and whilst they were far from ignorant teenagers, they were still adjusting.

Being comfortable with each other and with their superiors was vital to the process and if a light joke helped them to relax then it was worth it. Strangely, as much as Gileas could see it assisting his charges, he also felt his own private concerns fade into the background. Since his return to Varsavia, his idle moments had frequently led him to thoughts and concerns that were he to give them voice would be considered borderline blasphemous amongst the Chapter elders. For now, he kept his counsel. It was not his place to express them without something more tangible than a faint feeling of unease. Gileas made a mental note to visit Akando again when the Hunt was done.

'Movement.'

The single word was carried on the wind to the sergeant, pulling his attention back instantly. Within a heartbeat, Eclipse was in his hand and his thumb hovered over the activation stud. Through the swirling snows, he saw an indistinct shape, some distance away, but growing larger as it prowled towards them.

Gileas said nothing. The Scouts knew the rules of this expedition. He was there to guide them, not to lead them. In this early stage of their service, it was critical that they developed their own means of selecting a leader.

The wind was dropping now and at least gave the group a better chance to react, and Gileas could see the Scouts as every pair of eyes turned to Nicodemus. The psyker, to his immense credit, clearly noticed this and made no attempt to look the other way. He simply shot the sergeant a brief look and received a barely perceptible nod in reply.

'Do not stand together,' he said. 'We will be a more effective hunting force if we can encircle the beast rather than hold here and let it come straight at us as a group.' His tone held quiet authority and the others were clearly hanging on his every word. It was too soon to equate the boy's actions to evidence of a born leader, however. He may not have been a Prognosticator, he may not have been blessed with the gift of foresight, but he was a psyker nonetheless and formidable though Nicodemus's talent was, his inability to manage it with any predictability rendered him a largely unknown quantity in the field of battle.

If the Silver Skulls were lucky, though, the Prognosticatum would keep him and not let him go. His talents were still wild, crude and wielded with the impetuousness of youth, but they were talents that the Chapter treasured, and too many of Nicodemus's kind had been handed over under the terms of the agreement forged millennia ago with the Grey Knights. While it was considered a great honour to be selected by that secretive order, the lords of Varsavia lamented the loss of any of its warp-sensitive sons.

The group fanned out at Nicodemus's command into an approximate semicircle. Gileas heard the vox in his ear, which since the Thunderhawk had departed had been silent.

'Communicate by sub-vox for now, brothers,' said Nicodemus, his voice low enough not to be heard over the wind, but loud enough that the vox picked it up.

So far, Gileas thought as his more experienced eyes pierced the lessening snowstorm, so good. The shape that had been inching towards them was making the most of the trail forced through the snow by the passage of the Space Marines and now the shadow split three ways.

'Beasts,' came Motega's voice. 'Plural. Three of them.'

'Nivosus cats.' The positive identification came from Honon and Gileas felt the thrill of the upcoming fight. It would doubtless be over swiftly, three cats against the five of them, but nivosus were not always easy opponents. Standing nearly at the height of a Space Marine's chest, they were voracious hunters with razor-sharp, elongated fangs and jaws filled with equally deadly teeth.

He could make out their shapes properly now, the long, muscular bodies clad in fur that was as thick and tough as boiled hides. It was an effective defence against many of the beasts who shared the cats' hunting grounds on the Tsai Chator, but it would not last long against bolter rounds and the whining teeth of chainswords.

However, the cats were large, exceptionally heavy and could easily get enough power behind an attacking leap to drag down a lone warrior. If they were successful in toppling an individual who was slow or unprepared, they could swiftly strip flesh from bone with their claws and fangs. They would then attempt to lock their teeth around the victim's throat. Their bite and their jaws were so powerful that they could choke even armoured prey – and butcher naked flesh.

'Emperor's Throne,' observed Honon as the cats prowled closer. 'They *stink*.'

'They will smell worse when we gut them, Honon. Now keep circling.'

Gileas allowed Nicodemus to continue giving the orders. So far, the psyker was acting with wisdom and he was genuinely impressed. But Nicodemus was a survivor. As a psyker, he had to contend with the perils of the warp every moment of his life. It should have come as no surprise that he was able to adapt quickly.

The three animals had slowed their prowl and had dropped down, their shaggy chins resting on front paws that were easily the size of the Scouts' heads. Their white fur concealed them well against their natural element and all that could be clearly seen of them were slits of yellow and black glittering from narrow eyes. They were gauging the warriors silently, assessing the threat with an intelligence that seemed unnatural for wild animals.

Gileas had encountered nivosus on several occasions. The first time had been when he had been a child of eight, when he and his family had been travelling to the far north. The beast that had attempted to attack his family and which had been brought down by his fearless father had been little more than a cub in comparison to these monsters, and had been injured to boot. His hand went to the fang worn at his neck and he itched to go forth and face the cats.

But he had to heed his own advice. This was a hunt, not a war, and he was here to observe and to guide. The time for war would come soon enough for all of them.

'Nico?' Achak's voice through the vox was a hushed whisper of barely contained eagerness. 'What is your command, brother? Nicodemus!'

The psyker did not answer straight away. Just as the cats were assessing the Space Marines, so he was assessing them, attempting to pre-empt or guess what it was that they would do. Then he finalised his plan of attack in his mind.

'Follow my lead,' was all he said and Gileas shook his head. He would have to address that with Nicodemus when this encounter was complete. Improvisation was a desperate measure to employ when no other avenue remained open.

Nicodemus, in turn, had considered utilising his psychic talents but reluctantly determined they were too wildly unpredictable to channel in time. Instead, he unslung the bolter that he had been convinced to carry and levelled it at the cat. The barrel flared as he fired, and his brothers followed suit. The cats were fast, but one struck its target on the flank. It let out a roar of rage and the three cats began to slowly back away.

'You may have just succeeded in making them very angry,' observed Honon. 'But that might not have been the best plan. Wouldn't you say?'

'Don't speak too soon,' retorted the psyker. 'At least we can fight them away from the mountain's edge. The advantage of terrain is ours.'

Gaelyn let his gaze roam over the animals, then offered his opinion. 'The one in the centre is the alpha male,' he said. 'The other two are probably his females. Attack the male and the females will immediately turn on you. Eliminate the female cats first. Then unleash your full fury on the male.' Gileas made a noise of affirmation. The neophytes used their knowledge well. In the course of a day, they had gone from hesitant to confident with smooth ease.

'Yes, brother,' several of them replied, and the Scouts launched themselves straight into the fray. Gileas held back, although it took every ounce of self-control that he possessed. The months of training were nothing compared to a true fight in which blood was spilled and quarry was run to ground. But this Hunt belonged to the future battle-brothers, not to him.

The bark of gunfire echoed around the mountains as the

Scouts armed with bolters opened fire on the pair of smaller cats, whilst the whine of chainswords soon joined in the discordance. Added to the noise was the sudden growl and high-pitched yelp of the animals as they gamely returned the attack.

The huge alpha male, enraged at the attack on his small pride, instantly leaped at the psyker, any fear or uncertainty forgotten. Immense hind muscles bunched and the animal sprang. The leap carried it through the air, its claws reaching for Nicodemus. He firmed up his stance, planting his feet solidly on the ground to resist the inevitable.

It was a worthy attempt, but the beast was big, fast and exceptionally heavy. It knocked Nicodemus off balance with the impact. The psyker regained his feet swiftly and retaliated instinctively, planting a well-delivered punch to the animal's slavering jaw.

Its head cracked sideways and saliva sprayed from its mouth. Fully regaining his balance, Nicodemus brought up his bolter and levelled it at the animal. He squeezed on the trigger, sending a mass-reactive shell towards it. His aim was perfect and had the beast not crouched low for a second leap, it would have struck the cat right between the eyes. Instead, the projectile streaked over the animal's head and scudded across the ice before burying itself deeply in a snow bank. It detonated, sending an eruption of mist and vapour into the air. A slab of ice coating the side of the mountain splintered and broke away with a resounding *crack*.

The other Scouts were embroiled in their own combat. One of the female cats was already missing the end of her tail and dark crimson blood blossomed on the snow. Multiple lacerations bled through the pure white fur on her back, but she was clearly more than able to continue the fight.

These creatures were nothing more to her eyes than a means of feeding the pride and she would struggle to the last to bring them down. From the short, stilted conversations that came across the squad vox, Gileas noted that every one of the Scouts was conscious of this fact. Respect for their quarry was vital, even when that respect was charged with hatred.

Motega lunged forward, his leading leg sinking some way into the snow, and struck downwards with the chainsword in his hands. His aim was true and the weapon sank to the hilt in the nivosus cat's chest. Whirring teeth chewed through fur, flesh and bone and tore the creature apart before it could so much as yelp. It crumpled to the ground, Motega's chainsword trapped beneath it. He tugged at it and after a few attempts dislodged the heavy cat's corpse. The dead animal rolled away and the chainsword came free. Motega brandished the weapon triumphantly and turned his attentions immediately to the other female cat.

Gileas's attention returned to the psyker, who was still struggling with the big alpha. Quite literally in this instance. During the course of their deadly dance, he had lost hold of his bolter and resorted to fighting with bare fists. The animal, weakening, was starting to lose. A well-placed blow caused the creature to let out a shriek of fear and abruptly it turned its head away.

Immediately, the psyker lowered his shoulder, charging towards it. The psychic shield that he still maintained could be made out, a nimbus of greenish light that spat and hissed in the wind. He ploughed into the cat's flank in much the same way that the animal had attacked him before and the two of them went down in the snow, rolling over and over together. Jaws snapped, claws tore and the fists of a post-human warrior pounded their victim.

'Keep a hold of your temper, Nicodemus. Do not surrender to wild rage. Hone it into a precision weapon to turn upon your enemies. Your lack of control is already starting to affect your abilities.'

It was the only advice Gileas gave him during that battle and it was delivered in the kind of tone that invited neither discussion nor argument. The irony of it was not lost on him, either.

The alpha was not used to being grappled by its prey or any of the beasts of the wastes and was thus unprepared for the furious impacts that rained down upon it. Bones crunched under Nicodemus's frenzied assault and the animal's rear legs finally gave way.

It fought to the last, saliva dripping and watering down the blood that dribbled from its mouth. Finally, exhausted, it slumped into the snow and the light of life fled from its eyes.

The other female had long since been slaughtered by the other Scouts and as Nicodemus shakily extended his awareness once again, he become acutely conscious of his brothers staring at him.

'Your fists?'

Gileas stepped forward and yanked him to his feet. 'That is your weapon of choice? The ability to bend reality to your will, power enough to grind mountains into gravel... and you *punch* it to death?'

'It was... the most appropriate weapon of the moment, sergeant.' Nicodemus's frustration was very real. His talents with machinery were certainly formidable and in time might prove invaluable. Yet when faced with an unfamiliar situation poorly suited to his abilities... when unarmed and facing a predator, he had reacted instinctively and recklessly.

It was a development his mentors in the Prognosticatum would have to address.

'Yes,' agreed Gileas with a thoughtful expression. 'Perhaps it was, but it was a situation of your own making. Take your prizes, hunters, because that did not even remotely approach a challenge. That will come when we descend into the valleys.' His eyes narrowed as he took in the darkening night sky and the endless white horizon. 'That will come when we find whatever it was that drove these animals from their territory to seek refuge in higher hunting ground.'

SEVEN

THE LESSER EVIL

The valley was utterly soundless. The thick snow muffled everything, and sheltered from the driving wind the still, frozen air became oppressive. No cry of predators, no whisper of branches. Just a profound stillness that brought with it an eerie, sinister air all of its own.

Ancient trees, huge things that had endured the harshest of conditions, stooped beneath the crushing weight of the ice. They were bent double under the load of the snow that covered them, like a silent parade of hunched figures. In the fading light, they cast odd silhouettes in the new illumination brought by the Silver Skulls warriors trudging between the shadowy avenues they formed.

The pack ice was so old on Varsavia that there were few places one could sink into the snow-cover. Even the weight of an Adeptus Astartes was not enough to send them much further than shin-deep into the packed surface.

Their descent from the mountains had been spent in a

strange kind of silence. Two of the three cats had been skinned, and the head of the pack leader severed from its body and placed into a sack that Nicodemus wore tied to his waist. Rich, red blood seeped from what was left of it, making a gory mess of the fabric. He did not care. It was his first true battle trophy and would stand testament to his skill for as long as he survived.

The two pelts were being worn across the shoulders of two of the other Scouts - the third cat had been too torn apart for the fur to be worth saving. They were huge when parted from the bodies of their former owners, but then so were the warriors who wore them.

Gileas's ominous suggestion that something particularly dangerous must be at large in the valley had put them all on their guard. The sergeant had explained, during the descent, that the nivosus cats rarely moved up to the barren higher ground. The hunting was poor and the exposure to the elements brought a very grave risk with it. The caves they had briefly sheltered in had harboured a number of smaller, rodent-like animals who had hidden there, robbing the cats of their usual food source.

Gileas had primed every one of the neophytes to ensure their weapons were fully functional and had spent a little extra time ensuring that he had several of the grenades that he had brought with him.

Just to be sure.

The warriors moved through the forest in single file. Where they turned, the fading light traced across the deformed trees, casting long shadows over the ground. More than once, a Scout started in readiness, thinking that one of the moving shadows was something shifting in the trees.

They were fully alert for any kind of ambush that might be awaiting them, and the still air and stifling atmosphere necessitated a certain level of vox silence. Some idle banter was expected during long treks such as this, but the Scouts had all been quiet for upwards of thirty minutes now. Gileas watched their progress through the snow. Thus far, he had been reasonably satisfied with what he had seen. They had worked together and battled together long enough to be comfortable with one another. They had moved seamlessly and unconsciously into support and leadership roles and already they had ceased asking for orders. They were a good squad and Gileas was impressed with what Attellus was achieving.

Despite looking initially to their psyker for leadership, things had shifted subtly. Achak, the fair-skinned and fair-haired north-born, had assumed a natural leader's role amongst the boys and they were eagerly listening to his suggestions. There was a calm assurance about his manner and he had an ability to bring out the best in the others. Even the arrogant Nicodemus had deferred decisions to him without question. Achak was the eldest of the Scouts by over a year and that one difference seemed enough to set him apart. He moved with surety and confidence but retained enough sense to know when to ask his superior questions.

Gaelyn and Motega, the two youngest who were so like one another in appearance that Gileas had mistaken them for blood brothers at the beginning of the hunt, were not in fact related except now through the gift of their ascension. But they had a synchronicity of thought and action that impressed the sergeant as he kept a careful eye on them. Like Achak, they both wore their hair cropped close to the scalp and like their accepted group leader they were both Varsavian-born, with the colouring that went with it. Both were gifted with an ability to think several steps ahead and discard unwelcome outcomes. Strategic minds were every bit as welcome in the Silver Skulls as strong sword arms.

Honon was a different matter. He had struggled to find a place within the squad. He was not confident enough to lead and yet there was a core of resentment rippling through him that meant he found it difficult to be deferential to those he saw as his peers and equals. When they stopped to review their plans and direction, Honon always remained slightly apart from the others. Gileas knew that attitude well; he had not been so very different when he'd been Honon's age.

Honon was not a Varsavian. He had been drawn from the stock of one of the other recruiting planets, and his hair was red and his skin darker than the others'. There was a faint smattering of freckles across his face and he brought to memory Tikaye, of Gileas's own squad and another native-born of Honon's home world.

Nicodemus, for all his arrogance and nigh-on overbearing self-confidence, had noticed Honon's self-imposed distance as well and without Gileas needing to intervene, had begun to draw his battle-brother into the group. The sergeant was pleased to note that and marked it down mentally as one of Nicodemus's potentially redeeming qualities. Thus far, the list was not stacked heavily in that direction.

It was so hard to remember how it felt, he realised as he let his eyes search with practised ease around the snowy forest. How it had felt to step out of the apothecarion more than a foot taller and with radically altered physiology. He had become so accustomed to his implants that he had simply remembered the change as being instant. Now he realised it was not.

The silence here was eerie. There were no evident animal tracks in the crust of snow, but after they had walked some way into the forest, Achak pulled up short.

'Sergeant,' he said with a certain level of surprise in his voice. 'Looks like we are not the only hunters out this night.'

Approaching the Scout's position, Gileas saw the unmistakable flicker of a fire some way ahead of them and much deeper into the trees. He frowned and called up the mental map of the area. The Thunderhawk had dropped them just to the south of the landlocked sea. From his own long-distant experiences and from records kept meticulously by the Chapter, no tribes had moved their hunting grounds to this region of southern Varsavia.

The temperature around them notwithstanding, something chill gripped at Gileas's soul. He turned to Gaelyn and Motega and automatically assumed the tone of a commanding sergeant. The difference in his voice, where before he had been decidedly affable and easy-going, caused all five of the Scouts to stand to attention.

'Go ahead,' he ordered. 'The two of you get as close as you can to the camp and assess the situation. Do *not* engage unless it is absolutely necessary. It may simply be a wandering family who have taken shelter in the forest for the night, or it might be a whole tribe. Neither would give us any great problem, but you know how the Prognosticatum stands on interaction with the tribes who are not directly tithed.'

'They are hunters,' offered Nicodemus. Gileas glanced over at him.

'What makes you so certain?'

'There.' The group followed Nicodemus's finger to the broken spear that was half buried just below the snow. Gileas's lip twitched.

'Good eyes,' he said, approvingly. 'The orders remain unchanged. Go. We will hold here and observe the perimeter. Keep vox contact to a minimum and ensure you are out of earshot before you report back.'

With nods of affirmation, Gaelyn and Motega vanished out of sight between the trees.

The sergeant stooped to pick up the spear and considered it carefully. It was a hunter's instrument, sure enough. Plain, without any embellishment or etched design, it was an object that had been fashioned with the sole purpose of bringing down prey. He let his hand run across the roughly carved haft to the sharpened spear tip.

It was not a beautiful weapon. Its balance was poor and the metal point was not even particularly sharp. But there was something there… in the iron. He brought it closer to examine it carefully. The ice in his heart spread further through his body. He beckoned the remaining Scouts over to him.

'Opinions?'

Motega and Gaelyn were discovering that swift scouting was less easy than it had been before they had been gifted with their implants. Their increased height and bulk made a cautious approach challenging. They may not have been stealthy, but they were learning to adapt as best they could to their given terrain. Trees provided cover and whilst the snow laid their prints bare for any to follow, the deadening white also muted their approach.

The flickering fire that had caught Achak's attention was some way through the woods, a dancing wall of orange and yellow flames that contrasted brightly with the near-black velvet darkness. Using the comparative cover of the trees, the two Scouts approached with as much stealth as they could muster.

A break in the tree line afforded them an excellent glimpse of the encampment that they had been sent to assess and it took less than a minute to gauge what they saw there. Indicating to pull back, Motega picked up the pace noticeably.

'Did you see…?' Gaelyn's hushed question was answered before the words had even left his mouth.

'Aye, brother, I did.'

They both lapsed back into silence and continued to draw away from the encampment of approximately twenty-five warriors, each of whom had been very clearly marked with the tribal sign of the Xiz.

It began as a gentle tremor underfoot, so innocuous that it was hardly even worthy of notice. There were three active volcanoes across the planet's surface and seismic activity was not uncommon. So when the ground shook slightly beneath their feet, Gileas saw no immediate cause for concern. A proper earthquake brought acceptable risk: landslides, avalanches and all the other difficulties that nature liked to frequently deposit on the citizens of Varsavia. So the slight twitching beneath the sergeant's boots barely even registered on his scale of interest.

Nicodemus, however, sensed something was wrong immediately. He whipped his head around in the direction they had walked, his eyes narrowing and the sparks on his psychic hood glinting in the darkness. Gileas looked up at him.

'Something is out there,' muttered the psyker and he

exchanged a glance with Gileas. He did not have to wait for the sergeant's words and simply elaborated. 'There is a mind out there that I do not recognise. Animalistic.' He concentrated, but there was no more. Nicodemus berated himself for even trying. His powers were good, his skill exceptional, but there were so many things he did not know how to do. Had he been truly exceptional, he could have been more specific. As it was, he drew a blank. 'I don't believe it's human,' he tried. Gileas quirked an eyebrow.

'Nothing more?'

'No, brother-sergeant. Hunger, perhaps? There is a drive and determination there.'

'A hunter. Definitely not human. Not the tribesmen, then.' Gileas rubbed at his jaw.

'Brother-sergeant?' Motega's voice crackled through the vox-bead in his ear. 'Twenty-five tribesmen camped out here. All Xiz, sir.'

The concern that had slowly been crystallising since the discovery of the spear finally found its name. He shook his head to clear it of old prejudices that suddenly rose unbidden and instead focused on Nicodemus. Maybe the animal mind that the psyker was feeling *was* one that belonged to the tribesmen, in that case. Gileas felt a faint disappointment that the psyker's abilities were still so immature. If Nicodemus were less arrogant and more focused… the revenge that could be wrought…

Revenge.

Gileas allowed his breathing to slow again and controlled his thoughts. Revenge indeed. It was a thought unworthy of a battle-brother of the Silver Skulls and he knew it. But old memories, however deeply suppressed beneath the careful layers of mental conditioning and endless indoctrination, would not be denied. Particularly when they were the kind of memories that had been instrumental in the earliest days of forging the weapon that he had become.

The ground lurched beneath their feet again and this time Gileas noticed it. This was not what he had expected to find when he had set out to track down the predator that had displaced the nivosus cats from their regular territory. In the beat of a heart, the Silver Skulls had gone from being the hunters to potentially becoming the hunted.

The phenomenal encyclopaedic knowledge that was stored inside his mind had already worked out what it was that stalked them. Native Varsavian creatures such as the nivosus cats were reasonably prolific in the south but there were some things that were so rare that sighting them was considered at one and the same time a good omen and a dread curse. In this instance, Gileas's opinion was weighted very heavily in favour of the latter.

The quake was growing more intense now, cascading thick drifts of snow from the aged trees. The sergeant knew that he was going to have to act fast for all their sakes. He cast his gaze around the forest, his mind working furiously through a number of possible options. Activating his own vox, he assumed command of the squad. The moment he did so, the Scouts realised the seriousness of their situation. Until now, he had merely acted as a voice of experience. But this was the side to him that they were conditioned to respond to with instant obedience.

They slotted perfectly into the ordered machine of the Chapter. For all they had seemed a little unsure of themselves, the three young warriors still with Gileas had immediately and without question taken the roles they had been born to play.

'Motega, Gaelyn, fall back to this position immediately. If we do not regroup now, I cannot guarantee how easily we will get back to…'

He never finished the sentence. The persistent tremor underfoot became a rolling surge in the ice, which rippled beneath them like a wave and caused all of the Space Marines to stagger on the now uneven surface. Nicodemus stumbled sideways and Gileas reached out automatically to stop him falling. The ground bucked and heaved like a thing possessed and without any further warning, there was an ear-splitting *crack* as the deep ice beneath them suddenly ruptured.

From somewhere further in the forest they could hear the guttural sounds of human voices. Their Xiz hunter counterparts were evidently on the move as well, disturbed by the sudden activity.

'Motega! Gaelyn! Regroup. Now!'

'The Xiz are breaking camp, sergeant. The earthquake has disturbed them.'

'This is not an earthquake.'

And it was not. The ice creaked again and a great fissure split the surface, swallowing tons of snow and ancient trees into the lightless chasm. Great slabs sheared from the widening maw in the earth and tumbled away with a deafening crash.

With a sound like shattering bone, dozens of the snow-laden trees heaved into the air and burst apart as their frigid cores buckled under the strain, rising upwards in a spray of bark and pulped wood. Gileas's hand closed around his weapon, for all the good the chainsword was likely to do him. He cursed inwardly for the ambition that had driven him to seek the predator that had driven off the cats. That predator had now found *them*.

The earth seemed to inhale, a great bowl-shaped hollow suddenly falling away before being ejected into the air in a dirty shower of pulverised ice and fragmented vegetation. Rising from the pit came a monster that eclipsed the starlight and shook the heavens with the thunder of its voice. It towered two hundred metres into the night air and much of its bulk still lay concealed beneath the permafrost.

The broad, tubular body that drew to a taper at the top end was instantly identifiable. Thick, greyish fur covered its lumpy hide, punctuated by stubby and muscular claws that it employed to propel itself at startling velocity through the frozen earth. No eyes were visible, for there were none to see. The creature was completely blind.

'Solifugus worm,' breathed Nicodemus, who was caught between awe at the incredible beast that emerged before him and the need to ensure the continued survival of them all. The solifugus worm was a peculiar evolution of a species that had been indigenous to the planet long before the Silver Skulls had even come into being. Researchers and members of the Adeptus Biologicus had theorised that they might even have been the original dominant species on the world.

'The size of it,' muttered Achak. Gileas gave a humourless smile.

'This is nothing,' he said. 'See the greyish tint to its skin? *That* marks it as a juvenile.' Those words caused a ripple of disbelief that somewhere there was something bigger than this leviathan. The young warriors steeled themselves.

A cavernous mouth peeled back on its bullet-shaped head, revealing numerous rows of grinding teeth. These creatures were carnivorous and with its appearance it became instantly obvious what had caused the other predators to evacuate. The only mercy that Gileas could find in the situation was that the worms were solitary by nature and their territories were vast. There would be no more than one to deal with.

Should be. Luck had not favoured them so far.

There was no way they would be killing it. This was not a conclusion reached from any sort of misplaced sense of preservation, or a particular desire to spare the beast. It was pragmatism, pure and simple. The Silver Skulls were armed with the most basic weaponry. If they had had a lascannon or a plasma weapon of some kind they might have been able to incapacitate the worm. But they had bolters and chainswords. Bolt-rounds would never penetrate the thick hide and blades were of no use at all. Getting close enough to use one would have been challenge enough.

The sergeant noticed Nicodemus's psychic hood beginning to crackle with the eldritch power of the warp and put out a hand to stop him.

'Save your strength, brother,' he said softly. 'It will be wasted here.'

Looking startled, Nicodemus briefly pushed out mentally towards the solifugus. He felt that same desire for food he had touched before, an insatiable need to eat... and little else. The huge creature was nothing more complicated than a million nerve endings and reactive muscle. A giant eating machine with no capacity for or concept of fear at all. And Nicodemus was not yet strong or experienced enough to unleash the full power of his ability.

The flickering lights around his face ebbed and died as he heeded the sergeant's words.

Gileas had brought the Scouts out here to learn. It seemed that they would be forced to learn one of the key weapons of survival sooner rather than later. Strategic withdrawal.

It was more than a case of avoiding the gaping maw of the creature. The huge body was an effective hunting and killing machine. If the worm were to burrow back down, it could move with greater speed than even a Space Marine could achieve. But full retreat could not figure into Gileas's plans, not whilst two of his charges were still unaccounted for. He had no doubt of their ability to take care of themselves, but he had a responsibility that he would not shirk.

Unfortunately, he also had very little time in which to make his decision. The worm's bulk was extraordinary, but it was in its own terrain. It had risen far above them, huge and menacing in the night, and was already beginning its plunge towards them.

His mind working faster than humanly possible, Gileas assessed the situation and made his choice. The speed of the vast creature and the distance to the safety of the crags did not supply variables that combined to produce a favourable result under the circumstances. A life spent in eternal blindness meant that the creature was not even remotely handicapped by the gloom of the night: it sensed the body-heat of all living things and right now, Gileas and the three Scouts were its prey.

But being half out of the ice as it was also ensured that its manoeuvrability was limited, if only temporarily, and that was what Gileas used to their advantage. The worm opened its razor maw wide to swallow them whole as it plunged towards them.

'Scatter!'

The single-word command was issued in a barking tone and the four Silver Skulls darted in separate directions as the solifugus crashed down towards them. It struck the ice like a wrecking ball and tore a second hole as it once again burrowed into the depths. Honon, who was closest to the worm as it struck the ground, was thrown forwards, his arms outstretched, and landed badly in a tangled heap.

The Scout scrambled to his feet and struggled to maintain his balance. It was difficult with the ground still rolling unsteadily beneath him. All four of them watched in a kind of horrid fascination as the hump of the worm boiled up through the snow whilst it looped its body around for another pass.

'Distraction,' said Gileas. 'Distraction. Achak, explosives!'

The Scout nodded his understanding and pulled a pair of frag grenades from his webbing. He primed the charges on short fuses and hurled them into the trees. A few seconds later the detonations threw snow and ice into the air and shredded the frozen foliage with razor shards of hot shrapnel.

'Good,' said the sergeant. 'Good. Now fall back towards the Xiz encampment. Motega, Gaelyn – you as well.'

If any of the Scouts wondered why their sergeant had given this sudden and unexpected command, they didn't voice it. They began to run as fast as they were able in the direction of the camp. Honon spearheaded the retreat, since his unfortunate fall had thrown him further from the menacing creature.

The worm was burrowing its way beneath their feet towards the heat being given off by the explosions, the Scout's distraction apparently working as intended. The worm burst up through the surface again, the huge jaws gulping down the trees and ice at the site of the detonations with voracious rapidity. The monster had been fooled, but the respite was only fleeting.

In a movement that would have been incredible to observe under less dire circumstances, it arched its colossal body over backwards until it had reversed its momentum, its vast shadow falling over the fleeing Space Marines as it descended. Gileas, Nicodemus and Achak dived aside as it thundered back into the snow, their enhanced muscles carrying them clear of the crushing bulk.

Honon, caught in the worm's downward plunge, was taken down into the bowels of the ice in a massive gulp of snow and foliage. Gileas swore softly under his breath. There would be no chance of the Scout surviving the experience and whilst losing one or more novitiates whilst on a Hunt was considered more or less inevitable, the pang of guilt and the sudden sharp stab of grief were still unwelcome.

The worm had returned to its subterranean tunnels and the forest shook and rippled with its passage. By now the group had recovered Gaelyn and Motega, and Gileas gestured urgently to keep moving. Any moment now, the Space Marine party and the Xiz were going to collide.

A *distraction*, Gileas had said. Nicodemus cast a sidelong glance at the more experienced warrior as they ran. He saw the grim determination in his superior's expression and without much of a stretch of his imagination arrived at a complete understanding of what his ultimate goal in this course of action was. So simple and yet so remarkably effective.

Not for the first time in his young life and especially not since he had ascended to the ranks, Nicodemus began to appreciate the fact that not every problem could be solved by unleashing his psychic powers. Countless times that advice had been given to him and he had never heard it properly. Yet here, out in the wilds of Varsavia – under the command of a man he knew many considered to be little more than an animal in armour – it became clear.

Think. *Then* act.

The Xiz had not had a successful trip. The cannibalistic tribe who so dominated the south of Varsavia had discovered, as had the Space Marines, that something had driven the game out of the hunting grounds. Unable to find any meat, they had made camp for the night with a view to continuing when daylight returned.

Instead, the peace had been shattered by a quake and the deafening roar of something terrible. The tribesmen got to their feet and began jabbering at one another in a monosyllabic, guttural tongue that the Silver Skulls themselves frequently adopted as one of their battle languages. Some wanted to flee, to leave these cursed grounds at once and seek out fresh meat in more familiar territory. Others believed that the great noise and light in the woods was the work of spirits and that they should make the appropriate offerings.

The two parties collided barely seconds later. The Xiz, who had never encountered the silver giants of the north, were startled by the sudden appearance of five enormous humanoids running at a sprint towards them. Several let out war cries and raised their spears, ready to attack. Others scrambled to evade the running Silver Skulls.

'Keep moving,' bellowed Gileas across the vox and watched as his charges veered to avoid collision with the milling Xiz.

Afterwards, he could never fully recall the moment of intense hatred and the desperate need for retribution that overcame him. The desire to gain some measure of revenge on the descendants of those who had so long ago murdered a child's family and left him for dead in the ice took hold of his rational judgement and he plunged right through the middle of the pack.

Two died instantly as he barged them aside. Their skulls cracked under the force of the impact and their necks snapped like twigs. They fell to the ground, limp and lifeless, as several others turned on this rampaging monster with spears that did little more than scratch his superhuman flesh. Hands reached to grab him, to tackle this new threat to the ground, but Gileas simply lashed out without hesitation.

A Xiz warrior to his right had his face pulverised by the sergeant's gauntlet and one on the left began shrieking in agony after Gileas employed his Betcher's gland. The gobbet of acid burned at the man's face and he stumbled blindly around, screaming and clawing at his eyes.

Gileas continued his wild charge.

The brief slaughter complete, the Xiz were still reeling when the ground beneath their feet yawned open. Unprepared for the suddenness of the worm's appearance, the Xiz became the very distraction that Gileas had hoped for. He wiped blood from his face – very little of it his own – and glanced over his shoulder, witnessing the massacre. At his very heart, he felt the faintest twinge of respect for the dying tribesmen, who howled their defiance until the very end.

But only the *very* faintest twinge.

The Space Marines did not stop moving until they were several miles from the carnage. Although they were faster and more powerful than their human equivalents, this terrain did not make for fleet passage. They broke through the line of the snow forest back out onto the plains and thundered relentlessly towards a slope that led up to higher ground.

The fading shrieks and cries of the tribesmen as they died echoed into the night and when the Silver Skulls finally stopped and looked back, they did so with heavy hearts. One of their own was forever lost, an ignoble death that had no honour. His precious gene-seed had gone with him. Whilst all of the Scouts had encountered the death of a brother in one form or other throughout the course of their training, this was something different.

For Gileas, the years of experience meant that his sense of grief was greatly diminished. Honon's death had been unfortunate, yes. But far better the loss of a single battle-brother than the eradication of the whole squad.

'What now, sergeant?' After a period of silence during which the distant cries finally faded to silence, Nicodemus asked the question. He shifted the weight of the trophy bag on his belt and looked out over the stark landscape. A grey line on the horizon hinted at the coming dawn and the grim chill of night had lessened slightly.

'What now?' Gileas looked down the line from Scout to Scout. Each one of them had followed his orders without question and they had survived. They had witnessed the unfortunate demise of one of their own and they were taking it with the stoic determination and grim acceptance that was part of the harsh reality of becoming one of the Emperor's Angels. Honon had shown promise, but ultimately, he had not lived up to that. The other Scouts would mourn him in their own way when they returned to the fortress-monastery. The Hunt, it was said, had been designed to weed out those who were not strong enough in the Emperor's sight.

Honon was dead. The others remained. They were a credit to the name of the Chapter.

Gileas shouldered Eclipse and stared towards the creeping dawn. 'What now indeed? Now, Nicodemus, we continue the Hunt. We find what we can on this side of the mountain face.'

He began walking and the neophytes matched his stride easily. 'We have days yet. There are things out in the wastes that will hunt you just as ruthlessly as the solifugus. This was just the first encounter. We will find ourselves a worthy prize, I assure you.'

'Aye, sergeant,' affirmed Achak in a grim tone. 'A prize that we will take in Honon's name.'

'Well spoken, brother.' Gileas shot a long-fanged, wolfish grin at the youth and turned to walk into the winds of the Ice Wastes.

EIGHT

HERETICUS

Some people called them lucky. In truth, the Siculean Sixth Regiment were exceptionally skilled at what they did. Luck wasn't really a contributing factor for the most part. Canny strategy, strong bonds of brotherhood and an impressive ability to determine when the odds were turning against them had kept many of them alive through brutal theatres of war.

Under the command of Lord Commander Arnulf Meer, the regiment had been founded on the agri world of Siculi, in the Calixis Sector of the Segmentum Obscurus. The world bred solid men and women who were adaptable, loyal and keen to serve in the Astra Militarum. Particularly if it meant getting away from the tedium that was farming protoalgia. The slimy, moss-like plant was a vital ingredient in keeping those very armies marching, a protein constituent that was shipped all across the Segmentum.

Most of Siculi's youth were desperate to leave. Many

did so on the regular recruitment vessels that came to the planet. Some left in other, less pleasant ways. Once every generation or so, the Black Ships came. Whilst the psyker tithe of the planet may not have been large, Siculi still gave up its share of the warp-tainted to the bellies of the Terran-bound vessels.

The Sixth had served with loyalty and distinction for many years and had frequently been called into service as the military force for the Inquisition and its many activities in the Segmentum. One inquisitor in particular had all but adopted the regiment, frequently calling on their aid. The recognition of such service had merely enhanced the suitability of the moniker 'lucky'.

Nathaniel Gall contemplated this fact as he stared out of the ship's viewing port. Warp travel always left him feeling uncomfortable, as though he were being dragged through the ocean of Chaos like some piece of bait, a lure for the countless horrors that snapped in their wake. He could sometimes feel the shapes of the things that stalked him and when they were in the depths of the warp those things grew more solid. But he kept the fear under control. It was what he had to do.

He was not one of the regiment. He would never have been one of the regiment. Nathaniel had been too thin and too weak to ever have succeeded as a soldier. Instead, he had been resigned to a life of farming. Someone had to do it, his impatient father had said. Nathaniel would be that someone and he would damned well live with it.

Then the Black Ships had come and the sixteen-year-old Nathaniel Gall had left, whether he had wanted to go or not. Once he had been placed in the employ of the Inquisition, he had utilised his privileges – perhaps inappropriately – to determine what had happened to his family. He learned that his sister had been taken with a later tithe. Nathaniel had thought never to see pretty little Isara, the younger sister he had doted on, again. Her powers had not manifested in the way that Nathaniel's had. Not the long wait for puberty for Isara. No, her talent had become apparent at the same time as Nathaniel's.

Isara was a blank. Her destiny lay down an entirely different path to that of her brother. Even knowing that – once he understood the fundamentals of his 'gift' – Nathaniel's pain at the separation from his sister had been awful.

The chances that the Gall siblings should be brought together again so many years later were astronomical enough that Nathaniel had once attempted to calculate the odds. Eventually, and after extended discussion with others in the inquisitor's retinue, he concluded that it didn't matter. What would be would be. He also suspected a very deliberate move on the part of the inquisitor.

The psyker caught a glimpse of his reflection in the viewport and he turned his head to one side to avoid meeting his own gaze. No matter how many times he saw his own reflection, he could never accept that the face that looked back at him was truly his own. Only fifty-five years old, he looked perhaps twenty years older than that. Sallow skin that was prematurely lined and wrinkled, thinning hair that had turned grey when he had been sixteen and bloodshot pale blue eyes. The inquisitor had offered him rejuvenat treatments, but the first batch had made him so ill that no further offers had been forthcoming. His slight body was thin to the point of emaciation.

No, nobody could ever call Nathaniel Gall a handsome man. Even as a youth he had not been comely. All the good looks had gone to Isara.

Long robes covered his skinny frame, and his perpetually sour expression did not make him the kind of man people chose to speak with. The Inquisitorial brand of the sanctioned psyker was marked clearly for all to see, an intricate tattoo that took the standard Inquisition sigil and incorporated his left eye. It dominated his thin face, announcing to all he met what – and who – he was. Once, he had been ashamed of that brand. Now, though, he was proud to bear it.

He reached up and massaged his temples in irritation, trying to stave off the headache that was throbbing dully at the base of his skull. The Sixth hated warp travel as well, but for them it was about the boredom. Long stretches of nothing to do. All of them suffered from disturbed sleep and whilst strange noises were the norm, some heard things that left them cowering in terror. Used to having to maintain control under such circumstances, Nathaniel's headache was minor by comparison.

'I brought you a recaff.'

Nathaniel grunted something in response to the newcomer, but did not turn from the viewport. If he concentrated hard enough, the shadows fled from the darkest recesses of his mind. Distractions were not welcome. A steaming mug of the bitter drink was pressed into his hand and a figure shifted to stand next to him.

'Are you all right in here? You're not… about to explode, or burst into flames, or anything like that, are you?' The voice was well spoken; a cultured voice, as well it should be. Harild de Corso had been sent to the best tutors and had received the privilege due the rank of a hive world minor noble for his entire life. Strange, many people said, that such a man had become a soldier. His parents had hoped for politics, but Harild had chosen the solitary existence of a sniper.

'I'm still in control, if that's what you mean.' Nathaniel took a sip of the drink, welcoming its warmth, and looked forward to the caffeine hit that would follow soon. It would deaden the worst of the headache.

'You know that's not what I meant.' De Corso was actually wearing his uniform for once, but even so, his was cut from the best cloth and he had re-tailored parts of it to fit him even more flatteringly. For Harild de Corso, image was nine-tenths of the impression he made. Nathaniel had scorned his obsessive attitude to his appearance once. Why would a sniper care about how they looked?

'The victim doesn't know if their killer is immaculately dressed.' Nathaniel's argument had been reasonable and rational, as always. It didn't bother de Corso.

'Perhaps not,' he said. 'But *I* know, and I like to think of it as a courtesy.'

Nathaniel bit back his sharp words. De Corso was harmless enough and other than Isara and the inquisitor, the only one who ever so much as spoke to him when it wasn't absolutely necessary. Nathaniel held up the mug and shot a brief glance sideways. 'I apologise. Thank you.'

Harild nodded. 'You're welcome.' Nathaniel studied the sniper. Tall, slender, effortlessly handsome and with an even-toothed smile that he knew women fell for every time it was switched on, de Corso was excellent at what he did. And what he did was kill anybody he was told to, as long as they were a long way away.

'So. What's the word then, psyker? Did you get anything useful out of your... meeting with the inquisitor?' De Corso's eyebrows waggled in a decidedly suggestive manner that Nathaniel didn't like one little bit. He found the implication that his interest in the inquisitor was anything beyond professional to be insulting.

The fact that his interest *did* go beyond professional was not the point.

'When the inquisitor and I spoke,' he replied, a haughty tone coming into his voice, 'she told me nothing more than we already knew. And you should know better than to show such disrespect for her position. Or mine for that matter. You may be one of her retinue, but you're still new.'

De Corso held his hands up in mock surrender. 'I'm just making fun of you, Nate.' The psyker narrowed his eyes at the diminutive. He hated it. 'Try relaxing a little, would you? You'll burst something...' He tailed off, realising just how close to 'bursting something' the frail psyker had come in the past. 'I'm sorry. That was unnecessary.'

Nathaniel's cold blue eyes stared at de Corso for a few moments longer, evidently trying to decide if he was being mocked. Finally, he turned back to look out of the viewport again.

'We are heading to Varsavia. The inquisitor is confident that we will not be there for long. I hope not – I've read up on the place. It sounds horrible.'

'Ice world, right?' De Corso grinned, but there was no humour in the expression. 'Those places are about as grim as they come, Helbron reckons.'

'Helbron finds everything grim.' This was true enough. Curt Helbron was the inquisitor's pet bounty hunter and it was widely known that he hated everything and everyone.

'He doesn't find your sister grim,' teased de Corso gently. He was rewarded with the kind of look that could kill. Curt Helbron was a persistent thorn in Nathaniel's side.

The man was virtually silent most of the time unless he was addressed directly and although evidently proud to be a part of the inquisitor's retinue, did little in the way of getting to know his companions. Apart from Isara, much to Nathaniel's disapproval. To his further disapproval, he understood that Isara didn't find Helbron grim either.

Were things different, he would have spoken to Isara about it. But she was sure of her own mind and didn't care who knew it. On top of which, she necessarily avoided Nathaniel unless they had no choice but to be together.

Nathaniel reached up and toyed idly with one of the many rings that were pierced through his right ear. A Siculean tradition, each ring was meant to represent a personal mark of shame.

Nathaniel had a lot of them.

'Please do not speak of my sister in such a disrespectful way,' Nathaniel said disdainfully. 'She has devoted her life in service to the Emperor. Helbron distracts her from that purpose.'

De Corso thought better of his response and simply nodded. The two lapsed back into silence again, Nathaniel sipping on the recaff and staring at the shapeless *things* that leered through the viewport at him, defying him to lose control and join them. This was the lot of the psyker. The desperately important need to control themselves at all times and not to let that control waver, even for an instant. Nathaniel was concentrating so hard on this that it was a moment or two before de Corso's voice seeped into his consciousness.

'...ever dealt with the Adeptus Astartes before?'

'What?'

'I was asking, what's your experience of the Space Marines?'

'Limited.'

'Indeed. Well, do me a favour, would you? Do try not to be your usual forthright self. They can be pretty literal at times and frankly, some of the things you say would insult even the most forgiving saint in the chapel.' Nathaniel had a habit of speaking his mind without any intervention from his brain. It was a quality that his companions occasionally admired but more frequently dreaded. 'I enjoy working with you, you know. And despite being such a miserable bastard, you're quite good company. I'm fairly certain that none of us want to end our working relationship by scraping what's left of you from a Space Marine's boot.'

'I'll keep your advice in mind.' Nathaniel drained the last of the recaff and hugged the mug to his thin chest. De Corso watched him for a few moments longer and then quietly took his leave.

Isara Gall was a stately woman of forty-five. Tall and with neatly coiffed auburn hair that showed only the earliest hints of grey, she held herself with the pride of the nobles of any world. She had come into the inquisitor's service long before any of those who travelled with them now and as such considered herself the senior serving member of the retinue.

There was a fleeting resemblance to her brother across the brow, but those who didn't know their familial relationship would never have suspected any kind of connection other than the coincidence of their names. Isara was charming, witty, well educated and the inquisitor's closest confidante. She stood near the pulpit of the bridge, idly watching the hive of activity that buzzed around the consoles and workstations in the tiers beneath. She wore a finely tailored dress of shimmering scarlet, in stark contrast to the formal uniforms of the officers who occasionally hurried past. A few of them had thought to approach her, but had swiftly changed their minds with an obvious grimace. She forgave them. They could not have had any experience with her kind, or the unnatural sense of contempt that surrounded her. At least she supposed that was the reason for their reluctance. The presence of her companion could have been another.

The bounty hunter leaned on the polished brass railings and glared malevolently down at the mass of humanity and machines below. His face was a knotted mass of scar tissue and stubble, with a deep pucker running from his forehead to his chin. De Corso liked to joke that he was only an inch away from an augmetic nose, but Helbron didn't find it funny. He puffed on the stub of a battered lho-stick in open defiance of the bosun who had ruled that narcotics had no place on the ship, let alone the bridge. Curt had told him to come and take it if he wanted it and the topic had been abandoned.

'You look pensive, Curt,' Isara observed. 'Are you troubled by this visit to the Space Marine home world?'

The bounty hunter made a noise that suggested he didn't care either way. Isara gave him a warm smile. Sometimes getting an opinion out of him was like pulling a tooth.

'The hive world then. Has the inquisitor heard anything new?'

Helbron shook his head and spat the mangled remains of the lho onto the deck far below.

'No. But then you knew that,' he rumbled. He was a big man, with a voice like crushed gravel. Nathaniel had said openly that he couldn't see what Isara found so fascinating about him.

Helbron scratched at his jaw line and glared down at the bridge below. 'Just something not sitting right about this job.'

'You have said that about every mission we have ever been on and everything has always worked out.' Everything hadn't *always* worked out. Helbron and Isara had seen the end of more than one friend during their Inquisitorial careers, but they never spoke of the departed. You did not dwell upon the dead in their line of work. It would take too long.

Curt grunted his agreement.

'One of these days it won't, though.'

'Unknown vessel has translated into the system.'

It had taken only seven words relayed to the fortress-monastery from one of the orbital defence platforms high above Varsavia to generate a surge of activity. Servitors and Chapter-serfs began the job of ensuring that access to the armoury was clear whilst the Silver Skulls currently in residence at the fortress-monastery began mustering. Such preparation was necessary, for although more often than not such breaches of planetary security were nothing of consequence, there was always the chance that this might not be the case.

Lord Commander Argentius strode towards the central control room where the message had been received.

'Report.' He bellowed the single word through the vox that connected the fortress-monastery to the skies above.

'Sword class frigate, my lord.' The officer's voice was broken and distorted through the distance and thick walls that separated them. 'Translated fifteen minutes ago. There has not yet been any response to our hails.'

'Threat assessment?'

'Just the one vessel, my lord, and she is old. Threat assessment minimum.'

'Transmitting?'

'Old codes. Not so old that they are out of date, but it suggests that they have not been in this sector for quite some time.' Argentius nodded. That explained why the intruder vessel had not been simply vaporised the moment it had appeared. Still, there was no need for complacency. He transmitted through the vox, hailing the ship directly.

'I am Lord Commander Argentius of the Silver Skulls. Your ship is in danger of trespassing in forbidden territory. I suggest that you identify yourself within the next thirty seconds.'

A new voice was heard above the discordant noise that reigned supreme and it cut through the chaos like a knife. It was a female voice, smooth and lightly accented. Every syllable was as clear as crystal.

'...old codes and even older systems. Get this thing working, now!'

Argentius arched one eyebrow at the imperious tone and a few seconds later, the voice adopted a much less irritated and far more pleasant level. 'This is the Inquisitorial vessel *Callimachus*. Please accept my apologies for the delay in responding to your hails. Stand down your defences...'

'You will respond to my query before I do any such thing.'

'My name is Inquisitor Liandra Callis of the Ordo Hereticus,' came the reply. 'I am here on a matter of grave importance and request immediate audience with you. You need not scramble your fleet to meet me, Lord Commander. I assure you that the *Callimachus* represents no threat.'

Argentius did not let his surprise at the announcement change either the expression on his face or the stern quality that resounded through his words. There had been a situation in the Silver Skulls' history where a lone ship had been seemingly without threat and that had resulted in the near-decimation of Fourth Company.

There would be no repeat of such mistakes. Never again.

'Your arrival has caused quite a stir, Inquisitor Callis. Whilst you may give me your word that your vessel poses no threat, I am sure that you understand we have many protocols on this world. I will send out an escort vessel to bring you to the planet. I would ask you to wait until I have arranged this.'

'I did say "the utmost importance", Lord Commander.'

'Yes,' replied Argentius. 'I heard you. And until I am ready to receive you, I would request that you enter orbit and hold there until sent for.'

The vast distance that separated the Chapter Master and the inquisitor seemed to spark with the unspoken battle of wills and finally, the woman's voice came again, amusement evident.

'As you wish, Lord Commander. Just a question for you, though. Why didn't your Prognosticators foresee my coming? I hear that their gift of foresight is arguably the best in the galaxy.'

Argentius bristled a little at her implication and replied with the utmost politeness.

'Inquisitor, it is probable that my Prognosticators *did* foresee your arrival. I simply hadn't thought to ask them.'

There was a pause and the lightest of laughs before the communication was broken off. The Chapter Master shook his head grimly. The woman was yet to set foot on his world and already he did not like her attitude. Nonetheless, protocols were to be observed. 'Platform Theta, this is

Argentius. Stand down the security alert, but keep a close eye on them. I don't imagine for one moment that they are not who they say they are, but I would rather that we take every possible precaution against surprises.'

The fact that the Ordo Hereticus were coming into orbit around his Chapter's home world was unsettling enough, and most definitely not something that pleased him. The Silver Skulls had known only minimal contact with the majority of the Inquisition. Their history with the Ordo Malleus stretched back a long time of course, but they were still wary of the other ordos.

'Send word to Vashiro that I wish to see him,' said the Chapter Master as he strode from the control room, his expression grim. 'And make preparations to receive the inquisitor, I have no doubt she will wish to conduct a full inspection.'

'Yes, my lord.' The Chapter-serf bowed his head and scurried to carry out his lord and master's orders.

'The Inquisition does not simply arrive on a whim,' said Argentius as he paced the length of the War Room. Vashiro sat watching him thoughtfully. The Head Prognosticator had said very little since arriving at the Chapter Master's request, but had sat quietly. The bag of silver runes that he used to divine the most important threads of the Chapter's fate sat on the heavy wooden meeting-table in front of him. He had not even opened it.

Argentius dropped down heavily into the chair at the head of the table. He laced his hands together and leaned forward onto them. 'I am made… most uncomfortable by their presence. Particularly in light of the mission report filed by Kerelan and Bhehan on their return from Lyria.' Speaking of the younger Prognosticator gave Argentius a brief, welcome distraction from the matter at hand. 'How is he?'

'Bhehan? The boy has done countless hours of penance for what he sees as an unforgivable lapse of judgement,' noted Vashiro in his whispering voice. 'He strongly feels that he is irreversibly contaminated.'

'Because of the necessity of sharing minds with the eldar?'

'Precisely, my lord. As vital as it was to the success of his mission, by allying their forces and joining his Throne-given powers with the eldar witch, Bhehan claims he has opened his mind to forbidden knowledge.' Argentius sighed. 'He finds little peace in his decision to terminate the xenos. He questions his actions.'

'He is young,' Argentius said. 'Emotional. Easily swayed from his course. He did what he had to do for the necessary survival of our Chapter.'

'I agree,' said Vashiro nodding his head. 'He is beginning to see things far more objectively now. Kerelan has spent time with him and some of the heat of his shame is beginning to dissipate.' Vashiro paced slightly. 'Bhehan is a promising young Prognosticator, my lord. I am firmly convinced he is blessed with True Sight.'

Argentius pictured the youth: fair-haired and eager the first time he had been clad in his blue Librarian's wargear. Wary and noticeably more suspicious now. The loss of such energy to the realities of life as a Space Marine was something that Argentius expected but which never grew any easier to witness.

'He should take comfort from the fact that his direct decisions and actions led to the recovery of one of our most precious relics,' Vashiro added.

'The war banner is being carefully restored by the most

practised and skilled artisans as we speak,' said Argentius, his back straightening and a glow of pride coming into his eyes. 'Even the corrupting touch of Chaos could not destroy it. Its presence amongst our warriors will inspire them to acts of glory and honour.'

'You think the Inquisition is here for Bhehan.' It was not a question and a brief change in Argentius's face was all Vashiro needed to confirm his suspicion. 'I do not believe that to be the case. They have not been back on Varsavia for long and the report has yet to be committed to the records. I cannot fathom any way the Inquisition would have heard of what transpired.'

'They are the Inquisition, Vashiro. Who knows how they do anything?' The Chapter Master ran an agitated hand across his hair, standing once more and resuming his pacing. 'Well, if they are not here for him, then what in the Emperor's name could possibly bring them here?'

'You speak like a man with a guilty conscience, my friend.' Vashiro's heavily tattooed face crinkled into a smile. 'Guard your thoughts as best you can. It is possible that this inquisitor will have a psyker or two amongst her retinue and it would go poorly for us if the things that are going through your mind were on display for all to see.'

'I have nothing to hide,' retorted Argentius immediately. 'The Silver Skulls are loyal to the Throne. My warriors are stalwart defenders of mankind. They uphold the Imperial creed with honour and dignity. This Inquisitor Callis will find no heresy here.'

'Better,' said Vashiro with an approving nod. 'Now say it like you genuinely believe it.'

There was a moment's silence during which the Head Prognosticator registered his Chapter Master's shock at the words. Then the older Space Marine placed his hand down on the table.

'You have anxieties that the Inquisition will question our practices. *My* practices. Those of the Prognosticatum.' Again, it was not a question.

'They are our traditions. Looking to you, our advisers, has always been the way that we have divined our course. We have never had cause to explain this to anybody before. No, it cannot be that simple.'

'Do you believe so?'

The two warriors locked gazes for a while. Argentius looked away first, unable to submit to Vashiro's scrutiny for extended periods. It was as though he were transparent and every thought and feeling was on display for the psyker to see.

'We will discover the truth soon enough,' said Argentius. 'For now, she waits in orbit. I have heard nothing further from her so it appears that her "matter of grave importance" is not so very grave.'

'Settle yourself, my lord.' Vashiro opened the bag of runes and scattered them into an untidy pile on the table before him. 'Do not look upon this intrusion as a hindrance. Instead consider the honour that the Inquisition do our Chapter by arriving here.'

'The honour?' Argentius could not keep the incredulity from his voice.

'Aye, my lord.' Vashiro took up a single silver rune and let it dance across the back of his knuckles: a simple sleight-of-hand exercise, just one of many he employed to keep his senses sharp. 'What better opportunity to create a good impression than in front of one of the Ordo Hereticus? Do we know anything about her methods?'

'There is nothing available in current records,' replied the Chapter Master. In truth, Vashiro's words had pulled him up short. He had been so absorbed in considering all the negative reasons the Inquisition could have arrived on Varsavia that the positive element to their presence had not featured at all. 'But then, communications take a long time anywhere in the Imperium. Our most recent records do not return her name. She is either new, or simply more covert than those of whom we are aware.'

'Then it is vitally important that we impress upon her our fealty to the Golden Throne. That will not be a difficult task. Select your honour guard with care.' A ghost of a smile flickered across the psyker's face. 'I would avoid putting Brother Djul and Brother Gileas into that party... at least together.'

'You heard about that, then?' Argentius shook his head. Phrixus had been duty-bound to report the matter to the Chapter Master and as of yet, Argentius had not addressed the situation. Instead, he had engineered situations that had kept the two from coming into contact with one another until he could speak with them formally about it.

'I did. It is an unfortunate situation you have to deal with. Both of our brothers are headstrong and courageous. Both have very different outlooks on the future of the Chapter. Bringing those two viewpoints together into a shared vision will be an arduous task.' Vashiro studied the rune in his hand. 'Arduous, but certainly not impossible.'

'Wise words. I will leave both for now. Kerelan, obviously. Yourself. Phrixus. Bhehan?' The Head Prognosticator shook his head: a barely perceptible movement. 'Not him. Sensible.'

'Allow one of the new psychic intake to attend,' suggested

Vashiro. 'Nicodemus has great potential and is a good listener. He is young and observant and has not yet had time to settle into what some might perceive as our more... unusual habits.'

'Agreed. Of course, I may yet decide to greet her alone.'

Vashiro gave another of his enigmatic smiles and dropped the silver rune back into the bag at his waist.

'As my Chapter Master wishes,' he affirmed.

'Then I will send word to the inquisitor,' said Argentius. 'Time to fetch her down here and find out what it is that she wants with the Silver Skulls.'

NINE

DUTY'S CALL

Argentius had expected a full retinue to accompany Callis to the surface of Varsavia, but when the visitors emerged from the Thunderhawk, there were only three of them. Two were tall, one wearing a long black coat over the immaculate uniform of a soldier of Astra Militarum. Argentius did not recognise the heraldry on the breast of the man's coat. The other was a slight creature, swaying in the katabatic winds that gusted from the mountains with unbridled savagery. He was clad in thick, heavy robes that hung from his gaunt frame. Argentius studied him for a moment longer, taking in the body language: the set of the shoulders that spoke of disapproval, and the shadow of contempt on what could be seen of his face beneath the hood.

Standing between them was a petite, slim woman who seemed little more than a child swathed in a dark, floor-length hooded coat. As Argentius strode towards them her features came into sharp focus. She was in possession of flawless, alabaster-pale skin that was slightly reddened by the bite of the wind. 'A lazy wind,' Argentius remembered a long-dead battle-brother calling it once. 'Just as soon go through you as around you.'

The woman stood a little ahead of her two male companions, straight and proud, and her gaze turned towards the Chapter Master as he approached. One eye was augmetic, an obviously expensive implant that had no doubt been handcrafted at great cost for her. The other was bright blue, cold as the ice that surrounded them. Her lips pursed slightly as she boldly took in Argentius. Her eyes ranged over the Chapter Master of the Silver Skulls, weighing him up. He met her scrutiny with mild aloofness. She may have been an inquisitor, certainly... but he was a Space Marine. He was her superior in virtually every way.

He had chosen to meet her wearing his ceremonial plate. It was the same brushed steel as the rest of the Chapter livery, but with gold scrollwork that marked his position as an individual of note. A fur-edged cloak of deep wine-red fluttered from his shoulders, snapping in the wind where he stood.

On further consulting with Vashiro and based on his own instincts, Argentius had elected to meet the inquisitor alone. It would undoubtedly impress her more and help to convey that he had nothing to hide.

The inquisitor ceased her scrutiny and dropped a low, courteous bow. Her coat flared out behind her and when she rose again, there was nothing but respect on her face.

'Hail and well met, Lord Commander Argentius,' she said. 'I am Inquisitor Liandra Callis. Thank you for extending me the honour of meeting you here in this most sacred of places. I apologise for any inconvenience that my unexpected arrival in your system may have caused. My ship is… ageing, and our cogitators and communications are less than reliable. I trust that we did not put you to any trouble?'

Her formal greeting surprised Argentius. He had been expecting an immediate demand for escort indoors from the freezing air. He inclined his head and returned the formality in kind. If she was capable of making an effort, then it would cost him nothing to respond in like manner.

'You do me and my ancestors a great honour by recognising the sanctity of the fortress-monastery, Inquisitor Callis. Rest assured that the initial hostility that you may have felt we exhibited was nothing but precautionary.'

'Commendable,' she said with a terse nod. 'Such actions are preferable to allowing miscreants and traitors to roam freely through your sector.'

Argentius smiled and it was warm and honest. 'Formalities over, perhaps I might invite you within the fortress-monastery proper? The conditions here are not kind to those who are unused to them.' Out of the corner of his eye, he saw the robed man nod enthusiastically.

'That would be acceptable,' came the short response from the inquisitor. 'I ask that you extend the same courtesy to my companions.' She indicated the men at her side. 'These individuals are my chosen protectors and where I go, they go.'

The bigger of the two men stepped forward and made the sign of the aquila across his chest. 'Harild de Corso, regimental sniper, Siculean Sixth, my lord. An unfailing honour to meet you.' There was something instantly likeable about the man. There was charm oozing from every pore and his smile was warm, calculated to put people at their ease.

This may have been a tactic that worked on normal men, but Argentius did not count amongst that number. He saw the smile for what it was and filed a mental note not to trust this de Corso until he proved himself. Regardless, he bowed his head in acknowledgement of the man's perfectly rehearsed respect. He could play a role when it suited him as well.

'And this is Nathaniel,' the inquisitor said when the other man did not seem inclined to say anything. The scrawny figure finally looked up, the soft hood falling back enough to expose his face. Argentius immediately noted the brand across his eye. The inquisitor looked at the psyker, who lightly shrugged one shoulder. It was a barely noticeable gesture, but Argentius was used to spotting such things.

'Nathaniel Gall,' the psyker finally said, as though reluctant to give away something as important as his name.

'Nathaniel is one of my chief advisers,' said Inquisitor Callis, and Argentius kept a smile from his face at the look of pleasure this simple sentence brought to the psyker's eyes. 'Both him and *Captain* de Corso are cleared for maximum security and can be fully trusted.'

'Captain?' Argentius turned back to the sniper, who smiled broadly. This particular smile, however, was entirely honest and eminently more likeable for that simple fact. The Chapter Master's single-word question required no expansion and de Corso answered straight away.

'Imperial Guard,' he said, his pitch modest. 'I admit, I long fell out of the habit of using my rank when introducing myself. My role within the Inquisition is so far removed from what I was back then.'

The Chapter Master was intrigued by the offhand manner in which these three humans had reacted to the presence of a huge warrior of the Adeptus Astartes. Argentius was accustomed to those not of the fortress-monastery's complement of staff reacting with awe and instant respect when faced with the massive reality of an Emperor's Angel. The inquisitor and her bodyguards, however, seemed indifferent to him. They had dealt with Space Marines before, then. A useful nugget of information that he stored away.

'If you would care to follow me,' he said, 'I will take you to a place where you can warm yourselves. We have arranged refreshments and sustenance for you.' This at least sparked an obvious reaction in the psyker's eyes. 'When you are ready, we can talk.'

'I am ready to talk now, Lord Commander,' said Callis with a brief smile. 'But I would not wish to offend your sensibilities by refusing a gracious offer of hospitality. Please lead on.'

She was charming; there was no better word for it. Argentius had not crossed paths with many inquisitors, but this Callis was certainly different to the bombastic demagogues he had previously encountered. He did not doubt for one second that she was every bit as ruthless as her fellows; she would not have reached the rank that she held if she were weak. But she seemed oddly deferential. Perhaps she had adopted such an approach as her signature style of investigation.

He led the visitors in through the fortress-monastery gate, beneath the huge, vaulting entrance that opened into an enormous courtyard. Here, at ground level, were small dwellings designed for the Chapter's many serfs. The psyker seemed interested in the architecture and frequently pointed out things to the inquisitor in his soft voice. Here he would note the probable age of a curtain wall; there he would observe the style of a turret.

'You will have to forgive Nathaniel, my lord,' said Callis eventually with a small laugh. 'He likes to study, and the Space Marines are a subject open to very few.'

'He must be powerful.' The observation was candid. 'To face the perils of the Ruinous Powers and live so long.' The Chapter Master pitched the words very carefully towards the inquisitor, but it was the psyker who replied.

'I have my uses,' was all he said. Callis shot a silencing glare at him, the bionics in her eye clicking softly. In that one look, Argentius learned all he needed to learn about Liandra Callis. She might appear charming and refined on the surface, but there had been daggers in that stare.

'Nathaniel is one of my best operatives,' she said simply, as though Nathaniel himself were not even there. 'His devotion to the Golden Throne is without question and his skill is guided as much by his powers of observation as by his ability to channel power from the warp. His level of self-control has left me breathless before.' She frowned. 'He does, I'm afraid, have a tendency to open his mouth and speak without giving his brain a chance to intervene.' De Corso chuckled softly at this and picked up the thread seamlessly.

'Nathaniel has proven his worth over and over again. He asked specifically to accompany the inquisitor and myself here on this visit. He is greatly interested in your Prognosticatum, my lord.'

Now we come to it, thought Argentius as they passed through another vaulting archway that led to a vast stone staircase. Following this down would bring them out on the first of the fortress-monastery's many subterranean levels.

'A purely academic interest, my lord,' interjected Nathaniel with a swift smile. 'Nothing more.'

Argentius nodded. He'd not spoken the thought aloud. Strangely, the psyker plucking it from his mind did not bother him in the slightest. Vashiro did the same thing constantly. It did, however, remind him of the Head Prognosticator's words that he should guard his thoughts more carefully.

Three levels beneath the surface was the hall that the Silver Skulls had long since set aside for meeting off-world Imperial personnel. It was a plainly furnished room, with a polished table at its centre surrounded by a number of chairs. It was clear from their size and construction that they were designed for humans rather than Space Marines.

A tray containing refreshments had been left on the table, including a jug of steaming recaff, its bitter scent permeating the air of the room. Argentius indicated the table.

'Please sit,' he said formally. 'Help yourselves. I will fetch my senior council and bring them here to meet with you.' Callis bowed her head politely.

'You do me great honour, Chapter Master.' She indicated to de Corso and Nathaniel that they should get themselves a mug of recaff, which they both did with great enthusiasm. They may have been stoic above ground, but Argentius knew well how the cold of the planet bored into the bones. He noted also that the psyker fetched the inquisitor a drink before he got his own, and the look of pleasure on the pinched, warp-aged face when she thanked him. Argentius was not without his own powers of observation.

'Is it acceptable for me to smoke in here?' The sniper asked the question and waved a packet of lho-sticks around. Argentius turned a thoughtful gaze on the human.

'I have never understood why anybody would indulge in a pastime that polluted their lungs and invariably contributes to their early death,' he replied in the fullness of time, 'but please feel free to kill yourself.'

De Corso put the pack of lho-sticks away, visibly deflated by the Chapter Master's painfully clinical assessment of his vice.

Having so spoken, the Chapter Master left the inquisitorial retinue to their own devices and headed to fetch the rest of his party. Some of the uncertainty that he had known on hearing she was coming down to the planet had fled. If she had been desperate to pin heresy on a young Prognosticator who had done nothing more than what it had taken to deal with a clear and present danger, she would have come straight to the point.

Something else, then. Argentius had moved from cautious to intrigued.

'Are you sure you're comfortable, Chapter Master?'

The inquisitor's voice was filled with polite concern. She and her companions were seated at the long wooden table and the four attending Space Marines stood around them in a neat semicircle.

'Perfectly, inquisitor.'

'If you wished to reconvene in a room that was more suited to warriors of your...' She paused and Argentius had the fleeting impression that she had been going to say 'size'. Instead, she was more diplomatic with her words. '...warriors of your stature, then I would not be insulted.'

'Our comfort is not an issue, inquisitor. Please. Say what you have to say so that we may better understand what we may do to assist you.' Argentius had fought campaigns that had seen him standing on his feet for days, even weeks at a time. Standing in a room with three humans was no hardship.

He had introduced his three companions – Vashiro, Kerelan and the young Nicodemus – and each had said nothing
beyond simple words of formality before lapsing into stern
silence. They stood stock-still, like monochromatic statues. Nathaniel's eyes had lingered for a while on Vashiro
before switching to Nicodemus and it was evident even to
Argentius that the psykers were testing the limits of one
another's latent abilities. Eventually, the sanctioned psyker
seemed satisfied with whatever he had gleaned and leaned
back in his seat.

'As you wish, Chapter Master. I appreciate your desire for
candidness. The fact of the matter is exceptionally simple.
I need your assistance to quash an uprising.' She reached
into an inner pocket of her coat and drew out an exquisitely wrought silvery disc. The carvings on its exterior were
beautiful and she handled it with great care. She twisted it
slightly and set it in a new configuration before placing it
gently down on the table.

'The Valorian system,' she said as a hololithic display flickered into being. The quality was poor at best, but it was
possible to extract information. 'Specifically, this planet.
Valoria Quintus. Fifth planet from the sun and the source
of this information.' The hololith zoomed in on the planet
she described. There was nothing particularly special about
it – it was the same as any number of other blue-green planets that the Silver Skulls had encountered.

'Designation?' Argentius leaned forward and considered
the planet thoughtfully. 'What is its role?'

'Valoria Quintus is mostly industrial,' she replied. 'Terrain and atmospherics are better suited to sprawl-cities than
hives, but there are one or two habitation stacks on its surface. For now, focus your attention on Valoris City here, in

the south. It has always been a difficult zone. The inhabitants are notoriously independent. Fifteen years ago, Valoris was surrendered into the joint care of Governor Anatolus Gryce and his wife, Sinnaria.'

'Joint governorship? Unusual.' The Chapter Master studied the hololith without further comment.

'Yes, my lord. They were both young, but eminently capable. His devotion to the Golden Throne and his deeds in the service of the Imperium marked him as suitable for the position. His wife is a natural diplomat and their leadership has led Valoris out of a state of civil war and into a far more profitable and habitable state. Their rule has gone well...'

'So well that there is another alleged insurrection?' Kerelan had moved forward to study the hololith and interrupted the inquisitor's explanation. 'That does not translate as "well" under my understanding of language, Inquisitor Callis.'

The psyker at the inquisitor's side leaned forward and spoke in a mild tone. 'I would suggest that you learn to hold your tongue, first captain,' said Nathaniel. 'Remember to whom you are speaking.'

Kerelan let out a snort of derision and stepped back again, but did not comment further. Callis smiled slightly and without turning to look at the psyker, pushed him back into his seat. There was such control implicit in the action that it stalled the harsh retort on Argentius's tongue.

'The first captain is right, Nathaniel,' she said. 'Perhaps the truth of the matter is that we extended the governors of this world too much freedom and allowed things to get out of control. Say then, that the fault is ours. It is not an alleged uprising. It *is* an uprising.'

'Explain further.' Argentius had not appreciated the psyker's tone and his impatience told in the clipped response.

'Let me elaborate, if I may,' she replied, and rose gracefully to her feet. She paced the length of the table and every pair of eyes in the room followed her. She stopped at the far end and spoke without turning.

'The Imperium is an administrative nightmare, Chapter Master,' she replied. 'So many planets, so many citizens, so many wars. It is difficult to hold all of the leashes at any one time. Occasionally, something pressing captures the attention of those at a more... senior level.' She turned to look down the length of the table.

'Valoris was prospering,' she said, and her voice was quiet. 'The tithe was regular and reports were satisfactory. Governor Gryce was a superb administrator. Arrogant, certainly, but that was only to be expected. His wife ran the settlement alongside him, an effective behind-the-scenes administrator to his charm and presence. And eyes turned away from them for a while. I suspect they enjoyed the taste of autonomy.' She looked at the Chapter Master. 'You can see where this is going, I'm sure.'

'A few months ago, a representative of the Ecclesiarchy was bound for Valoris Hive.' De Corso picked up the story from the inquisitor with such ease that none of the Adeptus Astartes present had any doubt that they had long rehearsed how they were going to present this information. 'He never arrived. His shuttle was shot down during its descent.'

Kerelan scowled, a fearsome expression on his skull face. 'They murdered a member of the Ecclesiarchy in cold blood? Surely they knew that would provoke a response?'

'Indeed, first captain. Cold blood. The priest and his entourage were lost and the ship that carried them there was told to leave Valoria's orbit. The Gryce administrators appear to have claimed the world for themselves and the people seem all too keen to follow them.'

'Anatolus Gryce was exemplary in every way,' said Callis, picking up the story again. 'His behaviour seems... uncharacteristic. It is the belief of the Inquisition that the Ruinous Powers may have played a hand in this change of attitude. However, we cannot rule out simple sedition.' She laughed without humour. 'Although in my experience, sedition is *never* simple.'

De Corso spoke up again. 'The Siculean Sixth regiment of the Imperial Guard – my former regiment, as it happens – have been fighting and holding key points across Valoria. Here, here and... here.' As he spoke, bright spots glowed on the hololith indicating strategic locations. 'There are several lines of engagement surrounding Valoris City – I say city, a sprawl of factories and hab blocks is all it is, really. They call it the capital, but it has little to offer those outside its environs.' He flicked a button on the hololith and changed the angle. 'They had been managing to keep the worst of the fighting contained.'

'Had been?' Nicodemus spoke for the first time. 'You use the past tense.'

'Indeed I do, my lord. Had been. Things are beginning to escalate beyond the control of the Imperial forces on the planet. The rebels have brought in what can best be described as outside help.'

'Outside help that wears the trappings of traitors,' said Nathaniel in his cool, clipped voice. 'Traitor Space Marines, to be precise.'

Argentius nodded slowly. He found that he was not in the slightest bit surprised to discover the hand of Chaos at the heart of such treachery.

'And this is why you seek our assistance?'

'Yes,' she said, simply. 'And as the Silver Skulls are the closest Adeptus Astartes home world to my destination, I have come to request your aid.'

'Our efforts to contact the Gryces have repeatedly failed,' said de Corso, switching off the hololithic display. 'We have not heard back from them. The time has come to speak to them in person.' He sighed and took out his packet of lho-sticks absently. He prised one free and rolled it between his fingers. 'The walls of Valoris City, dull though it may be, are well guarded and well constructed and as such, are the most well defended. The fighting had been at a stale-mate until the arrival of the traitors.'

Argentius's eyes glittered, betraying nothing of the surge of anger that had bubbled up within him at the mention of the Archenemy. 'And our part in this?'

'Your Chapter have a good reputation, my lord, as noble warriors and siege breakers. You can provide us with the assistance we need to tear down the walls of Valoris City and then provide Valoria with the strength it needs to drive the shadows from the Emperor's shining star. And I am sure you can appreciate that such an action would speak well of your Chapter.' It was more than clear that de Corso felt little fondness for the city.

More interesting was the fleeting look that he had received from the inquisitor at his final words. Driven to a response, Argentius turned the full force of his own not-inconsiderable charisma on the sniper.

'Tell me, Harild de Corso, do you seek to flatter me with your words? Do you think you can buy the services of my Chapter with flowery speeches and promises of greatness? Services that we would give freely under such circumstances?

Because your words suggest that there is something we need to prove in this matter.'

'No, my lord.' De Corso's smile was guileless although it wavered slightly as Argentius moved to stand in front of him. The sniper was a tall man but even so, he still barely came up to the Chapter Master's chest. There was a flicker of uncertainty in his eyes. The sudden shift in the room's tension was subtle but felt by all.

'Forgive Captain de Corso, my lord,' said the inquisitor, rising to her feet. 'He has a pretty mouth, but a child's ignorance of dealing with the Adeptus Astartes. We have turned to you because nobody can deal with Traitor Space Marines as well as the Emperor's Angels.'

'I will commit to nothing without consulting my Prognosticator,' said Argentius, his eyes never leaving de Corso's. It brought a certain satisfaction to the Chapter Master that the man looked as though all his confidence had been sapped from him. 'Vashiro and I will confer on the matter and I will deliver the decision to you in due course.'

'Of course, Chapter Master, but I would beg swiftness. Time is of the essence. I have confidence that you will see reason in this matter.' She gazed up into Argentius's face, a face that had been altered and changed by the countless honour tattoos inked across its implacable canvas. He returned her scrutiny with resolute stoicism, giving away nothing. 'And I am sure that I should have no reason to doubt your loyalty, my lord.'

The meeting disbanded, the human contingent being led away to quarters where they would be able to eat and rest. Although the fortress-monastery was more suited to the lifestyle of the Space Marines, they ensured such provision was always made for regular humans whose constitutions necessitated sleep and sustenance.

'We cannot allow traitors to bring any Imperial world to ruin.' The first comment came from Kerelan and it was the precise response that Argentius had expected his fiery first captain to make. There was a special place in Kerelan's heart reserved for his hatred of those who had fallen to the taint of Chaos. 'If the inquisitor has proof that this planet is in danger of corruption, then it is our duty as loyal servants to assist in any way we can.'

'I agree,' replied Argentius. 'The inquisitor's trust in our Chapter is something we should not lightly set aside. If our presence on Valoria helps to quash a rebellion, then it will be a worthy goal. The opportunity to cut the threads of some of the fallen would be an additional bonus. My instinct is to accompany the inquisitor.' He swung his eyes to Vashiro, who had already taken out his tarot wafers from their soft velvet bag at his waist. 'But instinct counts for nothing if it must stand against the Emperor's will.'

Vashiro was holding one of the elegantly designed cards between his long, slender fingers, his face etched in deep concentration. Nicodemus watched eagerly. This was the first time he had been present during a reading given by Vashiro. The Prognosticator's eyes settled briefly on Nicodemus. The wafer continued to dance between his fingers in occasional flashes. It was a hypnotic motion that none of the others could help but watch. Their collective attentions were riveted on the Prognosticator.

'Tell me, boy. You must have felt the strength of will of that human psyker. What did you think?' Vashiro's question was pitched directly at Nicodemus, a shared moment between two men who were linked by the Emperor's gift.

169

'Startling,' said Nicodemus. He was still feeling pride at being invited to speak openly amongst such great men. He had carefully questioned why he had been chosen and had been rewarded with the ego-boosting comment that he had been given a chance because Vashiro had chosen him. Of course, the comment had been followed with the expected caveat that he was to remain silent unless spoken to, but still. Pride. And he *had* been spoken to.

'I could sense nothing from our visitors beyond surface thoughts. I suspect he was shielding all three of them. He was also... noticeably curious about our practices.' Argentius nodded. That was something he had observed as well.

Vashiro began to move the tarot wafers he had placed on the table with nimble dexterity. 'I would suggest you speak to him of our ways. Of the Prognosticatum and what it stands for. It would not do for people to misunderstand our intentions. You should go and consider the best way to broach the subject.' It was not exactly a dismissal or a command to proceed to such a questioning there and then, but Nicodemus was no fool. He bowed deeply to his three superiors and took his leave. Kerelan and Argentius moved to stand either side of the table, before Vashiro's tarot.

Kerelan's eyes rose to lock with those of the Chapter Master. Both men were warriors born and the desire to simply gather their forces and move en masse to Valoria to cull a threat of such magnitude was strong. But protocol demanded the intervention of the Prognosticator.

Vashiro's fingers reached over and he turned the first of the wafers. Normally he took his readings from the silver runes he favoured. Argentius knew from long association that the tarot was the method Vashiro preferred for more intense decision-making. He didn't understand why. He had still not understood when Vashiro had once tried to explain it. All Argentius knew was that his every action as Chapter Master was led and guided by the Emperor's will.

'A presence of Silver Skulls in the region would both show our loyalty to the Golden Throne and satisfy much of the inquisitor's curiosity,' said Vashiro quietly as he studied the wafer before him. 'It has the additional benefit of crushing the rebellion before it can spread to other systems.'

He turned over more cards, each one flickering into life as he did so, but said nothing. The expression on his heavily tattooed and ageing face was completely inscrutable. Kerelan shifted his weight from one foot to another as he waited. Argentius smiled slightly, willing his first captain to be still.

'In situations where the course of action seems obvious,' Vashiro said eventually, 'there is often a subtle undercurrent of danger. Behind the obvious battle, there is something more at work, something beyond our sight.' He ran a finger along the row of cards. 'Every way I study this layout, the answer is the same. The obvious reason for attending this planet is there. A display of strength, unity and power that will bring...'

He frowned, picked up one of the wafers and shook it gently. It flickered and then the symbol fuzzed back into being. He set the wafer down again. 'It will bring an end to the strife on Valoria, certainly. But this reading is also a warning. That our actions during this campaign will have far further-reaching consequences than we can imagine.'

'In summation?' Argentius was acutely aware of Kerelan's impatience.

'My instinct is as yours, Chapter Master.' Vashiro looked up from his study of the wafers. 'We must answer this

171

insurrection with the forces at our command. But the Emperor's will cautions me that there is a great deal at stake.'

'Consequences must always be expected,' said Kerelan. He didn't profess to understand the ways of the Prognosticator, but his simplistic viewpoint brought a nod from Vashiro.

'Aye, first captain. They must. But they cannot always be predicted. We should end this threat on Valoria.' The Prognosticator's finger tapped another card. 'This speaks of growth, self-awareness and repairing damage that has long caused problems.' He looked up at Argentius. 'An opportunity to forge new bonds, as it were.'

Argentius's lips twitched slightly and he smiled briefly. 'Bonds,' he repeated thoughtfully. 'Yes. A great opportunity to forge bonds. Kerelan, by the grace of the Emperor's will, we will be deploying as soon as we are prepared. I believe that the Talriktug should make the journey with the inquisitor directly as an escort. I will send word to the siege company to set course for Valoria. Take Nicodemus with you. It will give him the opportunity he needs to talk to the human psyker about our Chapter's beliefs.'

'As my lord commands.'

'First captain, it is the further will of the Emperor that you find and take Sergeant Ur'ten and elements of the Eighth. They have lingered overlong on Varsavia and are ready to return to action. I think that all of you will benefit from the experience.'

A universal hush fell. The only sound that could be heard was the gentle rustle of the tarot wafers as Vashiro gathered them up and dropped them back into his waist pouch. Finally, Kerelan spoke, directing his question to Vashiro.

'Permission to speak candidly, my lord?'

'Proceed, first captain.'

Kerelan thought carefully for a moment, putting his words into a sentence that properly conveyed his reaction. 'I have no wish to question your judgement or, with respect, your sense of humour. But I find myself questioning the wisdom of what you are saying. Do you believe that the enforced proximity that space travel brings is a sensible situation to put Djul and Gileas into?'

'It is an excellent situation. It is an opportunity for them to reforge their bonds of brotherhood, first captain,' replied Argentius smoothly. 'Can you think of anything else that Vashiro's words might indicate? If there is any chance that those two are going to mend their ways, it is going to be under the scrutiny of an inquisitor.'

Kerelan bowed his head and stepped backwards. 'Then it shall be as you command, Chapter Master,' he said.

It had not been hard to locate Gileas. During his tenure at the fortress-monastery, he was usually located on the training levels or, as was the case in this instance, the chapel. Kerelan stood quietly at the back of the vast chamber, waiting for the sergeant to complete his murmured prayers. When he finally rose to his feet, he turned his head slightly.

'Thank you for waiting, first captain,' he said. He did not look at Kerelan directly, but remained where he was. 'How may I be of service to you?'

Kerelan crossed the distance between them. It had been a few months since their bout in the training cages and he noted the subtle changes in the sergeant's stance. Gileas was wearing the sleeveless surplice that he usually chose to wear when not training and a new tattoo was evident on his arm. Kerelan's eyes roved across it: a beautifully rendered depiction of the Eighth Company's war banner, with the company's motto, *vincit qui patitur*, inscribed in flowing Gothic script. The new tattoo fully occupied the skin on Gileas's huge bicep. Kerelan noted that the other warrior was running out of free areas for his honour markings, an indication of just how many battle honours he had to his credit.

'Fine work,' commented the first captain, indicating the new tattoo. '"He conquers who endures", correct?'

Gileas gave a curt nod. 'Ignatius is very talented,' he replied.

'The Chapter Master's own tattooist? You are fortunate indeed. He is very selective about whose skin he marks.'

'He considered Captain Meyoran a friend,' replied Gileas. Ignatius was human; one of only a handful whose ability with body art rendered them suitable for induction into the Custodes Cruor, the Chapter's artisans. He had long been Lord Commander Argentius's favourite and rarely worked on other warriors. He was old now, but this did not seem to detract from the quality of his work; it merely meant it took longer. But Kerelan had not come here to admire his handiwork.

'Your squad is being recalled for active duty with immediate effect, sergeant.'

The single sentence brought a genuine smile to the sergeant's lips. 'This is... good news. Is Eighth Company returning for us?'

'In this instance, no. Your squad and the few elements still in residence will accompany mine on a mission to Valoria Quintus. We have been charged in this duty by the Inquisition directly.'

'I had heard that there was an inquisitor present in the fortress-monastery,' said Gileas, demonstrating no reaction at all to the fact that he would be accompanying the first captain. To most, this would be a great honour. Kerelan had expected surprise at the very least. He made a leap of logic that was not too difficult.

'Rumours spread faster in this place than I can comfortably keep up with.'

'Aye.' Again the smile, which flickered briefly and then became serious. Kerelan approved of this new and quiet dignity that Gileas seemed to have found from somewhere. 'I know what your concern will be. But I swear to you that I will strive to keep Brother Djul at a distance. My men will do likewise and you can be assured of nothing but absolute loyalty from them.'

'I do not doubt it, brother. You will retain command of your squad, but obviously overall command of the mission falls to me. Given the actions of the Valorian governors and their turncoats, we have assumed that we may encounter heavy resistance. As you may have heard, the Imperial Guard are already in place. We go to bolster their forces and to break the siege. We deal with what we find in our usual manner. It will be swift, efficient and clean. Locate your men and be ready to leave within the hour.'

Gileas bowed deeply.

'Aye, captain.'

Gileas strode from the chapel, leaving the first captain to his own prayers and litanies. The skull-faced warrior stared up at the statue of the God-Emperor of Mankind. The Father of All was so distant from this place. Only through the skills of the Prognosticators did He ever turn His gaze on His Varsavian children. Only through their divinations was His will brought to their ears.

It was the tenet by which Kerelan had served his entire

life. It was the way things *were*. For the first time he could remember, he tried to visualise how such a belief might be viewed from outside of his Chapter.

I am sure that I should have no reason to doubt your loyalty, my lord. Those had been the inquisitor's words and they had made him uncomfortable. He let his thoughts drift as he embraced the calm of the chapel. His eyes roved over countless silver trophies, many of which he had taken personally. This place was everything that the Silver Skulls were and it brought the same comfort that it always had.

But it did nothing to quiet the seed of doubt that the inquisitor's seemingly innocent words had planted in his mind.

TEN

VALORIA

Valoria Quintus, once the shining jewel of the Valorian system, was a ruined echo of its former self, a broken imitation of all it had once been. No longer a thriving, productive society, it was now a live warzone. The Governor's Palace, a baroque structure dominating the north face of the hive, was the only structure still largely intact and nobody understood why it had not been flattened.

Most of the populace who lived in the four quadrants of the inner city that hugged up to the hive had fled beyond the vast, crumbling curtain walls and tried to find their way to safety. Most had not succeeded. Corpses in varying stages of decomposition littered the once-pristine walkways that radiated from the massive complex.

The insurrection was not being put down on Valoria. The insurrection was alive and kicking.

For seven months now, the Siculean Sixth regiment had been just one of those who had fought against the rebels.

Under Lord Meer's command, they had entered the fray filled with the boundless optimism and certainty of success that marked every campaign they had undertaken. Indeed, at first, it seemed that they were fighting little more than disgruntled citizens. That assessment had swiftly devolved into the realisation that this was something more. Open pockets of resistance flared and were snuffed out to begin with, but then something insidious took hold and spread throughout the populace like a disease.

Disorganised cells of former workers and citizens became units acting with military precision, escalating from terrorist actions to urban guerrilla warfare. The Sixth, versatile and adaptable, altered their tactics in response and for a time, the heavy shelling of artillery fire was replaced by the sounds of multi-lasers and lasrifles echoing through dirty, abandoned streets.

They should not have been as tenacious as they were. The Sixth were fully trained and entirely competent soldiers. They were, after all, the Astra Militarum. More, they were the Siculean Sixth and they were invincible.

Or at least, this was what they liked to remind themselves.

But they had not succeeded in routing the rebels and this did not sit well with Lord Meer. He had dismissed the enemy as a mere rabble that required nothing more than several short, sharp shocks to bring them back in line. But that rabble was becoming increasingly strategically savvy. They tunnelled under the walls to sabotage the Sixth's artillery pieces, to devastating effect. One exploding gun had killed six men. They stole rations and poisoned water supplies until the Sixth had no choice but to post heavy guards around their supply points at all times.

Then the shelling had resumed, pounding what was

left standing outside the walls and leaving little cover to approach. The Sixth replied with focused and relentless airstrikes in an effort to break the siege, and the balance swung back in their favour. The campaign had an end in sight and the Sixth, renewed and replenished with fresh hope, doubled their efforts. They pushed back and they sensed victory.

Then the Traitor Space Marines had arrived, bringing their daemon-fuelled weapons, heavy armour and twisted sorcery to bear. Now the no-man's-land around the walls was littered with the burning hulks of Imperial tanks and the tattered remains of hundreds of soldiers and civilians. The Sixth were bloodied, but they still held firm. They would not abandon their posts. Lord Meer's frequently dictated order was 'until the last man drops' and they upheld that ideal.

The siege of Valoris City saw heavy losses on both sides. The Traitor Space Marines had dug themselves in around the palace and the central hive. They defended vigorously with heavy weapons pillaged from the conquered armouries and abominable warp-spawned creations.

A stalemate was reached. Beyond the reach of Valoris City, in other parts of the besieged world, uprisings dulled to angry, protesting throbs that were easily contained. Within the city's walls, however, untold horrors waited. From the heart of Valoris, the pitted flanks of the hive rose, marred by the endless weapons of war raging around it. Yet still the Governor's Palace remained untouched. It was whispered that the tower was warded by the vile sorcery of the Chaos Space Marines. Whispers became open rumour and rumour began to gnaw at the morale of the besieging and rapidly diminishing force. Soon, not even the fiery rhetoric of Lord Meer and his commissars could dislodge the growing sense of dread that leaked from the city, creeping into every living psyche like a tendril of all-pervading horror.

The unmistakable whistle of an incoming mortar sent the Guardsmen darting to take cover behind the burned-out stumps of rubble in front of them. They were on the outskirts of Valoris City, in a once-beautiful courtyard encircled with temples and Administratum buildings. Now those buildings were reduced to shattered debris, casting eerie shapes amidst the ever-present dust and smoke that filled the air.

The outlying habs and manufactories serving the outskirts of the city had quickly been abandoned by the people who lived there. Some had fled as soon as the insurrection had started, evacuating with the aid of the Imperial Guardsmen early on in the fighting. Many had been killed in the crossfire, attempting to make good their escape in a state of animal panic. The vast majority had joined the side of the rebels, bolstering their numbers. Now little in the way of humanity remained in the blasted streets and highways. Now there were just the ever-present sounds of war. Mortar bombs, distant gunfire and assorted transports screaming overhead formed a background cacophony that had become the norm.

'What I'll never get,' Achen said as he leaned up against a crumbling ruin, 'is why these bastards think they're going to win.'

'Blessed is the mind too small for doubt!' Commissar Gebhard quoted sternly. The black-coated officer paced the ragged firing line, heedless of the beams and solid shot peppering the position, shooting rebels with impunity like an avatar of Imperial zeal. The men kept their heads down as he passed, their attention fully given to the task of visiting divine retribution on those who had dared to turn from the God-Emperor's light.

A shabby figure rushed from hiding across the street, weaving as the Guardsmen attempted to pick it off. The runner made it halfway over the wrecked highway before a las-beam cut it down.

'Nice shot, Gerber,' Achen grunted. 'How many is that now?'

'Are you still counting? I stopped when I hit twenty or so.' It was an old competition, but such habits died hard. It was a standing tradition that whichever one of the squads killed the most enemies received the prize pot, or 'captain's fancy' as it was known. It was a collection of what passed for commodities among the Guardsmen: lho-sticks, drink, dried goods and holo-picts, usually donated by the various squad sergeants.

'Any word yet?' Gerber didn't have to elaborate on who he meant. Achen shook his head.

'Nothing yet. I just hope they manage to convince those Space Marines to come along as well. That'll crush these upstarts quick enough. And ultimately...' Achen dropped his voice rather than allow the commissar to overhear his next words. 'We're screwed if we don't get them on board. Those traitors in the red armour will tear us apart with sorcery before long.'

'I hope they get here soon,' replied Gerber. 'I don't imagine any of the Space Marines will be able to resist coming along to show us how it's done properly.' His chosen words caused both of them to grin broadly. 'For now, though, we have a job to do.'

They sprang back out of cover and resumed firing on the rebels. In this slow and methodical way, they had made small but important progress towards the gates of Valoris

City. The body count was lower than average; the rebels knew the territory and had adopted a loose guerrilla strategy that was slowing the advance. The Imperial Guard had won back a few strategic points, an old munitions depot amongst them. This small victory had brought fresh ammunition – although not a great deal of it – but its beneficial impact on morale was without question.

From some distance behind them, the sound of a Chimera's guns could be heard above the other noises. An answering report of weapons from the well-defended walls of the city sounded immediately. Shells tore through the air above their heads and detonated, sending shrapnel flying in all directions.

It began to rain.

Far removed from the fighting, atop the palace, another warrior stood. A cloak of smoking darkness fluttered around his ancient crimson battleplate in open defiance of the howling wind. Squirming, vile runes and numerous bone and crystal fetishes danced on threads looped around the living golden trim. Wherever the slashing rain touched him it hissed into vapour.

In his own way, he welcomed the foul weather.

He stood with his arms outstretched, embracing the unpredictable forces of nature. He was neither glad nor annoyed that the weather had changed. His attitude was best expressed as indifference. It was the manner in which he greeted most things.

He had lived for thousands of years and he had known much in his time. He had brought countless worlds to ruin and had taken more Imperial lives than he cared to remember in the name of the Great Deceiver. Blessed with the physique and the constitution of the Adeptus Astartes, further gifted with the powerful sorcerous ability that had been so common to those of his singular bloodline and then still further raised above others by the gift of Chaos, he had been charged in this duty by Lord Volkstein.

The champion had been known by many names in his lifetime. Before everything had changed, in the glory days of Prospero's sons, he had been known as Khenti. Then had come the forgotten years. Time had swallowed up much of who he had been. His memories had become shards: faint, distant things that he could never hope to reclaim. He remembered the shining spires of a home world laid to ruin by the hated sons of the Imperium. He remembered a beloved primarch wounded beyond human – or even Adeptus Astartes – comprehension. He had shared in that joined grief since the day Magnus the Red had been shunned by his own father.

Khenti had turned his face away from the Imperium of Man and embraced the new life that had become his. The benefits for his continued loyalty had been many and he had relished them. The rewards had been great and the contrasting costs immeasurable. His conscience had been the first to go. His emotions had not been long in following. He had been cast out along with many of his brothers at the culmination of the great ritual, when so many had been reduced to living husks in the hope of saving them from the flesh curse that had already claimed their brothers. When Volkstein had emerged from the ranks of the new, weakling Chapters he had set about building a new order at the behest of the Great Deceiver.

Or so he had claimed. Whether it was truth or a conceit, Khenti had chosen to join him.

In deference to his cold nature and lack of emotional response to any given stimulus, Volkstein had renamed his trusted lieutenant. He had become Karteitja, 'name thief' or 'taker of names' in Volkstein's own language. So Karteitja had buried the memory of Khenti far down in his thoughts. And now even that was forgotten. He had not removed his horned helm in countless millennia and it was whispered that there was nothing but an unholy, evil darkness behind its cold green lenses. Such rumour served to enhance his reputation and so he did nothing to dispel it.

He stood above the Governor's Palace on a platform that housed the planet's central communications array. For a while, he had indulged a deep-seated desire for satisfaction by looking down on the inspirational sight of a world falling to ruin. The ritual had taken a long time to prepare and he had spent many hours in deep meditation, ready to speak ancient words that would bring the process to its inevitable and glorious end.

The long cables and conduits that ran from the massive antennae at the very tip of the platform were shivering with what could easily be mistaken for the wind that was gusting this high up, battering at his battleplate. But he knew that the shuddering was an indication that his early preparations were bearing fruit. Once he opened up the psychic conduits, the power gathering below would feed directly into the array. The chaos, terror, hatred and confusion boiling through the population was close to fever pitch, the animal fear of an entire world gathering into a handful of sites prepared by the Oracles of Change for his purpose. Their own ignorance would prove to be their undoing. A fitting end, he felt.

Karteitja stood at the very edge of the platform, his arms

still stretched wide. He felt the shape of the winds as they toyed with him, threatening to blow harder at the slightest provocation, and dared them to send him tumbling. If he were to fall from here, he would surely impact on the highest point of the chapel below him, his body impaled forever. His blood would run down the ostentatious edifice, staining it with his disdain, and it would be a glorious thing. But it was still too soon for him. His time had not yet come.

'You would not dare,' he said aloud, a provocation to the unpredictable elements of the sky. His voice was a quiet, bestial growl that released curls of dark vapour to be ripped away by the gale.

And as he knew they would not, the winds did not claim him. He was an immovable figure, clad in the baroque armour of a Terminator that the storm could never have hoped to disturb.

There was a twisting of reality, and a similarly clad warrior stepped from nowhere and instantly dropped to one knee. Karteitja could sense the serpentine hate of the new arrival, like a caged predator thirsting for release. He had no need to turn to identify the other warrior.

'My lord,' said the newcomer.

'Speak, Unborn. We would hear you.'

'My lord.' Cirth Unborn rose to his feet, the show of deference complete. 'Garduul has spoken.' Karteitja turned and studied his fellow Oracle. Although Cirth was his chosen lieutenant, there was no bond between the two. A potent pyromancer, the other warrior hated his commander just as much as his commander disliked and distrusted him. Not for the Oracles of Change the precious commodity of brotherhood. Each of them vied for positions of power. Karteitja knew that Cirth Unborn would never move against him.

The pyromancer was too reticent, too aware of his short-comings to ever challenge for leadership. So instead, he served. But he did not do so eagerly.

The warrior's armour flickered as he moved, a constant wreath of warp flame raging beneath its surface. It glowed and smouldered in shades of crimson and yellow and other colours that were not recognisable on any mortal spectrum. They gave the impression that a creature made of living fire now stepped towards Karteitja.

'What does the First say?'

'The thralls are working to transcribe his latest prophecies. But amidst his raving, the Ancient One spoke something even I recognised. He sees that the False Emperor's pawns are even now journeying towards us.' Cirth wore his helmet but Karteitja could sense the look of cruel delight on the burned and twisted face beneath its protection. 'The Silver Skulls, my lord. They are coming.'

'Of course they are.' Staring down again at the world below, Karteitja turned from the platform's edge. 'We know of them well. The Silver Skulls are slaves to what they perceive as the words of their dead Emperor. They put far too much faith in those charlatans who claim to read the manifold weaves of fate's tapestry. They do not have the true gift. Not like Garduul.' Karteitja folded his arms across his massive chest. 'Work the thralls to death if you must, but we will have Garduul's divination within the hour. This is a vital task, Cirth. Do not disappoint me.'

'I would not dream of it, my lord.' Cirth stepped backwards and disappeared in a gout of flame. Karteitja maintained his stance for a while longer before he too was swallowed by the void.

* * *

Nathaniel Gall, as had been noted by so many of his peers, had a bit of a problem with tact, inasmuch as he possessed none at all. His ability to think about what he was saying before he said it was nonexistent and he frequently blurted out a question without stopping to consider whether it might be appropriate or not.

It was not a trait that Nicodemus found easy to deal with. And forced into continued proximity with the psyker, the young Silver Skulls warrior was wondering exactly what it was he had done to bring down this sentence upon his shoulders.

For the first day, he had been happy to answer Nathaniel's endless questions about the Prognosticatum. Nicodemus had explained how the Silver Skulls were structured: the Chapter Master at the head of the military arm, and Vashiro overseeing the psychic battle-brothers and Chaplains who made up the Prognosticatum.

Those questions had been easy enough to answer and Nicodemus had been open and honest. There was little point in being anything else. He had been primed on many responses by Vashiro prior to departure and until the third day, everything that Nathaniel had asked him had been anticipated.

Then he had asked the one question that had taken Nicodemus completely by surprise.

'Do you believe it? That the Prognosticators genuinely read the skeins of fate? That they read portents and predict the outcome of your engagements? That they divine the Emperor's will? Do you believe it?'

They were blunt words that caused the psyker to fall silent. He might only have been a youth, barely out of his teens, but he suddenly felt the rush of thousands of years of tradition. How *dare* this scrawny human speak to him with such disrespect? Pride rushed to the surface and it took every ounce of self-control not to crush the worm with his bare fists.

'Of course I do,' he replied in due course.

'Mmm,' Nathaniel said. 'I thought you might say that. Haven't you ever thought that a Prognosticator might be misguided? What happens when your Prognosticators get it wrong?'

'I am not the brother to whom you should be address-ing these questions, psyker,' Nicodemus replied, and there was ice in his voice. 'My experience is not as broad as that of my brothers. I am but recently ascended to the ranks.'

'Good point,' said the psyker, completely unfazed by the chill attitude he was receiving. 'I will go and speak with one of the other warriors. To whom do you feel my ques-tions would be best directed?'

It was very tempting to point Nathaniel in Djul's direc-tion. Nicodemus suspected that where he had stayed his hand and not delivered any physical blow to the human, Djul would bodily evict Nathaniel's crushed remains from the ship if he offered such an insult in his presence. The wrath of the Talriktug warrior would be beyond incandes-cent; something undoubtedly magnificent to behold. But Nicodemus still maintained compassion for those weaker than he was. He was only now starting to realise just how many people that encompassed.

For the sake of all of the Silver Skulls, he suggested Nath-aniel speak to Reuben. Of Gileas's squad, he seemed the most level-headed and approachable.

As he watched Nathaniel walk off, a pronounced limp causing him to move slowly down the corridor, Nicodemus felt a flicker of uncertainty. The psyker's questions had been plentiful and he did not think he had said anything that might have painted the Prognosticatum in a bad light, but one comment the outspoken Nathaniel had made echoed in his ears.

What happens when your Prognosticators get it wrong?

Liandra Callis walked the corridors of the *Prevision of Victory* alone. She had long given up any pretence of rest. Sleep was not something that came easily to her, and it had not done for more years than she cared to remember. Her mind was always active and as a consequence there was very little that she missed.

She wandered without any of her companions out of deliberate choice. Her thoughts were manifold and she processed them far better when she was alone. She was confident that no harm could befall her aboard the vessel and she had quite consciously allowed the psyker to carry out his uniquely irritating brand of questioning before she moved in and continued the task. Nathaniel was difficult to handle, but she respected his power and the strength that he displayed. Every day was a struggle for a sanctioned psyker and Nathaniel bore his burden without complaint.

She had grown surprisingly fond of him. She was many years his senior of course, although countless juvenat treatments and augmetics had enabled her to maintain the look of a woman in her early thirties. Her true age was unknown to any but her closest allies and the Inquisition.

Nathaniel knew. But then he had been extraordinary. As had been the coincidence of his sister already being one of those among her retinue. And it *had* been coincidence that had brought them back together, no matter what spin she might have chosen to put on it.

Liandra Callis had something in common with the dour warriors of the Silver Skulls Chapter. She believed that the Emperor's hand reached out and manipulated the course of fate far more frequently than others would believe. But she did not believe that things should happen only on His word. And that was where any harmony turned into discord.

She had shed the long, hooded coat that she typically favoured and reached up to run her fingers through her fair hair, which was beginning to grey at the temples. She chose to wear it cropped practically short for convenience and coupled with the confidence in her stride, there was something close to masculine in her overall manner. Clad in a black, sleeveless bodyglove, she prowled the corridors in silence.

The daughter of a noble house on the distant hive world of Siprix, Callis had demonstrated great articulacy and intelligence from an early age. Her education had been costly and had been worth every penny, or so her father had said.

Her father. He had been one of the first people she had investigated when she had been inducted into the Ordo Hereticus. She had investigated him, found him guilty of importing xenos technology to an underground movement of would-be seditionists and had arranged his execution within fifteen minutes. She had not regretted it. Not openly at least. But she had touched weakness in the wake of her father's death when she had mourned the loss of all he had once been.

Weakness was not something she cared to display but she had learned that demonstrating compassion – if only cosmetically – could encourage people to talk far more freely than if they were intimidated, and torture was such a time-consuming affair. Consequently, her results were sometimes startling in the extreme. This, coupled with the fact that Liandra Callis could be as cold-hearted and cruel as her role demanded at the flick of an internal switch, had ensured her success.

'Are you lost, inquisitor?'

The voice was a deep, sonorous rumble and she stopped, turning round to face the lone Space Marine who stood in the corridor behind her. Her excellent mental faculties immediately pulled his name to mind.

'Not at all, Sergeant Ur'ten,' she replied. 'I couldn't sleep, so I was merely familiarising myself with the layout of your marvellous ship. The Chapter Master did grant me security clearance to go wherever I needed to go.' She spoke the last sentence a little defensively, but the warrior merely nodded.

'As you wish.'

She watched him for a moment. Her prior research and simple powers of observation had listed this warrior as one of those she should investigate more closely. Fate or the Emperor's hand had put him in her path. Opportunities such as this should not be ignored. 'Perhaps you might tell me a little of its history as we walk?'

'I would be glad to.' He gave her a humourless smile and she hid the sudden shock at the sight of his sharpened incisors. That, combined with his choice to wear his hair long, made him seem like something savage, like he was some ancient beast of legend, not the noble warrior of countless battles that her reports had suggested. But Callis had lived long enough and made enough errors of judgement to know full well that first impressions were not always accurate.

'Thank you, my lord.'

He made a grunt of acknowledgement and folded his massive arms across his great barrel chest. Beneath the surplice he wore, she could make out the distorted shape of the fused ribcage. She knew Space Marine biology enough to be aware that beneath its protective shell pulsed both familiar organs and others that were completely unique to the Adeptus Astartes. He was so inhuman, so very different to her.

Of course, Callis was far too well bred to stare at him. She had known many different Adeptus Astartes over the years and they never failed to impress her. What a marvel these creations were, she thought. What a weapon the God-Emperor, beloved by all, gave us when He breathed life into His Angels.

Gileas recounted some of the vessel's noteworthy engagements as they walked together, an odd pairing. Standing not much higher than five feet tall, Callis was dwarfed by the giant at her side. She noted how he maintained a respectful distance between them, but always kept himself a few feet ahead of her. As was the case with all of the warriors aboard the vessel when they were not armoured, he carried only a bolt pistol secured in a holster at his thigh and a combat knife strapped to his shin.

'You fight with the assault company, is that correct?' It was a harmless enough question and Gileas nodded affirmation.

'Aye,' he replied. 'That is usually the case. I am assigned to Eighth Company for the most part.'

'But you are not out with them right now. Why is that?'

The warrior stopped and glanced over his shoulder, his dark eyebrows coming together in a look that was either surprise or displeasure. It was difficult to tell, particularly when his glittering dark blue eyes gave away no emotion at all.

'The Chapter Master ordered it,' he replied. 'And I obey my Lord Commander without question or selfishness of purpose.'

'You would have preferred to be with your own company.' She smiled. 'There is no shame in that, surely, sergeant?'

'None at all,' he replied, this time not hesitating at all. 'Of all the companies in the Chapter, the Eighth has been the one that has allowed me access to the most rewarding battle campaigns. With a jump pack and chainsword, I can find myself at the battle's heart before it even truly starts to beat.'

For a fleeting moment, his face became animate and alive. Callis made a mental note that despite his frankly savage appearance, Gileas Ur'ten was evidently far more than just a weapon. Such knowledge was important.

'You acquit yourself well, or so I have been led to understand. Your superiors speak highly of you.'

The stern facade returned and the moment of simple, open honesty seemed a distant dream. 'Thank you for your words, inquisitor. I have always aimed to be the best that I can be. But I must temper that with the understanding that no matter how strong I may be, no matter how proficient with a blade I become or even how well I develop my skills as a strategist, there is always room for improvement.'

'You strive for perfection?'

'No, because perfection is the domain of the Emperor alone. As I said, I... *we*... simply strive to be the best that we can be. To desire more would render us unworthy of the honour of our station.'

'And that is to be commended,' said the inquisitor, unable to keep the smile from her face.

'I am a son of Varsavia,' Gileas continued. 'And as such, you should know that my duty of care extends to you whilst we travel together. By tradition, the life of a guest is as the life of a brother. Honour demands that I serve the Inquisition as I would serve my Chapter while you are in our charge. Upon my oath, inquisitor.'

If she was startled by this open revelation of such a binding custom, it did not register in her expression. She merely inclined her head respectfully.

The two rounded a corner. They walked together in easy companionship through the ship and she absorbed it all. Idle glances took in far more information than she would admit to. Her ears listened with pleasure to the sounds of the tech-priests speaking arcane words to the ancient machinery they tended.

Gileas quietly and shrewdly pointed out persons of note and continued leading her onwards, beyond the bridge, through to the strategium, the mess area where the serfs ate – she was not surprised to see Curt there, smoking as always – and then in time back to the corridor where they had started.

His manners were impeccable, his courtesy perfect, and his level of eloquence surprised her. She had been led to understand that Gileas had been recruited from a tribe whose methods and lifestyle were cruel and harsh. But the warrior before her was articulate and clearly intelligent and his quiet pride and honesty were pleasing. Every question she asked him was answered without guile and no attempts were made to withhold anything from her. If she had been trying to interrogate him, however, she believed it might well have been difficult in the extreme.

She would have achieved it, of course, but it would have been a challenge.

As he strode away from her to continue with whatever

chore it was that she had disturbed him from, the inquisitor smiled coolly. Gileas Ur'ten was a useful link in the chain. For all his pleasantries and obviously rehearsed stock responses, he had answered one of her seemingly innocuous questions in a manner that he had not even been aware of. She could read body language, even in a post-human warrior. She had seen the look of discomfort on his face, the hesitation in his movement and the careful tone of his voice when he had replied. Despite having spent an hour or so in his company, she had learned everything she needed to within a heartbeat.

'Your faith is strong, Sergeant Ur'ten,' she had said. 'And of course, you honour the words of your Prognosticators like the rest of your Chapter.'

Then had come the telltale moment of uncertainty followed by his response.

'Of course, inquisitor.'

Things had not improved much for the Sixth. While they had tightened the cordon around the walls, the price in blood was rising by the hour. There was little cover from the shelling, and despite the Siculean artillery chewing at the defenders on the crenellated walls, they could not silence the guns beyond. Teams of rebel saboteurs had also been hard at work with mines and improvised explosives and those ruins that still stood often offered sudden death rather than respite.

The situation had been further confounded when the rebels had opened the gates in order to unleash mobs of stimm-crazed slum gangers on the Imperial Guardsmen. Throughout the engagement, the Guard had taken hundreds of rebel lives, but there was something unnerving about ending the life of a youth who was barely out of child-hood. The shots were fired in self-defence, but it brought little comfort to the Imperial Guardsmen who were, after all, only human.

'These are just kids,' Sergeant Cadoros growled during a respite in the attacks. It had followed a fairly predictable pattern so far: the rebels would attack, then scatter at the first sign they were being overwhelmed.

Particulate ferrocrete dust filled the air, the choking cloud all that remained of what had once been a bustling market. The zone had been levelled under the repeated onslaught of the Imperial Guard weapons and support vehicles. The traitors outnumbered the Guardsmen many times over, but lacked any sort of direction. Each gang seemed to oper-ate completely independently of its fellows. It made them ineffective but nigh on impossible to predict and they were tenacious to say the least.

'Ever thought they're leading us into something worse?' One of the Guardsmen nudged a nearby body with the toe of his boot. The corpse rolled over to reveal a girl of perhaps fourteen. She lay with her eyes open, staring into nothing. The scorch marks of a las burn marred her pale skin. The soldier's face set in a stony scowl.

'Stupid girl,' observed Sergeant Cadoros. 'These children have been blinded to the Imperial creed by the words of heresy that have been whispered amongst them. Don't let it get to you. They chose this fate for themselves. Think of their execution as a mercy. Far better they die and earn their redemption through blood, than to live in shame.'

'I think...'

Whatever it was that the soldier was thinking was cut off by the sudden impact of a missile barely feet away from where he stood. The sergeant was thrown off his feet and flung backwards into the side of a largely collapsed building. He righted himself swiftly and brought his weapon to bear.

'Another strike squad,' came the shout. 'And these ones are more prepared!'

'More prepared' turned out to mean the inclusion of several rocket tubes and a tripod-mounted stubber. A second shell screamed across the ruined commercia and detonated amongst a squad, hurling green-armoured bodies into the air.

'Get to cover!' Sergeant Cadoros bellowed. 'Wherever you can find! And get those heavy weapons up front and centre! Move!'

Men had already thrown themselves into the cover of the ruined markets and were returning fire. The snap of las-fire and hollow *thump* of a grenade launcher at work joined the chatter of rebel weapons. The sergeant tapped two of his men on their armoured shoulders and gestured to a row of fire-blackened stalls. The roar of battle concealed the noise as the trio crashed through the brittle frames until they were within sight of the enemy. Six rebels crouched behind a train of overturned carts, two bearing the weight of shoulder-mounted launchers while a third manned a belt-fed cannon. The others tended to bulging packs of missiles and a box of heavy brass shells.

Cadoros nodded to Veit, who nudged forward with the muzzle of his flamer. A moment later the gunner and his companion vanished in a torrent of hungry chemical fire. They didn't scream for long and Cadoros was already striding over their ruined bodies as the stunned survivors turned to meet their attackers.

'In His name!' the sergeant roared. He shot the closest

man through the throat and bisected the girl who had been loading for him with a savage swipe of his power sword. The other two fell with holes drilled neatly through their spines as they turned to run, his troopers finishing the slaughter in as many seconds.

There was no time to enjoy their victory. The very ground beneath their feet began to tremble and shake with the tread of heavy armoured feet and they found themselves facing a new enemy, one they had known was within the walls, but one which thus far had remained faceless.

There were eight of them, clad in armour the red of old, soured wine or dried blood, with details picked out in gold filigree that had once been splendid and beautiful but which was now tarnished and chipped. The gigantic warriors spread out into a line and halted, so still that they might as well have been statues. Sentinels of Valoris City, placed to prevent the ingress of intruders. They radiated a palpable aura of dread that froze the blood and knotted the guts, a sense of wrongness that clawed at the sane mind with ephemeral talons. Some of the younger troopers scrambled away in terror, falling over themselves in an effort to escape the monstrosities, while the weaker-willed simply fell where they stood, gibbering nonsense and clawing at their eyes. There was a deep rumble from the eight warriors as they spoke ancient, arcane words that crackled visibly before them and made mortal flesh crawl.

'Open fire!' Sergeant Cadoros would not allow his men to run from the sight, despite every nerve-ending in his body urging him to flee as fast and as far away as he could. The veterans began to fall back, snapping shots off at the hulking forms but to little effect. Those beams that found their mark slid harmlessly from the ancient battleplate.

The eight voices soared. It was not a choral sound, but the voices remained in perfect beat and eerie harmony. There was a certain cadence to their voices that dripped with a power all of its own. The unfortunate Sergeant Cadoros and his company were incinerated from within as their bones ignited, the coruscating warp fire reducing them to screaming, blackened scarecrows in a matter of seconds.

They were still several hours from their destination, but the Silver Skulls were already fully armoured. Most of them had resumed maintenance on their weapons, ensuring that the teeth of chainswords were sharp and the mechanisms anointed appropriately. The lower decks of the transport vessel were filled with the noise of battle preparation and it stirred the blood of everyone present. Chapter-serfs moved with greater purpose. The Silver Skulls themselves seemed to come alive, no longer merely cargo.

Inquisitor Callis called a meeting and Kerelan and Gileas attended her in the ship's strategium. As they made their way in, both fully battle-ready and armoured, she stared coolly over at them, her eyes as hard as granite. Callis nodded to Nathaniel, wasting no time. 'Deliver the report.'

'Yes, inquisitor.' The psyker looked around the small gathering and spoke quietly. 'Your ship's astropath received this transmission barely an hour ago. It has taken a little deciphering as the data has been badly corrupted on its way to us, but we have extracted its essence.' He tapped the data-slate in his hand. 'The Archenemy forces reported to be in residence in Valoris City have revealed themselves and have employed sorcery against the forces of the Imperial Guard. The battle is being lost.'

'There is more,' said Callis, and for the first time she did not immediately raise her head to meet the direct gaze of the Space Marines. 'There were reports of Chaos activity on the world. Specifically, of involvement from the planet's governorship. These rumours were under investigation when the rebellion started.' She looked up then, from Kerelan to Gileas and back again. 'We need to recover the governors and we need to subject them to a full Inquisitorial review.'

'Is there any reason why you left this important detail out of your initial briefing?'

'I am an inquisitor,' replied Callis. 'There are some things that I am required to hold close to my chest. My reasons are my own. What matters is that you know now.'

Kerelan snorted imperiously, turning to the sergeant. 'We should consider options,' he observed. 'Inquisitor – perhaps you should remain here on board the *Prevision of Victory* whilst we deal with this situation. Once we have the threat contained and have located the governors, *then* you can join us on the surface and commence conducting your investigations.'

I do not want you there was the unspoken subtext, and this time she didn't hesitate to square her shoulders.

'I will be coming with you,' she replied and there was a diamond edge to her words. 'Proceed, Nathaniel.'

The psyker nodded and continued with his report. He had to let out the breath he had been unaware he was holding whilst Callis fought a battle of wills with a Space Marine.

'Order must be restored to the city. If the governors have fallen to Chaos, or if they are dead, then the investigations will be long and arduous. As governor primus, Anatolus Gryce is our preliminary target. Failing that, his wife will do. Of course, it could well be that either or both of them are dead, in which case politically speaking, the planet is…'

'Nathaniel!' The inquisitor snapped the psyker's name and the man looked deeply wounded but curtailed his lengthy history lesson. 'If it transpires that the governor is dead – deemed highly likely from our predictions – then we must hope that we find Sinnaria alive to answer for the crimes they have allegedly committed. If we do not get this sorted quickly, the planet will fall. If it does not fall to Chaos, it will fall to civil strife.'

Kerelan scratched at his tattooed face. 'Your dedication to duty is highly commendable, inquisitor. But I do not wish to willingly deliver you into the heart of a pitched battle. To do so is anathema to my very service to the Golden Throne.'

She didn't flinch from his stern gaze and eventually he nodded. 'Very well. A compromise, then. You will deploy with the siege company here.' He jabbed a finger at the plans he had unrolled in front of him, a shaky and distorted printed image of a topographical study of the planet. 'The Siculean Sixth have set up a forward supply point and that is where we will leave you.'

She nodded. 'This is all acceptable. So far.'

Kerelan looked up and Gileas noted the irritation on the first captain's face at being interrupted in mid-flow. 'Sergeant Ur'ten. You and the members of the Eighth will continue on in the Thunderhawks and assault the city walls from the most appropriate angle…' He didn't finish the sentence, looking over at the sergeant who grinned.

'From the rebel angle, I presume, first captain.'

'Excellent understanding, sergeant. Exactly so. You will deploy along the walls and you will wrest control back.

The siege company are landing ahead of us so should be on the ground by the time we arrive. Once the fighting is quelled, then we can find the governors.'

'Yes, brother-captain.' Gileas looked ready to begin his assault right there and then. There was an eagerness and energy to him that was infectious and Kerelan felt a moment's sympathy for the warrior who had been cooped up in the fortress-monastery for the better part of a year. Gileas was a true fighter.

'Is this an appropriate plan, Inquisitor Callis?' The woman smiled slightly and nodded her affirmation. Kerelan straightened. 'Then we attack within the half-hour. Look to your wargear, brothers, and may the Emperor be with us.'

'I wondered how long it would be before you actually came to see me.'

Kerelan stood before the doorway to the small room that had served as Bhehan's quarters for the duration of the trip. The young Prognosticator had kept himself secluded and isolated from his brothers since he had returned from Lyria with the Talriktug.

'You are my squad Prognosticator, Bhehan. Of course I would come to see you.' Kerelan did not enter the cell, waiting to be invited. After a few moments, Bhehan raised a hand and beckoned the first captain in.

'That human psyker who travels with the inquisitor,' said the youth. 'His power is considerable. He has been letting tendrils of power drift around this ship and has been taking surface thoughts from those who are not prepared for it. An intrusion, first captain, that I am sure you will agree is unacceptable. Nicodemus has been keeping him occupied for the most part. I have avoided him.'

'*None* of us have anything to hide.' Bhehan winced slightly and Kerelan growled. 'Enough of this now. You have had time to wallow in self-pity. You came out of the encounter with the eldar unscathed. Discard this pointless melancholy and renew your faith in the fires of battle once more. I require that you perform your duty for the Chapter. Are you capable of doing so?'

Bhehan raised his head to stare at Kerelan and his eyes hardened. 'I already have done, first captain,' he responded, indicating the runes that lay spread out on the table before him. 'Take a seat and I will go through it with you.'

His response took the irritation straight out of Kerelan's attack, but he offered no apology – and Bhehan expected none. The first captain's annoyance was justified. The Prognosticator knew that he had lingered far too long on what he had experienced.

Bhehan forcibly pulled himself from his melancholy and turned instead to the layout of runes on the table. Every stone was exquisitely worked in silver-plated steel and each rune was an individual ancient Varsavian symbol.

Usually, Bhehan would cast the stones and divine meaning and gather portents from the manner in which they fell. But as he had the time, he had gone for a full reading of ten runes which he had laid out before him. Their patterns were as clear and familiar as anything he had ever known.

'Strength will prevail,' he began, tracing a finger across the first rune to the next. 'Yet during the course of this mission, we will arrive at a crucial juncture. Courage. Devotion. Although devotion…' He studied the fourth rune. 'Is inverted. A possible weakness. This is not a good rune.'

'Weakness? Ours?'

'I cannot say.' Bhehan continued. 'This rune symbolises

Sarah Cawkwell

the virtue of patience. These five stones together essentially represent the factors of the past that influence our future.'

'Strength, courage, devotion, patience…' repeated Kerelan.

'And change. Beware of the weak link in the chain is my advice here.' Bhehan tapped the second rune before sweeping the five of them aside. 'These others will give me a look at the present and, critically, the future as well.'

'Good,' said Kerelan. 'This is good so far. Although I am not sure exactly where this "weak link" you speak of may rest.'

'Really, first captain?' Incredulity filtered into the Prognosticator's tone.

'Please continue.'

Bhehan smiled briefly and turned his attention back to the runes. 'This rune here… this denotes future influences. In most Varsavian readings, this symbol is one of happiness, contentment. But the runes are never so straightforward. Taking into account all that I have looked at so far, this suggests that there is a price to this mission.'

'A price? In lives?'

'Unsure. The next rune applies specifically to me, the reader of the skeins of fate, and is for me and me alone.' The rune warned against the sin of pride; the focus upon the self to the exclusion of others. He bore its warning in mind as he moved on to the next rune.

'Factors in our surroundings,' he said and here, his brow furrowed. 'Like the runes of the past, change features heavily in this reading, but I am at a loss to fully understand it.'

'Are you able to divine the Emperor's will from these runes or not, Prognosticator? What is your decision?' Kerelan's impatience was rewarded with a cool stare.

'This blank rune… the ninth… it suggests that one of

the key outcomes of this encounter will be something that changes our perceptions. It symbolises a fresh start. New beginnings. And this final rune…'

'I know that symbol.'

'You do?'

'Yes.' Kerelan's face was sombre. 'Death.'

'Do not take it too literally, first captain. This does not necessarily mean death as in the absence of life. It can indicate the end of something and the start of something else. It would tie everything else I have read in the runes together neatly. I predict success in this mission.' He dropped the runes back into his pouch. 'The fates and portents are positive. We should employ caution of course, and we should…'

He hesitated. The next had not figured in his reading, but it was something he felt strongly. 'We should be wary of the inquisitor and her companions.'

'Then the Emperor's will and I agree on something,' responded Kerelan. 'I thank you for this reading, Bhehan. You should prepare yourself for the battle to come.'

ELEVEN

SIEGE

In the wake of the attack from the Chaos sorcerers that had seen all of Sergeant Cadoros and his detachment vaporised, things had fallen ominously quiet. The Guardsmen had been forced to pull back from the gates of Valoris City where even now the eight sorcerers remained standing, blades raised across their chests.

Until now, the Astra Militarum had been in nominal control of the ruins outside the walls. With the arrival of the sorcerers, the balance of power had shifted. Now forced into retreat, the Guard were becoming painfully aware of just how tenuous that control had actually been. In the wake of the rain which had blighted the day, the sky above them was leaden and sour with a peculiar yellowish tinge to the cloud that most associated with the prelude to snow. It seemed unlikely given the uncomfortable heat and humidity that lingered here. But it was that sort of sullen, heavy light that never grew any brighter. Dust particles hung in the air, choking and cloying and making the simple act of breathing a chore. The remaining Guardsmen were wearing rebreather masks and still found it uncomfortable.

The soldiers huddled in groups in whatever cover they could find. The constant pounding of the heavy guns as they attempted to pick the enemy off the walls was answered by the scream of missiles that were launched back at them. The enemy matched their firepower and was dug in behind a fortified position. It made any kind of advance suicidal even without the ominous threat of the sorcerers.

Sergeant Bernd surveyed his immediate surroundings. They had found shelter to the east of the main gate in what had once been a public park, a rare concession to aesthetics and greenery on the grey industrial world. There were the remains of synthetic flower beds, home to simulacra of rare species of plant. Most of them had been trampled into extinction during the fighting and the flagstones of the plaza were cracked and stained with the blood of both sides.

Bernd took off his helmet and ran his fingers through his damp hair. His own unit was still mostly intact, a fact for which he felt grateful. But their morale was beginning to flag. They had witnessed the destruction of their fellows and had suffered the residual effects of the fear that had come with observing sorcery in practice. It had taken every threat and promise he knew to ensure that his men did not run.

Colonel Oswin walked across the broken courtyard to his sergeant and patted the younger man awkwardly on the back. 'Have faith, sergeant. The Emperor will provide.'

Bernd bit back his sarcastic response. Oswin was merely attempting to do what he could to raise the squad's morale but the sergeant feared that it was now so low that nothing short of a miracle would lift their spirits.

The comms officer with his equipment in tow was kneeling apart from the rest of the cluster of men. His brow was deeply furrowed in concentration as he strove to extract a message from the static that he had largely met so far. The storm that was gathering on the distant horizon was having an adverse effect on his equipment, despite the proximity of the array within the city.

As he listened carefully, a change came upon his expression. A slow smile crept over his face, brightening his tired eyes, and he leaped up to race across to the officers.

'Ships in orbit, sir,' he said, snapping off a smart salute. 'News from Inquisitor Liandra Callis is that reinforcements are on their way. Two Space Marine strike cruisers. They're coming, sir! They're actually coming!' The young man was caught up in the thrill of the news, but none of his enthusiasm brought as much as a smile to Bernd's lips. He fixed the comms officer with a stony glare.

'And when exactly can we expect to be reprieved? An hour? Two? A day? Some of the men have been holding the line for nearly a week. They're all worn down into the ground. Not that they won't put up their best fight.' He added the last even though he didn't need to.

'Have faith, sergeant,' the grizzled colonel said again. 'Whilst we let the Space Marines break through the walls and storm the Governor's Palace, we can simply advance in their wake and mop up any rebels that they leave behind. Although I have to say...' He surveyed the carnage. 'Death's too good for most of them. For now though, we hold our position.' He stared up at the tower rising from the heart of the city. It was an impressive edifice of crenellated, blocky architecture, bristling with aerials and pitted with erosion. 'But hopefully not for too long.'

'This is worse than I could have imagined.'

The tone of the inquisitor's voice was not defeat, not exactly. But there was a strange mix of anger and sorrow that Kerelan had not expected to hear from the strong woman. They were gathered once again in the strategium, studying the pict-feeds being transmitted up from the planet below. Reception was poor at best, the images distorted and fragmented, making them difficult to discern. But the level of destruction was very plain.

Kerelan had received contact from Siege Captain Daviks that his company had just landed and should be deployed within what the stoic captain referred to as a short time. Kerelan had known Daviks for many years. 'A short time' could be anything from a few hours to a few days. He knew better than to press the matter and had trusted to Daviks's good sense to get them into position as swiftly as possible.

'We should not deploy until Captain Daviks and his siege teams are ready,' the first captain said, watching one feed that was on a repeat loop. He watched over and over as artillery shells impacted the ground a few short metres away from the observer. 'How recent are these images?'

The inquisitor examined the data-slate she held in her hands. 'Perhaps six hours,' she replied. 'The most recent of them, at least. Some are older.'

'A lot can change in six hours,' said Curt Helbron. The bounty hunter folded his arms across his barrel chest and glared at the screens as though simply staring at them could somehow make them not real. 'We have to trust that the regiment has kept its nerve and has not broken.'

'They will not break,' said the inquisitor, turning to the grizzled man. 'They are better than that. They will die, Curt, but they will not break. The commissars would never allow that to happen and well you know it. So mind your tongue.'

It was rare for the inquisitor to speak in such a manner to her retinue. She paused a moment or two to allow her words to sink in and then tapped the data-slate again. She called up another pict-feed and set it to playing, neatly breaking the moment of tension that had formed in the wake of her anger. 'I thought this one would be of particular interest to our Silver Skulls allies.'

An image fuzzed into being. Eight massive figures clad in abused and violated armour that had once been theirs by divine right. A low, rumbling growl started deep in Kerelan's chest and he forced himself immediately to calmness. The quality of the recording was so poor that he could not hope to make out any sort of markings or livery on the armour of the Traitor Space Marines. But when the blaze of fire snuffed out the life of the Guardsman who had been filming, he at least knew what they were up against.

Around the table, reactions were varied in terms of how the horror and revulsion were demonstrated, but the basic feeling was most certainly shared. Kerelan shook his head in disgust. Djul spoke words condemning the traitors to the darkest depths of eternal damnation. Curt Helbron simply stared at the spot where the image had flickered, his face saying far more than he could hope to ever give voice to. Then a single word shattered the stunned silence.

'Sorcery.'

Isara Gall's voice was fluting and hypnotic if she was given rein to speak for long enough. Right now, after sighting the atrocities on the feed before her, that voice was tinged with disgust and horror. She wiped her hands down the flak vest that had replaced her gown as though she could somehow divest herself of the taint of what she had seen. Her long hair fell down her back in a neat tail but now she reached up to toy with it, a nervous gesture that did not go unnoticed.

Kerelan swung his eyes to consider her. Nathaniel had not attended the gathering this morning on the inquisitor's orders and this was the first time Kerelan had properly had occasion to meet Isara. He had certainly seen her around the vessel, stalking along with haughty indifference as though she had spent her life surrounded by the Adeptus Astartes. He had not bought it for one second. Kerelan had long ago determined that any mortal with that air of arrogance was hiding something. He suspected now that he knew what it was.

Bhehan and the other psykers on board the ship had stayed well clear of her, finding her presence deeply disturbing. There had been several arguments about why she had been allowed to travel with them at all.

'As you say. Sorcery.' Kerelan nodded in agreement with Isara's assessment. 'We have our battle-psykers and Bhehan assures me they are capable of countering these abominations well enough. But your talents may be essential in the event of a daemonic incursion. Against the infernal creatures of the warp, any advantage we have will be invaluable.'

'My talents, as you describe them, First Captain Kerelan, are at your disposal of course,' she said. 'However, I take my orders from Inquisitor Callis and nobody else.' The inquisitor looked gratified at this assertion of her authority, but put out a hand to touch Isara's arm.

'In the matter of Valoris City,' she said, 'you will also answer to First Captain Kerelan.'

'As you wish,' Isara replied in a neutral tone.

'First captain?' A voice crackled across the vox-bead in Kerelan's ear and he turned away from the gathering to receive the message. 'Captain Daviks and Ninth Company have just deployed the last of the armoured elements.'

'Not before time,' said the first captain grimly. 'Transmit all the information we have to him and set up a dedicated vox-feed. We will get this situation dealt with as swiftly as we can.'

'You place great faith in your siege captain,' Helbron observed. Kerelan's bright eyes, sparkling jewels of intelligence in the skull-tattooed face, considered the scarred warrior.

'That, bounty hunter,' he said, 'is because I have seen him at work. It is said amongst my Chapter that there is not a wall standing that could not be demolished by Daviks and his company. Not a building erected that he could not just as easily dismantle. If anybody can break this siege, it is him. Captain Eddan Bourne once said "show me a fortress and I'll show you a ruin". It is an adage by which Daviks lives his life. If it can be broken, he will break it.'

Kerelan's smile was grim.

'Trust me on that.'

The order to halt the advance was gratefully received along the entire front, but the enemy within the city were not content to let the Guard simply wait it out. After three hours of awkward silence Colonel Oswin had been recalled from the front to give a direct appraisal of the situation to Lord Commander Meer, a summons that no soldier envied. The old warhorse at the head of the regiment was regarded with a peculiar mixture of reverence and fear among the men, a scarred embodiment of the Emperor's wrath and retribution. Then the shells had begun to fall again and another squad had been obliterated in the storm of fire, the ruin in which they had been sheltering shattered by the high-explosive barrage. One young soldier had survived, dragging his mangled body from the rubble, and had lain gasping and bleeding in the ceaseless rain.

Had a commissar not been on hand to deliver him the Emperor's mercy, he would have died a slow, lingering death over the next few hours as he bled out onto the cold ground. He had been spared that indignity via the swift and efficient method of a gunshot to the head. The incident had done nothing to improve the mood of the regiment as they sought cover among the shell holes and rubble.

When the first howls of tortured atmospherics split the gloomy skies, the Imperial Guardsmen merely took it to signal the coming of another aerial assault from their enemy and prepared to defend themselves. Within minutes however, the first of the steel-grey drop pods burst through the cloud layer, their superheated structures flash-boiling the ambient moisture and lending them fuming, incandescent comet-tails.

For the Imperial Guardsmen, it was the most welcome sight they had encountered in months. A cheer of relief swept through the beleaguered soldiers and even the stern-faced commissars permitted themselves a rare smile. The arrival of the Silver Skulls had energised the troops more than the deadliest threats or direst invective ever could.

'Raise command on the vox,' ordered Sergeant Bernd to the comms officer, who nodded vigorously. He had already sent out a repeating locator signal so that the newly arrived Adeptus Astartes could home in on their frequency. It was only minutes before a gruff voice came across the vox, but to the comms officer, it was even longer than the hours-long wait for their arrival.

'This is Siege Captain Rasheke Daviks of the Silver Skulls Ninth Company,' the Space Marine said. There was a metallic grate to it, the amplification module of his armour's helm distorting his voice into something less – or more – than human. 'Clear a path. We need room to work. And send me your commanding officers with all haste. Further reinforcements are on their way. I will be on your position in five minutes.'

In the wake of his words, the Imperial Guardsmen sprang into action as though they had been granted a new lease of life on the back of the single order. They moved seamlessly from bitter weariness to energised efficiency and prepared to withdraw from the south-west quadrant. The higher-ranked officers moved together and prepared to brief the siege captain on the situation.

More drop pods appeared in the sky, each signalling another injection of fresh hope. Most fell to earth behind Imperial lines, disgorging silver-clad giants bearing heavy weapons, tracked cannon units and the armoured bulk of Dreadnoughts. Gunfire opened from behind the walls of the Governor's Palace, attempting to pick off the Silver Skulls as they descended, and the air was swiftly filled with razoring lines of heavy bolter and missile fire.

One of the drop pods took a direct hit from a missile launcher and careened out of control, disappearing from view as it struck down beyond the line of sight of the city. There was the distant, muffled sound of an explosion and a collective groan went up from the Guardsmen.

'Gunships!' One of the soldiers was pointing upwards, her

eyes wide with renewed hope at the sight of three Thunderhawks flying in formation from the east side of the city towards them. The scream of their engines cut the air, bursting the few remaining windows and shaking the bones of the soldiers below with their sonic backwash. One of the three craft peeled off from the formation and rose in a graceful arc to circle around again. There was a clatter of autoloaders as cannons cycled up to speed and then the pilot opened fire on the main gate of the Governor's Palace, strafing the defences with a torrent of explosive shells.

The day had faded to little more than a bloody stain on the horizon, the fitful rain washing the colours from the sky. What little light remained reflected dully off the brushed steel of the drop-ship's hull, the strobing flare of its weapons throwing jerky silhouettes across its flanks. The pilot guided the craft with unmatched expertise, sweeping sections of the walls clear as the cavernous maw of the rear hatchway slowly began to open.

Moments later six Silver Skulls leapt from the ramp, their flaring jump packs bearing them easily through the darkening skies like avenging angels. Each giant in descent cast an ominous shadow over the ramparts and the waiting defenders.

The warriors dispersed as they fell, each plunging with intent towards the mounted wall guns. There were eight such weapons flanking the gates, hastily erected tripods bearing an array of assault cannons and heavy bolters. The rebel soldiers surviving after the Thunderhawk's initial barrage tried desperately to bring the weapons to bear on the approaching targets, but they had been placed to defend against foes from beyond the walls, not from above. The desultory bursts of fire that reached for the plummeting

Silver Skulls went wide of their mark or sparked harmlessly from their power armour. The Assault Marines wove deftly through what little resistance could be mustered with precise twitches of their descent jets as they prepared to bring death from above.

Gileas was the first to touch down on the wall, the impact cracking the plascrete beneath his armoured boots. His chainsword was already unsheathed and roaring as he landed. Three rebels who had been attempting to reload an assault cannon were decapitated before they could even draw breath to scream their resistance. The chainsword tore through their necks like a scythe through stalks of wheat and the severed heads plunged into the courtyard below, trailing fountains of gore. Their broken bodies swiftly followed as Gileas pushed ahead, tearing the cannon from its mount and pitching it over the edge.

From his new vantage point, Gileas took in the scene behind the fiercely contested outer gate. A broad avenue, what might once have been an arterial highway or parade plaza, was crawling with rebel soldiers. Seeing the Space Marines on the outer walls, they immediately rushed to the crude earthworks that pockmarked the area and began feeding belts of ammunition into a second rank of heavy weapons. A hail of shells began chewing up the wall around the six giants systematically butchering their way across the defences.

Gileas turned his attention to the nearest guns, a pair of high-calibre stubbers that were raining bullets on his position. He snatched a pair of grenades from his belt and primed them with a short fuse before tossing them into the shallow trenches. There was a chorus of screams a heartbeat before the explosives detonated, filling the earthworks with lethal shrapnel and throwing mud and pulverised flesh into the air.

'Threat neutralised,' the sergeant reported across the squad vox. He fired his jump pack again and bounded with graceful ease across the length of the wall to the next weapon team. Some of the rebels, terrified at what they had just witnessed, had already flung themselves from their positions. The distance was too great to survive without injury and they now lay with broken limbs in the courtyard below, adding their screams of pain to those already filling the air.

All along the wall, the assault squad duplicated the ferocity of their sergeant, slaughtering the enemy with singular purpose. Nicodemus, who had strapped into a jump pack for the deployment, had joined them and was, Gileas noted with the watchful eye of a veteran, hesitating. Knowing Nicodemus's talent, the sergeant understood precisely what the boy's thought process was and he took control of the situation with consummate ease.

'Brother Nicodemus,' he said into the vox as his chainsword tore yet another gun from its mountings and cut short the lives of two more rebels. 'In Eighth Company, we are proud that ours is the discipline of the blade. When you are under my command it will be your discipline also unless you are otherwise ordered. Hold back your psychic abilities until the situation demands them.'

'But brother-sergeant…' There was an air of smug confidence in Nicodemus's voice and it briefly sent a chill through Gileas. Such arrogance was the kind of attitude that had been the death of more than one initiate and in the case of Nicodemus, had already been instrumental in the death of a fellow acolyte during training.

'You will *not* question my orders, Nicodemus. This is blade-work. You will do as you are told. Are we clear?'

'But I…'

'Do it!' Gileas bellowed the last with such force that the two syllables drew a squeal of interference from the vox. He had moved further along the wall and was now level with the gate.

'Brother-Sergeant Ur'ten, this is Siege Captain Daviks. Report on your situation. Perhaps a little less loudly if you please.'

Gileas glanced around, assessing the damage. His battle-brothers were fighting fiercely and five of the wall guns were now smoking ruins, with three remaining: the one that Nicodemus was finally attacking with his force axe, and two between him and Jalonis.

'The emplacements are on the point of incapacitation and the gate is our next objective. Second and fifth squads have deployed at their objectives and are moving to clear the walls as expected. You focus on removing those sorcerers before they turn their attention on us.'

'I am well aware of *my* objectives, sergeant,' came the curt reply. 'Devastator squad Obsidian is moving in with supporting elements to engage them now. Daviks out.'

Gileas turned his attention back to his own task as more of the rebels, fearful of their corrupt masters, poured from the gatehouse. The sergeant smiled grimly beneath his helmet and raised his chainsword in salute.

The eight sorcerers had made no attempt to counter the warriors on the walls, leaving such work to their human minions. But they were no longer standing motionless as the Silver Skulls began their approach. Several Devastator teams armed with bolters and heavy weapons and lead by Siege Captain Daviks advanced on the red-armoured traitors. In their midst walked Isara Gall, tall and slender as a reed, carrying herself with arrogant pride – and it was all forced. False. Her stance effectively hid the creeping anxiety that flowed through her. Even the simple act of placing one foot in front of the other seemed much harder than it usually was. But she fought down the fear. It was what she must do.

Curt prowled at her side, his face hidden behind a featureless, armoured visor. He wore a suit of heavy black carapace plate and cradled a bulky meltagun, though a pair of pistols hung at his hips and a shotgun sat strapped across his back. The bounty hunter believed in being prepared and in his line of work being prepared meant being able to kill something at a moment's notice.

One of the eight Oracles moved forward away from his group and raised a hand to the skies. Purple lightning danced from his fingers as he seemingly drew it out of the very air. Behind him, his companions mirrored the movement until the sky above them fizzed and crackled with warp-tainted energy.

The sorcerers unleashed their attack as one, hurling a jagged spear of coruscating power at the Silver Skulls, who continued their advance, unwavering in their resolve as the sorcerous blast withered away several metres from their position. A few sparks rippled around the silver armour, grounding into the earth at their feet.

And still they pressed forward.

At the front of the squad, two of the warriors raised heavy bolters, training them on the sorcerers. With a scream of fury, the octet unleashed a second powerful bolt which caused no more damage than the first. They took several steps back as the realisation of what the Space Marines must have in their midst became apparent.

'Get me closer to them,' said Isara imperiously as aetheric sparks danced in the charged air. 'Get me close enough so that they can see me, know me for what I am.' The words held only the tiniest tremor, all that remained of her earlier terror. She had passed through the fear and clung onto the reassurance and satisfaction that her power brought her. People admired her and respected her. That was something to hold on to, shallow though it might be. And so she held on.

Curt advanced silently, his devastating weapon ready to destroy anything that strayed too close to his charge. The inquisitor had forbidden Isara from approaching the walls without a bodyguard, and since the Space Marines had objectives of their own the duty had fallen to the bounty hunter. The irony of having a bodyguard when surrounded by the Emperor's finest was not wasted on Isara.

The Devastators moved several more paces forward and at the sergeant's barked command altered their formation so that the pair had a clear view of the sorcerers and vice versa. Slowly, Isara let her lips part over her teeth in a predatory smile.

Her presence and the instant understanding of what she was had an immediate effect amongst the Oracles of Change. They threw aside all attempts at further arcane attacks and resorted to more direct means. Four of them drew weapons that were slung across their backs and the others unclamped boltguns.

The pause between Isara's exposure and the sorcerers' switch to conventional modes of assault was minuscule.

221

The Oracles aimed, but it was not quick enough. The pair of heavy bolters carried by the Devastators burst forth with stuttering fire.

Instinctively, the Oracles threw up a kinetic shield, their arts warding them from harm. The bubble of force was stippled with hundreds of small explosions as the torrent of shells poured over its surface. Isara was close, but not close enough that she could entirely blank their abilities. Unmasked faces rising from suits of crimson power armour were contorted with dark rage and the grim understanding that their warp-fuelled magic could very swiftly be undone.

Isara flinched at the thunderous roar of the heavy weapons. Auto-senses worked into a headband automatically compensated for her hearing, but the noise was still painfully loud. Without such protection, the experience would have ruptured her eardrums instantly. The Silver Skulls Devastators left a smoking carpet of brass casings in their wake as they continued their relentless advance, the bulky hoppers on the warriors' backs feeding ammunition to the guns at a terrifying rate.

The rain-washed gloom of the evening was suddenly eclipsed as the star-bright blast of the squad's plasma cannon illuminated the field. A blinding bolt of energy passed right through the failing shield and immolated a sorcerer where he stood. Molten fragments of armour painted the rubble in every direction and all that remained of the traitor was an ashen silhouette indelibly burned into the pock-marked wall.

Isara was acutely aware of the realities of the hideous war happening around her. She watched as though in a dream as an incoming salvo of bolter rounds caught a Silver Skulls warrior in its deadly path, chewing through his armour and spitting out gore and flesh in its wake. The Space Marine continued striding forward as though nothing had happened. Two men away from him, another giant clad in silver lost his head when a perfectly placed shot tore it from his neck. The headless corpse crashed to the ground, the helmet rolling in front of the line of advancing Space Marines. There was a creeping horror in the fact that they could not break stride and the unfortunate Silver Skulls warrior's head was crushed beneath marching ceramite boots.

Bolters roared, and the answering hail of fire from the Oracles' guns kicked up plumes of shattered stone and chewed great chunks out of the Devastators' plate armour. The Silver Skulls continued their advance with near-placid determination, intent on crushing the enemy warriors beneath the weight of their fire. Isara had taken cover behind the squad's sergeant, his bulk effectively shielding her from the enemy's wrath, but as the last scraps of the arcane shield drizzled away she knew that they had done their job well. They had brought her close enough to be known.

Now the heretics would answer for their treachery.

Gileas and his squad were winning their own battle on the walls. The rebels were plentiful and offered continuous resistance, swarming up onto the Space Marines like insects. The Adeptus Astartes were vastly outnumbered, but the rebel soldiers presented little threat to them. They were armed with weapons that could not hope to penetrate the Silver Skulls armour and they were culled with swift strokes and cool precision. Heads and limbs were severed, showering down from the curtain walls, and the screams joined the sounds of gunfire and chainswords in a perfect recital of destruction.

Reuben was matching his squad leader kill for kill and with the rest of the squad members rapidly slaughtering the remaining opposition they were converging on the central gatehouse. Captain Daviks and his warriors engaged the line of sorcerers on the ground outside the walls, their armoured bulk virtually obscuring the figures of the two Inquisitorial agents among them. Looking down on the battle, Gileas blinked away the reams of data that scrolled across his retinas informing him of enemy proximity, strategic objectives, armour integrity and ammunition levels. His eye-lenses focused on Isara Gall and the sight of her reminded him of another less obvious threat.

'Brother Nicodemus, withdraw from the gate,' he ordered into the vox. The last thing he needed to deal with was an incapacitated psyker. Gileas had experienced the effect of blanks before. He could see it in the increasingly frantic actions of the sorcerers below. He received a grunt of acknowledgement from the young warrior who was still carving his way through a knot of enemies. The wall guns had been stilled by the efforts of the assault squad, which would finally allow the beleaguered Imperial Guard to advance. Once the gatehouse was breached then they could press the attack on the earthworks. From what Gileas had seen it was likely to be close, brutal and bloody.

Reuben reached the gatehouse at the same time as Gileas, with Jalonis not too far behind; all three of them were blood-spattered, their armour stained with the deaths of the rebels who had dared attempt to hinder their progress. The blocky structure straddled the width of the wall and housed the controls for the massive inner and outer gates. The mural chamber beneath was filled with scanning and security equipment that would have kept a watchful eye on the masses passing through, but with both portals sealed tight nothing could be seen of the interior.

Down on the ground beyond the wall, Daviks and his team were still pouring fire onto the retreating sorcerers. Isara's presence was not enough to strip their abilities completely, but their powers were nonetheless reduced. Their draw on the warp was strained and difficult to maintain and the effects of the woman's proximity were starting to tell. Their fire had grown sporadic and wild as they attempted to fall back from the nullifying effect of her gift, with no bonds of brotherhood to unify them in the face of annihilation.

As each sorcerer concentrated on his own welfare, their attacks became increasingly uncoordinated. Even though they were Adeptus Astartes and just as strong and wily as their counterparts clad in silver, the lack of coordination was a hindrance. They separated, opening themselves up to attack. One of the sorcerers was sawn in half by the concentrated fire of the heavy bolters, his body rupturing like a burst fruit. In the split seconds before his gory death, he unleashed several accurate shots from his own weapon. Ceramite chips from Silver Skulls armour flew in all directions.

Death was the absolute right of every battle-brother who took to the field. No Silver Skulls warrior who had lived had ever believed in immortality. They were conditioned to accept the fact that they would die gloriously in service to the Emperor. During the fight with the sorcerers, four young battle-brothers went to the God-Emperor's side, cut down by the enemy. Each death was more grim and gory than the last and with each loss the Silver Skulls grew in determination, exalting the names of the fallen. The sorcerers were doomed by their own actions.

Another was vaporised by the searing beam of a lascannon directed by the captain. Pinned between the sealed gates and the advancing Silver Skulls, the surviving Oracles were sequentially isolated and destroyed.

The leader of the cabal made a wild charge for Isara, his snarling blade reaching for her skull even as shells plucked and tore at his armour. Curt raised his gun to fire but the weapon was still recharging after blasting one of the Chaos Space Marines. The enemy made it to within three steps of the Inquisitorial agent when a neat hole transfixed his forehead. Then the contents of his skull explosively evacuated from the back of his head as the high-velocity round finished its flight.

'Thank you, Captain de Corso,' Isara said as she released the breath she hadn't realised she was holding. She didn't know if she hid the shake in her voice. The whole ordeal was breaking her slowly apart and she was no longer completely convinced that she knew what was real and what was not.

'You're welcome.' The sniper's own voice was cool and calm as befitted his chosen speciality, and it calmed her. Isara had no idea where Harild de Corso currently was relative to her position, but she was glad that he was there on the vox for her.

'Captain Daviks, demolitions are ready for the inner gate on your orders.' Gileas gave his report, and received a curt affirmative in reply.

'Gileas.' Jalonis reached out and caught his sergeant's arm. 'We might need to deal with *that* before we take out the gate.'

Gileas looked down to where his battle-brother pointed. Inside the wall lay a plaza, an open space flanking the highway from the gates right up to the looming palace. It had been ripped apart: dug into a line of trenches and then fortified with numerous barricades, presumably as a measure against the kind of breach the Silver Skulls were attempting. Emerging from the earthworks with a heavy, unhurried stride was one of the largest Chaos Space Marines Gileas had ever seen. Held in his gauntleted hands was a long-hafted, double-edged sword with a wicked, serrated edge. The warrior wore a helmet with long, curling horns at the crown and as he approached the gate, he raised the sword in his right hand, a mock salute to the warriors on the walls.

'Slaves to the False Emperor!' His words resonated with the reverberation of a thousand voices. 'Know me now! I am Chuma, the blooded. I command these walls and I bring your death!' Reuben stared down at the warrior, and Gileas could feel the hatred seething from him. He shook his head once.

'Our orders are to hold the walls, not to engage the enemy.' Gileas looked down at the champion. 'We do not fight. We maintain our primary objective.'

Gileas's primary objective was subjected to a sudden re-evaluation when a moment later Chuma unleashed his sorcery and struck the sergeant with a crackling blast of warp lightning. Still trapped outside the walls, Isara's gift was too distant to shield him from the attack and a nimbus of purple-black energy bathed his battleplate in tainted power.

Jalonis and Reuben both put out their hands automatically as Gileas's body was wracked with convulsions. The sudden charge of warp energy wrapped around him in tendrils, shorting out senses, locking up vital joints and crazing his vision with screeds of nonsense data. He fought back against the attack valiantly, bellowing a litany of faith in a stuttering voice. Below, Chuma made a nonchalant gesture with one hand and dragged the sergeant from the wall, caught in a noose of unseen force. Gileas had sense enough to fire his jump pack in time to blunt the trauma of the impact, but his landing still ploughed a furrow in the ground and buckled his shoulder plate.

'Now we fight,' said Chuma, lowering his hand and swinging his massive sword in a menacing arc before him. 'I will prove my worth and you and all your miserable kin will die in this place, morsels for the furies to dine upon.'

Gileas dragged himself to his feet and thumbed the activation stud on his chainsword, letting it spit and roar into life. 'So be it, traitor,' he roared, already rushing to meet the hulking champion. Chainsword and hellblade came together with a tortured howl and a shower of sparks, weapons clashing as the warriors struggled to overcome one another through brute force. Superhuman muscles strained for several moments and then with a roar of fury Chuma hurled Gileas back, chasing him with his blade.

Firing his jump pack once again, Gileas retreated from Chuma's attack, but his options were limited. With his back quite literally to the wall and an opponent who could reach out to him with arcane power there was little to do but press forward. No matter, he reasoned. He had ever favoured the most direct approach.

Another arc of warp lightning lanced towards him, scorching the side of his helm and shorting out one of the thrusters in his pack. Unfazed, he cut the power to the remaining jet and allowed gravity to do the rest of the work. The plunge brought him down on top of Chuma, both boots slamming into the Traitor Space Marine's desecrated breastplate and pushing the other warrior back towards the trench line.

Chuma gave voice to his fury, venting it in a scream that made Gileas's ears whistle painfully before the auto-senses in his helmet shut it down, protecting him from its effects. The nearby rebels were not so fortunate. Seconds later, their skulls burst from the pressure generated by the attack. Gileas continued his advance, trading a succession of swift blows. The air was filled with sparks and the shriek of stressed blades. Then the swords locked, warp-forged steel vying for supremacy with sanctified technology.

With a titanic heave Gileas forced his weapon down, its teeth scraping against the ceramite of corrupted armour. Razor-edged chips spat as they ground in, but he could not get purchase. With warp-given strength, the sorcerer threw Gileas back and the sergeant narrowly kept his footing as he staggered away. In a swift motion, he drew his bolt pistol and fired, but his opponent deflected each round as easily as though he were swatting away flies.

Flashes of silver and heavy impacts either side of Gileas heralded the arrival of Jalonis and Reuben who, having slaughtered the occupants of the gatehouse, dropped from the walls to join in the fight. Both had their own chainswords active, and as a unit they converged on their enemy, who found himself suddenly at the mercy of three grimly determined warriors instead of just the one. The enforced slowing of his reactions proved costly.

Jalonis and Reuben circled the sorcerer and Gileas moved forward, his pistol raised before him. He emptied the magazine, the hail of fire pushing Chuma back still further towards the trenches. The final pair of shells found their way past his arcane defences and blasted craters in his crimson armour.

Chuma unleashed another psychic scream, killing more of the entrenched soldiers and fracturing one of Gileas's eye-lenses. The pain was intense, but Reuben silenced the piercing howl with a shot that smashed into the traitor's helmet and tore off one of the horns.

Jalonis threw a grenade at Chuma's feet and the three Silver Skulls hurled themselves away as the ensuing explosion engulfed their enemy. Dirt and smoke geysered into the air and blasted Chuma from the ground, his armour ruptured in a dozen places and weeping dark fluid: oils and chemicals and thick, richly oxygenated blood.

'Now, Reuben!' Gileas bellowed. 'Finish him!'

Snatching up his fallen sword and gazing hatefully at the surrounding Silver Skulls, Chuma spoke in his odd, multi-timbred voice. 'Nothing but death awaits you on this world, Silver Skulls. You cannot escape it. It has been foreseen and it must come to pass.'

Reuben's blade descended in a decapitating arc, but before the fatal blow could land Chuma spoke a single word and simply vanished from existence. The chainsword cleaved empty air and chewed a furrow in the soft earth, its purpose frustrated.

'Where…' Reuben's voice held a note of incredulity.

'There is no time for that question, brother. We must finish our job here. Get these gates down so that the siege company can move in and deal with the palace defences.' Gileas tossed a melta charge from his belt towards Reuben. 'Jalonis. Inform Captain Daviks that we are opening the way for him.'

TWELVE

THE EMPEROR'S GRACE

In his many years of service, Siege Captain Rasheke Daviks had seen many unusual things. The collapse of stars, the destruction of planets, alien species previously unknown. He had witnessed the horrors of the warp and he had lived through the deaths of countless battle-brothers. He had never once seen a Space Marine, traitor or not, so desperate to escape a battle.

He remained expressionless as he watched the wounded sorcerer struggle back towards the walls, armoured fingers scrabbling in the rain-slick rubble as he dragged himself agonisingly slowly. Heavy fire had cut the warrior into two ragged pieces held together by a thin strip of flesh. He left a dark trail of tainted gore in his wake. Every centimetre brought a fresh scream, but Daviks suspected that this had less to do with his fatal injury and more to do with Isara Gall, who was keeping pace beside him, negating his psychic ability.

The vox-bead in his ear chirped and Jalonis's voice sounded across the network.

'Melta charge primed and ready, Captain Daviks. The gate will be yours to claim in minutes.' Daviks nodded and his moment of reflection was replaced by his unerring sense of duty.

'Received and understood.' The captain turned his attention to positioning his squads effectively and laying the charges for the demolition of the outer gates. He placed squads on overwatch, protecting the flanks of the main battle force. Orders went out to Vindicators to sweep east in preparation for the upcoming breach whilst the Whirlwind batteries were primed to unleash barrage fire on the manufactory district.

He watched as a trio of blocky tanks rumbled away through the ruins, their armoured prows smashing aside the remains of the habs or grinding them beneath their treads. A Techmarine with a pair of Thunderfire cannons in tow moved them into place and signalled to the siege captain that they were ready to fire.

There was a shriek of atomised air as Curt finally grew tired of the screaming and turned his melta on the wounded traitor. Little remained afterwards other than a pool of liquid plascrete and an expanding cloud of vapour. Isara gave a short, barking laugh. It was not the laugh of a focused mind and alarm bells began to sound.

'Do you find something amusing about this, lady?' Daviks turned to the woman, studying her face. Her eyes were wide, staring and anxious, betraying her worry and disgust at what she had seen – and she had seen much today.

'No. I am simply relieved,' she said. 'They were overconfident. You and your men will soon cleanse them. I anticipate that we will celebrate a great victory, captain.' Her voice trembled and some of the terror began to seep from her face.

'I trust you are right in that assumption,' murmured the siege captain. He was not so sure. He had an extraordinarily bad feeling about the entire situation.

'Charge is counting.' Reuben's voice came across the airways. 'Detonation in fifteen seconds. Assault squad breaking clear of the gatehouse. Rendezvous inside.'

'Received and understood, brother.' Daviks fixed his eyes on the gatehouse. It was a vast structure, but given the height and breadth of the walls around the city that was not particularly surprising. What was bothering him right now was the fact that no further counter-attacks had been launched. That something waited for them was not in doubt.

What Daviks did not realise was that the 'something' would turn out to be far more unexpected than he had first considered.

'The silver tide has broken.'

He was named Garduul the First. An age ago, before Volkstein, during the lost years, he had been the Chapter's very first true oracle. Struck down by the piercing blades of the eldar and left for dead, Garduul's physical body had been beyond saving. Entombed within the sarcophagus of the Dreadnought, severed from the constraints of the physical world, Garduul's eyes had been fully opened by the Great Deceiver to the infinite skein of fate.

It was doubtful that Garduul remembered any of his former glories. Such knowledge was not meant for mortal minds, even genetically enhanced minds, and he

233

experienced reality now only in terms of what could be rather than what was. He babbled incoherently about the outcomes and probabilities of those around him, usually whilst he was cutting them down. But his prophetic ravings had proven themselves true over and over again and the warband treasured every word he spoke as though they were jewels of wisdom.

The voice was metallic and interspersed with binary white noise. The suddenness and clarity of its words heralded low rumbling and the clanking of the restraining chains. Deep in the heart of the palace, something was stirring.

As the noise began, a group of miserable thralls armed with an array of scrivener's tools scurried to be closer to the vast figure. When the creature spoke, it was their job to record his endless words of madness. For somewhere in those ramblings, the Oracles of Change believed all truths existed. Every utterance was recorded by the slave legion that attended him. Every phrase was parroted in the writings and scoured for omens and prophecies.

The slaves surrounded the ancient like an army of filthy children, swaddled in rags. They had no tongues, for they had only to listen, to record, to remember everything that was said. They communicated through sign language, their gnarled hands flashing in fluid motions, or via the tools they carried with them at all times.

A further barrage of unintelligible words came from the heart of the chained monstrosity. His massive bulk, thrown into sharp relief by the dim lighting of his prison, shook and strained as he spoke.

'The silver tide comes,' said Garduul, his voice a cracked, vox-distorted growl. 'The tide breaks, withdraws and breaks again. Now, it has broken. But the tide can be turned. It has turned, will be turned. It can be broken, can be split asunder. It flows, it winds, it turns in upon itself.' He rotated his massive body and the chains across the sarcophagus screeched against it with aching volume. An unblinking slit of fiery crimson stared down at the pack of scribes swarming like ants around its recumbent form. The words were gibberish, without context or form.

'The tide can be turned. The tide can be broken.'

Any sense of lucidity dissolved after this point and the madness took him once again. He began speaking in assorted languages that the scribes would painstakingly translate during one of his more subdued periods. One of the thralls peeled away from the group to deliver Garduul's words to Karteitja. It was not always a job that the slaves were willing to perform. At times, Garduul had predicted less than favourable outcomes for impending battle. These messages invariably ended in the death of the unfortunate slave delivering the news. But it didn't matter to Karteitja. There would always be slaves as long as there were humans to subvert. Garduul's scribes were sent out onto the battlefield with their master. If they fell, more would be found to take their place.

It was not considered a fortunate destiny.

Daviks had been right to feel concern. Fifteen seconds after Reuben's announcement, the melta bombs on both inner and outer doors detonated with a howl of tortured thermals. The roof of the gatehouse sagged in the heat and then ran molten as the armour-breaching charges did their work. Then the titanic hinges of the gates groaned, buckled and fell outwards with a rush of hot air. A cloud of dust and vapour billowed out ahead of the falling doors, eclipsing the waiting Silver Skulls, and then began to settle. Incredibly, most of the superstructure remained largely intact, with only the slightest evidence of wall collapse on either side. Daviks looked into the darkness of the gatehouse, and the darkness looked right back at him.

Two scarlet pin-pricks of light grew gradually larger and larger. Whatever had been ensconced within the gatehouse stepped forward with a hiss of hydraulics and a foul slithering of daemon flesh. The ground beneath Daviks's feet began to shake with the power of the thing's tread.

It was huge. It would have dwarfed even the Chapter's oldest relic Dreadnoughts. He had also seen such things before and knew all too well how much trouble they were in. All further thoughts of advance or careful manoeuvre fled in the face of the new enemy that roared its challenge to the rain-washed skies. Daviks's targeters locked on to the monstrous creation and illuminated it for the entire company.

'Daemon engine,' he bellowed. 'All squads, all support, fire on my mark! Bring it down! Gileas – we need the Talriktug down here *now*.'

There was no reply from the sergeant, whose vox had been compromised during his battle with the sorcerer, but Reuben answered on his commander's behalf.

'The beacon is in place, Captain Daviks. Support imminent. Your orders?'

'You heard me, brother. All support.' There was grim determination in the tone. Reuben hesitated for a long moment, his eyes drawn to the hissing, steaming rear of the daemonic machine, still partly shrouded by the haze of detonation as it pushed its way out of the gatehouse. Its attention was on the warriors outside the walls, not turned inwards to where the Assault Marines waited.

'Received and understood,' came the reluctant reply. Reuben turned to Gileas, who was kneeling before the device conducting the rites of appeasement and speaking the incantations of activation, and gave him a curt nod. It was the only cue that the sergeant needed. He murmured a final prayer to the machine-spirit housed within the beacon and activated it.

A slow, red light on the side began to wink regularly like a malevolent eye. Gileas took a few steps backwards and watched intently. He had used beacons before, of course, but they could not always be relied upon. On this occasion, however, he must have pleased the machine-spirits. The air and light around the beacon bent and distorted, folded inwards, and then without any further preamble, the five warriors simply *were*.

Even garbed as they were in their Terminator armour, Gileas knew one from the other. Each suit was a relic, handed down across the years, and the warrior spirits imbued within were ancient and fierce. The legacies of the Terminator suits were painstakingly etched in silver on every surface, and there were certain characteristics that made the hulking veterans unique. Djul in particular was distinguishable by the trailing skulls that he wore hanging from his belt.

'Brother-sergeant.' Kerelan already had his two-handed relic blade drawn and ready. 'Make your report swift and pertinent.'

Beneath Kerelan's words, like the thrum of a power generator, Djul's voice rumbled a constant litany. His words were largely indecipherable, but the tone and inflection of what could be heard were stirring the passions of the warriors even without them consciously being aware of it.

'The gates are breached, but their fall has released a

daemon engine hidden within.' Gileas nodded a head towards the sagging ruin of the gatehouse. The noise of heavy weapon fire crashed from beyond. 'In addition…' He indicated the numerous earthworks and fortifications lining the highway. The trenches and redoubts bristled with guns in anticipation of the coming assault.

There was no hesitation in Kerelan's reply. His battle plan was formed swiftly and without preamble. He delivered it across the company vox-channel so that Daviks would receive the orders as well. 'You take your men and deal with the human threat. All available units not presently engaged converge on this position in support. Death from above.' He gripped the sergeant's forearm in a brief gesture of camaraderie. 'May the battle be relentless. Let death come to these rebels. Pray that they find swift end and that we deliver them with due diligence to the hereafter. There can be no room in this world for heretics. They must burn, brother. By the Emperor's Grace, let us bring this insurrection to an end.'

'Burn the heretic,' responded Gileas, returning the grip. 'Purge the unclean.' The two squad commanders remained locked together for a moment and then without turning his head, Kerelan issued a single order, pointing his relic blade at the waiting enemy.

'Attack,' was all he said.

On a day of increasing horrors, Isara Gall had not expected to encounter anything more terrible than the atrocious acts of war that had seen men shredded before her eyes.

She could not have been more wrong.

The vile daemonic creature that stood before her ripped away at her crumbling reserves and it took everything she had not to turn and flee. In her time with the inquisitor, she had faced mutants, witches and debased cults, but had never been confronted by the vile reality of the warp given form. She didn't know whether the fear was of her own making or if it was some sort of projection put out by the thing. Whatever it was, she wanted nothing more than to run; to flee from the creature and put as much distance between them as she could humanly manage.

But there was no opportunity to retreat. Gunfire, missiles and shells sawed across the open ground, rattling off the monster's armour and turning the area into a killing ground. If she broke from the protective embrace of the Devastator squad she would certainly be cut down by the raging maelstrom.

Isara felt a scream boiling up inside her and fought to stay in control. She wanted hide; to curl up and weep at the vileness of what she was witnessing. Even as a blank, the raw evil of the monster still leeched the strength from her bones. It walked upright on two massive legs of knotted cabling and twisted daemon-meat, the knees hinged backwards like something lupine. Its massive weight shook the earth every time its segmented feet came down and it loped towards the Space Marines with terrifying speed. A vaguely humanoid mask hung between its colossal shoulders, not dissimilar to the design of Terminator armour such as she had seen before. But its eyes burned with a malevolent fire, not the righteousness of the Adeptus Astartes.

Dense, oily smoke coiled from the gaps between the thick plates that covered most of its bulk and living sinews writhed amongst the armour like purple worms. From what little Isara knew of such things, the monster was driven from within by a shackled daemon, bound to the machine by arcane sorcery too hideous to contemplate.

Her eyes were inescapably drawn to the terribly human-oid faces that screamed from the depths of its armour. They were etched or frozen in a state of permanent horror, their mouths stretched wide in screams of voiceless torment.

Finally, her eyes found its monstrous pincer-claw and she watched, helpless to act or even truly react as it lunged forward, its aura of terror making her want to empty the contents of her stomach. As it closed the distance she finally turned to run but Curt grabbed her around the waist and held her firm. The Devastator squad were firing, the roar of their weapons drowning out his shouted words. She screamed at him to let her run, but he would not release her.

The daemon engine lowered its massive shoulders and accelerated its pace towards the group of Silver Skulls. Shells hammered into it, dappling its armour with detonations but doing little to halt its wild charge. Spent casings clattered in a steady stream onto the ground at her feet and she watched, unable to so much as scream, as the vile thing crashed into the line of warriors before her. The Silver Skulls tumbled in all directions and the beast snapped up one of the fallen Space Marines in its killing claw.

Defiant even in the face of his certain demise, the warrior continued firing his bolter until the thing sheared him into two jagged pieces, slicing through his power armour like scissors through paper. The Silver Skull's body, now two uneven hunks of meat, thudded uselessly to the ground and was trampled beneath the daemon engine's mighty tread.

Isara thrashed in Curt's grip and faced with the carnage happening a few feet away the bounty hunter released her and turned his attention to the monstrosity. The Space Marines were attempting to rally, to bring their heavy weapons to bear again, but the thing was too close. Bolter shells pattered harmlessly from its hide and it swatted the Silver Skulls as if they were little more than irritating bugs. Daviks managed to roll beneath its thrashing arms and ram his power sword into its side and for a brief moment the daemon machine reared back in surprise and fury. Curt seized the opportunity as it was presented and shot it in the face with his melta.

The thing lashed out from within the expanding cloud of vapour and sent the siege captain sprawling, his breastplate cracked. Then the hideous, melted visage loomed out of the steam and it thrust its claw towards the other creature that had dared to injure it. The blades punched right through the bounty hunter with a crunch of armour and bone and flipped his body several metres through the air. Curt Helbron landed in a broken heap several feet behind Isara and suddenly all the fear went out of her to be replaced with a cold rage.

She screamed in fury as the monster peeled open the brutal pincer to reveal a maw dripping with greenish flames. Several Silver Skulls raced to her side, but the torrent of warp-fire immolated them in an instant. Her 'gift' held the holocaust at bay and Isara Gall remained unharmed, but she knew abrupt despair. How useless her ability seemed to her now. How useless and pointless, that she had failed to protect those around her. A cold hatred gripped her soul.

The fire subsided and she stared up into the hellish visage with terror that was tempered with utter contempt. Curt's body had been close enough for her to shield it and that small fact seemed somehow important, somehow redeemed her own sense of failure. She had been able to preserve him in death as she had been unable to do in life.

The daemon engine brought its other arm to bear with a rattle of autoloaders. The huge, double-barrelled cannon whined as the shells fed into it. Isara noticed that the muzzles were decorated with howling maws and that the darkness inside seemed to go on forever.

In the few seconds between realising she was going to die and the first salvo tearing into her, Isara found a peace she had never known. Her final thoughts, as she was ripped apart, were of her brother.

'Nathaniel…'

That was the moment at which the hulking forms of the Talriktug burst from the smoke of the gatehouse. They opened up with their storm bolters, Asterios sawing at the monster with a stream of fire from his assault cannon, and the creature screamed in rage before turning its attention on them.

Gileas turned away from the Terminator squad as they opened fire, feeling a moment's regret that he would not be engaging so mighty a foe. Not when the way to the palace was still thick with enemies.

A detonation in the east drew the sergeant's attention and he watched as a huge plume of dust billowed into the sky. A few moments later massive shells began raining down on the rebel fortifications, blowing them apart in great geysers of dirt and broken bodies. The Vindicator company crashed onto the plaza, their stubby cannons roaring as they demolished the eastern flank of the defenders. When Siege Captain Daviks ordered his men to assault a defended position, he did not do things in small measures.

As if prompted by the arrival of the heavy tanks, there was an overhead scream of engines and a further two squads of Daviks's company deployed from a Thunderhawk gunship. With the wall defences disabled the craft were able to deploy troops directly. None of Ninth Company wore jump packs, but they were low enough that the drop was little more than a minor inconvenience. With a succession of heavy thuds, they landed and grouped immediately with Gileas and his squad. Together, the warriors from Eighth and Ninth Companies joined as one and formed up to face the enemy. Warriors on both sides raised their weapons in defiance of each other and a short and bloody battle ensued.

The air filled with the staccato sound of bolters as the Silver Skulls downed the first line of rebels in a spray of mist and gore. Leaping forward into the fray, the melee fighters gunned their blades and the massacre continued without pause. Harild de Corso had joined in the fight from his hidden position – wherever it might have been – and more than one of the rebels was picked off by the sniper's incredible skill.

A few bold souls hurtled towards the Silver Skulls, waving their guns as though they believed that they were somehow capable of inflicting damage. Impact blows from their pistols and lasguns did little more than cause a brief hiatus in the advance of the Space Marines, who strode ever forwards with slow, steady purpose. Their chainswords sang with the promise of death and the enthusiastic charge of the rebels began to falter as the horror of what they faced dawned. They could only shift their gazes between the end of the bolt pistols and the cold, glaring reality of the approaching Silver Skulls. Every pair of blood-red lenses was keenly fixed on the targets the silver-clad giants were honour-bound to exterminate.

Gileas and Reuben peeled off from the rest of the group to head towards a frantic crossfire that had started up. The rebels were using the broken statues and fallen masonry from the walls for protection. Periodically one would break cover and unleash a hail of fire, but they were growing desperate. The two Space Marines continued their advance, their bolt pistols spitting out spent rounds on the ground.

As they got closer, the pair accelerated into a light run and fired the jets on their jump packs. They leaped forward, descending with deadly force, powerful enough to shatter the crazed flagstones beneath their feet. One rebel died immediately, crushed beneath Reuben's full weight. Bones popped and crunched and any screams of agony were stilled by the ribcage that had caved in and shredded his already crushed lungs.

Most of those who remained died swiftly and far from cleanly at the end of well-honed chainswords. Putting all his weight behind a killing stroke against one of the unfortunate men, Gileas virtually sliced his victim in half. The tungsten teeth of his blade chewed through shoulder and torso, splitting the rebel's body in an explosion of viscera and a spray of scarlet blood that spattered against the sergeant's armour. The rebel slumped to the ground, his enthusiastic advance forever stilled.

Gileas and Reuben fought side by side as they had done for decades, turning their attentions to the single artillery piece that continued to boom out defiance, lobbing huge shells in amongst the fighting that killed more rebels than they caused harm to the Silver Skulls. Elsewhere, Jalonis, Tikaye and Solomon discharged their own duty as they pressed forward at an unhurried pace. Their weapons poured a relentless stream of suppressing fire into the rebels' ranks. There was no discrimination at the receiving end of such relentless fury and men and women disintegrated in clouds of bloody mist and shredded meat, painting the ruined statuary with burst patterns of arterial gore.

Firing their jump packs once again, Gileas and Reuben launched themselves at the gun, their chainswords coming down in a shower of sparks to chew through the thing's yawning barrel, truncating it with a hot spray of shredded metal. The damage caused the cannon to explosively misfire, hurling one of the crew screaming upwards like a human flare and tumbling the second from cover. Reuben drove his chainsword through the rebel's sternum with a wet crunch of bone, and the pair continued their relentless advance.

Gradually, the rebels either fell beneath the scything blades of the Silver Skulls as they reaped their way through the onslaught, or threw themselves to the ground in weeping surrender. The numbers thinned until all that stood before Gileas and his warriors was the interior wall and vast, heavily fortified front door. The sergeant knew that Daviks and his Devastators would make short work of it.

'Tell Daviks that the way to the palace is open,' Gileas said to Reuben. His friend nodded and relayed the message.

'Excellent work.' Daviks's voice was taut with pain and Reuben suspected that the captain must have been badly wounded. 'I want the squads to begin sweeping the surrounding blocks and securing the area.'

'Yes, brother-captain.' Reuben passed Daviks's words on to his sergeant. Gileas felt ambivalent about the compliment from a senior officer, disappointed that he was left to herd the pitiable remains of a once numerous human threat that had now been dealt with. Beyond the walls, Daviks was in trouble and the Talriktug faced a much greater enemy. He yearned to join them in their battle.

A Techmarine who had been deployed with the others was moving amidst the Silver Skulls, tending to their weapons and armour. Gileas beckoned him over and unsealed his broken helm. Shaking his hair free, he thrust the helmet at the other warrior who took it with reverence. What was left of the broken lens tinkled free and showered down to the ground. There was a dent in the helmet that had he not been wearing it would have been in his skull instead.

'Do what you can with that, brother,' he said to the Techmarine, who looked at the helm with a critical eye. He gave Gileas a look of reproach which the sergeant returned with a cool stare of his own. The Techmarine shook his head and immediately set to work on the damaged piece of armour.

'Fortius quo fidelias!' Four voices, raised in the personal war cry of the Chapter's elite. *Strength through loyalty.* The sound of that particular quartet, their deep voices punctuated by the sounds of their weapons, bolstered the spirits of those who could hear them, and in their elite the Silver Skulls found purpose once again.

The Terminators poured their combined fire into the rampaging daemon engine, drawing it away from the injured captain and allowing some of the Devastators to open fire on it once again. Missiles and beams of energy stabbed at the monster's back, pitting and cracking its unnatural body and shattering the ammunition feed on its weapon arm. The beast clicked experimentally at the damaged gun and then screeched in rage before thundering directly towards the waiting Talriktug.

They separated as it approached and then closed in on it

from all sides. Vrakos took the brunt of the charge, the creature tearing deep furrows into his thick armour and pulling his storm bolter from his grip. He answered by smashing his power fist into one of its knee joints, pulverising the fusion of metal and meat in a rain of steel and black gore. The other three Terminators closed in, Djul ramming the snarling length of his chainfist into the beast's ribs and churning the knot of pipes into an oil-slick mess.

The machine staggered back under the assault, sweeping its claw around at the Silver Skulls tormenting it and ripping Varlen's helm from his head. They continued to pour fire into its wounded form, Asterios hammering the limping beast with a stream of shells until the barrels of his cannon glowed white-hot and the mechanism screamed in protest. They pushed it all the way back to the wall until it once again stood beneath the inner gate. Then Kerelan dropped onto it from above like an avenging angel.

Terminator armour was not built for speed or grace and so while his brothers did battle with the monster, the first captain had laboriously climbed to the top of the wall and waited until the daemon engine was beneath him. Once the moment was right, he stepped off the edge, his ancient blade turned point-first towards the spine of the beast. He drove every kilogram of his considerable weight behind the strike as he landed between whatever approximated as the thing's shoulders. His sword sheared through the chains that bound it and pierced into its vile body. There was a fizzing and popping of connections being severed and ruined.

The massive creature went suddenly still, as if every joint in its body had frozen at once. Then a thin wail echoed from within its hull, the cry rising in pitch and volume until it shook the ground and tumbled the surrounding ruins.

An ethereal mist gathered around the disabled engine, filled with roiling, tormented faces howling and gibbering in unholy anguish. Kerelan withdrew his blade and from his position atop the monster's body struck off its head with a single stroke. The fused and blackened mask tumbled to the ground and rolled to a stop.

Then the daemon engine exploded.

The shockwave toppled the already damaged gatehouse and hurled the first captain to the ground amidst a cloud of debris. His armour spared him the worst of the impact but he was still grateful for his enhanced physiology. A lesser being would have been crushed by such a blow. Once the smoke cleared, Asterios helped his commander to his feet and returned his fallen blade. Djul approached grimly, bearing the severed head of the defeated monster. Kerelan opened the vox and addressed the Silver Skulls forces.

'Brothers, this battle is won. Apothecaries, attend to the wounded. Let us now see to the winning of this war.'

THIRTEEN

DIVERSIONARY TACTICS

The psyker was in ruinous tears of grief by the end of the battle. Liandra Callis had been unable to prevent them. She had tried gentle remonstration through slapping him around the face, but Nathaniel had been rendered completely useless in the wake of the loss of his beloved sister. Once the daemon engine fell, he had made his way with an uncharacteristic turn of speed towards her corpse. He stumbled across the bodies of the fallen, slid in blood and entrails and crashed to the ground, crawling the remainder of the way.

He knelt by what remained of her, barely taking in the true extent of the damage. Her lower torso was mostly removed and one of her arms was missing, her blood mingling with the rain that still drizzled insistently. He gathered her up in his arms and drew her to him, the sobs leaving his throat red raw. For the first time in long years he was able to come close to her without the terrible pain that her proximity had always caused, and it was because she was dead.

He held her to him for a little longer before laying her back down on the ground. He reached up to take the silver necklace that she wore at her throat. It had once, so many years ago, belonged to their mother and for Nathaniel it was the only reminder he now had of the family that had once been everything to him. He took the decoration from her and slid it into a pouch. Then he knelt at her side and bowed his head, whispering fervent prayers to the God-Emperor to speed her spirit to His side.

Around him, the Silver Skulls were gathering together the corpses of their own fallen, reverentially moving those they could find to one side. There was no time for ceremony, but at least they could keep the dead free from those unworthy of honour or dignity. Captain Daviks surveyed the losses with a stoic heaviness in his heart. It could have been much worse, he reasoned. The arrival of the Terminators had secured their victory against the daemon engine – he was not blind to that fact.

'The inquisitor will not be pleased,' came a soft voice at his elbow. Daviks turned to see his company's Prognosticator, Inteus. The younger warrior reached up to scratch thoughtfully at the sandy beard that covered his chin. 'Half of her retinue are now little more than pieces.' He nodded his head towards the sobbing psyker.

'We would never have got as close as we did without Isara Gall,' replied Daviks in his deep rumble. 'We owe her a debt of gratitude. Ensure that her name and that of Curt Helbron are transmitted back to Varsavia for inclusion in the Halls of Remembrance.'

These words brought Nathaniel's head up, and for a brief moment the psyker's dull eyes shone with great pride.

Night had fallen now and the planet's twin moons throbbed dully behind the discoloured clouds, bathing the scene of carnage in an ambient, sickly glow that lent an air of additional horror to the scene, already painted strangely by the captain's infrared lenses. The planet's rotation meant that night lasted only a few short hours and dawn would swiftly be upon them.

Daviks looked at Inteus for a moment before turning his thoughts to the next task. 'We need to regroup and move in to secure the city. Our work here has hardly begun.' Inteus looked down at the bloody tear in the siege captain's armour and the way the warrior held himself awkwardly. He nodded towards a small, slender figure striding with absolute purpose towards the distraught psyker.

'Here she comes now. I will fetch an Apothecary to attend you.'

'Nathaniel, listen to me.'

The inquisitor's voice was not raised, and yet its tones were razor-sharp and conveyed the kind of menace that cut through the psyker's grief and brought him out of the cloud of misery back into the harsh reality of the slaughter around him.

'She's dead.'

'Do you take me for some kind of fool? I can see that. So is Curt. Two of my best operatives are gone. Set aside your childish grief. I need you to do your duty now, Nathaniel. Get up.'

The psyker wiped at his face with the back of his hand, streaking blood and dirt across it. He struggled to get up, but the inquisitor did not offer a hand to help him. With obvious difficulty, he dragged himself into an upright position. Inquisitor Callis studied him and the faintest trace of a sneer flickered across her features at his moment of weakness. 'There is still a lot of work to be done here and I can't afford for you to be at anything less than your best.'

The incessant rain had redoubled its efforts, the deluge deepening the gloomy night and rinsing out what little warmth remained. The psyker, now covered in mud and blood, began to shiver against the cold, his frail body shuddering violently. But he took his place at the inquisitor's side as she made her way through the devastation towards the towering figure of Captain Daviks. The siege captain turned his expressionless lenses on her. When he spoke, his voice was grave and contained no trace of the pain he was in.

'Inquisitor Callis. I extend deepest regrets for your loss. Mistress Gall and Master Helbron did their duty to the Throne. They–'

'Not well enough.' The inquisitor's voice cut across Daviks's irritably. 'But even the best have their flaws. I require the assistance of one of your men. Ideally, I would like it to be Sergeant Ur'ten. I have spoken at length with him and trust him to carry out this task for me.'

'Sergeant Ur'ten is occupied elsewhere at this time, inquisitor. What is your command?'

'Nathaniel had an idea which he discussed with me during the journey here. Tell them.' Her imperious voice invited no argument and it got none. Nathaniel nodded and took a deep, cleansing breath.

'Of course, inquisitor.' The slight man tipped his head back so that he was looking directly up at Daviks and Inteus. 'We need to solve the riddle of this insurrection and it occurred to me, after speaking with the inquisitor, that you people are perfectly placed to hel...'

'*You people?*' The insult was nothing short of shocking and Daviks shook his head, putting up his hand to stop the Prognosticator's retort. Inteus sucked in the stinging response that had formed on his lips. Inquisitor Callis folded her arms across her chest.

'Excuse my psyker,' she said and the sense of ownership explicit in the words was evident. 'He is not himself.' She gave Nathaniel the kind of stare that would have felled lesser men where they stood. Instead, he continued.

'I meant no offence,' he said. 'I beg your indulgence and assure you no insult was intended.' The psychic hood around Inteus's bared head glowed briefly and the Prognosticator scowled. He could pick up the nuances in Nathaniel's voice that suggested he had intended every syllable of insult.

'I merely thought,' continued the psyker, 'that perhaps if you were to apply one of your very *specific* talents to the problem, we might be able to find a swift solution.'

Rain drummed off the armour of the Silver Skulls in the silence left by Nathaniel's cryptic words. Around them, all that could be heard were the low voices of the Space Marines and the returning forces of the Astra Militarum as they began to muster ready for the push into the city. The ground beneath their feet released the bitter scent of scorched earth and the coppery odour of spilt blood; it was the familiar smell of war and set Inteus's nostrils to flaring.

'Speak plainly, psyker,' said Daviks in a clipped response. 'I am in no mood for simpering pomposity. So make your point. No insult intended.'

'He is speaking of the omophagea,' murmured Inteus. His eyes fixed on Nathaniel. 'Are you not?'

'I am.'

'And how is it that one such as you knows about the genetic secrets of the Emperor's Angels?' Inteus's eyes remained fixed on the psyker, who shifted awkwardly before shooting a glance towards the inquisitor. In an irritated tone, she answered Inteus's question.

'He knows, Prognosticator, because *I* know. This is not the time and place to debate the knowledge of the Inquisition. Will you aid us in this matter?'

Still shaking with the cold, Nathaniel cast a hand vaguely around the sea of dead rebels and the corpses of the sorcerers and ventured opening his mouth again. 'After all, there is plenty of choice for you here. A veritable *banquet* of opportunity. I am sure that if you were to employ your unique physiology, you could learn much of the enemy's plans.'

'No.'

The single word was spoken simultaneously by both Daviks and his Prognosticator. Inteus glanced up and nodded, a small gesture, allowing his commander to continue.

'No. We will not do this thing.' Daviks was stern and the words spoken were slow and careful as though he were addressing a child – or a fool.

'But I thought...' Nathaniel frowned. 'Or perhaps your Chapter is one of those who do not have all the...' Daviks took a step forward and stopped the psyker in full flow. Nathaniel's moment of bravado dissolved in the presence of a very large, very angry Space Marine in front of him.

'All of the Silver Skulls are gifted with *all* of the Emperor's Blessings,' said Daviks. 'From the Betcher's gland to the sacred progenoids that we carry within us, we have them all. We are complete in every way. But we do not employ the use of the omophagea unless there is no other alternative.'

'Is this another of your Chapter's beliefs?' The inquisitor's question was phrased artfully and politely enough and Inteus considered for a moment before he answered her. There was no particular emphasis placed on the final word and so he took her question as it was seemingly intended.

'Our views on the matter are strong,' he said. 'The practice of taking the flesh of another sentient being is considered abhorrent to us. We all bear a deep-seated hatred against one of our home world's native tribes.' A hint of disgust crept into his voice, colouring the words. 'They are cannibalistic by nature and so employing the use of the omophagea in any but the most dire of circumstances is considered distasteful at best, a deadly insult to our heritage at worst.'

'I appreciate your honesty, Prognosticator,' the inquisitor replied, her tone equally formal. 'Whatever else you may choose to think of me, I have a healthy respect for traditions. But I am sure you must agree that this *is* the most dire of circumstances. I accept that you find the request deeply offensive. Believe me, offending you is the furthest thing from my mind. But we could go around in circles asking "why" and "what if" and never progress to an answer. As an inquisitor of the Ordo Hereticus, I am trained to use *every* tool at my disposal.'

'Tools,' said the Prognosticator. 'So that is how you see us. Like Isara Gall. Like Curt Helbron.' Inteus said the words quietly and received a cold stare from Callis in return.

'Yes,' she said, defying him to question her lack of empathy. 'Just like them.' Her demeanour did not soften in the slightest and she stared at the Prognosticator without any emotion evident in her expression. Inteus could not help but admire the core of strength in this tiny woman, a strength that had no doubt been the root of her success.

Inteus's gaze shifted to Nathaniel, the psyker's teary, dirty face evidence that he at least had some compassion in his soul. He recalled that Isara had been Nathaniel's sister and, for a moment, allowed himself the brief luxury of touching the kind of grief he experienced whenever a battle-brother fell to the enemy.

'Why was it you wanted Sergeant Ur'ten to carry out this task?' Daviks's question was cool with an undertone of menace that for the first time caused a look of unease to ripple across her face.

'I got to know the sergeant reasonably well during the journey here,' was her reply. 'I admire his honesty and his integrity. I trust him not to be economical with the truth, though I do not intend that as a slight towards you, captain.'

'Then you did not get to know him as well as you think,' said Daviks. His voice, altered by the helm's modulator, was grave. 'He bears more hatred towards the cannibalistic Xiz than any other warrior I have ever known and for good reason. If you had asked this thing of him... the insult would have been infinitely greater than that which you have offered me or the Prognosticator.'

He was rewarded with a sudden shift of the inquisitor's posture. Her composure cracked for just a second as she considered the consequences of insulting a Space Marine to such a degree. Without any difficulty or hesitation, she regained that self-control. 'Then I ask this of you instead, Captain Daviks.'

'No.' Daviks's reply was quite certain, and Inteus laid a hand on his arm.

'The captain is correct. He will not do this,' the sandy-haired warrior said. The inquisitor looked at him, disappointment and contempt flickering in her eyes. Inteus cracked a slow, humourless smile.

'I will.'

Daviks's reaction was hidden by his helm and he passed no further comment on the subject. 'I am ordering the Eighth and Ninth to converge on the Celebrant's Square outside the palace. It is defensible and with elements of the Imperial Guard in support, will act as a staging ground from which to sweep the city of any further resistance. It will also allow you access to the palace and the grounds beyond.'

With that, he turned his back on the inquisitor and pointedly returned to the logistics of war.

The rain was now pouring down in a relentless torrent, and rising winds whipped it into sheets that battered continuously against the armour of the Silver Skulls patrolling the inner city and blasted earthworks. They met little further resistance from the rebels, who were now a broken force. Those who had not died in the onslaught were corralled together and now huddled tightly against the elements while they awaited the inevitable interrogation.

As Captain Daviks and his command moved off to secure the palace, the Talriktug, with Kerelan at their fore, rejoined Gileas and his squad. The sergeant was flattered to receive praise from the first captain for his efforts in securing the highway, but had not allowed that gratitude to show beyond a polite acknowledgement. Even the ever-critical Djul had been unable to find fault with Gileas's prosecution of the orders.

Much of the city was dark, the subterranean generators either sabotaged or simply offline, and the inky blackness was punctuated only by the glowing red eye-lenses of the

Silver Skulls warriors, gleaming like hot coals. Gileas's own eyesight pierced the gloom clearly, even without his helmet, which was still in the hands of the harried Techmarine.

Beyond the walls, the chemical lights of the Astra Militarum burned strongly. The mood amongst the Guardsmen had shifted from that of impending defeat to one of cautious optimism, but they all knew that there was still much fighting ahead of them.

'So. The Oracles of Change,' rumbled Djul. 'It has been some years since we found ourselves confronted by those traitorous cretins.'

'True,' agreed Kerelan, sheathing his massive relic blade and turning to the other warrior. 'And I am sure that the force defeated at the gates here today is barely a fraction of their presence on this planet. They always travelled in great numbers before. I see no reason to believe that is any different now.'

'Then why are they not here, facing their retribution?' Djul turned to stare up at the palace in silence. The trailing string of skulls that he wore at his waist were jostled by the motion and rattled against one another as he moved. His usually spotless armour was scored and dented from the battle with the daemon engine.

'We will face them soon enough, I am sure,' said Vrakos, who was checking the functionality of his storm bolter. He racked the slide, ejected a shell and then manually reloaded it before sighting along the barrel. 'And when we do, they will answer for their crimes here.'

'It will be difficult to answer anything when I am through with them,' retorted Djul. 'Dead men tend to have very little to say for themselves.'

Gileas listened to the fast-moving exchange between two

of the Chapter's heroes and took a strange sort of pride in the realisation that they all had far more in common than he might have thought. Kerelan's eyes remained on the sergeant.

'What do you know of the Oracles of Change, Brother-Sergeant Ur'ten?'

Gileas thought for a moment, rifling through the comprehensive knowledge he carried in his mind until he isolated the specifics. 'A band of itinerant sorcerers, most likely to have splintered from the Thousand Sons and made up of disparate rogue elements whose power is considered appropriate.'

'A textbook answer,' said Kerelan. 'And exactly right. We – my brothers and I – fought against a band of them some time ago. They believed they had a lot more in common with us than we were comfortable with.'

'First captain?' Gileas's nose wrinkled in distaste at the thought of sharing anything with a band of Chaos-tainted sorcerers.

'The Oracles of Change put great stock in prophecy and foresight,' said Kerelan. 'As do we. Just as we consult our Prognosticators to interpret the Emperor's will and decide on the right course of action, they do much the same with their heathen gods. They are unshakable in their beliefs. From what we learned, even the least of them has some psychic affinity and working in concert they present a formidable threat. We have… far fewer countermeasures at our disposal.'

'We have our faith in the Emperor,' replied Gileas instantly. 'We have our martial prowess and we will drive them from this world back into the twisted embrace of the Eye. That or we will slaughter them all in the Emperor's name.' Kerelan nodded his head, approving of the sergeant's heartfelt words.

'I hope that is true, sergeant,' he said. 'But we will have to track them down first. They aren't going to attack directly again, not now that they know we are powerful enough to defeat their monstrosities.'

'Within the palace, do you suppose?'

'Nowhere so obvious,' replied Kerelan. 'From what's been observed, many have the ability to translocate themselves at will, blinking through the empyrean the way we might employ the technologies of teleportation. Their next strike will come from an unexpected quarter, for they prefer deception over confrontation. They...'

'First Captain Kerelan, this is Captain Daviks.' Kerelan nodded and responded to the voice on his vox.

'Receiving you, captain.'

'Prognosticator Inteus is gathering useful intelligence about the enemy. You may wish to be present.'

'That is pretty disgusting. Really? They eat people's *brains*?'

The words were spoken by one of the Guardsmen who was close enough to watch as Inteus hunkered down by one of the mangled corpses of the Oracles of Change. It had been a simple enough matter to strip the traitor of its ornate helm, which had been cast carelessly to the side. The face beneath was a scaled horror of twisted features, with eyes that were wide and staring in death. Prominent veins traced the contours of the dead warrior's face making the pale, translucent skin seem blue and anaemic.

The Apothecary who had been tending to Daviks stepped forward, taking out his reductor. A tool more commonly utilised for the sacred recovery of progenoids from fallen warriors, this was not its only purpose.

'No,' said Inteus. He held up a hand to halt the Apothecary.

'Wait. We need to move the body somewhere less visible. Ritual should be observed, regardless of the location.' He shot a glance at the Guardsmen who were watching him with interest. Both of them feigned immediate fascination with a point somewhere over Inteus's right shoulder.

The Prognosticator and Apothecary were able to lug the bulk of the Chaos Space Marine between them and they retreated to the relative seclusion of a burned-out Administratum building that flanked the Celebrant's Square. The body was dropped without care on the ground and Inteus knelt, closing his eyes as he focused on the many words he had read on the use of his omophagea. Words were all he had. This was the first time the Prognosticator had been required to utilise the organ in the field of battle.

Crouching alongside the Prognosticator, the Apothecary positioned the reductor at the Oracle's temple. He engaged the mechanism and the razor-sharp spike shot through the flesh of the face and into the enemy's skull, straight into the prefrontal cortex.

Inteus watched as the Apothecary carefully withdrew a cylinder of the Oracle's brain matter. He dropped it into Inteus's hands and although the Prognosticator couldn't see the look on his battle-brother's face, he felt the distaste radiating from him.

Murmuring a soft prayer to the Emperor and a muted apology to any of his ancestors who might have been offended by what he was about to do, he opened his mouth and begun chewing on the meat of the dead Space Marine's brain.

The nameless soldier was right in his assessment, Inteus thought as he chewed grimly on the morsel. It *was* disgusting. It was also necessary.

Inteus chewed the rubbery mouthful slowly, allowing it to be dissolved and broken down with the aid of a slight injection of acid from his Betcher's gland. Nothing meaningful was forthcoming yet, but Inteus was patient. He knew it would not be instant.

He swallowed. The genetic matter slid down his throat to his stomach, and it was gone. He pushed back onto his heels and took a long breath. Now there was nothing to do but wait.

'They may have breached the city, but the Silver Skulls will not leave this place without hunting us down, my lord.' There was a certain smugness to the Unborn's voice that incensed the leader of the warband. Striding the short distance between them, Karteitja moved to stand before his lieutenant, now clad in broken and bloodied armour. The Unborn held his head high and refused to break his gaze from that of his leader. Contempt roiled from him.

The leader of the Oracles of Change warband brought up a fist. 'Do you take me for some kind of fool, Cirth? Whilst you have been *failing* in your task to transcribe the First's prophecy, we have been protecting our interests. Where were you when the Thresher fell? Your cabal were assigned the task of holding the gatehouse, yet they failed and you were not with them. Can you explain their inadequacy?'

'My lord, you commanded me to divine the meaning of the prophecy. I was simply following *that* order. I was engaging the Silver Skulls and learning something of their style, of their ways. They are fools and they will fall under the final onslaught.'

Karteitja hated him. It would be a matter of seconds to

cut Cirth Unborn down where he stood and he would feel no regret, only satisfaction.

'You were indulging your arrogance, nothing more. Return to the task that I set you on. Bring me the prophecy. Where is, it, Cirth? Still bound within the skeins of fate. You come here with the news that a dozen scribes are dead and you still do not bring me the words?'

'My lord, the First has been acting erratically...'

The two warriors stood within a shell of a hab block in the north-east quadrant of the city. Periodically, stone crumbled from the walls in a shower of dust and rock to add to the already choked atmosphere this deep into the warzone.

Due to the transitory nature of structures during a state of war, the Oracles of Change had not chosen a sanctum on the planet since their arrival. It was not truly necessary; their ability to move through the warp made communications and redeployment swift and sure. But it had been important to find somewhere for the First to be restrained safely and the half-ruined chapel here in this quadrant had proven the perfect place for him.

'I don't want your explanations, Cirth. I want success.' Karteitja turned away from his lieutenant and walked away. 'In the meantime, assemble the coven. We need to begin preparations.' He looked over his shoulder. 'You can manage that, can't you?'

As his master stepped out of reality and vanished, Cirth Unborn muttered beneath his breath before spinning on his heel and marching off to carry out his given orders.

'I must state my position on this, Inquisitor Callis.' Kerelan stood in front of the petite woman, his massive bulk an effective block to her passage. 'I would sooner you did this thing with a guard of Silver Skulls.'

The Space Marines had quickly and efficiently set up an armoured perimeter around the square before the palace, tanks and portable defence lines standing where statuary raised in praise of the Emperor once stood. The seat of the governor was a forbidding building climbing the northern face of the hive like a rash of buttresses and sculpted cherubim. The massive gates that had once stood tall, proudly displaying the Imperial aquila, now sagged open, blasted by demolition charges.

'Your concern is duly noted, first captain. However, I would prefer to take my own retinue.' The inquisitor's eyes flickered from Nathaniel to Harild, who had rejoined them. 'Or what I have left of them, at least. I know their strengths. There will also be a squad of Guardsmen coming with us. Don't worry about our safety. Your task is far graver than seeking out the governor of Valoris City.'

'Still, I would be made far more comfortable if you would take some of Daviks's men with you.'

'First captain, your concern is noted.' The inquisitor repeated the phrase, then she sighed wearily. 'I understand your worries and I respect them. But please stand aside and allow us passage into the palace. When your Prognosticator manages to find information about the Oracles, you will need all your resources to deal with them. I will keep in touch. We have done this before.'

She was so determined, so strong and self-assured that eventually Kerelan nodded his head and stepped aside to let the small group pass by. A detachment of Imperial Guardsmen, looking battered and weary, followed her as she made her way towards the ominously silent palace.

The rain was beginning to ease off a little and the darkness of the Valorian night was giving way to the grey reaches of dawn. The chill wind continued to blow and those Guardsmen who had spent the night drenched in rain and mud were shivering. Given the respite in the battle, they were able to rest a little and shared hot mugs of recaff that did little to warm the bones and less still to warm the spirit. In the washed-out light, the initial surge of triumph had evaporated. Looking around the muddied earthworks, littered with the bodies of the dead, they realised just how little there was to truly celebrate.

Gileas's helmet had been returned to him, functional once again although there was little that could be done in the field for the ugly dent in the back. The Techmarine had given the expected lecture about making sure it was properly attended to as soon as he returned to the ship and Gileas had nodded absently. Kerelan watched the sergeant, assessing the young warrior's attitude and capabilities as he had done since they had left Varsavia.

The sergeant and his squad, unable to simply stand down, were lending their aid to the Imperial Guardsmen tasked with reinforcing the defences, while Nicodemus directed newly arrived armour into optimal firing positions. It was not exactly glorious work but, as Daviks was always quick to point out, it was *necessary* work. Kerelan watched them for a few moments longer, then beckoned Gileas over to him.

'First captain?'

'Something troubling you, sergeant?'

There was a moment's hesitation. 'Perhaps, first captain.'

'Unburden yourself. Bearing doubts into battle leads to regrets in the aftermath.'

Gileas nodded. 'I know this to be truth,' he said. 'And yes.

265

There is something troubling me, but it is… not really of consequence and I should not linger on it.'

'It is to do with who you have been fighting, am I correct?'

'You believe correctly, first captain.' Gileas turned to look at the sight. Bodies of humans, some Imperial Guard, some rebels, still lay strewn amidst the ruins. Some were half-buried in mud, others lay broken and split apart. The grisly scene was a grim reminder to those amongst the Guardsmen of what became of traitors.

'Continue.'

'I have fought against illusions created to distract the eye. I have battled daemon-spawn and crushed the onslaught of the greenskin menace and never have I doubted my purpose. Yet every time I witness this… Whenever I wage war against citizens of the Imperium who have fallen into heresy, I cannot help but linger over the waste. Some of those rebels were barely into adulthood and we crushed them as though they were things of glass. I feel… senseless. Did you ever feel that way, first captain?'

Gileas regretted asking the question the moment it left his lips. It made him sound like an acolyte; a young warrior who had just stepped into the field for the first time. He began to retract his words, but Kerelan merely held up a hand.

'A long time ago, sergeant, I felt that way. A very long time ago.' Kerelan paused for a few moments. 'I have over three centuries of service to my name and perhaps that gives me a greater perspective.'

Gileas said nothing, letting Kerelan continue. 'We were designed to kill the enemies of the Imperium without remorse and many of our brethren, particularly those in some younger Chapters, seem beyond humanity. But though we wage war in ways that may seem inhuman, we do so to preserve the sanctity of man. We do what they cannot do, indeed what they *should* not do. To visit death upon another on such a scale, to be a weapon of retribution, is to set aside humanity. Sergeant Ur'ten, my shoulders… *your* shoulders are broad enough to bear the responsibility of these deaths which stain our armour with the blood of their treachery. Once the battle is ended, we rest assured that our cause was just and the delivery of that justice was our obligation, to both the Emperor and mankind.'

'You are wise, first captain.'

'No, Gileas.' Kerelan laughed lightly. 'I am merely pragmatic. Speak with the Prognosticator if you get a chance, or find Chaplain Akando on our return to the ship. Unburden yourself to him.' He fixed his gaze on the younger warrior. 'Are your troubles dealt with for now?'

'Yes, first captain.'

The inquisitor and her retinue entered the palace through the recently demolished front doors and walked into a vast, echoing and empty hallway that was one of the most ostentatiously decorated rooms that Nathaniel Gall could ever recall. Frescos were painstakingly hand-painted on the walls, each a beautiful work of art depicting famous scenes from Imperial history. Everywhere there were the words of the Imperial creed.

The palace was deserted. Their footfalls on the exquisite flooring, inlaid with mosaic tiles making up the Imperial aquila, echoed unnaturally loudly around the vaulting chamber. So loud were the acoustics in this silent place that it seemed forty or fifty marched into its confines, not the dozen there actually were. There was no sign of life and the air, whilst not choked with the dust and grime of the war beyond the doors, was still cloying and heavy.

They found only one thing, and that was enough to draw muttered oaths of preservation from several of the soldiers. They found Governor Gryce.

They found him at the end of the vestibule, but he was not in any position to give them the answers they sought. The man had been nailed to the wall, obscuring a great tapestry that was now blood-soaked and ruined beneath. His limbs and guts had been drawn out into the blasphemous image of the eightfold star of the Ruinous Powers. A jagged excision line ran down from neck to groin, opening him up like an obscene flower. No blood ran from the body and even the floor below was curiously free of what should have been an expansive pool. The unfortunate governor looked as though he had been drained dry. There were few signs of decay; the death had occurred only recently.

Worse, though, even worse than the appalling state of the cadaver, was the expression on the dead man's face. His eyes were open, staring down at some unseen horror beneath him, and his mouth was stretched wide in what must have been his last, terrible scream. He had been an attractive man in life. Now he was just a slab of meat that the inquisitor surveyed with a dispassionate eye.

The faint outline of markings on the floor was still visible and Nathaniel crouched with some difficulty to consider them. 'Ritualistic,' he observed. For a man who not so long ago had been wrapped in a state of unshakable grief, he was now once again the master of his emotions. A lifetime spent exercising control had simply come to the fore and pushed back the weaker part of his personality. 'In keeping with what we have come to expect from the presence of sorcerous traitors.'

'Such a find does not bode well for the longevity of Lady Gryce,' was the inquisitor's thoughtful response. 'If they have done this to him, then I don't imagine she will have fared any better.' She turned to the ashen-faced Guardsmen who were trying their utmost to avoid looking at the grisly scene. They had all been exposed to battle-wounded, but this was something else. This was clinical butchery that spoke of horrors beyond their comprehension.

'Get him down,' she said. 'Start sweeping the palace for Lady Gryce. We have the technology of the Space Marines at our fingertips, let us use it. If she is here, I want to find her. Nathaniel, see if you can trace her.'

It was merciful that the palace was a relatively small structure that represented barely a fraction of the hive, otherwise searching would have been something that could have taken days, even weeks. But the palace's function was diplomatic and it served primarily as a residence for the governor and his wife. There would not be many hiding places.

'Already looking. There is heavy residual disturbance present. I need to…'

'Just *do* it, psyker.' If the inquisitor saw how her snappish reply hurt him, she did nothing to show it, simply pushing past him to walk from the death tableau, her sharp eyes roaming up and down the vast hall. If Lady Gryce still lived, there was not much of a world left for her to inherit. But the bureaucratic machine had to run on regardless.

'Find her,' ordered the inquisitor. 'Dead or alive, it matters little now. Just find Sinnaria Gryce. She is going to have a lot of explaining to do.' Her eyes narrowed. 'Before she is executed for this heresy.'

* * *

There was no exact science to the use of the omophagea. Inteus knew this and yet he couldn't help but try to process it logically. The use of their ability to absorb genetic knowledge through ingestion was a serious matter and ethically, the Silver Skulls did not advocate it. Inteus's inexperience smarted, but he could access any number of texts on the matter. He knew the whys and the hows.

They chose the prefrontal cortex specifically to access any short-term memory they could find. Sometimes it worked, other times it did not. But the subject in question had not been purely human. He had been a Space Marine. Warped and twisted beyond recognition, certainly, but capable of utilising far more of his brain capacity than an unmodified mortal.

Seeking out the part of the brain that dealt with longer-term memory was a far more complicated process and Inteus knew that time was of the essence in the matter. But he could not hurry this. There was no way he could magically produce an outcome.

The world around him faded into a distant buzz of voices and activity. His nostrils flared with the assorted scents of mud and death, the smoke from the hastily erected funeral pyres and the lingering stench of promethium that wafted around every battlefield.

There were thoughts in his mind that he knew categorically were not his own. Thoughts that for him, a devout believer in the Imperial creed and lessons learned over decades of service to the Silver Skulls, were anathema. For several moments, he knew what it was to be filled with hatred so strong that it drummed inside his mind with a rhythm of its own. The rhythm thudded harder, more strongly, a driving force that meant he would do anything in the effort to bring chaos to order…

'No. This will not be.'

The Prognosticator drew in a deep, calming breath and exhaled slowly, purging these abhorrent thoughts. He was a Silver Skulls Prognosticator. He would not fall into the quagmire of this heresy. It was a mess that he had to unravel because somewhere in that memory – a memory that was already starting to fade – was a core piece of information that might just reveal the enemy's intentions and where they could be found.

He could feel it, the shape of it forming like a poorly received holo-transmission. Fuzzy at the edges, and indistinct. He reached through the haze to piece the thought together: as much as it turned his stomach and much as it went against everything he'd ever understood, he still reached for it.

I will know what you know, he thought.

And then he had the shape of it. A location, marked on the mental map of his knowledge of the city's layout, a knowledge that came from both his own studies prior to deployment and the mind of the traitor he now shared a brief but solid bond with.

You will die before you get there. The voice arrived in the back of his skull and was as loud as a shout in his ear. He started, his eyes flaring open, and the delicate frame of the psychic hood that rose from his shoulders sparked with life.

'Inteus?' Daviks stepped forward. 'Have you learned anything that can help us?'

The Prognosticator smiled grimly. 'A location, nothing more, but it is somewhere for us to begin.'

Kerelan nodded abruptly. 'Then consult the skeins of fate, Prognosticator, and we will set out immediately.'

* * *

The reading had been swift and efficient. It was always so with a Prognosticator's divinations in the field. There had been no sign that the party should not proceed and so the Talriktug, along with Gileas's squad, had left the battle-field and headed towards the ancient chapel that Inteus had identified.

The city was a mess: what had once been a bustling hive of industry had been reduced to ruins and blasted shells. Ferrocrete dust filled the air, motes flickering in the first watery rays of the morning sun. Here and there the Silver Skulls passed bodies of citizens and rebels alike, senseless deaths in the name of an evil cause. They found no signs of life.

The battle on Valoris had raged for many months and although a spate of early evacuations by the Imperial Guardsmen had seen some of the citizens to safety, it was clear given the number of bodies they passed that they had been relatively few in the grand scheme of things. Gileas crouched down at one point and picked up a child's doll, its face broken and one arm missing. He studied it without speaking before tossing it aside. It clattered against the broken stones and came to rest again, its sightless glass eyes fixed on the ponderous skies above. Somewhere beneath the rubble was its owner.

'A waste,' he said. There was a quiet anger smouldering deep inside him, something familiar and known and he welcomed it.

'First captain, look at this.' The voice was Tikaye's, and Kerelan's lumbering form moved over to join the other Space Marine who was standing before a generator. It was a standard Imperial design, or at least it would have been had the innards not been torn out. Evidence of tampering was clear: some wires had been re-routed and others left to spark uselessly. None of the party were privy to the secrets of the machine-spirits that dwelt within such things, but one thing was evident to them all. This damage was not accidental.

A trailing cable led from the generator, snaking its way back away through the ruins carrying whatever power it was leeching towards its new destination. With a snort of derision, Kerelan unsheathed his relic blade.

'Brother-Captain Kerelan, you should not...' Djul began to speak, but was silenced as Kerelan's blade came down and sliced through the conduits, severing the connection.

'That could have been a foolish action,' reprimanded Djul. 'It could have been a trap, laid for us to destroy ourselves.'

Kerelan shrugged. 'It could have been. But it was not. So get on with your task, brother.'

'As my captain commands.' Brother Djul, always diligent in his duties, murmured a prayer to the departed machine-spirit and nodded his head towards another generator, several metres away. The same thing was evident there, another cable stretching away into the gloom.

'Destroy what you can as we move,' ordered Kerelan. 'And pick up the pace.'

One of the lights had gone out.

The stuttering power from the city's damaged generators had been barely enough to produce an erratic glow and so it went unnoticed by all but one. In the darkness, the bulk of the First shifted, the shackles that bound him in place clanking against his vast form.

Garduul flexed one ancient limb and the chains that held him strained to contain the power of his artificial body.

273

The hulking Helbrute tugged against his shackles a second time and five of the twenty slaves set to record his mutterings backed away in alarm.

'The silver tide comes,' he rumbled from deep within the sarcophagus. 'The silver tide comes to me. But this is not the time of the conjunction. That time is now. It has passed. It will be. It will not be. This will not come to pass. The world fluxes, the outcome shifts...'

He ceased his motion and the chains fell silent again. Once more, the Dreadnought lapsed into its litany of madness and garbled divinations.

Another light went out.

FOURTEEN

REVELATIONS

Nathaniel allowed a single tendril of psychic thought to lazily probe ahead of him, keeping his senses finely tuned for the touch of life. Since the grisly discovery in the main chamber on the ground floor they had encountered increasing numbers of bodies: Administratum officials, judging by their robes of office.

The Imperial Guardsmen had already combed several levels of the palace and by the time they reached the fifteenth floor were growing visibly weary. Nathaniel had offered them one bright moment when he had caught the trace of a mind but the subsequent search and pursuit of that thread turned up nothing apart from a domesticated animal that had been found trembling beneath a chair. The moment one of the young soldiers had gone towards the creature, it had tried to bite him and then fled in terror.

That had not improved morale.

Everywhere there were signs of slaughter. Corpses were

piled high in various states of dismemberment, and all of them had shared the same fate as their governor, having been thoroughly exsanguinated. The beautiful decor of the Governor's Palace was stained crimson and the eight-pointed star of Chaos was daubed everywhere. Yet for all this, the building remained whole whilst so many others around it had fallen in ruin. The air was thick with the stench of butchery, the raw stink assailing them all until it clotted the air enough that rebreathers became necessary, even for the inquisitor.

It was around the twentieth floor, his hip screaming in agony from all the stairs he had climbed, when Nathaniel finally connected with an unmistakable spark of a living mind. He had been carefully tracing every scrap of biomass in the palace, examining each particle in what was rapidly becoming the unlikely hope of finding a trace of life.

'Nathaniel?' Inquisitor Callis's voice was sharp as she studied the psyker who had just stopped dead in the middle of a deserted corridor, causing at least two of the Guardsmen to walk into him. He held up a hand to silence her and for once, she made no comment. When Nathaniel was this deep in concentration, it was not advisable to interrupt.

His pinched face screwed up in effort and then he nodded. 'Definitely human this time,' he said and raised a long, thin finger to point. 'That way.'

'Listen.'

One of the young Guardsmen had spoken. He was standing beside one of the countless doors that lined the hallways. There was the faintest of sounds, as though the maker were trying and failing to control themselves, but now the party had fallen silent, they could all hear it quite clearly. It was the sound of sobbing.

'Open that door.'

The inquisitor pointed at the nearest soldier who did as she was ordered, heading for the door. It was not locked and swung open easily. The room within was a bedchamber of some kind, not anywhere near well-appointed enough to be one of the master suites. Perhaps a guest room of some kind. There was a bed, a simple dresser unit and a weeping woman ensconced in one corner. It was the latter that drew everyone's attention.

Her crying stopped immediately as the door swung open and she held up a pistol in shaking hands, pointing it at the door.

'Put down the weapon, Lady Gryce,' came the imperious instruction of the inquisitor. 'We are not here to hurt you.'

Sinnaria Gryce stared at the deputation at the door, scrabbling up against the wall as much as she could manage. She was a thin woman with a long, fox-like face framed by expensively treated blonde hair that had long since fallen into wild disarray. Her face was dirty and smeared and her eyes met those of Nathaniel for a fleeting second.

'We are here to help you,' said the inquisitor calmly, and pushed past the soldiers and Nathaniel to walk towards her. 'Are you Sinnaria Gryce? My name is Inquisitor Liandra Callis of the Ordo Hereticus. We are here to end this nightmare. You will give me your full cooperation.'

It was not that the inquisitor lacked sympathy for the woman's plight, Nathaniel observed. It was just that right at that moment it was the least of her concerns.

The woman stood up slowly, the long, bloodstained gown that she wore dropping to cover her feet. She stared at the inquisitor in terror. Her eyes were large and a pale blue, so pale that the irises were verging on white. They were not her natural eyes, Nathaniel was willing to bet, but augmetics of some kind. It was a strange sort of fashion, he decided, to want to look like a fish.

'Are you Sinnaria Gryce?' Again the snapped question, and the woman nodded her head slowly, her hair falling into her face.

The inquisitor smiled warmly and reached out a hand, switching from cold logic to compassion in the blink of an eye. 'Good,' she said. 'Come with me. We will get you to safety.' The words were not spoken in a gentle manner and the order in her tone was unmistakable.

Just like the inquisitor, Lady Gryce underwent a complete shift of mood, though in a different direction. The fear and anguish fled and were replaced by a righteous indignation. 'They shot me,' she declared furiously in a quavering voice. 'How *dare* they? They were my husband's personal house guard and the treacherous dogs turned on me. I managed to get myself in here…'

'When I want the minutiae, I will ask for them. If time permits, you can tell me your story later. For now, we leave.' She studied the woman with an impassive expression on her cold features. 'What happened to your husband? Do you have any idea?'

'No,' came the response. 'They took him several days ago. I had been able to conceal myself from his guard, but they found me. They shot at me… I ran and hid. I heard terrible screams and awful voices. Chanting. Singing? No. Not quite. Oh, it was…' She put her hands over her ears as though she could block out the memory.

'Inquisitor.' Nathaniel looked over at his mistress, who gave him a long, hard glare. The slight psyker gave an infinitesimal nod of his head which she returned in kind before reaching out and forcibly pulling the hands away.

'Lady Gryce, stop this. You are a woman, not a child. You have a civic duty to your people and to the Imperium.' The inquisitor snapped the remonstration, barking the words out. 'I am a representative of the Holy Inquisition and I demand nothing less than your full cooperation. You will be given enough time to refresh yourself and take sustenance, but matters are critical. There is no time for you to wallow in your misery.'

Lady Gryce looked shellshocked at such treatment. All her life she had been a pampered woman and now she was being commanded like a common serf.

'Nathaniel...' Inquisitor Callis turned to the psyker at her side but he had already moved forward and he reached a hand out towards the governor's wife.

'Don't touch me,' she said to him and her tone was veering on shrill. Nathaniel simply tipped his head on one side and studied her.

'All right,' he said. 'I have no real desire to anyway.' In a very vocal demonstration of his inability to engage socially, he continued with another biting comment. 'After all, you're terribly dirty.'

She looked insulted at this, particularly given Nathaniel's own current state of dishevelment. The psyker showed no indication that he cared. Or indeed that he had even noticed. 'I merely wanted to ask if you required assistance from me. Trust me. Far better you take it from me than wait for the inquisitor to order one of the soldiers to carry you.'

'Nathaniel, that's enough.' The inquisitor's tone was sharp and there was the kind of threat behind her words that suggested if he continued in this manner, she would gladly flay the skin from his scrawny bones. He shrugged in the off-hand manner that he had and fell silent. 'Lady Gryce, you will walk with Nathaniel. Take her downstairs and secure her in one of the vehicles. Get what you can from her and compare the information to what we already know. I will join you shortly.'

'I will, inquisitor.'

'And then, Lady Gryce, you and I will have a friendly discussion.' The inquisitor reached out a hand and patted the woman's cheek in a manner that was gentle, but far from friendly. 'About a lot of things.'

A fuel tank had been ripped open by one of the many projectiles that had torn down this quadrant and although it had long since drooled its contents into a slick of chemical waste that oozed a rainbow path across the damp ground, the smell of promethium was still strong. Kerelan studied the retinal feed from his helmet as they continued their progress towards the chapel.

They followed the course of the parasitic cables through the decrepit city, their route revealing yet more hijacked generators and violated machinery. Each was destroyed in turn, but even Djul, diligent in the execution of Kerelan's order to disrupt the enemy activity, began to question the point of their actions.

'These are treacherous scum, Kerelan,' he said in his bass rumble. 'They have no sense of honour. They will not meet us on the field of battle. They will draw us into the shadows where their strength is greater and their advantage greater still.'

'I am aware of that, brother,' said Kerelan in a flat tone. He gripped his relic blade more tightly and his shoulders visibly tensed. 'I have battled against the forces of Chaos countless times, just as you have. But we cannot safely ignore these works. It may be nothing more than a distraction or it may be that we are moving towards...'

Whatever it was that the first captain thought they were moving towards would never be revealed. Reality howled and buckled as the air protested at the unnatural abuse that suddenly assaulted it. There was a tortured heave of energy and a crackling ozone stink as something huge was vomited into existence. Moments later, a figure clad in ancient power armour coloured deep, arterial red was standing where before there had been an empty alley. The helm that it wore was crowned with a pair of curving horns and the decals and etchings on the armour were chased in writhing gold.

Most obvious of all of these was the eight-pointed star design that was worn in pride of place on the shoulder pad where the Chapter's insignia would once have been. In the centre, a slitted daemonic eye throbbed with evil light. The Talriktug already had their weapons trained and the roar of storm bolters filled the damp air, explosive shells chewing the ferrocrete into dust and fragments.

Reality shrieked again and another Adeptus Astartes was standing there, this time to the group's right. A third stepped from nowhere behind them. A fourth. Fifth. Within a heartbeat, the Talriktug were surrounded, an island of muzzle flares and gunfire in the gloom.

'Sergeant Ur'ten...'

'Already moving on your position.' Kerelan could hear the roar of a number of jump packs firing and knew that within seconds, more warriors would arrive to support them.

Death from above.

Gileas and his squad had moved ahead to act as a scouting

force and Kerelan enjoyed the briefest moment of satisfaction that the young sergeant had obviously been monitoring the vox-channel closely.

Kerelan was by far the most seasoned of the warriors present, but for each of them there was the rush of righteous hatred that only the presence of traitors to the Imperium brought. The Silver Skulls had many enemies and a particular contempt for the foul eldar, but Adeptus Astartes who had lived on and perpetuated the vile treachery of the long-dead Warmaster Horus were abhorred above all others.

'No mercy, Talriktug,' ordered Kerelan. 'Destroy them all. Now.' He held aloft his relic blade and roared his command. 'Now! For Varsavia!'

The unit bellowed their assent and joined in the battle cry. As a single group, they moved forward, weapons at the ready, and began their assault. They were joined bare moments later by the assault squad who roared down from the heavens to bolster the attacking fury.

The traitors' movements were hard to follow, their motions flickering like a badly tuned pict. They wove their way between the Terminators' assaults and pressed the attack. One gave a short barking laugh and raised a hand. He released a wave of sizzling power towards Gileas's squad, swatting three of the Assault Marines from the air and even staggering a pair of the Talriktug caught in the backwash. Motes of energy danced across the ornate skin of their ancient battleplate, but did little more than cause momentary disruption in their retinal feeds.

Resuming his approach, Kerelan whirled the relic blade above his head, the ancient weapon arcing for a killing strike. His aim was true, but his adversary intercepted the blow with a conjured shield of white-blue energy.

'Imperial slaves,' growled the red-clad warrior, speaking for the first time. 'So blinded by your creed, so easily led. The Great Deceiver will witness your demise at our hands.'

'Our demise, traitor?' Kerelan shifted position, spinning his sword low into another attack. 'Just try it.'

'You should not test your betters,' the traitor taunted as he moved. He fired a pair of shots into the first captain's armour, the tainted blue projectiles blistering the sacred battleplate. 'We know more and have seen more than you could possibly imagine.'

Kerelan drove everything he had into his next swing, a precise and well-honed killing blow that was aimed with unerring accuracy at his enemy. By all rights it should have cleaved the Oracle's head in two.

It would have done as well, had his opponent, and the one Djul had been trading blows with, not simply vanished.

Kerelan lowered his relic blade warily. He did not ask the obvious question, merely turned to join in the fight going on elsewhere. The others, seemingly taking a cue from their leader, also disengaged and disappeared.

'Teleportation?' Djul lunged forward to the spot where the Space Marine with whom he had been fighting had been standing.

'Warp powers.' Kerelan said the words with obvious distaste. 'Chaos-tainted *filth*.'

Djul swore and curled his huge hands into fists. His rage at losing his quarry was palpable.

Nicodemus stepped forward and stared through his lenses at the surrounding area. Particulate dust, propellant and vapour hung heavily in the aftermath and the eyes of his helm glowed softly in the gloom. He reached a hand out in front of him and swiped it downwards as though grabbing at a cobweb. The axe in his hand throbbed a bitter shade of blue.

'I would suggest that… they are stepping sideways through the warp,' he suggested in a low voice. 'They must have great power, or some kind of arcane technology to achieve it, but that's the only possible explanation. They…'

The psyker had sensed, rather than heard, the sound of a weapon being unsheathed. Spinning on his heel he poured power into his blade, sending spears of lightning flickering along its edge.

Another Chaos Space Marine had appeared behind them. Whether it was one of the original forces or a new arrival hardly mattered in Nicodemus's mind. As he ate up the short distance between him and his enemy, he had to alter his path to avoid the double-headed axe that was swung in his direction.

'You can claim no victory here,' the Oracle said. His voice had the distortion that all of the Adeptus Astartes had when wearing their helms, but there was something else there too. Something strange and unnatural. His voice was not the deep bass rumble of a Space Marine; rather, there seemed to be a chorus of voices coming from his throat, a maddening, impossible sound. He opened his free hand and snaking tendrils of power lashed from his armoured fingers. Nicodemus was sent flying, his psychic hood blazing as it countered the sorcerous attack. He crashed to the ground several metres away and dazedly scrambled to his feet. The young psyker rushed to the offensive again, but Gileas had already raced ahead and swung furiously at the waiting Oracle.

His chainsword met the axe with a scream of metal and sparks, the teeth whining furiously as they tried to gain purchase in the hell-forged steel. Putting all his weight behind the strike, Gileas pressed his foe back. The Oracle matched Gileas in strength and the two were locked in stalemate for a few seconds before the Oracle barked a short laugh, releasing his grip. Gileas staggered and nearly fell. His opponent unclamped a bolt pistol, aimed it and fired in a single motion.

The shell struck Gileas's shoulder and he stumbled backwards. His armour absorbed the worst of the impact and the shot had little effect. Before he regained his balance and returned to the fight, the Oracle of Change was falling back, his flickering image fading in and out of existence as he retreated through the ruins.

Without hesitation, Gileas bounded after him, joined by Reuben. Even as the two warriors pursued him, the Oracle tore open another rent in reality before him, vanishing as easily as if the world had simply swallowed him up.

'He's gone,' reported Reuben across the vox, but Gileas's senses prickled with unease and he spun to confront the anticipated attack. Sure enough, his enemy reappeared, only this time he was charging along the crumbling wall of the nearby hab, parallel to the ground in open defiance of gravity.

'You are slow to learn, Silver Skulls!'

In reply, all of the Space Marines opened fire. The resulting hail of shells tore the wall of the hab to pieces and carved an interior stairwell to shards. Splinters of red and gold armour went spinning in all directions accompanied by a spray of black ichor, and the enemy roared something in a language Gileas did not know before vanishing again.

'You winged him, brothers. At least now we will know it is him if he chooses to reappear.'

An eerie silence settled around the abandoned ruins of

the once glorious Valoris City in the wake of the noise that the brief skirmish had brought, and after several minutes had passed without any further incidents, Gileas voiced the thought that was on every pair of lips.

'We have been duped.'

'I concur, brother,' said Kerelan. He looked around and nodded, challenging anybody to counter Gileas's deduction.

Nobody did.

Kerelan nodded again. 'We move on.'

'Are you sure?'

Nathaniel nodded. 'I sensed it the moment that we found her.'

'You must be wrong. There's nothing in her records to suggest any...'

'Inquisitor...' Nathaniel was snappish in response. 'I know it to be the truth. You are not gifted with my talents. For once, I advise that you don't question what I am telling you. Sinnaria Gryce is a psyker.' The pinched features of the gaunt man fixed on the inquisitor and she paused before nodding. This new revelation did not bode well for the future of the investigation.

'How powerful is she?'

'I can't tell. She must be either barely strong enough for me to have picked up the traces of it, or so powerful that she is effectively able to ward herself.'

Inquisitor Callis looked up at the Chimera where they had sequestered the governor's wife. She had been put inside with an armed guard – not to stop her escaping, the inquisitor had explained, but to stop anything getting in with her. Now she wondered if she had got the decision the wrong way around.

'Then our line of enquiry may have to change,' she said. 'And we must be more guarded than we would otherwise have been. I want you with me during her interrogation, Nathaniel.'

'Where else would I go, inquisitor?' The unspoken words that passed between them were weighted with the psyker's melancholy.

And with whom?

They headed for the Chimera holding Lady Gryce and entered it.

'Why must *that* be with us?'

Sinnaria Gryce pointed a finger at Nathaniel. Her manner was imperious, with no trace of the terror she had exhibited when they had found her in the palace. Inquisitor Callis had dropped any veneer of politeness and courtesy and had become entirely more aggressive in her approach to questioning. She'd barely even entered the Chimera before she'd started to talk.

The inquisitor's questions came thick and fast, and so rapidly that Sinnaria could not draw breath between her answers. When had she last seen her husband? With whom had he consorted? Had he made any unpopular legislative decisions in recent weeks? Questions, questions, questions and Sinnaria could not answer them all.

She seemed deeply unnerved by Nathaniel's presence. The psyker had simply settled down, cross-legged on the floor, and was watching her closely with his head tipped thoughtfully to one side. Occasionally, his lids would close as though he were simply dropping off to sleep. Whenever that happened, she felt the telltale probe at the edges of her mind.

'Make it stop,' she said to Inquisitor Callis. 'Make it stop doing what it's doing.'

'*He* is working under my orders, Lady Gryce,' snapped the inquisitor. 'I need to establish the truth behind what you tell me and his abilities are perfect for that job. Don't worry yourself that he will somehow harm you. Nathaniel's power is considerable but so is his self-control. He will not hurt you. On that you have my word. Others have… far less control over their abilities.'

'Really.' It was a statement rather than a question and something in its cadence made Nathaniel's eyes snap open and he stared straight at Sinnaria Gryce. 'Well, I wouldn't know about that, would I?' Her lips curled in a cruel smile.

'Nathaniel has reason to believe that you yourself may have some psychic talents, Lady Gryce. I'm sure I don't need to explain the importance of being candid with me in this matter.' Callis hesitated. 'You are a woman of breeding and intelligence, however, and so I am prepared to give you this one chance for confession before I have to resort to more … direct methods.'

'Flattery *and* threats?'

'Observation.'

The air between the two crackled palpably and although the inquisitor was the smaller of the two, it was Sinnaria Gryce who looked away first. When she turned her head back, that cruel smile had gone from her face and there was something entirely colder there.

'Easier by far to show you than to tell you,' was all she said and Nathaniel felt the hairs on the back of his neck rise. He was not even able to jump to his feet and shout a warning. He opened his mouth to speak and then choked for breath as his throat began to constrict. A translucent paw shimmered in front of him, fastened around his neck, and he felt phantasmal talons pricking at his skin.

'Release him now.' Inquisitor Callis had already drawn her pistol. 'I will kill you if you don't.' The soldier who was standing guard also pointed his rifle at the governor's wife.

Nathaniel was struggling to breathe. He reached up to pull at his throat as though he could somehow fight the insubstantial hand that was crushing the life from him. His pale face was starting to turn dark purple and he kicked and thrashed against his own suffocation.

'Have I answered your question as to whether I am a psyker or not, Inquisitor Callis?'

The inquisitor fired but Sinnaria Gryce made a nonchalant gesture with her free hand, flicking the projectile onto a new trajectory. It buried itself in the soldier's eye and the man pitched backwards with a gasp, dead before he hit the ground. His weapon discharged, burning a scar across the inquisitor's back and spinning her from her feet with a cry of pain. Despite his own predicament, Nathaniel stared over at her, his eyes widening in shock.

'Now that I am finally free of your tiresome meddling I can get back to work,' purred Sinnaria. 'I have such plans for your beloved inquisitor. Don't think I haven't read your mind and seen into the heart of your feelings for her. Does she know? Have you ever told her? You will never get the chance now. By the time you find her, it will be far too...'

She broke off as she felt Nathaniel's will gathering. He may have been weakened and on the verge of collapse, but the psyker was gathering every scrap of strength he could muster. The power slithered around in his mind as he tried to grasp it with his failing senses but he refused to surrender. If he could just hold on to it long enough to wield, to throw at the woman, maybe he could burn her mind to cinders. The thought was that of a desperate man. But despite the spark of rebellion, he could feel his consciousness begin to fade. His body was beginning to betray him even as his mind shrieked in rebellion. The killing bolt slipped away from him, the energy fraying away like so much chaff on the aetheric wind.

His vision must be failing. It was the only explanation he could muster to explain what happened next. The air between him and the thin, fox-faced woman began to blur at the edges, becoming unreal and indistinct. Gryce and the inquisitor seemed lost in a heat haze that had risen between them.

Lady Gryce looked around, moved towards the inquisitor and wrapped an arm around the smaller woman's neck. 'Time to go,' she said. 'There is much to do.'

She whispered arcane words that chilled the blood in the inquisitor's marrow. There was a sudden searing flash of light and the bend in reality widened to swallow the two women. When the light died, there was nothing to be seen.

The invisible force that had been choking Nathaniel ceased abruptly, but he was weakened already and the damage that had been done took its toll on his frail body. As he fell to the floor, he got a hand to his vox-bead. He smacked at it in a burst pattern – three… four… two… four – with his right hand before the darkness finally claimed him.

The bursts of static on his vox summoned Harild de Corso instantly. He had been waiting outside of the Chimera, ready to squeeze off a clean shot should the woman attempt to flee. The armoured vehicle had deadened all sound and he heard nothing of the altercation within.

The static code he had received from the psyker meant only one thing and it filled him with creeping dread. He had thought their business in this place largely concluded. The Guardsmen could not hope to deal with the Traitor Space Marine threat – that would be the domain of the Silver Skulls. De Corso had been looking forward to leaving this worthless rock. Now it seemed things had gone catastrophically wrong.

'Nate,' he said into his comm. 'Nate. Talk to me!' But there was no response forthcoming from the psyker. Inquisitor Callis's team had long ago established the emergency code sequences and this one was the second highest on the list.

'Nate! For once in your life I want you to open that mouth of yours!'

Silence.

De Corso swore and ripped open the door of the Chimera, diving inside.

Karteitja plunged his hand deep into the abdominal cavity of the thrall and drew out a handful of ropey intestines. They spilled between his armoured fingers in a sticky mass and he tore them free from the corpse.

For countless centuries he had glimpsed the designs of the Great Deceiver in this way. Not for him the need to communicate with the imaginary voice of a far-distant corpse. For Karteitja, his ability to perceive the threads of destiny came from contact with the corporeal. But he was not looking to divine a future he knew would be glorious. He was looking to satiate those powers which would drive that change.

He discarded the blood-soaked guts onto the platform and they slithered into a gory heap. Rummaging his hand inside the man's body, the sorcerer tore out other organs. Kidneys. The liver. The bladder was ripped out and tossed to one side. With effortless ease, he broke open the ribcage and closed his gauntleted fist around the man's heart.

It still beat slowly, the rune of suffering carved into the man's face keeping him alive despite the horrific mutilation. Karteitja snapped the man's neck with a shake. For a few seconds after the heart was plucked like a ripe fruit from its thoracic home, it continued to pulse dully, a seemingly tiny thing in the palm of his massive hand. The sorcerer rose to his feet and kicked the corpse over the edge of the platform. It plummeted to the ground far below, soon lost within the low-lying cloud that misted around the pinnacle of the palace. The sorcerer strode to the bank of sealed cogitators that controlled the array and the strange device he had placed amongst the antennae and cabling. The adept's heart fitted snugly into the machine and he drove plugs deep into the flesh. The techno-organic conduits burrowed hungrily into the meat, threading it with black veins of living circuitry.

The first stolen life was little more than a symbol. It was a beginning, a catalyst, an ignition for the change to come. But symbols had power. The right symbols had enormous power. Now he needed fuel. The heart of one of the city's denizens would beat at the heart of the machine that would destroy the heart of the planet. It was an unholy trinity that brought great satisfaction to the sorcerer.

Infused with a sudden rush of unnatural vigour, the thrall's heart began to beat with an unearthly rhythm.

'Excellent,' said Karteitja. He turned to the warriors who had joined him. 'Slaughter as many of the Imperial dogs as you wish, but leave some alive to fuel the change and bear witness to the rebirth.' He turned his head up to stare at the gathering clouds. 'The ritual is begun and the thousand eyes of the Deceiver turn upon this world. The children of change swarm about us and I can smell their hunger. Soon they will join us. Let the Silver Skulls suffer in their impotent rage as they thrash in fate's web. They have been snared, and now they will learn the price of their insolence and their blindness.'

Karteitja turned back to his warriors. 'Let them burn. Let them all burn.'

They all raised their weapons in mute acknowledgement of their leader's order, took a step sideways and were gone, leaving Karteitja alone once more at the peak of Valoris City.

FIFTEEN

SKYFIRE

'First Captain Kerelan, we have a few problems up here.'

'Go ahead, Captain Daviks.'

'Switching to closed channel now. Encryption protocols active.'

There had been no further sign of the Oracles of Change, but none of the Silver Skulls had sheathed their weapons as they paused in the blasted shell of a manufactory. Every last one of them remained alert, falling swiftly and without the necessity of orders into pairs, allowing one brother to guard the other against further ambush. They had traversed only a little deeper into the city, still pursuing the trail of generators.

Gileas exchanged a glance with Reuben. That Daviks had requested a private audience with the first captain was a bad sign in and of itself. That they were now deep into the city, some distance away from their battle-brothers, was not much more encouraging. Sporadic gunfire still echoed through the crumbling streets as the kill teams purged pockets of resistance, and the bass rumble of a Vindicator as it demolished rebel positions shook motes of dust from the ruins. The siege company had fragmented, breaking down by squad to sweep the city of remaining enemies. The air filled periodically with the howl of rockets and Thunderfire shells as strongpoints were encountered and bombarded.

'I am going to guess that you are thinking what I am thinking, brother,' murmured Reuben, and Gileas nodded.

'This is a waste of our time,' said the sergeant in a low voice. 'We were lured here for nothing other than presumably some kind of distraction. The real threat remains at large elsewhere.' He shifted his gaze to Bhehan. The young Prognosticator, who had been largely silent up until the initial arrival of the Oracles of Change, was carefully examining the tears in reality that only his psychic senses could detect. Gileas watched him without comment, trying to fight back the words that trickled into his mind, tickling the edges of his awareness.

What happens if the Prognosticators are wrong?

The thought skirted the edges of blasphemy and Gileas shook his head as though the action could dislodge the notion. It had been on a Prognosticator's word that they pursued their current course of action and they had walked directly into an ambush. On the other hand, they were now acutely aware of the Oracles' capabilities.

It occurred to Gileas – not for the first time – just how much ambiguity there was in the comparative success of the Prognosticatum and their efforts to foresee outcomes. Retrospectively, it could easily be argued that the entire point of this journey to the city's old quarter had been purely to determine that the Oracles of Change had a hand in what was happening on Valoria. But what had that fragment of knowledge cost them in time? What had it cost them that was so grave it meant the siege captain and the first captain were speaking privately?

'Sergeant Ur'ten, with me. Now.' Kerelan's voice crackled over the vox and frequency details scrolled across Gileas's retinal feed.

'Go ahead, first captain.'

'The inquisitor has been abducted,' Kerelan reported in a low voice, and Gileas drew in a sharp breath.

'So we are returning to the palace? We should focus our efforts on ensuring her safe return. It is our sworn duty, first captain, I–' Kerelan's voice interrupted him and Gileas did not miss the note of annoyance.

'Do not forget your place, sergeant. I am perfectly aware of my duty. I do not need reminding.'

'My apologies, first captain. I meant no insult.'

'None taken,' Kerelan smoothly replied. The lie was galling, but Gileas did not comment. 'Your zeal does you credit, sergeant, but do not let it govern you. The Oracles of Change take the blessed Emperor's gift and distort it beyond anything we could imagine. It is a grave foe we face and compared to the greater threat, the inquisitor's safety is the least of our concerns.'

'Permission to speak freely, first captain?'

'Granted, sergeant, but be warned that my patience is already thin. I would not suggest testing it further.'

'I gave the inquisitor the Oath of Hospitality as our guest,' he said. 'I respect that you may not have done the same, but it was an oath given freely. I know what some of your men think of me...' Here, Gileas allowed his gaze to drift briefly to Djul who was kneeling in prayer, his voice murmuring repeated litanies. 'But I am nothing if not honourable. I must fulfil that oath and prosecute my duty as best I can. I cannot do that if I am engaged on a pointless chase through the bowels of this accursed city. With your permission, sir, I will take my squad and go in pursuit of the inquisitor.'

It was a speech which came at a great cost to Gileas Ur'ten. To actively question his first captain's judgement was anathema to his way of thinking. But, witnessed or otherwise, he had bound his honour to the Inquisition. He had little choice but to fulfil his duty.

'I am concerned for her safety, and the reasons for her abduction rather than simple assassination, Gileas.' When Kerelan finally responded, there was a sympathetic edge to his voice. 'But the Oracles of Change present the greater threat. The Imperial Guard are capable of conducting the search while we focus our efforts on the Archenemy. I need your support here, Gileas.'

'I cannot easily give it. In so doing, you ask me to become an oathbreaker.'

'Then we must ask Bhehan which path we follow,' said Kerelan. 'A decision lies before us, brother, and it is vital that we choose correctly if our efforts here are to be successful. If we seek the missing inquisitor we might once again find ourselves led astray by the traitors. We must be cautious, Gileas. Who knows what destruction the Oracles of Change may bring about while we chase phantoms?'

'And if we simply leave this in the hands of others,' Gileas added, 'who knows what fate may befall the inquisitor, or the consequences of not recovering her?' He began to catch the essence of Kerelan's thoughts. 'Can I not simply take my squad and search for her? The Talriktug are more than capable of...'

'We don't know their numbers, brother. We know nothing of their motives. The enemy we face is twisted in thought as well as in body and it is at times such as these that we must rely upon the Emperor for guidance.' The first captain switched back to the Chapter's regular vox-channel.

'Brother-Prognosticator, you are needed.'

Bhehan knelt on the ground, studying the runes he had drawn from the soft leather bag. He had considered them for a time, but had said nothing. Kerelan and Gileas stood over him, their mutual agitation growing. Above them, dark clouds were gathering once again and although the sun was now up, they muted the feeble daylight as though some-one had simply drawn a curtain across the sky.

Whilst the Prognosticator had been thus engaged, the rest of the Silver Skulls had performed a number of peri-meter sweeps, but there had been no sign of the Oracles of Change. Whatever hell they had come from, it seemed that they had returned to its depths.

'Brother-Prognosticator, with respect to your position, I need to know your decision.' Kerelan's voice was tight with irritation.

'I cannot divine a path, first captain.' It was the first time Gileas could recall hearing complete uncertainty in the young psyker's voice. 'The runes are not granting me guidance on this matter.' Bhehan had never, to Gileas's knowledge, experienced the psychic blindness known as the Deep Dark. The condition was the moment every Prog-nosticator of the Silver Skulls dreaded. The moment the Emperor's light turned from them. It was rarely a lasting thing, but seen as an indication that the Emperor was displeased enough with the individual to withdraw his guidance for a time.

Invariably it resulted in the psyker in question spending countless hours, often weeks, in prayer and penance in an effort to rededicate himself to the Emperor and to prove his loyalty. There was certainly no chance of that happening here.

'Then we have delayed here long enough,' said Gileas in a low tone to Kerelan. 'I will do as I suggested, return to the palace. Sweep it floor by floor until every traitor is dead and the inquisitor is found.'

'We do nothing until the Prognosticator gives the word.' This latter statement came from Djul, who had approached the gathering and was looking down at the scattered silver runes. 'Are you deliberately attempting to provoke me into a response, brother-sergeant? Your attitude continues to live up to its reputation.'

Bhehan briefly shot a look up at the veteran warrior before resuming poring over the runes. No matter how hard he tried, the arrangement of etched stones made no sense at all. Everything he knew about rune lore was strained to the utmost. The complex web of meanings was so interwoven that teasing out the single strand of divination was impossible.

'I am merely making an observation, Brother Djul.' It was hard to miss the anger in Gileas's voice.

'Peace, both of you. Djul, return to your patrol. Gileas, keep your concentration on the question at hand.'

With a snort of derision, Djul moved off again, his huge form lumbering away.

'You do nothing to help yourself where he is concerned,

brother,' observed Kerelan in a tone that suggested response was not required.

'I will try one last time,' said Bhehan, gathering up the runes. 'There is endless contradiction here and nothing is easy to divine. Perhaps if Sergeant Ur'ten were to try concentrating a little harder on the issue in question ...'

'Very well.' Kerelan snapped the words. 'But do so swiftly. The Archenemy may return at any time and I have little wish to lose an excellent Prognosticator as he is struck down by traitors whilst communing with the Emperor.'

Bhehan felt a swell of anger building within him and took a deep breath to control it. He had turned the runes one at a time, but still everything was divinatory gibberish. Paths that should never cross were intertwined with one another. It was either a failure on his part or the worst of omens. He made a decision based on the instincts warring within him.

'I cannot rule based on this reading, first captain. I suggest we regroup with Daviks and see what evidence, if any, exists to inform our next course of action. If the inquisitor is still alive and can be recovered she may have learned something of the nature of the enemy's plans. If we cannot... then I have to say that the omens for this venture have turned black. If we remain on this world, the future bodes poorly for us.'

Even to speak the words aloud made his shame feel very real. He gathered up the runes and dropped them back into the leather pouch. Drawing tight the string that held it closed, he shook his head.

'I did my best,' he said. 'I am sorry.'

Gileas folded his arms across his chest and shrugged his shoulders easily. 'It cannot be helped, brother,' he said in what he hoped was a conciliatory tone. As far as he was concerned, the outcome was good enough.

'I will try a random reading when we reach the plaza,' the Prognosticator continued, grateful for Gileas's easy acceptance of his failure. Kerelan had said nothing, but he could feel the first captain's disappointment as something tangible. 'Perhaps the situation here is simply too unstable.'

'Perhaps,' said Kerelan flatly. 'Very well then. Brothers, we are returning to the palace. Mark the location of that chapel for the purgation teams and the moment we have the chance to return, we will do so. If the Oracles of Change return to hamper our passage, engage with extreme prejudice.'

Across the surface of Valoria, the fighting had raged for days. The battle for the Governor's Palace had been just one tiny conflict in a war that had been carefully orchestrated throughout the cities over many months. The seeds of treachery that had been planted in the populace had burst into full bloom and even now the rage and hatred of an entire planet boiled and seethed, feeding upon itself and fuelling the dark sorcery that was claiming them.

Karteitja watched in unvoiced pleasure as the biomechanical cables and daemon-flesh bound to the antennae of his device began to thrash violently, soaking up an entire planet's worth of hate, pain, grief and horror. The blood-soaked heart of the thrall throbbed with the surge of power that came from such emotions; emotions that the sorcerer lord revelled in and which would ultimately fuel the change that would soon wrack the planet. This world would belong to the Oracles of Change and their warp-spawned masters.

'It is time to give Valoria a taste of what is to come,' he

said, running a hand across the slick surface of the device. It was straining now, imbued with so much energy that it could barely contain the forces that raged within it. Once the chosen heart of the anointed was installed, it would be far worse. This was simply the beginning, nothing more. He would turn Valoria inside out, drag it into the tides of the warp, and it would become home to beings far greater than the insects that crawled its surface now.

Karteitja knelt before the antenna and lowered his head, murmuring words in an ancient language that countless thousands had once spoken but was now known to but a few. The lenses of his helm began to glow softly in the same pulsing rhythm as the disembodied heart and a ripple of arcane power coruscated across the surface of his armour. He felt the always-welcome thrill of his own might and raised his head to the skies. The gathering clouds were black-edged and bloated as though they brought a deluge with them. But this storm would unleash something far more than torrential rain.

'This world will be ours,' he said in his deep, monstrous growl. 'Let us take it.'

With those words, Karteitja channelled the restrained power in the psychic conduits and it burst upwards to the clouds in a single column of pulsating green-blue light. It pierced the roiling clouds and rent a mighty tear through the thin fabric of space and time that separated this world from the realms of Chaos. The sky boiled, the cloud churning into a froth of colour-bruised foam that spread like ripples in a pond from epicentres around the globe.

There was an earth-shattering sonic boom, like a thunderclap, and Karteitja gasped at the sudden pain that seared through him. But he was a creature of Chaos now. He was used to the agony that always came with the onset of a warp storm.

There were others on the world who were less prepared.

The Silver Skulls had all but made it back to the palace when the clap of psychic thunder rumbled around the city, shivering the souls of all within its walls and crumbled structures. The ground shook: a tremor that Gileas at first mistook for a seismic shock. Bhehan stumbled suddenly and fell against Djul. The Terminator turned to pass a comment, but stopped immediately.

'Brothers!' Bhehan and Nicodemus were convulsing violently, the echoes of the sudden blast of tainted power affecting them even down here. Bhehan gripped onto Djul as though he were a drowning man clinging to his last hope of rescue.

'So much... power,' he said through gritted teeth. 'Someone is... vile sorcery... ah!' He broke off and released Djul's arm, clutching at his helm. He made a move as though he would tear it off, but the zealous Terminator pushed him hard up against the wall.

'Whatever this evil is that threatens your sanity, Prognosticator, you must fight it. You are better than this. Do not disappoint me. Look to your faith. Trust in your own strength and power.'

Kerelan had joined them while Gileas grappled with the fallen Nicodemus. The first captain noted the sudden play of lights on the Prognosticator's crystalline psychic hood. 'What is he talking about?'

Bhehan was stuttering, struggling to force back the power that threatened to boil his brain and shatter his soul. When he was finally able to speak, his words were slurred as though he were drugged. He gripped onto Kerelan's forearm and spoke slowly and desperately.

'The warp is bleeding out onto this planet,' he said with obvious difficulty. 'I can feel the evil within it clawing, tearing... pushing through. They will be here soon, if they are not here already.'

Kerelan looked around at the gathered Silver Skulls. There was still no evidence that the Oracles of Change would return and events were starting to spiral out of control.

'Stand firm, brothers,' he said. 'I understand that you are in pain, but you are sons of Varsavia both by birthright. Brother Djul is right. You are stronger than this.' The words were spoken in a hard tone, but they were not without compassion. 'Guard your soul and control your mind. We must regroup with the Ninth and begin an immediate sweep of the palace. The outer city is in ruins, the seat of the governor is the only place left they could be hiding. We will find them. And we will exterminate them. Brothers, make all haste. Gileas... carry Nicodemus if you must. We run.'

The effects of boring a hole through reality were profound, but they were slow to spread. Karteitja, however, was eternally patient. He had been granted millennia to develop the art and he excelled at it. True Chaos, in its raw form, was not a tool that could be easily bent to the will of the one who used it.

He suffered the effects of the initial tear in reality as much as any other psyker on the planet. Even his own warriors were forced to their knees at the sheer tidal surge of the empyrean. But unlike the Imperial forces, the Oracles of Change welcomed such pain with howls of adulation. They did not fight it, they embraced it. It was that acceptance which had given them so much power over the stuff of creation.

The clouds above the war-torn planet had distorted completely now, tinged with purple and blue, and the sky beneath was turning a virulent shade of yellow. It seemed as though the heavens themselves had been wounded.

The rain began to pour, spattering on the armour of the Oracles in a sticky mess of scarlet. No longer the dirty water of Valoria, this was a rain of blood that had started to fall. Vile as it was, the storm of gore was nothing compared to the streaks of pink and cerulean fire that soon replaced it. What remained of the buildings below were slow to catch aflame, but gradually, the world would burn.

Karteitja began to laugh. It was a deep and guttural sound that carried no humour. Flinging out his arms he raised his helmed and visored face to the skies, welcoming the maelstrom.

Far below him, the Imperial Guardsmen who had been mustering their forces in readiness for redeployment found themselves caught in a sudden deluge. When the realisation came that they were being soaked in blood, uproar broke out. When the blood became incendiary, things got worse. Where the unnatural fires touched flesh, it bubbled and contorted into obscene new shapes. Men dissolved into thrashing tangles of eyes, limbs and flailing pseudopods.

There was no escaping the insidious touch of the warp's terrible power. Those who stared up into the clouds saw daemonic faces etched there, faces that stretched into grotesque, alien shapes and whispered words of damnation to any who were weak enough to listen. Many of the younger and less experienced amongst the soldiers fell prey swiftly to such suggestions and even those who had rallied before in the face of corruption found themselves struggling not to succumb to the power.

Weapons were drawn as comrades turned on one another in their madness. Shots rang out and blades were thrust into flesh, and above it all rang the stentorian voices of the commissars as they vainly attempted to bring order to the chaos. The *crack* of execution shots joined the growing din of battle as the regiment slowly but surely turned upon itself.

The rain sizzled down, igniting drums and fuel tanks with violent explosions that rocked the streets and threw broken men and women in all directions. And the chaos and horror unfurling across the city fed the power upon which the Oracles of Change drew. Violence begat violence and terror begat terror until the entire area around the Governor's Palace had dissolved into complete and glorious madness.

The Talriktug were just about in sight of the Celebrant's Square when three Oracles of Change stepped from their hiding places. A tide of madness was rising across Valoria and the surviving population was drowning in it, choking the rubble-strewn alleys with crazed rebels and hapless survivors. The all-pervading chaos blunted the Oracles' surprise attack, as not only did Bhehan detect the peculiar shift in the aether even over the growing storm, but the emerging warriors had to smash aside howling madmen to reach their foes.

'Attack,' Bhehan bellowed out across the squad vox and lowered his force axe before him. The word had barely left his lips before the first flash of deep red armour had emerged from nowhere. Then another... then another.

The bolt pistols of every Assault Marine fired simultaneously, the shells cracking against the archaic armour of these most hated of enemies.

Bhehan could feel the traitor warriors gathering their will, drawing power from the burning air around them, and prepared to deploy a psychic shield of his own. He was sick and weakened by the effects of the backlash that had torn at his consciousness, but he was tenacious.

The Terminators reacted less quickly than Gileas and his squad, their massive bulk slowing them considerably. Kerelan's sword was already drawn and he held it before him. Many an enemy had died on the point of that blade and he was more than willing to increase that body count on this battlefield today. His cloak fluttered behind him, whipped into a frenzy by the furious winds, and he held his position rigidly. He was the very image of the stubbornness the Silver Skulls were renowned for.

The Oracle of Change closest to the Talriktug thrust a hand out in front of him and a rippling ball of energy slammed into Asterios's chestplate. The Terminator staggered and would have fallen had Djul not been standing directly behind him. The zealot pushed his battle-brother back to his feet with a sputtered oath. There was the crackle of cooling metal as the armour did its job of protecting the man within its shell. But Asterios's armour was damaged. Djul moved as rapidly as his restrictive plate allowed in such a small place to shift positions with his battle-brother.

Levelling his own storm bolter before the Oracle could unleash another attack, Djul fired. As the weapon stuttered out its reply to the enemy, ceramite shards of the traitor's armour flew. At this range, the weapon did enough damage to tear one of the red-clad warrior's arms from his body. The limb clattered away and a spray of hot Adeptus Astartes blood gushed from the stump. The Oracle let out a scream of fury and pain, stepping backwards.

But he did not vanish. He said something in some old, forgotten language that grated on the senses and which was quite obviously a curse of some kind. The two warriors with him replied in kind and then they were both gone.

'Do your worst, Silver Skulls,' the Oracle said in his rasping voice.

Behind Djul, Bhehan was on his knees, his voice coming in a strangled gasp of effort and energy. 'I can hold only one tear for so long, brother. Now is your chance.'

Djul did not hesitate. He stepped to one side, allowing Vrakos to stand beside him. Both storm bolters fired simultaneously and the Oracle of Change was gradually pressed back under the fusillade before finally a well-placed shot chewed through his damaged helm. His skull evaporated in a spray of fine red mist and grey matter.

Bhehan collapsed in a state of complete exhaustion and was dragged up to his feet by Vrakos.

'Fight now,' said the near-silent battle-brother in his customary serious tone. 'Fight now and you can rest all you want when we are back on Varsavian soil, Brother-Prognosticator.' He paused for moment, then nodded. It was a curious gesture of camaraderie from the deeply introverted man.

Amidst the fire and flames of the horror that had become Valoria, they moved off once again towards the Celebrant's Square.

SIXTEEN

MADNESS

Bhehan had regained his composure swiftly following the psychic shockwave, but Gileas was concerned for Nicodemus. The young psyker lacked the experience of the Prognosticator and was clearly suffering under the onslaught. As the squads retreated towards the palace, Nicodemus groaned and several sparks coughed from his protective hood. He was able to mumble a few words of thanks before slipping back into delirium once again. Bhehan, still pale from shock, nodded in approval of the warrior's fortitude. 'He will owe you a debt of honour should he survive this ordeal,' he observed to Gileas.

'It is my duty, brother. You are both too valuable. If it should come to it, I would carry you both to the palace across my back.'

'What are you going to do about the inquisitor, Gileas?' The question was not entirely unexpected and Gileas did not look at the Prognosticator. 'You know that I must consult the runes when we get back before a decision can be made.'

'If your runes are not burned away,' retorted Gileas, then his tone softened slightly. 'I will wait and see,' the sergeant said eventually in a neutral but verging on dangerous tone that Bhehan knew well. 'What else can I do, after all?'

They finally reached the edge of the Celebrant's Square and were greeted by a horrific sight: the charnel house that had ensued in their absence. The rain of fire seemed to have abated, but the damage had been done. The madness and mutation that had spread throughout the human ranks was doing more damage in a single blow than months of warfare had accomplished. The streets were choked with soldiers shooting, biting and clawing at each other, their twisted minds and bodies driving them into an orgy of slaughter. A few islands of sanity remained amidst the chaos, drawn up around a handful of officers or the instantly recognisable commissars. Blood ran freely, mingling with the rainwater on the blasted ground. It congealed and created a vile, stinking miasma that seemed to twitch and gurgle with a life of its own.

They barely had to fight their way through the melee. Nobody even seemed to notice the Space Marines as they passed through the riots. As they moved through the cordon of vehicles, one Guardsman, engaged in a brawl with one of his fellows, collided with Gileas and rebounded from the Assault Marine without even seeming to notice the transgression. Djul crushed the offender beneath his chainfist in contempt.

'You will forgive me for voicing this opinion, I am sure, but the regiment is in need of discipline,' commented Vrakos in his usual deadpan manner. His lenses were fixed on the battle with obvious interest. The others swung their heads towards him and he shrugged easily. 'Merely an observation.'

'With the Oracles of Change behind this unnatural affliction, we should expect the worst from all encounters,' said Kerelan from behind gritted teeth. 'Vrakos, Varlen – go and offer whatever assistance you can to the survivors. Take two of Gileas's squad…' The first captain tailed off and shot a glance at the sergeant, a cue for him to delegate.

'Reuben, Tikaye – you're with me.' Gileas's squad took their positions without comment, those who remained with him and those who went with the Terminators.

The rest of them made their way towards the broken entrance to the palace. The buttresses and spires of the building still remained largely untouched by the fighting, but the shower of gore had given the north face of the palace a macabre aspect. Blood streamed in rivulets down its pillars and columns and poured from the shattered doorway that hung open like some kind of obscene maw. Standing before the grisly tableau, Daviks waited for them, his Devastators flanking him and their weapons covering the chaos of the square. The siege captain had removed his helm and his dark face was one of sombre self-control lined with lingering pain from his wounds.

'As you no doubt saw, things have gone from bad to worse,' he said without any preamble. 'The majority of the siege company managed to fall back into the palace grounds when the storm struck and I have contact with units around the city who have likewise entrenched themselves. I have twenty per cent loss of armoured support due to catastrophic failure and the Thunderhawk *Sigil* went down beyond the city limits. We have had no further contact. The inquisitor was abducted by Sinnaria Gryce, and you saw what has happened to the regiment.' Daviks ran a hand over his scalp. 'The inquisitor's psyker was injured too – and he and our own psychic brothers suffered some kind of attack that affected them gravely.'

'We noticed that,' responded Kerelan, shooting a glance at Bhehan and the groggy, but recovering, Nicodemus.

'The Oracles have remained curiously absent. I do not have any idea what their strategy might be beyond the obvious carnage.'

'Corruption,' boomed Djul. 'Heresy. How bad is the human psyker? How close to failure is he?'

'He isn't some sort of machine, you know.' The voice was Harild de Corso's, his perfectly polished veneer decidedly cracked. He stood several feet away, a supporting arm around the frail psyker who was leaning heavily on the only friend he had left. 'Nathaniel is disoriented and confused, but otherwise well.'

'If he is a danger to himself and more importantly to others…' Djul persisted with his train of thought, not wanting it to be derailed. Gileas could not help but get the impression that the Terminator was out for blood.

'He is remarkably resilient,' interjected Daviks. 'I have already addressed the matter with de Corso here. I agree that he does not present a danger. Not at this time. He is merely agitated. He does not possess the same potency of psychic defence as do our own men.' Daviks indicated Nicodemus, who was finally managing to regain his feet unsupported. The young warrior's psychic hood was occasionally spiking with energy as he struggled to contain the forces flowing through him. It was more active than the one on Bhehan's armour but such was the price of youth and inexperience.

'What of the inquisitor?' Kerelan took command of

the situation before Djul and Daviks could descend into some sort of theological discussion on the state of the party's psykers. 'Do we have any idea where she has been taken?'

'She just vanished.' Nathaniel spoke, his quiet voice a half-octave shriller than his usual speech. His words were clear and lucid however and that was undoubtedly promising. 'The governor's wife summoned daemonic strength from the warp. She tried to strangle me... then she took the inquisitor and they were gone. She is a sorcerer in her own right.'

'Then we need to find her.' Kerelan's response was short, indicative of the increased impatience the first captain felt.

'I can... I can maybe help with that,' said Nathaniel instantly, then flushed as all eyes turned to him. 'I am well attuned to the inquisitor. We have worked together long enough for me to be able to recognise her...' He hesitated. 'I know her mind. I can recognise her psychic patterns better than anybody.'

'You will not be going anywhere, witch...' Djul began to say in his booming voice. The psyker held up a hand to forestall the argument and Djul stopped in his tracks, more from surprise than anything else.

'Am I calm, my lord?'

'You appear to be so, but...'

'Am I rational, my lord?' He said these words with no hint of irony despite the fact that he had a twitch under his left eye and his right leg was jiggling uncontrollably. Gileas watched the exchange and for the first time since he had known the man, felt something like respect for Nathaniel kindle in his breast.

'I would dispute that,' growled Djul, but he did not

continue. Nathaniel nodded, turning to stand before the first captain, a molehill approaching the mountain.

'I can help,' he said again.

'He is a liability.' Djul's voice across the private vox was more than a little outraged. 'He is barely strong enough to stand on his own two feet!'

'He is offering his help. Bhehan is exhausted from his efforts and Nicodemus is in little better condition. Nathaniel is the only other psyker I would trust with this task.' Kerelan was snappish in response and Gileas carefully interjected.

'With permission, first captain, I would like to lead the search for the inquisitor. As we discussed.' Djul began to say something else, but Kerelan held up a hand, speaking aloud again.

'I appreciate the offers of assistance in this matter,' he said, 'but there are rituals that must be observed regardless of what happens. Prognosticator?'

'Yes, first captain.' Bhehan wearily drew the rune bag once again from his waist, ignoring the look of fury that the human psyker shot him. It was all Nathaniel could do to keep from hopping up and down in rage.

'This is wasting time! I think–'

Whatever it was that Nathaniel thought was cut off in a yelp as Gileas reached down and lifted the psyker by the shoulders until he was at eye level.

'I am every bit as anxious as you are to locate and recover the inquisitor, Master Gall. However, you will wait until we have made our observance. Do you understand me? I say this not to intimidate you, but to protect you from those whose patience is far less than mine.'

Gileas ignored the barely stifled snort of amusement from

Reuben and continued. 'Do we have an accord, Nathaniel Gall?'

'Fine,' squeaked Nathaniel, his legs waving helplessly. 'Just... please put me down now?'

'Of course,' said Gileas and set the psyker down as gently as if he were a child. 'Now if you would just wait a moment longer?'

Nathaniel said nothing else, merely nodding, his eyes wild and alarmed.

'You continue to surprise me, Sergeant Ur'ten,' murmured Kerelan.

'Thank you for the compliment, sir,' replied Gileas and waited for Bhehan to commence his task.

He saw nothing.

With a sinking heart, Bhehan realised that his ability to commune with the Emperor was severely hampered by the rising warp storm that was raging around him. The inside of his skull itched madly and his eyes felt as though the optic nerves had been set alight. He closed them and breathed deeply, feeling his lungs fill with the sour, tainted air of the city.

In. Out. In. Out.

The calm that he sought remained elusive, however, and he began to know a moment's panic. For the second time, the Deep Dark was upon him. Had he fallen out of the Emperor's favour somehow?

+No, Bhehan. It is circumstantial. Just keep your calm, boy.+

It was Vashiro's voice he heard, the great Prognosticator's calm and dulcet tones permeating the phantasmal horrors that had formed inside his mind. Bhehan reached for that cool voice and held onto it tightly. This had formed part of his training, after all, dealing with a situation beyond his control. He breathed again.

In. Out.

If you ever truly know the Deep Dark, you must never let that show to your battle-brothers. They rely on your advice in the thick of battle. To admit to them that the Emperor did not turn his gaze upon them would be detrimental.

There were planned methods for this. The obvious one was simply to consider the situation and suggest the most logical strategy accordingly. Bhehan had never once had to fall back on this method, but that was because Bhehan was one of the rarest of Prognosticators. He did genuinely possess the gift of foresight, even if only a fleeting glimpse. That, combined with a quick-thinking mind, meant that he had never failed to give wise advice.

Many of the other Prognosticators, had he but known it, experienced a blank at times. When this happened, they drew on their strategic minds far more than anybody would ever have suspected. As a result, Prognosticators were a great deal more than simply spiritual and psychic advisers. They were brilliant and gifted tacticians. They were invaluable, and over the years the Silver Skulls had built up a dependency upon their psykers.

Bhehan took another shuddering breath and opened his eyes, drawing a single rune from the bag. He ran his fingers across the engraving on its silver surface and stared down at the iconography that he knew as well as his own gauntlets. A rune in the shape of a lightning strike. One of the most powerful, representing the sun.

'A potent rune,' he murmured, working through the possible interpretations of its appearance and applying them to what he knew must be right. 'It can be seen as both positive and negative. As dangerous as the heart of the sun whilst in every way as enlightening.'

'The practical upshot, Prognosticator? The best course of action?'

Bhehan gently palmed the rune and stared down at it. He raised his head, the red lenses in his helmet glowing softly.

'Given the circumstantial evidence all around us, I would be inclined to lean towards the negative aspect of this rune,' he said, carefully avoiding Gileas's gaze. 'The lightning strike symbolises the potential for something that is on the verge of being obliterated. We need to make our way off this planet and we need to do it soon.'

'But the inquisitor!' Nathaniel had been standing quietly after his alarming moment at the sergeant's hands, but the Prognosticator's words sparked him back into vocal resistance. 'We have to find her! You said that she is probably here somewhere... I could look for her. In fact, I'm going to look for her and I don't care what you think about it.' He began to move, as though he would limp towards the palace, but de Corso reached over and grabbed him around the waist, hauling him back again.

'In this matter, my choice lies with the psyker,' said Gileas quietly. 'I have an oath to fulfil and I will not leave Valoria before it is realised. That is a simple fact.'

'The Prognosticator has given his advice, Gileas.' Kerelan spoke in just as quiet a voice. 'You realise that to pursue any other course of action will not be perceived well when we return to Varsavia?'

'With respect, first captain, I think a fairer assessment would be *if* we return to Varsavia. There is no way you will contact the *Prevision of Victory* through this warp storm. For all the good standing around here debating the relevance of a carved nugget of silver will do us, I could already have been searching for the inquisitor. In the event we return to Varsavia, I will deal with the repercussions then.'

'You dare stray into the realms of blasphemy?' Djul's modulated voice quivered with a deep-seated rage that he no longer cared to disguise.

'Brother Djul, your continued low opinion of me is hardly a matter for discussion now,' responded Gileas, his voice level. 'We are beset on all sides, we cannot evacuate from this planet whilst a warp storm threatens to tear it apart. There are enough of us here that we should be seeking out the heart of this threat – and there are enough of us here that you can spare me to fulfil my sworn duty.'

Djul's hands balled briefly into fists, but he was a veteran of hundreds of years of service. He reined back his fury and simply asked a question in a carefully pitched manner.

'Why do you do this against the word of a Prognosticator, sergeant?'

'Did you never swear an oath, Brother Djul?'

Djul stiffened and took a step forward. The two warriors were nose to nose and Gileas leaned in until the ceramite of his helm was practically touching Djul's. Clad as he was in his Terminator battleplate, Djul was a hulking monster of an Adeptus Astartes. Most of the regularly armoured brethren came barely to his shoulder. But Gileas Ur'ten was bigger than most. He was just shy of the same height and whilst he had nowhere near the same mass as Djul, his presence was every bit as intimidating. If the Assault Marine sergeant were ever to find himself among the ranks of the Chapter's elite, he would be one of the most impressive warriors ever to don the ancient wargear.

'This should not be an issue, sergeant. The inquisitor is likely already dead anyway.' Djul was dismissive. 'If you want to waste your time on a fruitless hunt instead of visiting retribution upon heretics, go right ahead.'

'There is an issue, Brother Djul,' replied Gileas. 'Imagine if I were to find out later that the inquisitor had been alive and I had abandoned her to her fate, or worse, the Oracles had corrupted her with their sorcery? How would I ever look my battle-brothers in the eye again, knowing that I had forsworn my oath-bound duty? I respect the runes. I respect the word of the Emperor, but this situation does not favour us in any way. If death is my destiny during this mission, then I will not hide from it.'

'Your oath? When did this happen? Who witnessed such a thing?'

'I spoke to Inquisitor Callis directly. I gave the Oath of Hospitality. And my word, Brother Djul, was ever my bond.'

There was a gruff snort of derision and Djul stepped back. 'We will not come for you, Ur'ten.'

'I know that, and I appreciate it. As such, I do not expect any of you to follow me on this path.'

His words fell into a silence as Djul considered him. 'I am a son of Varsavia, Djul,' continued Gileas. 'I know you do not wish to accept that at times, but that is the simple fact.'

When the Terminator spoke again there was something new in the pitch of his words. Something that bordered on respect. 'Aye, sergeant. I start to see that perhaps you are.'

It was as close to acceptance as Gileas was likely to get. The sergeant let out a long breath that he had not even noticed he had been holding.

'Your observation is likely accurate, Sergeant Ur'ten.' Kerelan's eyes were on Djul, but he spoke to Gileas. 'We need to establish the epicentre and causes of this warp storm and then we need to do whatever we can to end it.' He turned to the youngest Silver Skull present.

'Brother Nicodemus. The time has come for you to take up your birthright and embrace the challenges that it brings. As of this moment, you are our most powerful psychic battle-brother. The Prognosticator is drained and still recovering from his recent exertions and if anybody is going to be able to help us with this matter, it will be you.'

'I understand, first captain. I am ready,' Nicodemus managed to reply.

'Of course you are, boy. Do you really believe that you would have been deployed on this mission if your instructors or my brothers and I had not thought so as well? Very well, Gileas. If you must do this thing, then do it. But you do not go alone. Take Reuben and Tikaye with you and remain in contact as much as communications will allow. Brother Djul is right. Do you understand that if we are able to make an extraction, we will not come for you? The runes have given us our path. We *must* heed His word. You know that.'

'I do, first captain, and I welcome the chance to at least try.' He did not thank Kerelan, but the gratitude was there nonetheless.

'I am going as well.' It was not unexpected. Nathaniel had moved from the corner where he had been cowering following Gileas's reprimand. 'I know you all think I am incapable of providing assistance, but I am stronger than you think.' His voice shook only a little, which for the second time increased the respect Gileas felt for him. 'This is me accepting my duty as a member of the Inquisition. Sergeant Ur'ten, I will defer to your command.'

'Nate…' Harild de Corso shook his head.

'With the inquisitor gone, who has seniority?'

'You do.'

'Then I am ordering you right now to leave this world in the care of the Silver Skulls.'

The sniper looked as though he would argue for a few moments, then shook his head and hurried off towards one of the nearby vehicles. Yes, there was a core of strength running through Nathaniel Gall, and Gileas finally nodded.

'Very well. Reuben, keep an eye on the psyker. He's your responsibility. First captain, we will conduct a search of the palace. Nathaniel will be well attuned to the inquisitor's psychic trace. Taking him is a wise idea.'

'Go, then. Strength and honour, brothers. We will try to maintain whatever passes for order here and attempt to contact the ship in orbit to arrange evacuation as soon as we can.'

If we can, was the unspoken phrase that lingered between them.

'Aye, first captain.' Gileas made the sign of the aquila across his chest, then turned to the small group who would be following him. Tikaye and Reuben had been his battle-brothers for so long that he had never envisioned what it would be like to fight without them. Nathaniel Gall he neither knew nor fully trusted.

'We will perform an auspex sweep of the palace,' he said. 'If you could use your abilities to see if you can…'

'I know what I have to do,' said Nathaniel irritably. He was immediately contrite. 'Apologies.'

'Apology accepted. This time.' Gileas reloaded his bolt pistol and unsheathed his bloodied chainsword. 'We go.' He glanced at his battle-brothers. 'How is your faith, brothers?'

How is your faith?

He could hear the words of the Chaplain in the back of his mind and realised that he spoke the same words he had heard from Akando's lips so many times before. They felt strange coming from him, but he said the ritual lines anyway. With every word, his pride grew stronger and his fervour more determined.

'How is your faith, brothers? Repeat the litanies. Assess your strengths, defy your weaknesses. See the corruption active in all things and challenge it boldly. You are a son of Varsavia, a warrior of the Silver Skulls and you *will* prevail!'

'My faith is strong. In my brothers I trust. I will uphold the Emperor's ideals. I am a son of Varsavia. For Argentius, for Varsavia and for the Emperor!' They chorused the reply in perfect unison and raised their weapons high.

Nathaniel said nothing, merely pressing his lips together so tightly that his mouth was little more than a narrow slit across his face.

'They come. Just as the First predicted they would.'

'The Silver Skulls are deluded fools,' said Karteitja. 'It disappoints me that they have not already succumbed to the Primordial Truth.' He turned from the edge of the platform and picked his way around the heavy cables snaking across its surface. The massive antenna array at its centre trembled in the unnatural winds of the rising storm and with the power being fed to it by the arcane machine wired into it like an ugly parasite. The heart that had been inserted into it was shrivelled and the stench of burning meat was strong, its strength dying even as the planet died. For each failing beat of the organ, another surge of

324

power coursed through the myriad cables, further feeding the growing maelstrom.

The more the skin of reality buckled the more the Imperial forces and inhabitants of Valoria descended into madness. The rain of fire followed the spreading storm like a curtain, and while it had abated over the palace it had been replaced by equally disturbing phenomena. The air was greasy, thick with warp-channelled power, and the stink of blood pervaded everything. Now far worse things were pressing through the abused fabric of the planet.

Far below them, fighting amongst the remaining population and the Imperial Guardsmen continued to escalate. The throaty screams and wails of humanity losing their minds to the relentless warp storm were like a delicious melody to the Oracles of Change, a beautifully orchestrated requiem for sanity.

The mutations triggered by the touch of the fire had run riot. Cackling madmen with flesh of pink and blue capered through the howling mass of humanity while others screamed and gibbered, little more than knots of tortured meat that bit and tore at their former comrades. The Silver Skulls present on the planet might have a better chance of resisting the changes that would be wrought on the weak and pliant, but they too would ultimately fall. And the more they fought and screamed and struggled against the inevitable, the more the machine soaked up their suffering, hatred and pain and further fuelled the widening rift. There was a beautiful symmetry to the self-destructive nature of the process that pleased Karteitja greatly.

'Do you have no interest in taking these Imperial souls for yourself, my lord?' Cirth Unborn hissed. In the past whenever the sorcerer had confronted servants of the Imperial creed, he had taken a perverse pleasure in attempting to bend them to his will. Most of the time he was successful and the last thing seen by many human victims of machinations wrought by the Oracles of Change had been a rampaging Adeptus Astartes. It brought a shiver of gratification to see the humans slaughtered by the very hands they had believed would be their salvation.

'I know the Silver Skulls of old,' Karteitja replied eventually. 'Once, perhaps, they were worthy of consideration. In times long past...' He broke off for a moment, his lightning-fast mind peeling back the years. He had encountered the Silver Skulls perhaps three times in several thousand years. They had been a force for such a long time, it seemed impossible that their paths had not crossed more frequently.

But then, following the last meeting, the Oracles of Change had retreated to nurse their quite considerable wounds. Stalwart warriors the Silver Skulls might be but as far as Karteitja was concerned, that merely made them a nuisance. 'In times long past they were a force of considerable might,' he continued. 'But they have fallen into disarray. Their leaders are dying and they are losing their way. In time, perhaps, what remains of their pitiful force will find their way to our side anyway.'

He extended a forefinger and stroked it gently along the length of the withered heart. He would need to make another sacrifice soon, before the dying flesh failed and the gods turned their eyes from Valoria. The Silver Skulls were a distraction he could not afford to invest time considering. 'No, Cirth, there is nothing they can offer me. They can be consumed with the rest of this worthless planet. When Valoria is reborn as a world for our lord and master, they will simply become slaves to its new order. Or die. Either result is satisfactory.'

Nathaniel could feel nothing. He had been seeking evidence of the inquisitor's psychic trace as they moved through the floors of the palace but there was none to be found. The auspex had identified a number of life signs as they climbed, but thus far all they had found was a mob of crazed servants and a menagerie of xenos pets. His frustration with the situation was impairing his own ability to concentrate and he paused, breathing deeply.

He had spent many years being instructed in the means to control his powers and yet here, when he needed to employ the less confrontational spectrum of his abilities, he could hardly remember any of that advice.

'Master Gall?' The voice belonged to the brutish sergeant who had picked him up and reprimanded him as though he were no better than a child. Nathaniel felt a heavy, gauntleted hand beneath his armpit, dragging him into a more upright position. 'Are you well?'

'I am fine,' he snapped in reply. 'I just need… a moment to gather my thoughts.'

'As you wish, but time is not something we can afford to squander. Brothers, hold.' Gileas's manner was, if not deferential, at least respectful and Nathaniel let this fact squirrel itself away at the back of his mind to deal with later. If there *was* a later. He did not claim the gift of foresight, not like his post-human counterparts, but still he had a very bad feeling about this situation. That, coupled with the endless whispers of the Things Beyond that were constantly trying to break through his waning defence, left him feeling weak and feeble.

He closed his eyes and took several deep breaths. He

could feel the psychic spoor of the warriors who accompanied him. It was an ability he had always had and the visualisation in his mind's eye had always been that of cord-like tendrils that connected his mind to the individual concerned. Whilst each of the Silver Skulls bore traces of similarity due to their shared genetic brotherhood, there were also subtle nuances; variances in the effect.

The sergeant's echo for example would best be described as a silver thread with flecks of red and black rage running through it. The others bore notable differences that marked them out: Reuben's had a golden glow, something that Nathaniel had always attributed to a protector spirit, whilst Tikaye's was a stoic and solid silver, untainted by anything but purity of thought.

He knew Liandra Callis's psychic trace well. Scarlet, with no imperfections. Her sheer determination and single-mindedness had long been part of the attraction for Nathaniel; an attraction that he had only ever acted on once and which had cost him dearly. But there was nothing other than the three silvery threads and the varicoloured, complex tendril of his own psychic trace.

'Keep moving, sergeant,' he said in due course, his heart heavy. 'I still do not sense her.'

She was in considerable pain, of that she was certain. With regard to everything else around her, the inquisitor had no idea what was happening. The return to consciousness had come with considerable suffering. Slow awareness crept through her body and she realised that she was lying face down on a cool surface with her hands bound behind her back. A crude gag of torn material had been forced into her mouth. It tasted vile.

Her head ached and she remembered the suddenness with which she had been flung against the wall. For decades she had been trained in the art of self-defence and at the last, she had fallen victim to a duplicitous, scheming witch…

'Awake at last. I had hoped it would only be in time to hear your own screams as they opened your flesh,' came Sinnaria Gryce's voice. 'But no matter.'

The inquisitor lifted her head from the floor. She could feel the taut muscles in her abdomen complain at this sudden use of them, but ignored it. She took in the peculiarity of her current surroundings with little more than a widening of the eyes. The room was vaguely octagonal, but it was difficult to tell exactly how large because the walls were lined with flawless mirrors. It was impossible to determine where one started and the next began as each surface reflected its opposite number into an eternity of distorted images.

Standing in the middle of the room was Sinnaria Gryce, dirtied and bruised. She turned this way and that, admiring her many reflected forms in the mirrors.

The inquisitor could not raise her head far enough to see her own reflection, but she could see those of the traitorous witch and what she saw made her heart hammer harder in her chest.

The reflected images of Sinnaria Gryce were each subtly different to the woman who stood before them. As Callis's eyes moved from reflective surface to reflective surface, she felt a prickle of nausea. From her prone position, she could barely make out more than two images clearly. The first one showed Gryce not as she was, but as she clearly preferred to see herself. Tall and slender, endowed with womanly curves that were far more becoming than the rake-thin creature she actually was. The reflection held itself with all of the strength and dignity that befitted a wife of a planetary governor.

But the eyes…

Was this the woman she believed herself to be? The inquisitor recognised the nature of the Dark Powers at work and her stomach turned in revulsion and hatred. You needed to be a fool not to determine that from the image of the staggeringly beautiful woman in the mirror. Her eyes moved to the reflection behind Sinnaria and a stifled cry of pain left her lips as the hexagrammic wards branded across her back flared into life.

Sinnaria turned to see what it was that the inquisitor was so shocked by and her smile grew broader and crueller. The image was that of an avian daemon, shimmering blue and ethereal, with cold eyes and a sharp, wicked beak that curved into an evil-looking hook. Sinnaria reached up a hand and stroked it lovingly across the glass.

'Are they not beautiful? They have such plans for this world! They have granted me their power and they have given me a task. I am to take you to their greatest and best and you will be the key to this planet's salvation. But I am weary.' She sighed theatrically. 'The Oracles are attending to the ritual and it took a lot of my power to bring you this far unspoiled. This room…' Waving a hand around dismissively, a thousand or more Sinnarias waved back. 'This room sustains me. Gives me strength.'

She preened for a while longer, her bird-like movements more exaggerated the longer the inquisitor watched her. 'My idiot husband did not agree with me that we should embrace the will of such greatness, but then he was ever the short-sighted fool.'

It was you that killed him.

Unable to give voice to the accusation, Callis stared at the madwoman with malevolence and contempt. The pain in her head was forgotten. All she wanted to do now was be free from her bonds and break the woman's neck with her bare hands. Such heresy was anathema to the inquisitor and hatred unlike anything she had ever experienced was racing through her veins.

Sinnaria's brow furrowed briefly as she picked up a psychic echo that she recognised. A small smile played about her lips as another piece of the design fell into place. 'Your pet psyker is still alive,' she said. 'And he brings the Emperor's lackeys with him. They are looking for you.'

Inquisitor Liandra Callis had never been helpless in her entire life, but as she lay there, her arms tightly bound and her captor giving her the look a predator gives its meal just before tearing out its throat, she finally knew how it felt.

Nathaniel, she thought furiously, pushing out her mind with everything she had towards the old man. *Nate. Find me.*

'Oh, please do call to them.' Sinnaria stepped away from the mirrors, although the bird-creature lingered awhile, staring after her with its unfathomable eyes. 'You have been annoyingly difficult to capture, inquisitor. Do you really think you would still be alive if there was not some purpose to it?' She let that thought sink in for a few moments. 'You are *supposed* to lead them here, my pet, it is all just another part of fate's grand tapestry. So please, call him, call all of them… call out to your little pawn.'

The inquisitor shook her head desperately, but the damage was already done. She had reached out to Nathaniel and the psyker would no doubt hear her cry and lead the Space Marines into whatever snare Sinnaria had set for them.

SEVENTEEN

THE ENEMY WITHIN

'I sense her.'

They were making their way steadily up through the floors of the palace and were approaching the audience hall when the psyker suddenly stopped. During the ascent the structure had been eerily quiet, with only a handful of crazed retainers still in residence. The auspex and Nathaniel's senses had detected little of worth until now.

Nathaniel, when he spoke, did so with the easy confidence of a man who knew he was quite correct. Gileas liked that trait as much in the psyker as he did in any individual: a sense of absolute certainty. There was no hesitation about him and he knew from his own dealings with those endowed with the Emperor's gift that hesitation was something that could cost the wielder dearly if indulged.

'Good,' replied the sergeant, shouldering his chainsword. 'Would you care to share some sort of direction with the rest of us?' He spoke without mocking and Nathaniel glanced up briefly to see if the sergeant was jesting at his expense. There was nothing he could read in those glowing red eye-lenses.

'I can lead you,' he replied. 'If you imagine the inquisitor's psychic trace is like an uncoiled ball of string that I'm winding back in behind her...' He tailed off and gave a rueful, self-deprecating smile. 'I'm sorry,' he said. 'This way.'

He had felt the inquisitor's cry in his mind as something barely tangible; a butterfly wing of thought that had brushed the surface of his senses through the building maelstrom of horror. But it was a voice he had come to respect so deeply that it was instantly recognisable.

Nate. Find me.

Liandra.

Nathaniel raised his head and turned slightly, veering towards the massive stairs that would carry them to the last few floors of the palace. 'She's up there. I'm certain of it.'

'Then we had better get moving.'

The three Space Marines and the psyker began to wind their way upwards.

His lungs were fit to burst by the time they finally reached the top staircase, but Nathaniel struggled on with the determination that had so marked his entire life. He was not unfit, not by any stretch of the imagination, but his human body had limitations. He couldn't keep up with the three Space Marines no matter how hard he tried – and yet he had tried. Worse was the pain in his twisted leg.

'Wait,' he called out, pausing briefly. 'Wait a moment, Sergeant Ur'ten.'

Gileas turned and moved to stand beside him. 'Are you well enough to continue?' The question was harmless enough, but it triggered a response in Nathaniel Gall that fired up his pride.

'Of course I am. Just give me a moment to... to... gather my thoughts.'

'Indeed.' Gileas surveyed the psyker, the scroll of his retinal feed noting that there was a marked increase in the psyker's body heat and that his jugular vein was visibly pulsing. Gileas watched in silence until the man's heart rate slowed a little, then spoke again. 'Which way do your senses tell you we should go?'

The psyker concentrated and nodded. 'There. The inquisitor's trace leads through that doorway there.' He raised a bony finger and pointed at one of the many portals that lined this richly decorated residential level of the palace. There was something unsettling about the door that he couldn't put his finger on.

Reuben put a hand to the door. 'Locked,' he reported.

Gileas strode forward and punched his way through. He tore the door from its frame, sending it flying down the corridor, and then squeezed his massive bulk through the opening.

'Unlocked,' observed Reuben with heavy sarcasm.

'Wait!' Nathaniel called as the Space Marines barged their way inside. As the last of the squad pushed through the entrance he managed to identify the sense of disquiet. The psychic trace of the inquisitor did not just feel like it was in the next room, it felt like it was incredibly far away, everywhere and nowhere all at once. The space beyond the door could not possibly exist in any conventional sense. Realising that the Silver Skulls were completely unprepared for what they might face, he rushed after them. But his warning cry came too late.

The room opened out into an impossibly large chamber and for the briefest of seconds, Gileas was quite disoriented. The hairs on his neck tingled and he stepped further into the hall. He sensed his brothers enter the chamber behind him and turned to address them, but they were no longer there.

All he saw were infinite reflections of Gileas Ur'ten. Reflections of reflections that poured into each other like water into an ocean. He took another pace forward and stepped into a nightmare.

He saw himself as he was. A stalwart hero of the Imperium; a warrior of the Silver Skulls Chapter who carried out his duty commendably. One of the Emperor's finest. His battleplate was worn but well cared for and polished to a mirror shine. He carried a Chapter relic, the chainsword Eclipse, in his hand and his face was hidden behind an expressionless helm.

He turned.

He knew the warrior who stood before him now as well as he knew the previous one. The differences were so subtle as to be barely noticeable. He concentrated hard and stared. He had seen that aspect in countless dreams and flashes of what he had always taken to be déjà vu. The stance was the same, the prideful set to the shoulders, and he nodded. This was a fine warrior. A perfect example of his breed.

His reflection nodded back, but that was where the mirror image ended. Reaching up to pull free its helmet, the reflection of Gileas exposed its face to the sergeant.

He recoiled in sudden disgust as the daemonic being beneath the armour gave him a leery, toothy grin. And despite its very alien nature, a skull-like face that was bronze-skinned and studded with spines, there was still something he recognised.

The Gileas-thing raised Eclipse in salute and stepped back, allowing more reflections to fill his vision. Somewhere on the very edge of his awareness, he could hear a low moan of horror, but it did not register straight away. He was too absorbed in the sorcery trapped within this mirror room to even remember that he had not entered alone.

The moan came again and he spun around with his chainsword at the ready to deal with the intrusion on this moment of revelation. But he saw nothing but Gileas Ur'ten, reflected again and again.

He was falling into this deep well of infinity and he was helpless to stop it. He was seeing the man he was, the man he could be... his *potential*...

Serve my needs, Gileas Ur'ten Da'chamoren, and you will be well rewarded.

The voice was a thing of nightmares, a shivering sound, wet and breathy as though the words were wheezed through collapsing lungs.

Da'chamoren. Son of the Waxing Moon. The tribal name of his father. A name he had only ever spoken to a handful of brothers. A name from a past he had long forgotten. The daemonic face in the mirror warped and twisted and became someone he had not seen for many years. His soul swelled with fraternal affection and delight.

'Captain,' he said, joy bubbling to his lips. He took a step forward and reached out a hand. The reflection was no longer his; now, the face of Andreas Kulle looked out at him. His former mentor did not reply, but merely smiled a little sadly and reached up a hand. Gileas raised his own in response.

This is wrong.

The thought came unbidden from the well of his piety and he was startled at its determined emphasis. *This is wrong. You must not fall, Gileas.*

He stared at the man he had thought of as a father-figure for long moments. It would be the easiest thing in the world to step forward and fall into the darkness beyond the mirror, but he did not touch the surface of the glass. The long years of service and loyalty combined with his own fervent nature prevented him from taking the damning step.

Do not touch the glass.

'No,' he said and there was something like regret in his tone. 'No. This is not real. This cannot be.'

Then his world shattered.

'Sergeant, you must hear my voice!'

Nathaniel was agitated beyond belief. The moment the four of them had walked into this room, the Space Marines had all become entranced by whatever it was they saw in the mirrors. Gileas had been the last to be caught in the mesmerising trap, as first Tikaye and then Reuben had stopped dead, staring into their reflections. Nathaniel could see them shaking as they strained to free themselves from whatever spell had snared them, arms struggling to lift their weapons against a foe they could not see, but only experienced in their minds.

None of them were gifted with psychic abilities and so they had all fallen into the cunning trap that had been laid for them. But Nathaniel had sensed the seeping horror that oozed from the countless silvered surfaces. The years of building up his psychic defences had ensured that he had seen nothing in the mirrors but his own image. He knew the face that stared back at him well, a gaunt man aged and haggard before his time, his youth stolen too early by the harshness of his life.

But the three Silver Skulls had no such bulwarks and they fell one after the other, gazing into the void, trapped by the entity that lurked beyond the skein of reality. Nathaniel had screamed, yelled and attempted to physically push the Adeptus Astartes warriors to no avail. It was like trying to shake a mountain. The taunt of the inquisitor's proximity had made him more and more agitated until he had attempted to communicate in a psychic whisper. He poured all of his attention onto Gileas and sent the thought deep into the sergeant's mind.

Do not touch the glass.

It had come as a surprise to Nathaniel when it apparently worked. The sergeant's hand, which had been half raised to the mirror, stopped, and Nathaniel dared to hope that he had succeeded. But he had to break this power and there was only one way he knew he could do that.

Do not touch the glass.

Gileas's head turned towards Nathaniel, and the psyker stared up into the unreadable mask of the sergeant's helmet and smiled slowly. It was a sad expression.

'Save her,' he said. 'Please.'

He summoned every ounce of power he possessed – and with the storm raging above, it poured in like a flood – and closed his eyes. He let out a small sigh and, as Gileas stepped towards him, let the unfettered strength of the warp flow through him. His thin body shook in unnatural ecstasy and a faint nimbus of blue glowed about him. Then he threw back his head and roared out his defiance.

There was a deep, ominous rumbling and then an ear-splitting sound of cracking glass. Nathaniel could feel the taint of the power being utilised in this foul place and it turned his stomach to the point of making him want to vomit. But he did not. He could not afford to give way to physical weakness, not now. Not for the first time in his life, Nathaniel Gall was filled with hate for his slight build and poor constitution, but he pressed past it into something he had never thought he could accomplish.

'No,' he bellowed. 'No! I defy you!'

He flung his arms out, and the energy gathered within him erupted in a coruscating shockwave that burst the closest mirrors apart. Silver, razor-edged shards chimed from the Space Marines' armour as the hall filled with lethal shrapnel. The blast continued to spread, the psychic nova ripping the sorcerous artefacts apart throughout the chamber.

Nathaniel barely noticed the lacerations that the flying glass from the mirrors wrought on his body. He was too focused on ensuring that they were utterly destroyed. The taste of the foul Chaos taint in their enchantment brought bile to his throat again and he spat it out. Blood ran in rivers down his face and there was a terrible burning in his chest. He was certain that he must have ruptured something. His clothing was torn to shreds that hung in ragged strips from his body.

He laughed. He had done it. He had freed the three Space Marines from the trap that had been laid for them. He had accomplished it. Gileas and Tikaye took abrupt steps backwards, both speaking soft words of Varsavian. From the tone of their voices, Nathaniel could only guess that they were wondering what had happened.

He glanced around, noting that Reuben was still standing stock-still, staring at the empty space where moments before he had been confronted with his own reflection.

Nathaniel watched, his consciousness beginning slowly to slip away from him as the sergeant moved towards the frozen Space Marine. Then Nathaniel wrapped his arms around his body. The temperature in the room dropped noticeably and he saw Gileas's breath ghost before him as he called out the psyker's name.

'Nathaniel!'

Gileas caught him as he fell. Nathaniel was gravely wounded and bleeding from countless injuries on his body. Smoke curled from his eyes and ears from the backwash of the power he had unleashed. Blood ran in a scarlet river from his nose and there were trickles coming from his ears as well. Gileas laid the man on the ground and stared in consternation at him. 'What happened?'

'No time,' gasped Nathaniel. 'No time. Save her. Please.' He pointed a shaking, bloodstained finger in the direction of the inquisitor's scarlet trace. He could feel his own life slipping away from him, but he had perhaps bought the Silver Skulls enough time to ensure the inquisitor's continued survival. 'She is still alive. And she is here. Close by. I see her thread, still. Go. Get…'

He let out a rattling breath as darkness reached up to claim him. Unresisting, Nathaniel let it swallow him and he fell gladly into its welcoming embrace.

'Is he dead?' Tikaye had moved to stand behind him.

Gileas shook his head. An unsteady pulse still fluttered weakly in the psyker's throat. 'He is not,' replied the sergeant, 'but he has paid a terrible price in order to release us from the grip of this evil. Reuben, see what you can do for him and try to raise de Corso on the vox.'

No answer came to his order and he swivelled his head

to stare at his other battle-brother. Reuben still had not moved from the spot where he had been standing. Like Gileas, his hand had also been raised and from where the sergeant was crouched beside Nathaniel, it seemed that his brother's hand was trembling slightly.

'Reuben!'

'Of course. Yes, brother.' Reuben seemed to snap out of whatever trance he had been in and took a step back. He stared at the blank wall a moment longer, then turned to Gileas. The sergeant studied him before speaking.

'Are you quite well, brother?'

There was a fraction of a hesitation before Reuben replied. 'I am. I... think. I saw...'

'We have no time to discuss it, brother. Raise de Corso on the vox and see if there are any medics free to attend Nathaniel, if any have endured the madness. This man needs to be treated quickly if he is going to live.' Gileas trailed off and seemed to consider his words. 'Although he may well be better off if he does not survive.' It was remarkably pessimistic and highly unlike Gileas to sound so inclined. Even the sergeant seemed startled by his own pronouncement.

He shook his head again and turned to his other battle-brother. 'Tikaye – with me. He sensed the inquisitor's presence nearby.'

'Aye, sergeant.'

Gileas rose to his feet. 'I grow weary of the treachery of this Gryce woman. Let us see an end to her so that we might turn our attention to the Archenemy.'

Tikaye let his thumb linger on the activation stud of his chainsword. 'There is very little that would give me greater satisfaction at this point, brother.'

Reuben did not enter into the discussion, and that

concerned Gileas. He wondered what it had been that Reuben had seen in the mirror that had left his stalwart, logical battle-brother so very shaken. He even wondered what the stoic and dependable Tikaye had seen. But he would not ask them. He would never ask, lest they ask to know what it was he saw as well. That daemonic face troubled him. Was he capable of falling to the Ruinous Powers? Perhaps. They were all fallible – he knew that as well as any other. But he also knew, or at least he was confident, that his battle-brothers would see him dead before he turned.

It was the closest Gileas had ever – or would ever – come to a crisis of faith and with the practice of decades, he pushed the uncertainties down. He buried them deeply beneath the physical armour that wrapped his genhanced body and the mental armour that he had built up over his years of service.

'I am a son of Varsavia,' he said aloud. 'And I will prevail.'

The last of the broken mirrors crashed to the floor, the silvered fragments melting into insubstantial mist. Nothing but abject darkness waited beyond the fallen panes, its liquid surface rippling with the suggestion of movement. The Space Marines tensed, expecting some new horror to assail them. As they watched, the gloom seemed to sigh and drain away, leaving them standing in an empty chamber. Every inch of the walls, floor and ceiling was painted with arcane symbols, their twisted designs now scuffed and flaked.

'This trap may simply have been put in place to delay us, Gileas,' suggested Tikaye, answering his sergeant's unspoken thoughts. 'They could be anywhere.'

'The psyker said he could sense her nearby. She's here. Somewhere.'

* * *

They were closer than they could have imagined. Karteitja stood only a few floors above them, separated from his hunters by bare metres of ferrocrete, and they were oblivious to the fact. His stance told of unimaginable rage as he faced the warrior opposite him.

'The scrying chamber is destroyed!'

'My lord, the Silver Skulls must have been… stronger than we first believed. The flesh pawn cannot hope to turn them now, or even contain them. They will be upon us soon.'

'Her powers are barely enough to part the veil, let alone bring Space Marines to heel. Her failure to awaken the Silver Skulls to the Deceiver's truth has cost us the heart of the anointed. The third ritual is too far advanced now to be stopped. The powers are gathering and we must bring the rite of desecration to its conclusion. This planet will be ours soon.' He strode towards the warrior who stood proudly, eyes fixed on his leader. 'We will purge the unworthy from its face. We will reveal to them the glory of the Changer of Ways and usher them into his embrace.'

'I understand that, my lord. That is why I have come to you.' The Oracle of Change tore off his helmet to expose the twisted, scarred face beneath. 'Take what you must. I will serve as a conduit. Our masters will welcome my flesh gladly.'

'You understand the price I must exact from you? That is good. It would have been needlessly wasteful to have to break you.' Karteitja surveyed his loyal warrior just the once, and nodded. 'It is good that you are willing, it adds potency. So be it. Prepare to give me your hearts.'

A cursory examination of the room revealed nothing beyond the fact that the runes were old and had been carefully inscribed in human blood. The treachery of Lady Gryce had been going on far longer than the current insurrection. Gileas observed that she must have had at least some assistance in disposing of the bodies such ritual inevitably left in its wake. The inquisitor, however, was not to be found.

'There!' Tikaye pointed at something. He had seen a shimmer, an undulation in the fabric of reality. It was similar to that which they had all observed in the streets of the city and which had heralded the arrival of the Oracles of Change. Gileas turned, his thumb on the activation stud of his chainsword, but saw nothing.

'I see nothing. I... Wait.' Gileas allowed his lenses to focus on the area where Tikaye was pointing and adjusted the visual gain. Then he saw it too. The air shimmered, much as it did whenever the Oracles slipped in and out of existence, but this seemed slower, less controlled. Darkness wept from the growing breach and a rising shriek of anguish leaked into the chamber from a place beyond common reality.

'I think all we need to do is wait, brother.'

Gileas's assessment was accurate. Within a few moments the growing rift ruptured to reveal a pair of indistinct figures shrouded with crawling tendrils of warp-stuff. The shapes became Sinnaria Gryce and Liandra Callis, and eventually the governor's wife could no longer maintain the tiny pocket of space that had kept them hidden.

She fell forward onto her hands, wailing pathetically. Her face was one of haggard weariness and the keening sound she made was the noise of a cornered animal. Gileas was reminded sharply of the cats that he had hunted across the tundra with the initiates only a few short weeks before.

The inquisitor had fallen too, her hands still bound behind her back, but she was on her feet in an instant and moved to stand before the woman. Gileas reached over and with the knife at his belt cut her bonds free. She tore the gag from her mouth and spat on Gryce.

The pitiful woman looked up at her. 'I have no strength left,' she said in a wheedling plea. 'Please, inquisitor. Show me mercy. I was a fool. They promised me…' Her eyes welled with tears. 'I am sorry. I am so sorry.'

'Your pleas mean nothing to me, *Lady* Gryce.' Callis's response was biting and filled with hatred and anger. 'Give me your pistol, sergeant.' She opened her hands expectantly and Gileas passed her the weapon. The bulky firearm looked huge in her grasp, but she levelled it at the crumpled woman on the ground.

'Sinnaria Gryce, in the name of His Holy Inquisition I find you guilty of heresy in extremis and therefore declare you to be tainted beyond salvation.'

'Then the warp take you!' Lady Gryce hissed, all trace of her former misery suddenly gone. She lunged at the inquisitor, her fingers lengthening into claws and her skin suddenly iridescent.

There was a single shot, and Lady Gryce's skull burst apart in a fountain of gore and cranial matter. The inquisitor thrust the weapon back into the sergeant's grip.

'You stand as witness to the execution, Gileas Ur'ten.' Her manner was completely professional; she acted as though she had merely taken a brief pause in the proceedings. Her eyes went to the broken psyker lying nearby on the marble floor.

'Nate…?' Gileas heard the question in her voice and shook his head.

'He lives, inquisitor, although I fear that may not remain the case for much longer. Reuben has called for help.'

'Of course.' Any sign of emotion that may have been

shown in the previous syllable was gone and Callis was once again all business. 'What's happened whilst that cursed woman had me in her thrall? I need information, now.'

Reuben was kneeling by Nathaniel's side and if Callis was at all interested in whether the Silver Skull was doing anything to keep her companion alive, she gave no sign of it. In a steady voice, Gileas relayed the events that had transpired.

'What is it that the Oracles of Change are doing?' It was a rhetorical question but she asked it aloud regardless. 'What do they want with Valoria? It is not of strategic importance.'

'To change it, inquisitor.' Tikaye, who rarely commented unless directly asked a question, gave his response. 'I do not mean to be rude and I see how what I say could be construed as such, but I mean that quite literally. They are tearing down the walls that exist between this world and the empyrean.'

'Then we have to stop them.' She drew a deep breath and her face hardened once more. 'Sergeant Ur'ten, I will see to Nathaniel. You should find your captain and combat this threat as best you can.'

'You will be safe here for now,' replied Gileas. 'But I can make no guarantees as to your continued safety. The Oracles of Change have the ability to slip through the warp to wherever they choose to be.'

'I know,' Callis replied with a visible shudder. 'I may have been unconscious for some of it, but...' She remembered the nightmarish visions that had jerked her to wakefulness. Even with only that tiny moment of exposure to the horrors, even with the sorcerous protection afforded to the both of them, and her own wards, she had still felt its effects. 'She wanted me for some reason, but I never found out what for. She told me... that she was going to take me to their greatest, their best and that I was anointed by betrayal to be the very heart of the planet's salvation.'

'Do you know what that means?'

'Not at all,' she said. 'But if it comes to it, I am more than capable of ensuring neither I nor Nathaniel fall into their hands.' Her pistol had been taken by the dead woman at her feet and Callis stooped to snatch it free from Gryce's belt.

'I hope it does not come to that, inquisitor.'

'Then make sure it doesn't, Sergeant Ur'ten. Go and do whatever it is that you have to do to stop them.'

'As you command, inquisitor.' Gileas nodded his head respectfully and gestured to Tikaye and Reuben to come with him. The latter got to his feet, making room for the inquisitor to kneel beside the gravely injured Nathaniel. She glanced up and waved them away.

'Begone,' she snapped. 'I am more than capable of dealing with my own people. Go and take care of *yours*.'

The three Assault Marines left the two humans lying in a pool of blood, some of it Nathaniel's, some of it Sinnaria Gryce's, and Gileas found he hoped fervently that this would not be their final farewell.

EIGHTEEN

AGAINST THE TIDE

Beyond the palace walls, anarchy reigned. The growing warp rift had spread to encompass the entire city. Those citizens who had thus far stubbornly survived both the bombardment and the ongoing street battles had nowhere they could hide from themselves.

Ragged madmen and twisted horrors boiled out of crumbling hab blocks, hidden basements and forgotten warehouses. They took to the streets in a howling, raging riot of madness, biting and tearing at each other and anything they found. The Space Marine purgation teams, already forced into cover by the arcane deluge, found their positions assaulted by the mutant mobs. Scarred Vindicators crushed their way through the chaos, armoured siege shields swatting heretics aside as they sought to regroup with their company.

Daviks and the Talriktug had fortified the staging point in the Celebrant's Square as best they could, rallying the

Sarah Cawkwell

scant remains of the Imperial Guard. They had turned the open plaza into a killing ground. Heavy weapons teams and massed bolter fire slaughtered the attackers by the hundreds, but countless more still scrambled over the carpet of ruptured flesh and bloody meat heedless of their fate.

The siege captain coordinated at a furious rate as reports poured in from units isolated throughout the city. He linked stranded squads and directed barrage fire from the Whirlwind and Thunderfire batteries outside the walls, each strike designed to block an avenue of approach or inflict maximum casualties. Despite his efforts, he knew that it would be in vain if the widening hole in reality could not be closed. He had already begun to see leering faces as they strained to push through into reality and spectral claw marks had begun to manifest on the Imperial iconography, as if raked by avian talons.

The Silver Skulls would need nothing short of a miracle to win this battle, but Daviks refused to allow such thoughts of defeatism to linger, banishing them with a fresh set of bellowed orders.

'Have you raised the *Prevision of Victory* yet?' Kerelan's words came out in a bark as he held one of the breaches in the defence lines. His relic sword crackled with energy as he lifted it for yet another swing. Its blade glinted as it fell in a deadly arc, connecting with the mutated creature that had flung itself bodily at the Space Marines. Numerous monsters already lay at their feet, some still wearing the tattered rags of the Imperial Guard or the clothing of those who had been caught in the unfortunate crossfire.

'No,' came the curt reply from Asterios, who was engaged in a swirling melee of his own. 'At least, not for anything longer than a second or two. They are trying now to reach us. I keep receiving undefined transmission bursts from orbit, but not much more.'

Asterios side-stepped to avoid another mutant, a young woman who had once worn the colours of the Siculean Sixth regiment. Her face was hideously deformed on one side, the skin sagging and apparently melting from her bones, as though someone had held her by the ankles in a vat of acid. A green eye stared balefully from the mass of flesh and sinew and there was utter madness in its emerald depths.

She had long since discarded whatever weapon she had been carrying, probably as a result of the knotted masses of tissue that had once been her arms. Her humanity had fled along with her sense of self-preservation. She flung herself towards Asterios, a low moaning coming from her ruined throat.

He obliterated her with a squeeze of the trigger.

All around them, horrors like this were taking form. Some of the Astra Militarum were on their knees, howling words of prayer to the God-Emperor. Commissars were bellowing litanies and delivering killing shots to those whose faith showed any sign of wavering. Their resolve could not last forever, even under the unflinching guidance of Lord Meer, but their actions were commendable nonetheless.

Somewhere, Kerelan could hear the voice of Inteus giving a continuous sermon, constantly reminding the Silver Skulls of the need now, more than ever, to assert their faith and renew the fires of loyalty to their Emperor. Djul echoed everything virtually word for word, delivering a double dose of pure Varsavian faith that fired the spirits of all.

Kerelan's thoughts strayed briefly to the missing sergeant

and his team. He had no doubt that Gileas Ur'ten would achieve his objective. The warrior was far less impetuous and far more in control of his temper than rumour would have had him believe. In the short time that he had fought alongside the Assault Marine, Kerelan's opinions had changed considerably.

He hoped fervently that they would have a chance to discuss the matter on the return home. Of course, there would be the matter of Gileas defying a Prognosticator's orders, but there were already ideas percolating in Kerelan's mind regarding that thorny issue.

'The mutations are getting worse,' observed Varlen. The Terminator stood beside his first captain, the power fist he wore thrumming with energy. He had crushed numerous skulls already with his weapon and the twin barrels of his storm bolter glowed like coals from overuse. He nodded his head towards the far end of the plaza where three former local citizens were on their knees, screaming in anguish as their bodies twisted together into a monstrous hybrid of limbs. Flesh seemed to melt from their bones as the taint in their souls finally manifested as taint in their bodies, given over wholly to the Ruinous Powers.

'End it,' said Kerelan, who was swinging his relic blade yet again towards another wave of attackers. 'Varlen…'

The other Terminator had already begun lumbering towards the tortured Valorians and opened fire. Their warped bodies were ripped to shreds by the storm of explosive bolts and they died with their screams still on their lips.

'Be sure they are dead, brother.' Kerelan roared as he cleaved into a fresh wave of foes. Varlen brought his power fist down on the remains of the thrashing creature, squashing the skulls of the fallen like they were overripe fruit.

'I am quite sure, first captain.'

The two Terminators moved on through the sea of carnage, unaware that their very actions were making things worse. Caught in a vicious cycle of violent horror, the power that Karteitja was drawing from the slaughter and mayhem was feeding the growing rift, pushing the planet deeper into the grip of the Archenemy as its influence spread. The harder they fought, the further victory slipped from their grasp.

Similar scenes of carnage played out across the planet as unholy techno-sorcery harnessed the anguish of a population, funnelling it into similar rifts that were spreading like cancers to encompass the globe. Regiments of Guardsmen who had fought to contain the rebels in other urban sprawls suddenly found themselves overwhelmed by frenzied Valorians and mutation within their own ranks.

On the outskirts of Boreal City in the southern hemisphere, the Harpthian Fusiliers were slaughtered practically to a man. Their commanding officer had ordered their armoured columns into the narrow ravines of the sprawling geothermal facility before launching a Manticore bombardment on the area. He had then used his own pistol to terminate his existence. The senior commissar discovered writhing brands beneath the dead man's skin and reported that their position was compromised before all contact was lost.

The Valar Agridomes, responsible for feeding ninety per cent of the population, were overrun by gangs of feathered monstrosities who spread unquenchable blue fire in their wake. The ensuing inferno towered hundreds of metres into the air, flames coiling into leering, avian faces that seared the eyes and minds of those who dared to look upon them.

Communication was lost with the sprawling manufactory complex that covered the northern pole, only for the vox-channel to come alive several hours later with a continuous, inhuman scream that burst unprotected eardrums and drove men into paroxysms of madness before shorting out the delicate vox equipment.

The mining community of Holt simply congealed into an amalgamated morass of weeping, mewling flesh and limbs that bubbled and seethed across the landscape leaving a blighted scar in its wake.

All of Valoria groaned under the unholy assault and the Oracles of Change strode unopposed, spreading mutation and insanity in their wake. Crimson-armoured killers marched openly through the streets, their fell sorcery fuelled by the raw stuff of the empyrean that leaked out over the world. The only resistance remained in Valoris City, along with the only hope of salvation.

The two psychic battle-brothers moved through the horror of the plaza side by side. Bhehan's mental reserves were drained but not completely exhausted and Nicodemus complemented his skills well, but both of them were taxed by the excessive use of their talents and the growing mental pressure of the rift above. They could feel the black things of the empyrean, sense them as shadows at the very edge of their awareness: predators just waiting for a moment of laxity.

Bhehan's crackling axe cleaved a path amongst the damned people of Valoria and he stood back to back with Nicodemus as the two of them fought off the steady stream of abominations.

'Where are they all coming from?' Nicodemus's question

was simple enough, but Bhehan didn't want to acknowledge what he believed to be the answer. His junior's question deserved a reply, however.

'It is the people, brother, all of them,' he said grimly as the blade of his axe neatly decapitated another. 'So be silent and keep fighting.'

'Yes, Brother-Prognosticator.'

Bhehan nodded to himself, pleased at the deference, impressed by the certainty of it. The young Prognosticar may just have been obeying the orders of his superior, but he was doing so with comfortable confidence. There was real potential in Nicodemus. Bhehan offered up a brief, silent prayer to the God-Emperor, asking that they be guided through this day so that potential could be fully realised.

Every lesson the pair of them had ever learned about managing their gift, every single time emphasis had been placed on the fact that their minds were little more than portals to the evils and terror of the Ruinous Powers, bubbled back to the surface. Where the other Silver Skulls fought purely on the physical plane, the psykers also had to defend themselves spiritually.

For Bhehan, his concentration focused on sending power sizzling through his force axe. The weapon sang as it scythed through those who stood in his way, imbued with a fury that he dared not unleash fully. He could feel forces far beyond his comprehension pressing at the barriers of his psyche, a feeling best likened to standing with his back against a door that bulged under the strain of enemies attempting to push their way through. For now at least, his mental bulwarks were holding.

Nicodemus, who was younger and less experienced – but

no less well trained – fought with a grim determination. For him, the focus came in the form of each kill that he made. At the moment of death, he captured the expression on the face of his enemy, committing it to memory, using their hatred to fuel his own contempt of the unclean. Some were very human in their shock but most simply flung open their arms and accepted death.

Horribly, some even rose and continued to fight beyond the moment of their supposed demise. Nicodemus felt no fear towards the thrashing mutants, only a sense of complete revulsion. They were an insult to life and whilst he took no pleasure in destroying them completely, he took satisfaction in the knowledge that he had done so.

Like Bhehan, he felt the forces of the warp growing ever stronger, tugging on his psychic senses like children at their mother's skirts. They were begging, plaintive thoughts that were urging him to give in to his true power. That he should cease struggling and simply embrace what he was and all that he could be.

The temptation was strong, and beneath the helmet his face ran with rivulets of sweat. He was filled with a compulsion to tear off the mask that hid him from the world and to scream his defiance into the air.

But he did not. He *could* not.

And it was then that he felt the hateful pulse of the daemon machine.

Karteitja watched as Cirth Unborn stood, his arms folded across his chest. The warp fire continued to wreathe his armoured body in flame, a flame that his abilities as a pyromancer allowed him to control with precision and deadly accuracy. He faced his superior and there was the kind of smugness and arrogance in his tone that Karteitja had come to loathe over the centuries.

He should just kill the Unborn. But he had his skills and his uses and so Karteitja had continually spared him. He didn't doubt for one moment that every time he turned his back on his lieutenant, the warrior was waiting for the chance to plant a weapon there.

'The design is failing, my lord.' With six words, the Unborn delivered a curse so damning that each syllable slammed into Karteitja as a new insult. His hands curled into fists. 'The anointed is lost to us. The pawn has failed in her task. You were a fool to ever trust her.'

She had been an easy puppet; simple to manipulate. It had been Gryce who had suggested the ritual slaughter of her husband. It would prove her allegiance to her new masters, she had insisted. She had been mesmerised by Karteitja's eloquent words and cunning articulation. She had believed wholeheartedly that he had the ability to tease out more of her latent power. She never once considered that she had been a piece in a larger game. She had never known that her treacherous heart had been one of the final two intended for the great machine. Gryce and the inquisitor. The betrayer and the betrayed.

The hearts of the dead Oracle of Change were stronger by far than any mortal thrall's, but they was not part of the ritual. They would feed the Powers for a while until they were nothing more than shrivelled black husks.

'It seems that the Silver Skulls are more of a threat than you originally believed, my lord. Perhaps the time has come to add our own powers to those of the engine. The change must surely be hastened. We should begin the last rite.'

A plan such as this took time to execute perfectly, but

despite his misgivings, Karteitja could see the sense in the Unborn's words.

'Perhaps,' was all he said. 'I will need only four others to assist me in the ritual. As for you…' He studied the flaming sorcerer. He could sense the Unborn's consuming hunger and base passions and for once, he gave the sorcerer what he sought. He gave permission for indulgence. 'Unleash the First. Lead the others and destroy the Silver Skulls, Cirth. Break their will in whichever way you see fit.'

'Yes, my lord.' Cirth Unborn strode away and dissolved into the warp. Karteitja knelt by the growling machine and laid his armoured hands on it. There was such power emanating from it now that he could feel it like knives in his flesh. He did not shy from it, but embraced it. The pain reminded him that this mission would not fail; that things were too close to success now. The Silver Skulls had been given their chance to embrace the truth and they had rejected it.

Therefore, they had to die.

Karteitja poured a surge of tainted power into the machine, adding a little of his own strength to its growing might. A pulse of aetheric energy spread outwards, not as potent as the moment he had awakened the engine for the first time, but enough to drive two Adeptus Astartes psykers far below him to their knees as the renewed shockwave hammered at their mental wards.

Bhehan was being pummelled by fists and blunt objects. He felt weapons fire discharge against his armour and slowly, painfully slowly, his senses returned to him. His mind was on fire and the bulging door that he had been so carefully holding back was struggling to bear the weight of the force pressing behind it. He got to his feet and blinked rapidly, the sensors in his armour feeding back the status of his battleplate.

Two breaches in the armour's outer skin. Failure in the left knee joint. Fluid leak. Some damage to his generator, but no major systems compromised. Overall assessment, seventy per cent functionality and falling. All of this information was taken in and absorbed within a second, the psyker adjusting his battle stance and position to compensate.

By his side, he felt Nicodemus shuddering and was aware that his battle-brother was struggling just as much as he was to deal with the renewed assault that had nearly claimed him. He was not much older than Nicodemus, not really, but his field experience had given him skills that his younger counterpart could not yet have learned.

'Stay steady, lad,' he said, keeping his eyes carefully on the younger psyker. 'It will pass. Hold fast against the onslaught.'

For a response, Nicodemus groaned softly. He wanted nothing more than to tear his own head off his shoulders and scratch the inside of his skull. The itching was maddening and he was walking close to a precipice. He hazed out of awareness.

His mind's eye zooms out, leaving him standing with his weapon clenched in hands that have lost all feeling. It pans out across the broken city of Valoris. He sees every last one of his battle-brothers, silver-clad warriors wrestling with terrors that should not be. He can't recognise them individually, but he senses them; feels the pulse of their dual hearts drumming a ceaseless rhythm to which they march and battle. It is a glorious sound. It stirs his blood.

But there is something drawing him away. Something familiar, yet unknown. A machine. A device unlike anything the psyker has ever encountered. He must seek it out. He feels the familiar sensation of seeing into a mechanism as though its blueprints are etched on its surface. He doesn't recognise it.

He probes deeper.

He still doesn't recognise it.

With a deep breath and an arrogant push of his ability, Nico-demus drives forward into the heart of the daemon engine and instantly feels as though he is being swept away by the sheer vile horror of its nature. He mentally backtracks, scrabbling desperately to escape. He tugs loose from tendrils of scalding darkness that have wrapped around his astral projection and he tumbles free. In a blink of an eye, he snatches the location of the machine.

Then he has a sudden vision of falling into an eternity of fire. He is falling. He will die.

And then, out of nowhere, an image of Varsavia creeps into his thoughts. The icy ridges that had been treacherous in the white-outs. How he had found his way by use of his other senses; he grabs the focus like a drowning man. An image of home. Something to connect him to the here and now.

Slowly, agonisingly slowly, he slams his mind shut against the creeping horrors that threaten to overwhelm him.

He gasps.

'...Nicodemus. Speak to me.'

'The top of the palace. It's at the top of the palace.'

Bhehan nodded. 'Report it to First Captain Kerelan. Then resume your defensive position. We are far from done here.'

The last Silver Skulls Thunderhawk roared through the boiling clouds, lightning strikes licking against its grey hull. The pilot within was juddered unpleasantly, but maintained his course with stoic determination. The gunship's main cannon and several subsystems were already smoking ruins, trails of debris marking the ship's passage across the skies of Valoria. But the pilot flew on regardless.

The other two gunships that had descended to the surface were gone. One had returned to the orbiting cruiser, having exhausted its ordnance flying bombing runs early during the assault. The other had gone down when the storm began and its landing site was overrun. Both it and its crew were now recorded missing in action.

The last gunship had made a pass over the entire city. The pilot had located the chapel that the Talriktug had flagged for investigation and found it crawling with mutants and crazed citizens. As the crumbling walls had been shorn away under the barrage of the gunship's remaining firepower, something had shot back.

Something had traced his passage with deadly accuracy and all but destroyed the Thunderhawk's starboard engine and most of the wing. With the controls failing and losing altitude, the chances of making it to the ground in anything other than a crash dive were decreasing all the time.

But he flew on, not looking back. The wounded ship's systems were registering a cascade of failures as the central engine coughed, struggling to remain functional despite the best efforts of the surviving tech-adepts. He flew on and he crested the Governor's Palace.

And he *saw*. To his loss, he was also seen. A tall mast of aerials and antennae reached from the top of the palace, supported by a nest of cables and platforms. But it was not the communications array that drew his attention. Tiny figures moved slowly around the device, lit by flickering ethereal fires. As he soared above them one of the figures turned and fingers of crackling black lightning reached into the sky. The blast ripped into the remains of the starboard engine and blew it apart, scattering armour and debris into the air as the wing went spinning away. The pilot had just a few seconds to transmit what he had seen as his craft tumbled wildly out of control.

The final words from the gunship as it plunged to its fiery death reached Kerelan at the same time as the words from Nicodemus.

'The top of the palace. The traitors are on top of the palace.'

The final transmission from the Thunderhawk and the separate report from the young psyker were heard by everyone both on the ground and in the palace. Every last Silver Skulls Space Marine sensed the urgency in both messages as they were broadcast simultaneously. Nicodemus's voice was broken and distorted as it cracked across the vox, the syllables chopped and fuzzy with interference from whatever dark powers had this planet in their thrall.

'We hear you, Nicodemus. Be more specific.' Kerelan spoke, his own usually crystal-clear tones also juddering and otherworldly. 'What is at the top of the palace? Sergeant Ur'ten, are you receiving this transmission? Respond to the Prognosticar. We cannot...' The first captain's voice died out and Gileas took up the situation without pause.

'Receiving, if only barely. Go ahead, Nicodemus. What do you need from us? We are inside the palace.'

'The source of these horrors we face,' came the response. 'It is above you.'

'You are sure of this, lad?' Gileas was cautious, but respectfully so. Nicodemus was young, certainly. But he was also a psyker, a budding Prognosticar, and as such, his word needed taking into consideration.

'I guarantee it.' The certainty was in his tone and Gileas nodded.

'Then that is where we will go.' He indicated that his battle-brothers should move out. Nicodemus's voice came across the vox again.

'I am coming up to join you. It feels like a machine and if that's the case, I can be of assistance.'

'Nicodemus will follow as soon as we have spoken about the matter.' It was Bhehan's voice this time. The Prognosticator's youthful voice was so filled with command that it took a second or two for Gileas to recognise it. 'Proceed, sergeant, but use your caution and discretion.'

'Received and understood, Prognosticator.' Bhehan was no longer the raw recruit that he had been only a year before and Gileas deferred to the warrior's command without question. 'Ur'ten out.'

'On the roof of the palace. How they must be laughing at us.' Tikaye spoke, which was a rare occurrence. Reuben had remained reticent and practically silent since the mirror chamber. Tikaye waved a hand indolently. 'There is nothing above us but cogitators and antennae, the workings of the Mechanicus. What would the Oracles of Change want with such things?' Such disdain was remarkably out of character for him.

Gileas stared at him. Despite the unpleasant memories of what he had seen in those Chaos-tainted mirrors, he had come out the other side of the ordeal with his faith and belief intact. He was beginning to feel a knot of concern form in his stomach that the others had not fared so well. He steeled himself and addressed the matter as he always did – head on.

'Pull yourself together, Tikaye. What has happened cannot

be changed, but what is to come may yet be altered by our actions. Not our inactivity and bitterness.'

Tikaye nodded reluctantly, but Gileas sensed the shift in his mood from dark and inward-turning to tuned in to the situation once more. 'Their plan is strategically brilliant, I suppose,' Tikaye said, admitting it aloud. 'Unnoticed from below and unassailable from above without a passing ship. We should proceed with all haste.'

'Hold position before the final ascent. We must wait for Nicodemus. If there is some sort of machine… you know where his talent lies, brother. His knowledge may be necessary. Curb your impatience if you can. Just for a little longer.' Gileas hoped that his brothers fighting far below *had* a little longer. From what fragments he could extract from the vox-chatter, the battle below was increasingly becoming a nightmare. The Terminators were failing to reach the *Prevision of Victory*. They needed reinforcements or an extraction and the latter was looking increasingly unlikely.

The three Space Marines began moving to the access corridors that would take them to the roof-space generators and ultimately out onto the roof of the Governor's Palace where communications arrays and further emergency systems were installed.

'Gileas?' Reuben's voice was subdued and the sergeant moved to stand beside his friend.

'Speak your mind, Reuben.'

'What did you see?'

'It is of no importance,' Gileas forced command into his tone. 'Calm yourself. I need you by my side for this battle, Reuben. With the Talriktug otherwise engaged, it falls to us to confront the evil that waits for us up there. You must cast out any doubts that witch may have fostered in you. You and Tikaye have been my battle-brothers for many years and neither of you have ever had any hesitation in your duty.'

'I...' Although he couldn't see the other warrior's face, Gileas knew that Reuben had closed his eyes. He knew the way his friend composed himself. 'You are right, of course. Forgive me.'

'Nothing to forgive, Reuben. We will speak of this later. I promise you.'

'Yes,' said Reuben, but Gileas could hear his despondency. 'Later.'

'If it's a machine, then I can deal with it, Brother. You know that. It's my talent. Let me handle it.' Nicodemus's insistence was beginning to try Bhehan's already tested patience.

'Nicodemus...' Bhehan and Nicodemus continued to battle the mutated horrors that swarmed around them. They had begun to move across the jagged, broken paving to join up with another row of Silver Skulls who were cutting down line after line of the living and dead in equal measure. 'Your arrogance in assuming you can do this is foolhardy.'

'You need to trust me, Prognosticator. I swear to you that I am not being foolish. *I* trust my instincts. If you cannot trust in those, what can you trust in? Have you not said those words to me many times before?'

'Yes.' The response was instant and there was no doubt in the voice. 'I have. Then I trust you, Nicodemus. I can provide a temporary window of opportunity for you to get to the palace. Make your contribution to this effort count, brother.'

'I will, Prognosticator.' There was a heartbeat's pause. 'Thank you, brother.'

Bhehan nodded once and then he held his force axe in front of him, one hand stacked atop the other, holding it close to his chest. His shoulders rose up as he drew a deep breath and with all the remaining power at his command, he unleashed a psychic shriek that rippled out in a shockwave around him. For twenty metres in every direction around the psyker, assailants fell like corn beneath a scythe, their minds and senses blasted by the assault. Nicodemus took his chance and ran.

The psyker ran harder than he had ever done before. His jump pack carried him to the doors of the palace in a few bounds and he rushed inside. While his brothers had slowly made their way up the structure, searching for the inquisitor, Nicodemus knew precisely where he was going. He made directly for the transit elevators that would carry him to the roof and the waiting enemy.

'First Captain Kerelan, this is the *Prevision of Victory*. We… interference. There is… send a gunship down… repeat, do you… assistance?'

The message was garbled and distorted but its meaning was clear and its very presence greatly welcomed. There had been a momentary break in the tumult that had interfered with their communications off-world and fortune had favoured them.

'Yes,' bellowed the first captain. 'Yes. On my coordinates.' He transmitted his current position to the *Prevision of Victory*. There was nothing more he could do. They were too few, their enemies too many. They were losing the battle.

'Message… understood… erelan. Backup in…'

Varlen and Kerelan had fought their way across the square to join the rest of the Terminator squad and the Talriktug as a complete unit had crunched booted feet over those who had been disabled by Bhehan's shriek. They stood together with Daviks and his surviving warriors while the tattered survivors of the Imperial Guard commended their souls to the Emperor. The defenders had been pushed back in a tightening ring around the palace, a thin line of armour and soldiers anchored by islands of bloodstained silver.

Even as he fought, the young Prognosticator reached into his pouch and withdrew a single rune. He stared down at it, dreading another moment of denial from the Emperor. That the Deep Dark should have settled upon him at such a critical moment was galling.

The sight of the rune marked with the Aquila Ascendant made his heart sing. The Emperor was with them.

The singing turned to a discordant note the moment he raised his head again and saw a building tumble into ruins under the onslaught of something huge. It emerged from the debris dripping chains, its crimson armour streaked with dust and gore and surrounded by a swarm of ragged creatures that fluttered with hateful scripture. Flanking the Dreadnought monster was a force of Oracles led by a sorcerer whose armour seethed with living flames. The traitors roared their fury at the Silver Skulls and advanced as a well-structured unit towards the defenders.

'Brothers,' said Kerelan in a grim voice. 'Emperor's grace go with you.' He raised his sword above his head and the Silver Skulls came to meet them. Around them, the chaotic swirl of the horrors continued to boil and churn as the walls of reality groaned under the strain. He suspected it would not be long before Valoria was nothing more than an open portal to the powers of Chaos: a daemon world. It would see the end of all life on the planet and should the *Prevision of Victory* be unable to extract the warriors, Kerelan knew well what would happen.

Best, he thought as they came within range of the enemy, to focus on the present and worry about Exterminatus later.

'Weapons free,' he bellowed. 'In the name of the Emperor, destroy them all!'

NINETEEN

FALLING STAR

The roof of the Governor's Palace was a veritable forest of communications equipment, antennae and generators that thrummed with life and activity. There were several elevated platforms piled atop each other in a maddeningly complex array. These were interconnected via steel-reinforced gantries strung from platform to platform. They created a series of swooping arcs where they remained intact, a direct if precarious way to access the higher reaches of the towering mass of aerials, dishes and masts.

Emerging from the stairwell onto the roof, Gileas's first thoughts were that they had walked into a hurricane. The winds whipped around them, intent on hurling these newcomers from the palace, and unnatural lightning crackled around the tower top. Fell voices howled and gibbered in the gale and reality stretched thin as the storm intensified. Gileas adjusted his weight to bear the brunt of the relentless battering and looked around. From far below he could hear the faint sounds of the battle that raged; a potent and heady drug. Gileas felt the welcoming shot of stimulants from his armour, preparing his muscles and his whole being for the battle to come.

He growled softly, the noise echoing around the interior of his helm. The odds were not good. They were massively outnumbered on the ground and they were going up to this encounter without any tactical information. But these were the kind of odds that Gileas Ur'ten had always lived for, the kind of challenge that brought his every sense to life. The churning world around him seemed to fade into obscurity and all that mattered, all that was in sharp focus, were the antennae ahead of him. Behind him were his battle-brothers. Before him…

Before him was whatever fate had placed there to test him. They would each face it with the stoic determination that drove every last one of them. The aberrant storm lashed at the platform, clawing at the warriors with savage ferocity and battering at their minds with infernal promises. A storm that would grow to swallow the world.

'I can feel the nature of it,' murmured Nicodemus. The psyker had caught up at the rear of the group and had said very little as they had approached the communications platform. 'There is a great evil at work here, something the Oracles have brought with them or bound to this place. And it is mechanical, but it is alive. I can end this thing.'

'Are you telling me or reassuring yourself, brother?'

The young psyker tipped his head thoughtfully to one side. 'A little of both, Sergeant Ur'ten,' he admitted in a regretful voice.

* * *

The last rite had begun but Karteitja knew that they were forced into completing the incantations in a limited time frame. The machine, fed by the hearts of the sacrificed and his own sorcery, had done the majority of the work, but the ritual to tear the fabric of reality fully open, to allow the true invasion to begin, took more than machinery. It took skill and dedication. Arcane sigils surrounded the device in spiralling, eightfold patterns that circled the platform before converging at its centre. Tainted light pulsed from the runes, casting weird shadows from the chanting sorcerers as they invoked the names of the Great Deceiver.

Karteitja heard the small group of enemies exit onto the roof above the Governor's Palace before his psychic senses found them but he paid them no heed. He could not afford to let this ritual fail. It would spell disaster for the Oracles of Change and particularly it would spell disaster for him. The arrival of the small Silver Skulls force was a hindrance that he did not need at this critical juncture. He had invested too much time and effort into this plan to see it all fail at the last.

Karteitja, his machine and four other Oracles of Change were firmly settled on one of the satellite platforms a few gantries away. The five of them were arranged in exact points around the device, knelt with their heads bowed. The arrangement for the ritual was perfect and Karteitja craved perfection in this. He *chose* perfection. In another lifetime he had been meticulous and his attention to detail had often been lauded. Such habits had always stayed with him. Through service to the Changer of Ways, he had learned that fate could be changed by the smallest of differences. Such had been his plan for powering the machine.

The heart of an Imperial citizen was one thing, but the heart of a fanatical Imperial inquisitor would have been another. As it was, it barely mattered now. He had only to raise his head to the skies, see the boiling clouds and feel the power of the warp whipping around him, to know his success was assured.

He would not fail. He *could* not fail. It was simply impossible.

His plans for the devastation of this Imperial planet should have been executed without the interference of the Imperium. Breed enough discontent and chaos and the human populace would resort to their most basic instincts. Small cells hidden among the menials would plant the seeds of discord. Mistrust would grow. Out of that would grow resentment and finally rebellion, violence and anarchy, the psychic fuel for the glorious transformation. It had all worked according to his plan.

He should have been exultant. The process had reached a point of no return. The machine was channelling the anguish and suffering of the world and was tearing a great hole deeper and deeper into the warp. With the success of this ritual, hurried though it must necessarily be, the Great Deceiver would reach out and snatch Valoria from the heavens and make it eternally His. It would be a world steeped in the power of sorcery. A world to rival even that of the Cyclops.

His four warriors knelt in supplication, their voices raised in discordant harmony, and Karteitja joined them, his stentorian tones thundering into the tumultuous sky. Aetheric energies began to crawl up and down the cluster of masts and antennae as the power of the spell took effect. Arcs of cerulean energy and purple-pink fire danced from the spars and gathered at the tips of the aerials as the sorcerer's chant built to a dreadful climax.

Then Karteitja roared an ancient and terrible name to the heavens. The gathered power leapt from the array like a spear, a column of corrupted light reaching into the storm and ripping open a gateway into the realm of madness, spilling its vile contents out onto the world of Valoria below.

Lord Commander Meer was dead. The hulking Helbrute had burst from the ruins of the city and was charging its way through the press of mutants in the Celebrant's Square, crushing them with its stride and tearing into the Imperial Guard position. The loss of their commander had had the expected effect of causing a momentary lack of cohesion amongst the troops. To their credit, they pulled themselves together with impressive speed, but the damage was done.

Kerelan stared at the machine. It had a Dreadnought's shape and form, but the clean lines of its hull had long since been erased by snaking cables of daemonic meat, loops of chain and writhing brass iconography. One of its arms terminated in a double-barrelled cannon which was barking a torrent of shells at a tremendous rate, turning the Guardsmen into puffs of gore and ragged flesh, while its other arm was a knotted mass of barbed tendrils, lashing at everything within reach.

The armoured behemoth droned a constant babble of nonsense from its vox-horns as it killed, and the first captain was sure he had heard it rumble something about sacrifice to the powers even as it ripped Arnulf Meer apart with its flail. Then it flipped a Chimera onto its side and tore the belly from the tank before shunting the wreck out of the way and advancing on the Talriktug's position.

The Oracles of Change were in amongst the defenders, slaughtering Guardsmen and locking blades with Silver Skulls. Daviks barked orders into the vox, directing his fire teams even as he traded blows with a giant wielding a two-handed chainsword. The siege captain's ancient power sword shed blue sparks as it met the hell-forged teeth of the traitor's blade, but the targeting array on his pack was locked firmly on the advancing monster.

Bolt shells, missiles and a brilliant star of plasma energy converged on the rampaging monster but it emerged from the storm of fire trailing smoke, its armour blackened but unbroken. Kerelan rammed his relic blade through the traitor in front of him, ripping it upwards to saw the Oracle apart in a shower of gore. He turned, hacking his way directly towards the approaching juggernaut.

'Faith is my shield!' the first captain bellowed as he killed. 'Hatred my weapon!'

Asterios had long ago exhausted the ammunition in his assault cannon and was now crushing enemies with the might of his power fist. Varlen and Vrakos cut down foes with controlled bursts from their storm bolters. Djul was nowhere to be seen, but his brothers could still hear his constant litany droning over the squad vox and the occasional roar of his chainfist as it chewed up traitors.

Bhehan was in trouble. He had seen the infernal sorcerer immolate a squad of Guardsmen and burn down two battle-brothers before he managed to cut his way to the heretic. The Oracle gave the Prognosticator a predatory grin, acrid smoke curling from between his teeth, and then hurled a ball of fire with deadly accuracy. Bhehan barely managed to turn the attack aside, his psychic abilities frayed and exhausted, before launching forward at the pyromancer.

The sorcerer blocked the youth's clumsy attack with a sweep of his blazing spear, shattering one of the Silver Skull's shoulder guards with the return swing. The shock of the impact was tremendous, throwing Bhehan to the ground in a shower of molten ceramite and ruined plasteel. He managed to scramble to his feet in time to block the next attack with his axe, but the crystal matrix cracked under the blow and tainted fire washed over his gauntlets, blistering the flesh beneath.

Bhehan began to doubt he could have bested the Oracle even at full strength and he was far from that now. He was wounded, and made sick by the creatures of the empyrean clawing at his senses. He tried to throw up a kine-shield to intercept the next attack, but the fiery weapon blasted it aside with an explosion of force that burned the purity seals on his armour and sent his axe spinning away into the melee. He staggered back, senses reeling, and saw the chaos that had engulfed the plaza.

Close by he watched, helpless to act, as Varlen fell, his ancient armour lashed open by the rampaging Chaos Dreadnought despite Kerelan's best efforts to halt it, his blade hacking repeatedly into the thing's cannons.

He saw Asterios and Vrakos standing back to back, surrounded by a pile of mangled dead. Their armour was soaked in gore, their power fists rose and fell and Oracles swarmed around them.

His eyes roamed around the battlefield and fixed on Daviks, one arm gone below the elbow, as he used his good hand to ram his sword through a horned enemy champion. The twisted brute grappled with the siege captain even when faced with his own inevitable death.

Further afield, his gaze locked on Inteus, the other psyker

whipping his staff about in a frenzy, his blows hurling mutants into the air like broken rag dolls while motes of lightning danced from his eyes.

Bhehan fell to one knee, tasted his own blood in his mouth and felt his hearts throb painfully in his chest. He heard the whine of the spear as it whirled behind him and roared in defiance. He would not let this moment take him. It was not his time. This was not his day to die and Chaos was most certainly not going to claim him. The painful truth of his own mortality had come to him in a vision years ago. Bhehan knew when and he knew how he would die.

And it would not be today.

'For the Emperor!'

Nicodemus's words resounded across the vox, strong, sure and leaving no room for doubt. Even Reuben and Tikaye, both of whom still seemed subdued and withdrawn after the experience in the mirror room, drew their weapons and fired their jump packs. The Silver Skulls wasted no more time. They began to make their way up the gantries leading from the roof to the platforms.

There was a sudden whine of protest and the entire catwalk shuddered underfoot.

There was a blur in the air and one of the Oracles of Change sorcerers shimmered into being at the head of the walkway, a heavy chainaxe raised above his head ready to bring down the reinforced steel cabling of the gantry. He struck. The bridge would shortly be nothing more than scrap. It was testament to the workmanship of the construction that it had held at all under the onslaught of such a weapon.

The second strike produced an even more violent shudder

and the cable's individual strands began to lose cohesion. The walkway gave a sudden lurch and dropped a few feet, but the Space Marines' mag-locks held them firmly in place.

'It will take too long to go another way around,' said Gileas, nodding ahead. 'Fire your jets, but short burn only. These crosswinds could easily throw us over the edge. Be ready to engage the moment we land.'

The sorcerer's chainaxe bit into the reinforced steel cables of the walkway with a metal-on-metal shriek that would have set even the most robust human's teeth on edge. Blue sparks spat out where the weapon connected with the steel and in three solid blows, the cable was severed. The walkway fell out from beneath their feet and they fired the jets on their jump packs, soaring into the air.

'They still approach, my lord.' Karteitja cursed roundly and unsheathed his own weapon, brandishing it before him. The huge, double-headed axe that he chose to wield was a monstrous thing, the eight-pointed star motif chased in red bronze on its surface. Spectral faces writhed leering and screaming beneath the surface of its warp-forged blades and the air moaned at its cursed touch. A malevolent sentience deep within the weapon teased at Karteitja's awareness. It was an ancient and hateful thing that he had long since dominated, but still it tested the boundaries of its prison.

'Let them come,' he snarled. 'They are too late anyway, the ritual is complete, the wheels set in motion. They will be no match for our combined strength and ability. Destroy them utterly. Then we will see this world reborn.'

The sheer force of the negative energy pulsing from the machine atop the communications array was making Nicodemus's forehead throb. He had begun to seek the core of the construction in his mind as they had approached, but it was like nothing he had ever encountered. There was a tarry blackness surrounding it like a murky halo; an impenetrable fog of dark power that made him want to vomit. But he had to stop whatever it was that it was doing. His attention broke as Reuben and Tikaye caught him under each arm to carry him from the toppling gantry.

The Space Marines descended to the next platform where Gileas met the first of the sorcerers in a clash of ceramite and screaming chainblades. Nicodemus was dropped behind them and immediately set about countering and protecting them from the worst of the Oracles of Change's sorcerous attacks. Already the enemy had vanished again, whether into the warp or utilising unknown cloaking technology Nicodemus didn't know.

He did not linger on it, because from other platforms other Oracles of Change appeared and unleashed a relentless assault. They employed their power in its most brutal forms, lashing at the Silver Skulls with kinetic bolts, arcs of black lightning and sheets of iridescent flame. The strain of deflection was enormous and the young psyker was only able to turn aside the worst of the blows assailing his brothers, while others chipped and hammered at their battleplate.

He needed to focus his energy on the foul machine squatting at the heart of the array. The beam of agony spearing into the ruined sky originated there and if he could only reach it with his senses then he knew he could end it.

'Hold fast, brothers,' Nicodemus growled through gritted teeth.

It only took a handful of seconds to push his awareness through the greasy foulness that shrouded the machine, a handful of seconds to find the right points to twist and break, but he well knew that a handful of seconds in battle could be costly.

The proud silver sigil on Reuben's shoulder burned and melted away, the ceramite bubbling and sloughing under the assault. Tikaye lost an eye-lens and half his helmet to a punishing sledgehammer of force that nearly toppled him from the platform and Gileas was stung by half a dozen tongues of crackling warp lightning. The three of them fought on against the punishing assault.

Forced back to solid defence, the moment was lost. Nicodemus's realisation of the machine's construction slipped away in the effort of concentrating on the battle and he had to begin the process again, his impatience growing with each passing second.

Time slowed to a crawl as he pushed his senses into the miasma of darkness, grappling for the monstrous heart shrouded within. It felt like he was swimming in razors, the crystalline hate of the thing flaying his strength and his resistance as he strove to break it. He felt his teeth crack. His vision dimmed and his secondary heart beat erratically in his chest. He could see dark conduits feeding the device like twisted arteries and reached for them with all his might. His astral flesh blistered and burned, but with a final gasp of effort he seized the veins of darkness and twisted until they broke.

He strained so hard against the psychic resistance that it felt as though he might implode. Then, a whining so ultra-high frequency that it only just registered on the edges of his aural senses distracted him.

Gileas felt a warm trickle of blood from his ears and nostrils and gritted his teeth against it. He pressed his attack harder against the Oracle of Change he faced. His opponent was every bit as skilled as the sergeant was. In addition, the frequent bolts of power were slowly but surely wearing Gileas down whilst the Oracle of Change was clearly drawing strength from them. The Silver Skull's chainsword was working to maximum efficiency but had its limits. Gileas could feel it shuddering in his grip and knew that he was driving it harder than it had ever been driven. But it paid off.

Bringing down the weapon on the weakened elbow joint of his enemy's armour, Gileas bellowed out a prayer to the Emperor – and the Emperor answered. The tungsten teeth chewed and spat their way through the wires and cables, sending a spray of sparks as the connections shorted out. The Oracle of Change lost his chainsword hand a moment later, the limb severed. A roar of pain and fury left his mouth.

He brought up the bolt pistol in his left hand and pointed it at Gileas, squeezing a finger on the trigger. At point-blank range the damage to his armour would have been horrendous.

But nothing happened. The bolt pistol clicked a few times and then the traitor threw it away, disgusted. He began to mutter words in a hideous arcane tongue and Gileas moved quickly before he could unleash any more of his tainted power. He snatched up the chainsword that now lay on the floor and spun at his enemy with a screaming blade in each hand. Swinging them together like snarling shears, the pair of blades bit and worked their way through the Oracle's battleplate until he felt them bite into the flesh beneath the armour. He exerted every bit of strength and was rewarded with the sensation of subcutaneous fat and muscle giving way beneath his attack.

The last thing the Oracle of Change ever did was release the aetheric charge he had been gathering for his attack. It arced around Gileas in a display of lightning strikes that caused every sensor in his armour to go into overdrive. The rune display in his helmet flickered and came back with lines of nonsense and he was flung backwards. He stopped short of falling from the platform, his armour screeching along the floor and slowing him down. Stunned, it took him a moment or two to get back up.

He was rewarded with the sight of the Oracle of Change toppling over before him, his ruptured body a bloody mess of cracked armour, torn skin and stringy muscle. His armour drizzled smoke from damaged joints and blood pooled beneath him. As Gileas struggled to his feet, he kicked the corpse over the edge. He turned his head to Nicodemus.

'Well done,' he said.

'What, sergeant?' the psyker slurred.

'Your talent. Seizing up his pistol. Thank you.'

'Sergeant, I...' Nicodemus had no chance to tell Gileas he had done nothing of the sort, because another of the Oracles of Change had come charging towards him. Side-stepping the attack, the young psyker was once again hard-pressed by his enemy. Tikaye joined him and the two Silver Skulls fought furiously against the traitor.

'The storm, Gil.' Reuben's voice was subdued, where once Gileas had heard his brother's voice sing out at the sheer joy that battle brought. 'It is raging.'

'The machine is still working. Nicodemus needs our support to get closer. We should...' They could no longer continue the conversation. There were still three warriors battling against them for the supremacy of this alarmingly small space. With Nicodemus once again holding the worst of the ethereal attacks at bay, Gileas pressed the assault forward with customary ferocity. The four Silver Skulls pounded across the gantry that separated them from the next platform.

Again, the Oracles of Change phased out of the warp, ready to take on their opponents. There was a clashing screech of blades and the bark of bolt pistols as the battle resumed. Reuben was the next to get the better of his foe as the Oracle of Change attempted to reload his depleted weapon. The Silver Skull backhanded the traitor with the butt of his own bolt pistol, snapping the warrior's helm back and leaving him vulnerable. The Oracle instinctively raised his sword, expecting a decapitating blow, but instead Reuben thrust the tip of his snarling weapon into the exposed joint beneath the arm. The sword chewed into armour and chest cavity with a grind of bone and a mist of blood erupted from the traitor's armour. Reuben wrenched his blade free and without waiting for his enemy to fall, charged on towards the waiting champion. The monster stood on the innermost platform, motionless as a statue, and the temptation was too great.

'Reuben, wait!' Gileas's order was drowned out by the roar of battle and he could only watch helplessly as his brother half ran and half launched himself at the hulking warrior. The thrusters in the jump pack flared and roared as he landed heavily on the platform, weapon ready.

Karteitja met the assault with a lazy, one-handed parry. Reuben retaliated with a shot from his pistol that was deflected with a casual flick. Then the Chaos champion headbutted him. The movement was slow and languid, but for Reuben, it felt as though a tank had fallen on him. The massive, curling tusks the traitor sported as part of his helm design gouged twin furrows in Reuben's chestplate and the front of the Silver Skull's helmet caved in.

Gileas saw his brother stagger from the blow, saw him fall to one knee under the impact, but could do nothing to aid him. The Oracle he faced was a skilled warrior and trying to break away would be potentially fatal.

Reuben, swaying unsteadily, miraculously managed to block a blow that would otherwise have split him in two and fired a pair of shots at his enemy. Both were scattered harmlessly aside. Through his cracked lenses he saw the axe swinging ponderously at the warrior's side and once again he reached out, managing to catch it on his chainsword. The blade shrieked as the last of its teeth tore uselessly at the daemonic weapon. It was ripped from his hand and spun away, clattering across the platform to lie useless.

Something hit him in the head again and he lost vision in his left eye. Then something sharp and agonisingly cold slid into his body and as he was lifted into the air, he screamed. It was a noise born of terrible pain, frustration and suffering the like of which he could never have imagined.

Nicodemus's skull felt like it was cracking with the effort of blocking the Oracles' sorcerous assaults. It had become less painful as his brothers had defeated some of their enemies, but the incessant pressure of the boiling warp storm had not abated and continued to grow. He had to push past it. He had to do this thing.

He looked up at the beam of power reaching from the antennae into the heavens and finally realised the truth. The process had become self-sustaining. The storm brought madness, death and misery to the people below which in turn fed the daemon within the machine that fuelled the storm. Destruction of the machine, the skill that was his and his alone, was the only remaining way to win this war.

For a moment, Nicodemus felt a surge of uncertainty. He was the only one with any kind of shielding against the horrors of the warp and even that was dying. The only way to stop this thing from happening now was to bring the entire array down and hope it was enough to disrupt the delicate balance of energies.

The young psyker looked around at his brothers. Tikaye and Gileas were locked in battle with their enemies and could do nothing, while Reuben hung impaled on the vicious blade that tipped the champion's vile axe.

Nothing he could do here would make a difference, but up there he had a chance to do something. The antenna array was a pillar of plasteel bristling with aerials and spars, a spear pointed at the heavens. A spear he could break. He glanced again at Reuben and shook his head. 'I'm sorry, my brothers,' he murmured softly.

Nicodemus bounded forward, making his own way across the network of gantries until he was on the platform where Karteitja and Reuben were locked in battle. He offered no assistance to the older warrior and Karteitja barely spared the psyker more than a glance.

'So keen to die, boy? Your turn will come.'

'Warp take you,' fired back Nicodemus and with a gravity-defying bound, he leaped at the antenna array. He punched his hands and feet into the structure as he landed. Then, with all the strength he could muster, he began to climb.

Karteitja withdrew the blade and gave the massive axe an effortless shake. It bit into the Space Marine's armour with a crunch, shearing through his hip and thigh with contemptuous ease. The Silver Skull fell, his enhanced body struggling to stem the arterial flow from his amputated limb.

Gileas watched him fall and reacted with the instincts of a child raised amongst warriors. He went berserk.

Gileas lunged at the Oracle who was blocking passage to his fallen brother, taking a shot to the chest for his efforts. The shell scattered armour chips in all directions but failed to penetrate the battleplate. Then he grabbed the traitor's armoured collar and smashed him in the face with the studded guard of his chainsword. Three times Eclipse rose and fell, three piston-motion punches that crumpled the baroque decoration of the Oracle's helm. The fourth downward swing removed his opponent's blade hand, sending him stumbling away. Then Gileas raised his bolt pistol and emptied the magazine into the wounded warrior's face.

The sergeant stepped through the raining gobbets of meat and ceramite in time to see the enemy champion hurling crackling bolts of force at a figure high up on the flank of the array.

Nicodemus climbed, the air growing thick with the ozone taint of psychic power as projectile burst after projectile burst struck the young psyker. Even from this distance, Gileas could see that the youth's armour was beginning to peel in places and there was only so much more it could take before its systems were fully compromised.

The traitor in front of Tikaye let out an ululating cry and sidestepped, dropping like a stone from the platform. There was a sudden prickling of the air and that now-familiar sound of an Adeptus Astartes stepping into the warp. The Oracle of Change had made good his escape. Stirred at last from the apathy brought on by the mirror room, Tikaye bellowed curses into the cloud-bank that had swirled beneath them. One by one, they were departing.

'Sergeant.' Tikaye attempted to raise Gileas on the vox, but he knew it was a futile effort. He could see his superior carving his way towards the enemy with relentless determination. The enemy seemed disinterested, focused as he was on another target.

Tikaye had little choice but to follow Gileas and deal with the situation as it happened. Reuben lay still and seemingly lifeless, although his life rune glowed faintly in the corner of Tikaye's helm. His brother lived still, but was in the deep embrace of a sus-an coma. His sergeant also lived – but was in the grip of a red-rimmed cloud of absolute rage that Tikaye had seen before.

'Sergeant,' he said again, reaching out a hand to grab the bigger warrior by the shoulder. 'Gileas!'

The voice of his battle-brother... his *friend*... finally penetrated the scarlet haze and Gileas turned to look at Tikaye. The battle helm that the Techmarine had spent so long carefully fixing up was broken and shattered, both eye-lenses lost now, and Gileas's dark blue eyes slowly bled fury until it was evident he had come to his senses.

'Their escape route is assured,' said Tikaye, indicating Karteitja with his weapon. 'The minute he thinks he is beaten, he will step off into the warp.'

'So pessimistic, Tikaye,' said Gileas. 'Then you and I must kill him before we can allow that to happen.' His eyes cast upwards to where Nicodemus was still clinging with determination to the highest antenna array. 'We need to buy that boy the time he needs.'

They considered Karteitja for a moment. Then they

launched their attack in perfect synchronicity. The jets on their jump packs burned fiercely and they lifted with effortless ease into the air, throwing themselves with reckless abandon at the sorcerer.

His goal was within a few feet.

The furious psychic attacks being hurled at him by the horned warrior champion far below were taking their toll on his systems. His generator was starting to fail, its functionality now intermittent at best, and this added to his climbing burden. Having to bear the weight of his own armour without the generator's aid meant that extra chemicals and stimulants were flooding his system. But bear it he did, his expression grim beneath the helm.

He too had seen Reuben's life sign fade to a dull throb and knew that far below him, a respected and admired battle-brother was fighting for his life. He had been indoctrinated and trained for live combat and instinctively knew how he should be reacting in this situation. But the extraneous factors were far harder to compartmentalise than training had ever promised.

He climbed. He poured everything he had into climbing. It became the only thing that mattered. As he gathered his psychic will on the antenna in preparation to destroy it once and for all, he saw more clearly than he had ever seen in his young life. Everything that he had absorbed through the hypno-doctrination sessions during his ascension... every training fight he had ever battled... every word of advice or any moment of fraternity that had passed his way... he remembered it all.

Steeling his every thought against what he knew must follow, he offered up a whispered prayer to the God-Emperor, so far beyond his reach on distant Terra. Energy trembled through his limbs and ignited his fists with argent flames of blinding purity. He thrust them into the guts of the massive antenna and seized the corrupted, vitreous core with both hands. The raw agony of a million tortured souls assailed him, the psychic backlash shattering his helm and blowing the matrices of his hood apart in a spray of crystal and ceramite.

Nicodemus had often heard that your entire life was supposed to flash before your eyes at the moment of death. But no amount of indoctrination or any wise words from his more experienced battle-brothers could ever have prepared him for the reality of that fact. In the blink of an eye, he saw everything he had been, all that he had become.

He did not see what he would be, and he smiled. 'I have done well,' he said. 'I have prevailed.'

The entire array shuddered, throwing the warriors below off their feet as the structure groaned in protest. The pillar of warped energy spearing into the heavens wobbled and shook as Nicodemus strained to kill it at its source. The shaking got steadily stronger and the antenna to which he clung began to crack loudly as it broke away from its fellows.

'More,' he urged through gritted teeth. He strained, psychic might, enhanced muscle and powered armour focused in that one moment of pure purpose. He could feel the forces of the warp playing about him, stripping away his battleplate, scorching his flesh and hammering at his psyche. But in that one perfect moment he found the flaw in the design and his gift broke it open. He was rewarded with a glaring, searing white flash of light that whilst it blinded him, nonetheless brought with it the knowledge that he had succeeded.

The torrent of hateful energy sputtered and died in a catastrophic backlash, blowing the top level of the array apart in a dazzling flash of white and silver. The mast listed drunkenly to one side before tearing from its moorings completely and plunging past the platform to the plaza far below. Burning debris rained down from the explosion, including a lone blue comet with a tail of argent fire that guttered out as it fell hundreds of feet to the distant ground.

The killing stroke did not come. Bhehan surged to his feet and whirled about. In every direction he looked across the plaza the Oracles of Change were gone. Even the hulking Chaos Dreadnought and its attendants had disappeared like nothing more than a bad memory.

Mutants and heretics still clogged the Celebrant's Square, but without the threat of the sorcerers they were wild and uncoordinated and the surviving Silver Skulls set about slaughtering them despite still being greatly outnumbered. The Prognosticator staggered over to the first captain, retrieving his fallen axe. Kerelan said nothing, his grim expression amply conveying his feelings on the subject, and then the pair set to work on the twisted hordes of Valoria.

'Nicodemus, no!'

Gileas was unable to prevent the yell that escaped his lips, the momentary denial of his brother's demise. He had been nothing more than a boy. Promising, eager, everything he had once been. To see him fall, damaged and broken, was enough to bring that surge of furious rage burning back through the calm he had gathered. Tikaye heard the

Chaos champion snarl in rage as his works were undone and wondered for a moment why he had not simply fled as his brethren so often did. Treachery was in their nature, however, so perhaps he had been abandoned to his fate for his failure.

Nicodemus was gone, but his efforts at least had borne fruit. The billowing black clouds that had gathered at the top of the antenna rig began to disperse. The warp storm would take some time to clear, but here at its epicentre, the driving force behind it was damaged beyond repair.

The two Silver Skulls were on their feet before their opponent was; Terminator armour had never loaned itself to agility and Gileas was grateful for that fact. The Oracle of Change had dropped forward onto his knees. Both Gileas and Tikaye struggled for a moment to regain their balance on the platform as it groaned in the wind and blast shock.

The two warriors exchanged brief glances, their unspoken bond of brotherhood connecting them more than it had ever done before. 'He will probably kill us, Gileas,' said Tikaye, a statement of fact rather than a concern.

'Probably.' Gileas's acceptance was spoken in a voice that was calm and reasoned.

'It was always going to come down to this. You, me and Reuben against an insurmountable challenge. Reuben's going to be beside himself with rage that he missed it.' Even now, even at the moment of certain defeat, Tikaye's dry humour brought a smile to Gileas's face.

'We can regale him with stories of our final heroic foolishness when we reach the Emperor's side,' said the sergeant. 'But I have a mind to drag that traitor with us.'

* * *

For the first time, Karteitja considered the very real possibility of defeat. His warriors were gone; dead or made good their escape into the warp.

'So you betray me at the last, Cirth,' he said aloud and a gale of bitter laughter burst forth from him. He was left to face the Silver Skulls alone.

It was hardly a challenge. He had defeated worthier rivals in his long lifetime, champions of the Four and Imperial dogs alike. The problem for him now was how he was going to get out of this place. Somebody had sealed the blessed ways behind them, effectively preventing escape by sorcerous means. Only the Unborn would dare, only the Unborn had such ambition.

He would have to fight these two warriors, but little matter. It would not take long to deprive them of their worthless souls.

TWENTY

WE SHALL PREVAIL

'I have not managed to raise Sergeant Ur'ten on the vox,' Kerelan said. 'I would suggest that we work on an assumption that our battle-brothers have fallen and have been unsuccessful in their endeavour.'

The first captain's words came in response to yet another failed attempt to communicate with Gileas's squad. Evidence certainly suggested that they had failed; the skies above them still swirled and boiled and vile creatures continued to rampage throughout the city and beyond.

The battle in the plaza had been horrific and arduous; the Astra Militarum had been butchered, with only a handful of men and vehicles remaining. It had been difficult for the Silver Skulls to bear witness to something that was far out of their hands, but they had been hard-pressed to defend themselves against the Oracles' onslaught. Apart from the one break in the storm, there had been no word from the *Prevision of Victory* since its brief transmission and Kerelan was unsure whether he had even heard them or if it had just been a moment of battle madness.

Bhehan and Inteus had all but exhausted their psychic energies protecting themselves from the attacks directed at them by the Oracles of Change. They had hoarded what little strength they had remaining to guard themselves against the perils of the encroaching empyrean. Tactically, they were next to useless.

The remnants of the Talriktug, fragmented squads of the siege company and a handful of men and armour were all that remained of the palace defence. As the waves of mutants broke up under the concentrated fire of the survivors, Bhehan wearily voiced his concern regarding the disappearance of the Oracles.

'They knew they could not hope to win,' asserted Vrakos with the unshakable confidence of the terminally arrogant.

'More likely that they are planning something worse,' responded Asterios, needing to shout over the roar of battle.

But the Oracles of Change did not return.

'You are surprisingly tenacious, Silver Skulls.' Karteitja was not paying them a compliment when he spoke the words. 'But then… you always were. Even the course of thousands of years has not eroded that stubborn streak in you and your brethren.' He hefted the daemonically possessed axe in his hands.

Gileas and Tikaye did not bother to engage their enemy in conversation. They had hurled themselves towards the Terminator, Tikaye with his bolt pistol on semi-automatic and Gileas with his chainsword throbbing hungrily. He set his stance ready for what he fully anticipated to be a ferocious battle. Even the razor teeth of the well-honed chainsword would be hard-pressed to make so much as a scratch in desecrated Terminator armour, but he would not fail through lack of trying.

The two Silver Skulls pushed forward, keeping themselves at just enough distance so that the sweep of the Terminator's axe could not reach them. They had yet to see what the weapon was fully capable of, but it had revealed itself to be lethal enough to carve through sacred battleplate.

With a barking laugh, the sorcerer thrust his free hand out before him, the gauntleted fingers spread wide. Unseen and invisible forces gathered around the two silver-clad warriors and clamped tightly round their armour, dragging them backwards with a power they could not hope to resist. They were both dumped unceremoniously over the edge of the platform, falling a few feet before they fired their jump packs and soared back onto the unstable surface.

They found Karteitja ready and waiting for them, his axe held out before him and with an arrogant set to his stance. He spoke in his strange, other-worldly voice. 'I forget. You are far less than my brothers and I. We have the gift. You have nothing but a legacy of deceit and lies. Your Prognosticators have misled you from the day your wretched Chapter was born. They cannot possibly hope to divine the future, for there will *be* no future for your kind.'

With those words, he lumbered forward, the heavy armour slowing his movements considerably. The axe sketched a complicated figure and a flare of sudden light burst forth from its twin heads. It dazzled even the eyes of the two Space Marines and they were forced to turn away whilst their sight adapted to block out the worst of it.

Before that process had even finished – and it took barely a second – the axe had connected with Gileas's shoulder and carved through the thick ceramite guard, burying itself in the plates beneath. The power armour prevented the weapon from biting into his flesh, but it was not his body that was threatened by the possessed blade. Its whispering voice seemed to creep beneath his skin and run through his entire body as though taking passage in his very veins.

You saw what you could have been.

He had. He had witnessed the power of Gryce's mirrors. He had seen a warped, tainted version of everything he believed himself to be. He had seen, if he would but admit it, the Gileas Ur'ten that he could easily become if he were ever allowed to fall victim to the visceral and violent rage that burned in his soul.

You saw what you could have.

Again, the whisper shuddered through him and he felt, for the second time that day and in over a hundred years, physically sick. Nausea rose in the pit of his stomach, filling his mouth with the taste of acidic bile, and he swallowed it back.

You saw what?

It was coaxing, pleading, begging him to answer, flirting with him to submit to a fundamental change of direction, gnawing ceaselessly at his resolve. He remembered the warrior in the mirror and for a heartbeat, he tasted temptation. Faith, he thought. My faith is my shield.

The voice of Andreas Kulle, so long dead, echoed in his mind. *'Without faith, what are we but a bundle of impulses and blood vessels in complicated armour? Ah, Gileas, to be a warrior of the Silver Skulls Chapter is to embody that faith. We are so much more than the Emperor's strong arm, my boy. We are His beating heart. His will made flesh.'*

As if in unconscious response to those words, spoken to

him decades before, Gileas felt the dual thump of his twin hearts as he fought off the encroaching darkness. The suddenness of them, reminding him once and for all that he was *alive*, brought him back to his senses.

You saw. There was triumph now in the voice, and perhaps it was indignation at the idea of losing, or perhaps it was that sudden vivid memory of his former mentor, that gave Gileas the push he needed to drag free of the axe's bite.

'Yes,' he said aloud. 'I saw. And that was not me. That will *never* be me.'

A pity.

The axe swung again and this time Gileas had enough presence of mind to avoid it. The thing seemed to twist and change before his eyes and he could see screaming faces in the heart of the steel. It was an impossible thing, a creation so alien to his own mindset that all he wanted to do was snatch it from the enemy's hands and fling it as far away as he could. He suspected, however, that were he to lay a grip on the thing, it would claim him.

'Why do you not fight back, Silver Skulls?' There was taunting in the voice. 'Are you so susceptible to the power of the warp that your brains have become soft already?' The sorcerer exerted his powers again and for the second time, the two Assault Marines were gathered up by unseen hands. Rather than throw them casually from the platform, this time the powers at Karteitja's command grasped them in a crushing embrace that slowly began to squeeze the life out of them. Joints popped and ancient plates cracked under the strain as Karteitja strove to pulverise the Silver Skulls in their own armour.

'I cannot move!' Tikaye's voice came as a gasp across the vox. The remaining half of his helm fell from his head and crumpled in. The warrior slowly turned his head to look at Gileas, bloodshot eyes staring at his brother from a face tight with effort.

'Hold on, brother!' Gileas struggled to get the words out. His chest felt as though it were about to burst. His armour creaked under the strain of the onslaught and the damage it had already suffered. Again, the two Assault Marines were dropped to their knees and Karteitja snatched back his power with a resonant laugh that rumbled deep in his crimson armour.

'You have no hope here, whelps. You have neither the strength nor the experience to match me. One way or another I will make you see the truth. You have already glimpsed it and felt a fraction of that exaltation. Even if all three of you were fresh and able,' he pointed the axe at the fallen Reuben, 'you would be little more than a temporary inconvenience. But that would be such a waste of promising new recruits.' He unleashed the power of the warp again.

He could feel a sense of hopelessness and despair closing in around him, but Gileas was stronger than that. He would fight and he *would* win. He drew on every resource he possessed and he focused his strength and his will.

There was a thunderous *crack* and a bolter shell thudded into the melted and fused communications array. It exploded, sending more of the equipment tumbling to the ground below and another shower of electronic and mechanical parts raining down over Gileas and Tikaye. Karteitja released his power over them in an instant and the two of them fell to the ground gasping for breath.

'You wish to talk of inconvenience?' Djul stamped up the last of the walkway. All of them, Karteitja and the other Silver Skulls, had been so caught up in their struggle that Djul had managed to negotiate the ascent unseen, the sound of his approach hidden by the lashing storm. 'I will happily discuss such matters with you, traitor filth. And then, when you have exhausted your worthless opinion, I will remove your head from your shoulders and end the discussion.'

Wheeling around to face this new enemy, Karteitja was knocked off balance by the impact of the storm bolter's next explosive impact. With a roar of fury, he straightened, brandishing the daemonic axe before him. As he pounded across the platform towards Djul, Gileas and Tikaye took the opportunity to steady themselves. Both of them were still struggling for breath, but their sheer determination carried them forward.

'Gileas, look.' Tikaye caught his sergeant's arm and pointed upwards. Where several minutes before there had been nothing but a swirling morass of dark clouds in a sickly yellow-tinged sky, there were now occasional clear patches. The worst of the warp storm was clearing and through the rents in the vile clouds, they could see the familiar shapes of drop pods ripping their way through the atmosphere.

'Backup.' Gileas grinned, exposing his sharpened incisors. It was a predatory expression. 'Now the tide will turn.'

'This is far from over, brother,' snapped Djul, and Gileas was not sure whether he was more startled at the fact that the champion had even been listening to him or the unlikely reality that Djul had just called him 'brother'.

Djul spoke no further as a barrage of psychic lightning was unleashed from the hands of his enemy. The energy arced around the Terminator's ancient battleplate with a crackle, scorching and blistering its surface. Gileas had been on the receiving end of that power and he knew how it felt. But Djul kept on walking towards Karteitja, chainfist held high and his voice resuming the endless repeating litanies of faith.

'My faith,' he was saying, 'is my shield. The Emperor protects the faithful.' He said the words with such passion and such unshakable belief that Gileas and Tikaye too were stirred to speak along with him.

'I shall know no fear. Fear denies faith. My faith is my shield. The Emperor protects the faithful.'

Karteitja let out a marrow-curdling laugh, a sound that came from another world. 'The Emperor protects the faithful? You fool yourselves. Your Emperor has long been dead. Your entire world is built around nothing but lies and deceit and you are too ignorant, too *foolish* to see the truth. You will die here and in your final moments, you will see the faces of the True Gods. And the pain of that, the realisation of the truth, will be *exquisite!*'

He unleashed a second wave of energy at Djul and the Terminator paused briefly, visibly shook himself and then continued to advance.

'Gileas.' Tikaye's voice held a note of urgency. The sergeant turned to his battle-brother, a quizzical set to his shoulders. 'If we strike at his flanks then we can buy our brother enough time to strike the killing blow.'

'Circle around,' Gileas replied. 'I will bear the brunt of that axe of his. Aim for the joint beneath the arm.'

'I can still hear you both,' snarled Djul. 'Ur'ten, this is *my* fight now. Fall back whilst you are still able and take our fallen brother to safety. Emperor willing he will continue to bring honour to the Chapter.' He spoke the words even as the killing lightning flickered about him and Gileas could hear the strain in the veteran brother's voice. '*Now*, Ur'ten. Before I change my mind. I do not have time to waste in idle prattle.'

'The first captain said you could not come back for me.' Gileas pushed the issue as he seized Reuben's recumbent body. For a moment, an unfamiliar noise sounded from within Djul's helmet. It took a fraction of a second to real-ise that it was a deep, amused chuckle. Yet another barrage of smoking black power was clinging to Djul's armour as though trying to find purchase and there was something sinister about his continued approach despite the Oracles of Change sorcerer heaping torment upon him in an effort to still his advance. That he was laughing merely added to the macabre nature of the confrontation.

'I did not,' said Djul. 'I came back for the others. That you are still alive is merely *your* good fortune. Now get out of here.'

'Should I consider that an order?'

'Yes, if it will compel you to do what you're told.'

With those final words, Djul fell back into his recitation of the litanies. The Catechism of Hate boomed from his vox-grille, amplified to levels that would have been agonis-ing for mortal ears. The Castigation of Sin, the Scourge of Faith and the Benediction of the Righteous thundered from the platform, echoing in the plaza below like an Ecclesiar-chal sermon. Vile energies played across his armour, melting silver script, blackening the gilt aquila and darkening the brushed steel with ugly burns. Smoke seeped from the joints of the ancient suit and an eye-lens popped under the strain.

Despite Djul's order to leave, Gileas and Tikaye found themselves riveted to the spot, torn by the desire to aid him in his struggle against the monstrous champion and the duty to obey the order to leave and save their wounded brother.

Ultimately, however, Gileas's overriding sense of obligation won the conflict and he shifted Reuben's weight on his shoulder. His unconscious battle-brother's life rune was barely visible in the corner of his helm now; only the faintest of glows even hinted at life still flowing through his veins. With some difficulty, he got his friend's body slung over his shoulder. His jump pack would not bear the weight of both of them and so he would have to return to the plaza by foot.

'Go, Tikaye,' he said. 'Assist the others below. Tell them what has transpired here.'

'Yes, sergeant.' Tikaye bowed his head and made the sign of the aquila. 'Nicodemus will not be forgotten. It will be both our honour and our duty to ensure it.'

Behind them, there was a clashing sound as Djul and Karteitja finally came together with a crash of armour. The Silver Skull had his chainfist poised above the Chaos champion's tusked helm but was held at bay by his enemy's free hand. At such close range Karteitja could not bring his axe to bear and instead had its head locked around Djul's storm bolter. In this way, he could keep the muzzle of the weapon pointed safely at the deck. Even as Djul struggled he maintained his endless recitation.

'Go,' Gileas ordered. 'I will be there as swiftly as I can.' Tikaye jumped off the edge of the roof and made a controlled drop to the plaza far below. He was out of sight even quicker than Gileas had imagined.

He shifted Reuben's weight and moved towards the gantry that Djul had used to access the platform. Without even taking his eyes from his opponent, Karteitja gripped his daemon axe tightly in his right hand and lashed Gileas with a tendril of dark will. Instantly his body spasmed, every muscle and tendon clenching in an involuntary response to the assault, agonisingly locking him in place so that he could do little more than move his eyes.

'No,' said Karteitja. 'I don't think so.'

Perhaps it was simply his righteous indignation or perhaps it was something stronger, but Gileas fought the unnatural paralysis with every fibre of his being. His closest friend and most valued squad member was dying across his shoulder and he was not going to bear the weight of another death. He *would* defy this sorcery. If Djul could overcome it through sheer force of will, then so could he.

Every effort he made to step forward was met with solid resistance and every muscle in his body screamed at him in searing agony. He could feel them straining to the point of bursting, but still he fought against it. Blood was pumping harder through his veins as his enhanced physiology struggled to aid him, but the power of the Oracle was too strong for him. He had the overwhelming sensation of the veins in his neck standing out against his skin beneath the armour, fit to burst. The blinding feeling was that he was on the verge of an aneurysm.

But still he tried.

Karteitja could not maintain his concentration on the Assault Marine for long, not when Brother Djul was intent on his destruction. When the release came, Gileas nearly went over the edge of the platform. His reflexes saved him and he gasped audibly.

Despite the pain in his muscles and the slow realisation that the physical strain of trying to press through the enemy's psychic block had torn tendons and ligaments,

Gileas resumed his passage to the walkway. The Oracle of Change Terminator was no longer interested in him and he moved onwards, trusting to his own body to heal the damage enough to get him down to the plaza.

Djul and Karteitja remained locked together for a few moments more, each straining for supremacy over the other, before breaking the stalemate. The champion turned his axe slowly in his fist as he cautiously circled the Silver Skull. He did not waste any words on this one; the booming litanies of faith denied any temptation and any threat he cared to make. No, this one would have to die.

The Oracle lunged and Djul swayed back, the bladed tip of the evil weapon carving a furrow in his battleplate. He stepped past the swing and punched his snarling chainfist at the traitor. The warrior turned so that the killing blade simply screamed from the curved armour in a shower of crimson chips.

Karteitja howled with rage and punched at Djul with his free hand, snapping the Terminator's head to one side. Once again inside the arc of the axe, the Chaos champion struggled to bring his weapon to bear on his adversary and the Silver Skull used the opportunity to press the barrels of his storm bolter into the champion's damaged chest.

Then he emptied the magazine in one long salvo.

Karteitja reeled under the assault, the hail of explosive bolts obliterating the numerous obscene icons adorning his armour and biting huge craters into the red ceramite. He staggered to a halt as the weapon clicked dry and the Silver Skull dropped the smoking gun to the deck.

'A weapon is no substitute for zeal,' he quoted and advanced once again on the Oracle of Change.

Wisps of darkness curled from his damaged armour and billowed from his helmet grille as Karteitja clashed again with his enemy. This time the axe blurred faster than Djul could follow, its brutal head burying itself in the thick armour of his torso. It failed to bite flesh, the venerable suit holding the evil blade at bay, but a scatter of critical failures danced across his display as the compromised systems protested.

'And zeal,' Karteitja grunted as he tugged the weapon free, 'is no substitute for a good weapon!'

He drew back his head with the intention of smashing his tusked helm into the Silver Skull's already damaged face, but Djul grabbed one of the horns and twisted it savagely to one side. Karteitja stumbled, dropping to one knee as the enemy Terminator used his own weapon against him. The chainfist came up, its teeth growling as it started to bite into the weakened armour of his torso.

The Chaos champion grabbed the Silver Skull's wrist and held it with all the strength he could muster, arresting the killing stroke. He rotated the axe in his grip and using it like a spear jabbed the blade into the narrow shoulder joint of his opponent's armour.

Djul grunted in pain but did not relent as the evil weapon bit into his flesh. He pushed against Karteitja's grip with his considerable might, his armoured boots gouging dents in the decking as he threw his entire weight behind his fist.

'Suffer... not...' he growled as the buzzing saw inched closer to its target. Karteitja screamed in fury. 'The... unclean!' Djul surged forward, the chainfist plunging deep into the torso of the Chaos champion. The Oracle of Change bellowed in rage and pain as he was torn apart, but the Silver Skull levered the weapon upwards, shearing through collar and gorget until it chewed into the twisted helm from beneath.

There was a single shrill and inhuman shriek and a great cloud of stinking darkness erupted from the broken armour. Then Karteitja crashed to the deck and lay still, nothing more than a suit of empty armour that had once protected an unspeakable evil.

Drop pods fell like steel rain, their armoured shells peeling open to disgorge the warriors of Eighth Company. They slammed into the mutant horde with righteous fury. The newly elevated Assault Captain Kyaerus spearheaded the charge, his lightning claw flashing in the sun that slowly started to break through the dispersing clouds.

As soon as contact had been lost with the surface, the *Prevision of Victory* had called for aid from the rest of the Chapter and the *Silver Arrow* had been the first to arrive. Engines burning hot as she ripped her way from warp space, the strike cruiser had been ready to deploy its payload of drop pods as soon as it had achieved orbit, but had been forced to wait out the growing storm.

Kerelan was relieved when Tikaye dropped from the heavens and turned his sword on the mutants, but the appalling damage to his armour clearly showed the struggle he had endured. Gileas, carrying the mutilated Reuben, emerged from the palace along with the scarred and battered Djul in time to meet Kyaerus as he and his warriors swept the last of the horrors from the plaza.

The officers clasped forearms in a warriors' greeting but there was little warmth in the assembly. As the Thunderhawks descended to extract the dead and wounded Kerelan cast his eyes over the devastated city and listened to the sounds of chaos that still echoed throughout the streets.

'We have prevailed this day, brothers,' he growled quietly, then he strode into the waiting gunship. The Talriktug followed, the broken body of Varlen carried between them.

TWENTY-ONE

THE CAPTAIN'S CHOICE

At the head of the party walked Inquisitor Callis, a pronounced limp marking her passage across the battle-torn grounds. The procession behind her wore grim faces as they bore their various burdens. Nathaniel, his body a shredded mass of flesh, had long since lost consciousness but somehow continued clinging to life with a remarkable tenacity. The shrouded bodies on the other stretchers borne by exhausted-looking survivors from the Siculean Sixth were less inclined to induce optimism. The remains of Isara and Curt had been recovered at the inquisitor's order.

Harild de Corso walked just behind the inquisitor, his head bowed in weariness and his usually jovial mood dark and sombre. At a word from Callis, he peeled away from her side and conducted the parade of the injured and the dead to the transport ship.

The inquisitor continued on until she was standing in

front of the Silver Skulls, a tiny, frail-seeming thing compared to the might of the Space Marines. She looked from Gileas to Kerelan and back again and bowed her head, making the sign of the aquila across her chest.

'The Inquisition will be sending its formal thanks to the Silver Skulls, first captain. But I could not depart without extending my own personal gratitude for all you have done in this place.'

'Your will is my duty, inquisitor,' said Kerelan.

'Not now,' she replied, with the faintest of smiles. 'This matter is resolved satisfactorily. My own masters will be pleased that the objectives were achieved.'

All this she said whilst around her the insane were being dealt with in the most efficient manner left to the Silver Skulls. The sheer indifference to the executions that were taking place was cold and calculated and nothing less than Kerelan had expected of an inquisitor.

'Therefore, first captain,' she continued, 'once your ship escorts me to my next destination, our alliance is effectively over. I will return to my own life and you will return to yours. For some…' Her eyes drifted to Nathaniel as he was carried in through the rear ramp of the transport and they hardened. If she felt any sympathy for her psyker's plight, she certainly did not show it. 'For some, life will never be the same. I will be in touch to give you my instructions regarding our destination in a few hours. There are reports that I must make. Excuse me.'

Once more she made the sign of the aquila and bowed in respect before joining her own people in the transport. It lifted from the broken city and took to the skies where it was soon lost to the dark and mists.

* * *

They conducted a thorough search of the plaza and the surrounding area, but in the wake of the battle Eighth Company were unable to find any trace of Nicodemus's body. At the request of the first captain, they had spent hours trying to find a trace of the young psyker, even searching further afield among the ruined suburbs of the city. They swept the ruins for two full days employing means both mundane and psychic but to no avail. The Apothecaries finally concluded, after an extensive description of his final actions, that Nicodemus had been utterly destroyed by the explosion.

'It pains me to record the loss of Brother Nicodemus in the battle of Valoris City,' said Kerelan. He sat alone in the strategium of the *Prevision of Victory*, a servo-skull meticulously recording his detailing of recent events. 'As we have been unable to find his body, we must record that he is missing, presumed dead. Brother Reuben of Eighth Company is in a stable condition, awaiting the implantation of bionics on our return to Varsavia along with Siege Captain Daviks and several other battle-brothers who suffered major injury. Sergeant Ur'ten and Brother Tikaye of Eighth Company also sustained a number of superficial injuries...'

Kerelan tailed off and a humourless smile flickered across his tattooed face. Gileas had refused any medical attention until he was satisfied that Reuben was not going to die. The sergeant's own injuries had completely healed anyway by the time he had stood down guard over his friend's inert body. His loyalty to his battle-brothers was commendable and it was a point in Gileas's favour.

He was going to need those.

'Inquisitor Callis has yet to report the full body count from the Siculean Sixth regiment who were initially responsible for Valoris City. My own observations are that the survivors are no longer numerous enough to make an effective fighting force, and will likely be decommissioned into an auxilia unit when, and if, the inquisitor clears them for release. It is not the honour that they deserve. Of the three other regiments deployed to pacify the world no survivors have been found. Among her personal retinue, the psyker Nathaniel Gall...'

The skull made a chittering sound as it dutifully recorded Kerelan's words and the first captain let out a small sigh of regret. Recording deaths in this clinical way had always had an adverse effect on his mood. Nicodemus had shown great promise and his courage, whilst impetuous, had been outstanding. The similarities to Gileas Ur'ten had been remarkable, further underlining the fact that those battle-brothers who were born to the southern tribes were fiercely unpredictable. That Gileas had lived as long as he had was nothing short of miraculous.

It had been a trying couple of days and the mood aboard the *Prevision of Victory* was sombre to say the least. True to her word, it was only a matter of hours before the inquisitor informed the first captain that the Ordo Malleus had been notified of the incident and that a purgation fleet had been dispatched. She had also made it clear that it would simplify matters considerably if the Silver Skulls were long gone by the time they arrived.

Kerelan suspected that Valoria would remain a closely monitored and quarantined world for many years and that it would be subject to a careful repopulation programme once all evidence of the Oracles and their influence had been expunged. There had been nothing left of the original citizenry worth saving.

Kerelan continued his report from where he had left off as though there had been no interruption.

'...will also make a full physical recovery, although as he is yet to regain consciousness, his mental state remains in question.' On discovering that the frail human psyker had been responsible for saving if not the lives, then certainly the souls of three of his battle-brothers, Kerelan had been deeply regretful of his earlier disdainful opinion of the man.

'Harild de Corso also survived the battle, and I am led to believe that he was responsible for snuffing out the lives of an admirable number of heretics before he was forced to abandon his sniping position due to exhaustion of ammunition. I believe the close and immediate ire of the Oracles of Change may also have been a contributing factor.'

Having failed to escape the planet following Nathaniel's orders, the sniper had intended to return to the palace when the storm brought his shuttle down among the suburbs. The soldier had pulled clear of the wreckage and scaled the highest ruin he could find before picking off targets of opportunity. He had been doing well until a glancing hit attracted the attention of one of the Oracles who translocated to Harild's location. The game of cat and mouse that followed had been somewhat one-sided and the sniper had barely escaped with his life when the Oracles abruptly abandoned the battle.

Kerelan watched the cogitator spew out his thoughts in closely spaced High Gothic script and let his thoughts drift a little. There was much that needed to be undertaken before the *Prevision of Victory* broke orbit with this forsaken world and returned to Varsavia. Of the contingent of Silver Skulls who had answered the inquisitor's call, many would not be returning. Had it not been for Nicodemus's sacrifice it was doubtful that any of them would have survived and for that mercy, the first captain was grateful.

'You need to wake up, Nathaniel.'

Harild was making his customary visit to his unconscious companion's bedside. He had visited regularly every three hours or so, more frequently when his own duties permitted him, and was annoyed that Nate was still refusing to respond to any sort of stimuli. He had resorted to taunting the psyker, the only thing he had not tried.

'If you don't wake up,' he was saying, his tone grim, 'then I'm going to have to find new owners for all your things. Do you have any idea how difficult it's going to be to get rid of clothes that used to belong to a psyker? There are all sorts of strange beliefs about that, you know. Though I suppose I could just blast all your junk out of the airlock.'

The psyker offered no response. There was not even a hint of a flicker beneath the eyelids. Nathaniel was an absolute mess. The damage done to his flesh by the flying glass had been considerable and the scars would fade, but never heal. The medicae who had worked on removing the numerous shards of mirror from the psyker's body had expressed amazement that the tiny projectiles had not cut major arteries. Some had been buried so deep in his flesh that open surgery had been necessary. *He will probably die before we get it all out,* Harild had been told candidly.

He had known the psyker was more stubborn than that. He was as tough as old leather.

'You really *want* me to launch your tarot cards into space? Damn it, Nate, wake up.'

But Nathaniel didn't stir.

Harild sat next to his friend for a while longer and then got to his feet in exasperation, heading to the viewport. He took out a packet of lho-sticks, trying not to notice how much his hand was shaking. He had not realised how badly the events of the last two days had affected him. Isara and Curt were gone. He didn't want to be the only survivor; there were all sorts of stories of ill-fortune associated with sole survivors and he didn't want to be that man.

He shook his head and lifted the lho-stick to his mouth. He stared moodily out of the viewport.

'You can't smoke in here.' The voice was quiet.

'I know that.' Irritated at the interruption, Harild folded his arms across his chest. 'I wasn't even going to light it.'

'Liar.'

There was a weak cough and Harild turned to the psyker, hardly daring to believe that the unexpected had occurred. Sure enough, Nathaniel's eyes were open.

'How long have you actually been awake?' Harild attempted to hide his relief. Nathaniel shook his head. It didn't matter. All that mattered was that he *was* awake.

Once Djul had looked down on Gileas, considering him worthy of nothing but the most cursory of attention. Now, he actively sought the Assault Marine. He found him in his arming chamber, working out the many dents in his battleplate.

'Ur'ten.'

His bulk filled the small doorway and Gileas looked up. Out of the respect he felt for all the Chapter's veterans, he began to set aside his work and stand, but Djul waved a hand dismissively.

'Sit down, brother. I will not detain you for long. I wished

415

merely to exchange words with you regarding your actions on Valoria.'

'I know, sir,' said Gileas, a dull edge to his voice. 'I effectively disobeyed orders and I am both prepared and willing to accept whatever punishment is levied for those actions.'

'You are right, of course,' said Djul and the Terminator's lined and scarred face was stern. 'The Prognosticator advised us not to go after the inquisitor. You chose to ignore that advice and went anyway.'

'I am well aware of my failings, brother.' Gileas was bristling now. 'If you have come merely to…'

Djul held up a hand to stem his tirade.

'You went after the inquisitor based on the Oath of Hospitality. There is no wrong in that. You did go against the advice of a Prognosticator and I am sure that Vashiro will have more than a little to say on the matter. I merely wanted you to understand something, Ur'ten.' Djul waited until he had Gileas's full attention. 'Based on your actions, I came to realise that a Prognosticator's words may be… considered as guidance rather than an instruction.'

Gileas was taken aback. Djul, the most zealous of them all. Djul, the most faithful and the most respectful of the Prognosticators and their place within the Chapter, was openly admitting that he too had used ambiguity to his own advantage. He could find no words so he chose to remain silent.

'You fought well down there,' said Djul eventually. 'Clearly the lesson I gave you made some inroads into your thick skull. But do not rest on your laurels, brother. We must all strive to be the best we can be. Imagine what you could do if…'

'…if I could do all that I can,' finished Gileas quietly. 'They were Captain Kulle's last words to me.'

'I know. Andreas never had anything but praise for you. I scorned him. I poured disdain on his words. You are a barbarian, Ur'ten. You are a dangerous commodity. But there is a promise of fate that hangs around you that you do not have to be a Prognosticator to see. You have great potential. Do not let your temper take that away from you.'

Djul looked a little uncomfortable at the words he was speaking. 'You will have the grace and good sense not to repeat any of the praise I have given you, I am sure?'

'You were never here, brother.'

'Excellent.' Djul nodded. 'You *do* learn quickly.'

Some weeks later, the *Prevision of Victory* entered orbit around the fourth planet in the Anaximenes system. It was a scheduled pause on the return leg to Varsavia, and it was here that Inquisitor Callis and her retinue parted company with the Silver Skulls.

Nathaniel's recovery had been slow and at times extremely painful for him. But he was far more determined and more resilient than his thin frame suggested. He had found an unlikely recuperation partner in the shape of Reuben, who had been adjusting to using his newly fitted augmetic limb. The device was excellent but only the most basic of models that would certainly be of little use were they to fall to war again. A far better augmetic would be fitted once they returned home. The temporary limb was enough to get Reuben up and about and he had offered quiet and solid support when it seemed that Nathaniel was on the verge of giving up.

Nathaniel sat now staring out at the rich sapphire oceans of Anaximenes IV and marvelling at the distant star's cast of light that highlighted every geographical feature on the world's surface. The ridge line of mountains that encircled the globe was picked out in heart-achingly beautiful detail and the outlines of the continental masses where countless citizens of the Imperium lived and worked were edged in sharp relief. It was so beautiful, so lovely, that Nathaniel felt emotion welling up.

Between his fingers, the chain of his sister's necklace was wrapped. Since her death, he had drawn an odd kind of comfort from its proximity. There was the faintest trace of her strange aura about it, an fluctuation in the warp energies that surrounded all living things and made the necklace invisible to his psyker-sight. It was as though a part of her remained with him, too weak to negate his powers, but strong enough in her essence to console him in his lingering grief.

Valoria had looked beautiful, too, when they had first entered orbit around it. From so high up, the taint that had polluted its heart could not be seen, the treachery that had eaten the planet away from within. From so far away, its beauty had been utterly flawless. Once you got beneath the surface of such exquisiteness… then the truth would out. Reality would always find a way to hold up a mirror to the superficial and reveal it for what it truly was.

Thinking of mirrors brought an involuntary shudder to Nathaniel's body. Only one of the three Space Marines whose very souls he had saved had spoken to him of what had transpired in the chamber of mirrors and he would never betray that confidence.

He had undergone long and arduous testing at Inquisitor Callis's hands, conversations that had drained him emotionally. It would be some time before he would be permitted to use his abilities and further testing awaited him here on

Anaximenes IV; a planet that for all its beauty was a grim place for a psyker.

His hand went up to the null collar that he had chosen to wear. Its edges had not been well filed and were rough against the skin of his neck. It was frustrating, it was uncomfortable, but it was necessary.

He could have refused to wear it, of course, but had he done so, the inquisitor would only have forced him into it – or worse. Accepting it was the sensible thing for him to do. He claimed that he trusted his mind had not suffered any ill effects from the taint of Chaos, and his willingness to submit to the questioning and indignity that the collar meant would count highly in his favour. He hated the thing, though. More than once he had yearned to tear it off. He knew that would have resulted in a bolt-round to the brain, however, and Nathaniel Gall was not yet ready to meet that fate.

He sighed inwardly. He didn't even know what his fate might be any more. Before they had travelled to Valoria, everything had been clear cut. He had built up a near-perfect working relationship with Inquisitor Callis and it had all been snatched away in a heartbeat. The closeness and even affection that he had been sure the inquisitor had harboured towards him was gone. She was closed to him, now. The friendship that he had come close to finding in her had frozen solid and she treated him with a clinical detachment that hurt more than the healing scars on his body.

'They are looking for you.' The deep voice came from behind him and he turned – still with obvious stiffness – to lock his gaze with that of Gileas Ur'ten. 'It is time to leave, Master Gall.'

'You still use that form of address,' observed Nathaniel.

'Why is it that you still have respect for me? For what I was? When nobody else does, I mean?'

'I have respect for what you did for me and my brothers. I have respect for what you might be again.' Gileas's face was solemn.

'Your confidence in me is flattering, sergeant.' Nathaniel managed a smile. 'Why are you always so certain that everything will turn out for the best? The trials down on Anaximenes IV are notorious for weeding out the incompetent and the weak.' He got slowly to his feet and leaned heavily on his staff. He walked slowly towards the Space Marine and Gileas was struck by how frail he seemed.

'I have spoken with Brother-Prognosticator Bhehan,' responded Gileas. 'He consulted the runes on your behalf. The portents are good.' Gileas nodded. 'Have faith, Master Gall. Faith and fortitude. Prevail. You ask me why it is that I am always so certain things will turn out for the best? It is because I hold fast to the most basic of our Chapter's beliefs. We will prevail.' He smiled. 'We *must* prevail.'

'Thank you.' Nathaniel was genuinely touched by Gileas's words. 'And the same to you.' The psyker limped slowly out of the doorway, then stopped and turned. 'Will you ever tell them what happened? What it was that you saw in that chamber?'

'Never,' came the reply. 'It was a lure. An illusion. Designed to ensnare my mind and devour my soul. No more, no less. But I am a son of Varsavia.' A crack appeared in the stern facade he wore, but it was fleeting. 'My faith is my shield. It will take more than a vision to turn me against everything I stand for.'

Nathaniel nodded slowly. 'I understand, sergeant,' he said. 'But speak with Reuben about it if you find the opportunity.

As far as I know, he hasn't spoken to anybody about what it was that he saw, but you would need to be a fool not to appreciate that whatever it was does not sit well with him.' He offered one last smile and hobbled away, leaving Gileas to brood about what he had said.

'Your men behaved in an exemplary fashion from the moment we left Varsavia,' Inquisitor Callis said. 'On behalf of the Inquisition, I extend thanks and gratitude. Without them, I would be dead and the traitors would have succeeded in their plan. I regret the losses amongst my agents, but their service will be remembered and with proper... re-education... Nathaniel will once again prove his worth.'

Her physical recovery had been swift and had brought with it the same arrogance that had so marked her when they had first met. She held herself with superior indifference, clad in a stiff-collared coat that meant her head was held high.

'I am gratified you feel we discharged our duty admirably,' said Kerelan. He stood on the hangar deck, towering above the tiny woman. The skull tattoo on his face lent gravitas to him as he made the formal farewell to the inquisitor.

'More than admirably,' she responded. 'Every last one of you. Now that I have seen your reports on the battle, I extend my regrets as to the losses amongst your brothers. Nicodemus was a fine warrior and a prime example of your Chapter. I hope that there will be words spoken on his behalf.'

'We do not mourn the deaths of those who are lost in service to the Emperor,' said Kerelan. 'We celebrate their lives instead. They will all receive their honours in the Halls of Remembrance, of that you may be assured.'

'You return to Varsavia, then?'

'Only to rearm and resupply. The armouries of the Eighth and Ninth are much diminished on the back of this campaign.'

The inquisitor hesitated for a moment. 'And the matter of Sergeant Ur'ten's defiance?'

'The Lord Commander gave me leave to address that matter myself. It was with regret earlier that I advised Sergeant Gileas Ur'ten that he will not be going back to his home world, but will instead be returned to the Eighth Company battle lines.'

Kerelan's face was completely expressionless. 'I am sure you can imagine how this sat with him. A terrible punishment, being turned away from the fortress-monastery.'

Her smile became broader. Gileas had told her how he had yearned to return to his brothers of Eighth Company.

'A harsh punishment indeed,' she said, seriously.

'Quite so.'

'In time, I suspect, first captain, Gileas Ur'ten will rise through the ranks. Perhaps one day he will fight by your side as your peer rather than your support. He would make a formidable Terminator.'

'Djul would not let him within fifty metres of a suit of Terminator armour. I have no concerns in that regard.'

Argentius had been pleased to hear of the uneasy truce that Gileas and Djul had formed, however tentative. Kerelan did not mention this. Nor did he mention that Vashiro had once again denied a recommendation for Gileas to be considered for a captaincy. The sergeant had acted with integrity and honour and proven that he was more than worthy as a leader of men. The first captain's recommendation was the highest accolade that Gileas would likely ever receive. But he had been denied.

His time is not yet come.

Six words. That had been all Vashiro had had to say on the matter and they had sent a shudder of anticipation through the first captain.

A silence fell between Kerelan and the inquisitor whilst those who were departing for the planet's surface boarded the transport. When she was certain that she was the only one remaining on the hangar deck, she nodded.

'There is one last thing,' she said and from within the depths of her dark coat, she withdrew a data crystal. 'A transcript of a coded astropathic message I sent an hour past. There are things contained within that I feel…' She offered the item and Kerelan took it. 'Sometimes, words are not enough. But by way of gratitude…'

She shook her head and thrust her hands back in the deep pockets of her coat. Her artificially youthful face took on the stern expression he had come to recognise on her. 'Of course I have never given you this.'

Kerelan raised an eyebrow quizzically, but she offered no further explanation. He looked at the crystal, then at the inquisitor. 'While we speak of gratitude, perhaps you could answer a question for me. While Valoria was indeed in dire need of our aid, did you have ulterior motives for choosing to travel in our company?'

She gave him another mysterious smile by way of response. 'We all do what we must,' she replied neutrally. 'The Silver Skulls will prevail against overwhelming odds, First Captain Kerelan. Of that I am sure. In the Emperor's name.' She bowed, briefly, and made the sign of the aquila across her breast.

'In His name.'

Kerelan returned the gesture and the bow and watched as

she strode up the ramp of the vessel. The door slid shut on grating hydraulics that had seen better days and the engines began whining as they cycled for launch. The first captain of the Silver Skulls Chapter turned and walked from the hangar as the inquisitor's ship prepared to depart, the air-tight hangar door sealing closed behind him.

'And she gave this to you freely?' The Prognosticator studied Kerelan carefully, but the first captain's face did not change. His voice, though. It was all in his voice.

'Yes,' replied Kerelan grimly. 'She did. And whilst I am sure that she has not disclosed all that she could have and that I should forget what it is that I have seen, there are some things that are impossible to unsee.' His fingers wrapped around the data crystal in the palm of his hand and he opened them out again. 'This is one of them.'

The two, warrior and psyker, sat in the strategium. The light levels had been reduced to the bare minimum, the simulation of shipboard night, and a hazy mauve swathed the vast area. The small amount of light thrown out by a data-slate's screen was the only other form of illumination in the room. The human contingent aboard the vessel may have required light, but the two Adeptus Astartes did not. Beyond the ship, the Geller field held back the roiling madness of the warp, an uncomfortable reminder of the skies over Valoria and how close they had come to catastrophe.

Once they had left Anaximenes IV, Kerelan had retired to his personal chambers and viewed the contents of the data crystal. What he had read within had disturbed him deeply and he had been unable to rest. He had turned to Bhehan for advice. The Prognosticator was many centuries his junior, but the boy was wise beyond his years.

'She put herself in a dangerous position allowing you to see the contents of this crystal,' observed Bhehan. He reached and took the object from the flat of Kerelan's hand. 'Why would she do that, do you think?'

'I have asked myself that question over and again,' said Kerelan. 'And every time, I come to the same answer. Because she felt she owed us this much. And perhaps because she sees to the heart of our Chapter's issues more clearly than we do ourselves.' He shook his head. 'Perhaps she did it for some other reason that is beyond our comprehension. The ordo moves in mysterious ways, after all. I do not like feeling as though I am a pawn in some greater game of the Imperium.'

Bhehan rose from his seat, feeling the damning weight of the data crystal in his hand. He stared out at the muted, raging energies of the warp. He had rarely had reason to consider why it was that humans did anything. Their behaviour patterns were erratic at best, unpredictable at worst. He had been conditioned to expect inquisitors to behave in a certain way and Liandra Callis had broken that pattern.

'Do we divulge its contents to Vashiro? To Argentius?'

The first captain's voice contained a note of uncertainty and Bhehan let his mind drift lightly over the potential ramifications of bringing this information to the attention of the Chapter's most influential adviser. What he sensed there unsettled him more than he already was in the wake of reading the inquisitor's words. He foresaw a time of upheaval and great change, just as he had predicted in the rune casting before this mission had deployed.

Bhehan knew that he was gifted with genuine foresight. Too many things had come to pass that he had envisioned for it to be a mere coincidence. The visions, if that was the right word to describe them, were not always accurate, of course, and he had come to learn in the past few weeks that there had to be room for interpretation. Otherwise, the majority of the Silver Skulls would willingly follow the guidance of the chosen few until disaster occurred.

For the first time, Bhehan genuinely questioned the manner in which his Chapter operated and the divergence of his faith and loyalty left a hollow in the pit of his gut that he did not like. Not one bit.

'I do not honestly know,' he said in time. 'I am unsure that it would be wise to bring this information to Vashiro's attention. The inquisitor has given us a warning and we need to consider long and hard the outcome of sharing this knowledge.' He turned from the viewport and looked at Kerelan, his young face lined with concern. 'We can ill afford a schism within our Chapter and this is where the road leads.'

'Do all roads lead to that ending? Is it something that we must accept and confront openly, armed with what we know?'

'You would fight your own brothers over this matter? First Captain Kerelan, would you really set aside the millennia of tradition over the contents of a single crystal that may not even be true? Had you considered the possibility that the inquisitor's report is a carefully constructed ruse? There is a certain ambiguity to the words. She does not name the...' A scowl marred his features. 'The ones who made this claim, after all.'

Kerelan looked ashamed. That very thought had indeed coloured his reckoning. He had served the Silver Skulls for centuries, boy and warrior, and the thought of change was alien to him. But he had truly seen how he and his battle-brothers were perceived through the eyes of others for the first time. He had been awakened to the realisation that beyond the impenetrable walls of Varsavia's fortress-monastery, the Silver Skulls were sometimes considered in a less than favourable light.

'My advice, first captain, is that we wait.' Bhehan's blue eyes flared with intensity for a moment. 'We wait and we watch. What I have seen may not come to pass. The inquisitor may have given us the means to change the future of our Chapter.' He measured the weight of the crystal in his hand. The motion was more metaphorical than anything else and he did not like the outcome of the balance. He offered it back to Kerelan. 'This may appear to damn us, but in the same context, we are exonerated. How we choose to read her warning can be our redemption or our undoing. Whether we share this knowledge… cannot be my decision.'

Kerelan took the crystal from the young Prognosticator and looked thoughtfully at it for a long while.

'Thank you, Bhehan,' he said, effectively dismissing the Prognosticator from his presence. The younger warrior sketched a salute and strode from the strategium. Kerelan tossed the data crystal back onto the table and dropped back down in his seat but found he was entirely unable to take his gaze from it.

He could share the contents of the inquisitor's message with his superiors, or he could obliterate the words. But whatever he did, the inquisitor had set things in motion. He would be damned if he brought this information higher up and he would forever wonder what would have happened if he did not. The wrong decision could unwittingly spell downfall for the entire Chapter.

The decision had to be his and his alone and he did

not make it for several hours. He could only hope that he chose wisely.

= Priority Transmission =
From: Inquisitor Callis, Ordo Hereticus

+++

Security Level Maxima Ultra.
Breach of this code is considered
an act of traitoris extremis.
Any non-authorised individual attempting to view
these documents will be dealt
with severely.

+++

Transmission Begins

+++

Thought for the day: Serve the Emperor today,
tomorrow you may be dead.

Subject: Mission Alpha Forty-Seven

As instructed, I am transmitting under separate cover my final report on the matter of the Silver Skulls Chapter as tasked to me by your esteemed selves several months ago. I have had occasion to spend a great deal longer with these noble warriors than previously anticipated and I feel I would be doing a disservice to them as a Chapter and to myself as a woman of integrity not to impart my full and frank assessment.

There are matters that must be addressed. However, let me state the positive first.

In the matter of the situation on Valoria, I feel it essential that I report that the warriors of the Silver Skulls Chapter who accompanied me and my interrogators carried out their duties with due diligence and true excellence. I have nothing but praise for their actions and their dedication in ensuring that the situation was dealt with swiftly and effectively.

The outcome of the events on Valoria has necessitated a stop at the psykana facility on Anaximenes IV whilst I ensure that Nathaniel Gall remains untainted and suitable for continued service in my employ. Should this not be the case, then I would like to request his fate be a merciful one. He has served well and risked his life to ensure my continued survival.

Returning to the matter of the Silver Skulls, and in particular the grievance stated by the Contestor: I feel that the ritualistic — and traditional — practice of consulting their Prognosticators is in many ways no more alarming than other rituals associated with the trappings of war. They pay due homage to the God-Emperor, they maintain themselves with honour and dignity and they are as fearless as true Emperor's Angels should be. I cannot deny, however, that from an external point of view, their apparent dependency on the Prognosticators may yet require further scrutiny. I recommend the intervention of their parent Chapter as they are perhaps best placed to deal with such a matter.

I would submit this question in rhetoric, my lords. Is it right to point the accusing finger at strategic minds? If so, then there are other Chapters of the Adeptus Astartes who could also be considered for deeper investigation.

I assure you of my due care and attention in all things.

Ave Imperator!

Inquisitor L. Callis
Ordo Hereticus

+ + +

Transmission Ends

+ + +

ABOUT THE AUTHOR

Sarah Cawkwell is a freelance writer
based in north-east England. Her work
for Black Library includes the Silver Skulls
novels *The Gildar Rift* and *Portents*, and the
Architect of Fate novella, *Accursed Eternity*.
For Warhammer, she is best known for her
stories featuring the daemon princess of
Khorne, Valkia the Bloody.